GEORGE HAWKINS SPACE CAMPER

·

Space Between Space

FOURTH ROTATION

L. A. Bissonnette

BISMIL LLC
2012

Also by L.A. Bissonnette:
It Comes From Within - 1ˢᵗ Rotation
Past and Present Fear – 2ⁿᵈ Rotation
Dark Secrets - 3ʳᵈ Rotation

For previews of upcoming books by L.A. Bissonnette and more information about the author, visit **www.georgehawkinsspacecamper.com**

Copyright © 2012 by L.A. Bissonnette

All rights reserved. Except as permitted under the U.S. Copyright Act of 1976, no part of this publication may be reproduced, or stored in a retrieval system, or transmitted in any form or by any means, electronic, mechanical, photocopying, recording, or otherwise, without written permission of the publisher and/or author.

BISMIL LLC
GHSC Book Group

Visit our website at **www.georgehawkinsspacecamper.com**

Illustration by Tyson Mangelsdorf

The characters and events in this book are fictitious. Any similarity to real persons, living or dead, is coincidental and not intended by the author.

ISBN 978-0-9823961-3-1   0-9823961-3-9

Printed in the U.S.A.
First American edition   September 2012

For all who believe that one person,
one team, one group,
can make a difference in the lives
of those around them.

Thanks to family and friends
across the planet.

Compassion

Contents

Prologue

3RD ROTATION

George's birthday and the beginning of summer vacation had fallen on the same day last year. In his wildest dreams, he never imagined he would be going to a summer camp in space on a faraway moon filled with summer campers like himself. In one short day, he went from being a regular teenager on Earth to being a cadet on a space station. After three summer camps in space, George and his team of amazing friends were learning to trust their instincts and each others.

Andy Penteado was a tall muscular boy with dark brown hair. He had grown up in the wilds of Brazil on the family's farm. Over the summer, Andy was learning to be George's second in command and the defender of their team.

Gus Reiter was from central Germany, a bit rounder than the others and was as strong as an ox. Andy seemed more seasoned than Gus, like he had grown up faster. Gus was their cook and keeper of their strongest weapon, the seeds of hope.

Emily Miller was from Great Britain. She was about George's height, with light brown hair that curled over her shoulders. Her mom had died when she was very young; Emily had grown up lonely, the closest thing Emily had to a friend was her computer. Emily created intricate computer programs that would help save their lives.

Anna Jhang was a short girl from Japan with long, straight black hair braided down her back. When she was very little, her grandmother had taught her all about the universe and the stars. Anna had become their navigator through the caves of Ganymede moon.

Sara O' Conner was from Ireland and was from a large family of six older brothers, with no sisters. She had learned about medicines from her grandfather and herbs from her grandmother. She was now the team's healer.

Pete Petrosky was their team captain and in charge of their training. He and his team of captains had become their friends over the last year. Yet George knew there was something their captain had not told them, something was missing, unsaid. George and his team had taken the Oath of Odin with Pete's team and

George's older brother Frank's team and Toma, a Thorean team. Together they formed a triad.

George's tenth-grade year in High School was winding down and soon summer vacation would start. On a Friday afternoon in the spring, the evil that hunted George and his team found him on Earth. George and his dad narrowly escaped the minions of evil. Now, Andy was pulled from his High School and sent to George's High School to protect George. With many visitors coming and going from the Hawkins home, George and Andy soon learned of an ancient prophecy that foretold of a team to unify the galaxies. Emily started to investigate the legend.

Before long, school was over and George and Andy were on their way to Jupiter station when they were captured by evil's minions. They escaped their captors and headed to the Calshene cadet station, Asteria. "They hate us," Andy complained. "No, they just don't understand us," George replied as they landed.

On Asteria station their whole team was reunited. By accident they discovered the Asteria stations officer's library and met a Celestian librarian. They found the original prophecy scroll in the library and read it using one of Emily's computer programs. Max, a being of white light, stopped them from reading about themselves. The Galactic council found out they had taken a copy of the prophecy from the library and punished them by making them train at the captains level.

While on a training mission in space, the Galactic council asteroid was attacked by the Mahadean slave traders. George,Äôs team and Pete's team traveled to Mahadean in training scout ships, accidentally attached to the side of the enormous Mahadean galactic cruiser.

On Mahadean, George and the others planned their rescue of the Galactic council from the Magistrate's fortress. They would race through the molten center of the planet's core and win the "Turns" race. As their prize, they would free all of the slaves. To earn money on Mahadean, Sara healed the sick and Gus cooked, feeding thousands of people.

Free from Mahadean, they returned to Asteria station and for a while, life returned to normal. However, the center Senior Viceroy of the Galactic council was infected by evil and attacked George and his team. They ended up in the officer's library once again, infected by evil and reading the prophecy and forbidden scrolls. Their triad rescued them and with the help of the beings of white light, freed George and the others from the grip of pure evil.

The team discovered a tunnel hog cave as old as time and found a way to contact the beings of white light. In the end, the center Senior Viceroy of the Galactic council was stopped and George"s team and triad were honored for savings the lives of the Galactic council. In their last week of summer vacation, they met a retired Senior Viceroy named David Lu. He taught them how to use the raw energy of the universe!

Chapter 1

COUNTRY VIEW

Last year, when Andy came to live with George and his family for the last month of school, George thought Andy had been exaggerating about having a car and driver to get to high school each week. Andy wasn't kidding!

The Galactic council did let George, and his team, return to Earth for their junior year at high school in the fall. However, because evil had found George at his home in the middle of the states last spring, George was sent to Andy's family's farm for safekeeping.

The farm was enormous and located in central Brazil. The farm had every kind of fruit orchard, herb garden, vegetable, and grain field. It was unlike anything George had ever seen. Down the small hill from the main house, was the pool terrace, flower gardens, vegetable gardens, the main barns, and many houses for the farmhand families. Further out, across the valley, the farm had fields to raise hay, alfalfa, and oats and barns for the cattle, goats, chickens, horses, and lamas. The enormous farm needed more than two hundred farmhands working to keep it running well.

Andy and George were enrolled in a boarding high school with two of Andy's younger sisters, half a dozen of his cousins, and two dozen farmhand children. The students all stayed at the high school during the week and came home to the farm with loads of laundry and homework each weekend.

The high school had more than two thousand students who, like Andy and George, came and left every weekend. Some students traveled up to six hours by bus to and from school each weekend to see their families. Often the student's family homes were high in the mountains, making travel by car, bus, and truck difficult. Most of the students at the school had been home schooled from kindergarten through seventh grade because of the difficult travel. Once in eighth grade, the students were old enough to go to the mountain boarding high school during the week.

For three hundred years, the school in central Brazil had been teaching the students of the central mountains and the valleys. Long ago, the school's founders had set up scholarships for all students that attended the school. The high school's acceptance criteria were based on the student's test grades and not on money; yet, Andy knew no student that had applied had ever been turned away. The children of central Brazil studied hard to get accepted, as it was a great honor for the families.

Andy's family's farm was large and remote, deep in the wilds of central Brazil. It provided the local economy with many good jobs. On the weekends during the school year, Andy spent a lot of time teaching George about the cultures of South America. How the ancient tribes and the modern people of the valleys lived on the edge of the rainforest and co-existed with wildlife and the plants.

Andy's cousins and the farmhand children rode in one of the farm buses that transported farmhands during the week and carried the children to and from the high school each weekend. However, Andy and George were different and rode in a beige, four-door car. Most thought it was because they were the sons of the farm owner, but the boys knew it was because if evil found them, the Galactic council wanted to be able to get them away quickly and not endanger any innocent people.

As the boys traveled to and from school each week, Andy often had their driver stop so he could teach George about the rainforest animals and plants. George was amazed at how much Andy knew about the valleys and mountains around him. Andy was so in tune with nature as he told George about each plant and animal and the part that plant or animal played in the web of life in the rainforest. He missed nothing and could blend into the forests and disappear easily.

On one trip back from school, George recalled his escape with his dad from the people in black suits last spring. At the time, he didn't even know the name of the stream they had escape into or where it went. At that moment, he felt so small, as if he had so much more to learn. He was sure Andy's knowledge was why he was always in-tune with his surrounds on the cadet stations and missed almost nothing that happened around them.

As Andy had said the year before, his mom took the whole family, brothers, sisters, cousins, nieces, nephews, and farm children on historical outings each month. They filled a bus each month with moms, children, and picnic lunches. Sometimes the journeys were short and sometimes they travelled a long distance, returning home late at night. On each trip this year, George and Andy paid attention to the guides and learned to read more of the symbols of the ancient tribes and civilizations of Earth.

"Not so dumb anymore," they agreed on one outing to the main Natural History museums in the city where Andy's father worked as a judge.

The age and history of the South American cultures were amazing to George. The North America culture and history was all shiny and new, a blaze in the lights of progress and industry, its' native history long-ago hidden by western expansion. Here, in central South America, life was simpler. Yet, both the ancient and modern cultures benefited from the progress of the cities with vaccines and new medicines and the peace and tranquility of the countryside. To George, it was a fascinating blending of new and old.

Between the high school and the family farm were two great valleys that were used as trade routes across the country for more than five thousand years. Twice, during the school year, George and Andy had been allowed to walk alone along the paths and dirt roads for the ten-mile journey home.

Many of the farmhands, who worked on the farm, had come from the surrounding valleys and mountains. During the week, they lived in the small clusters of homes Andy's dad and grandfather had built on the farmland to house them. Some of the people moved into the homes permanently and left the forest and mountain life behind, others came only for the work and went home to their families on their weekends off.

The boys walk home took them through two of the valley's small housing groups his family had built. The white washed buildings with red tile roofs glistened in the afternoon sun as young children ran around, playing ball. George felt privileged to hear many of the ancient stories and folklore from the elders as they passed down the stories from generation to generation in this culture. Every time they heard a new legend from one of the village elders, it reminded George of Nick's stories, about his grandfather's American Indian heritage,. In the mountain valleys, life was simpler.

As sons of a wealthy landowner, Andy, and now George, were treated well. Yet, it had its drawbacks. There was nothing they could do that everyone didn't know they had done the next day. Everyone knew them by sight and made sure they were always safe, even if they didn't want to be.

In the fall, Andy and George tried to escape from their CORE officer watchers by running through a banana field on one of the few times they had been allowed to walk home from school. Ducking down into a drainage ditch and crossing through a second banana field, the boys escaped their watchers and found a small waterfall and pool of crystal-clear water. The boys swam and chased fish around the pool that afternoon oblivious to the manhunt Andy's mother had started when the boys went missing. A few farmhands, coming down from their mountain homes, saw the boys at the waterfall, and reported the boy's location when they got to the farm late in the afternoon.

Salo, the lead farmhand who helped run the farm for Andy's father, retrieved the boys and brought them to the main farmhouse. Andy's mom was angry to say the least! While she never raised her voice at the two boys, her disappointment was obvious.

"You both have responsibilities and duties to your family and the people around you. Your privileges are earned in this house, not given to you because of your birth into this family. If the two of you have so much free time, perhaps cleaning out the stables will help fill your weekends for the next month," she said firmly, nodding to Salo.

Salo nodded. He would make sure her wishes were carried out and the boy's work would be sufficiently difficult, so that they would learn their lesson. This was the countryside, the wilds of Brazil, and disappearing for hours at a time was not acceptable; to say nothing of how dangerous it could be.

"No more foolishness. You are not children. You both have responsibilities," Andy's mom said firmly, and Salo led the boys away toward the lower barns to begin their new chores.

"The life may be simpler here, but I am always watched and kept out of trouble. I must always be aware of where I am and the family I represent when I speak," Andy said, repeating his mom's words as he and George cleaned the stables that evening.

They both knew Andy's mom was right; however, it didn't make them happy.

"I know she is right, but...," Andy whined, shoveling another scoop from one of the barn stalls. "It's like we can never just have any fun anymore. We are always watched! We have no freedom," he said and sighed.

"You mean without someone, well you know, mad at us for, well, for anything we do," George said wistfully, as he shoved used straw from another horse stall.

That fall, the boys completed Salo's list of grueling chores without complaint. Salo chose the chores and the farm workers the boys would be working alongside of carefully. The boys had much to learn and Salo wasn't going to waste the opportunity.

As they worked, the boys listened and learned from the farmhands working with them. George learned more that fall about diplomacy while speaking with the poorest of labors than he had in all the summer camps he had attended in the previous years. If they were not careful, they could end up with the only food a laborer had; and his family would go hunger that night~ simply because he said, he liked the man's chickens or corn.

Like last year at George's house, the boys' driver to and from high school, each week was a CORE officer who watched them. Yet, Andy had no idea why when everyone else in the valleys always watched them. In the spring, the driver let the boys walk home along the road again. However, this time the CORE officer followed a short distance behind them in the car~never losing sight of the two boys since last fall's banana field incident was not yet a distant memory to the CORE officer. It wasn't much freedom, however, it was Earth. They could breathe the air and eat the food without dying.

Andy's dad was gone most of the time now, and his older brother, Persio, was running the farm with only the occasional interference from his dad. Andy loved the farm; however, it had never been his desire to stay. His older brother had always wanted to farm and had not wanted to be a judicial court judge like their dad. What different paths they had taken, and yet, they were both happy.

One Friday in early spring, Andy's dad came home a week early as a big court case had ended sooner than expected. With unexpected free time, Andy's dad brought some friends from the University and the National Museum in the city out to stay at the farmhouse with their families for the weekend. It was a nice break for everyone's family. They could get out of the hot city for a while and enjoy the peace and quiet of the countryside.

Andy's father and the company arrived before the boys returned home from school on a Friday afternoon. Andy's mom and her helping women had set up tables and chairs for a large picnic on the swimming pool terrace for the guests to eat dinner outside that evening. Andy's brother, Persio, had a large fire, burning in the fire pit, off to the side of his mom's flower garden, just down a small sloping hill below the upper pool terrace.

George thought the backyard had to be five acres of gardens and walkways, not including the pool terrace. The gardens were beautiful and many of the workers had had their weddings and wedding receptions on the terraces.

Andy explained that by having a large garden and yard to tend, his mother could keep more people working and paid. She was taking care of the people of the valleys and the mountains the best way she could. She knew they were a proud people and wouldn't take money without working for it. It was her way of protecting her part of the planet. If the people had good work, then they could feed their families and were less likely to poach the endangered wildlife or do other things to make a living.

It was late Friday afternoon, when the CORE driver dropped the boys off in front of the sprawling one story stone farm-style house in early May. The red tile roof glistened in the sunlight as they stepped out of the beige car. They were greeted by Malone; the eldest son of Salo. Malone was about Persio's age and was destined to take over his father's position as the head farm manager when Salo retired.

"Your parents are waiting for your arrival to begin. Your mother is on the pool terrace now," Malone said politely.

"Thanks, Malone," the boys chorused.

Salo over saw the care of the house and farm for Andy's family and Malone was learning to do the same; yet, like Persio, both were waiting for their fathers to retire.

George thought about Salo as their lifted their backpacks out of the trunk of the car. Salo was more of a guide to Andy and himself. He was always looking out for them, covering for them when they did something wrong and keeping them out of trouble with Andy's mom.

Salo taught them about the traditions and mysteries of the people of the mountains and valleys from long ago. The stories he told often taught lessons about life in the mountains, and what was important to the people who lived there. He had become more of their friend and teacher to them. George smiled at the thought as they hurried across the front driveway.

"Malone will help your brother like Salo has helped your dad?" George signed as they ran up the two front stairs of the house, sliding into the front door.

"Yes, I'm sure. You know, there was a time when Malone and Persio were both younger and my dad was gone even more than now. Salo ran nearly everything on the farm alone. He was really busy for a few years. I don't know how we would have ever done it without him," Andy said, reaching for the door handles.

The two carved wooden doors were blocked open by two matching carved stones. The hand carved wooden screen doors were swinging slightly open and closed with the afternoon breeze blowing through the house. Hurrying inside, the boys raced down the hallway to their bedroom. They slid their bags of clothes and books across the black stone floor of the bedroom. The breeze in the hallway slammed the door shut as the boys spun around and raced down the hallway to get to the pool terrace and not be too late for Andy's mom.

Racing back toward the main living area, they swung around the corner wall, into the front entrance, and crashed head-long into Andy's older brother, Persio. Their impact sent Persio and the boys flying through the air and colliding with the closed library doors. The doors burst open, slamming hard against the inside walls. Together, they all tumbled across the stone floor, sliding to a stop at the base of Andy's dad's heavy wooden desk. Three sets of shoes stood in front of them as they scrambled to their feet. They had landed at the feet of Andy's dad and two of his guests. Persio jumped up and grabbed Andy and George's shirt collars. Quickly, he dragged the boys from the library before they could even straighten their clothes.

"Sorry sir. My apologies sir," Persio said, dragging Andy and George out of the library and closing the doors before the boys could see their fathers' guest's faces and disturb him further.

"Who were they?" Andy asked, ducking down as Persio took a casual swipe over his head.

"Andy, you and George need to be more careful. We have guests, you have responsibilities," Persio said firmly, sounding more and more like Andy's mom and dad.

"Ya, ya who were they? Dad looked so serious," Andy asked, pressing and ignoring his brother's advice.

"No one you need to know right now. It's business, and mom is steaming because you're late," Persio said, helping Andy and George hurry through the family room.

Andy and George shrugged their shoulders at each other.

"We have gotten home at nearly the same time every Friday. How could we be late? It has to be one of those parent things. Where you're late no matter what time it is," Andy signed, as they hurried through the family room. George nodded in agreement.

The three walked quickly across the red-tiled family room and left the house through the sliding screen doors that opened onto the terrace by the pool. Andy's mom saw them enter the terrace with Andy's dad and his two other guests following close behind. She raised her hands and the helping men and women uncovered the trays of food that lined one side of the pool terrace.

Before them, there were over flowing dishes and trays of homegrown vegetables and fruits, with homemade breads, meats, and soups.

"Gus, would be in heaven," George whispered and Andy laughed.

"Oh ya, a feast meant for Gus," Andy replied and they laughed.

Gus had feed them many meals of rations on their adventures over the last three years. Yet, every time Gus got the chance to cook, he had made their team the most amazing meals.

A second table across from the main food table had small cakes, cookies, and pies. Andy and George instantly stared at each other.

"Pies!" they said in unison and then laughed again.

They spun around looking over the guests; they were both looking to see if grandfather was there. Their existence had been calm and quiet this year. Emily had linked their computers together so they could instantly communicate at anytime. George could sense the presence of each of them and knew they were all OK. However, he couldn't communicate with them by thought, like, he had done during their last rotation. It seemed weird to have lost the ability to communicate by thought in a link. George would need to find out why when they finished the school year and returned to space for their fourth rotation.

Other than their team, the boys had little communication with anyone from space and the cadet stations except for their CORE driver for the entire school year. George had spent Christmas in Brazil with Andy's family. His mom and dad didn't come and every time he and Andy had tried to make a link with their triad, they could only sense their presence. No connection to their triad was ever made and George couldn't send any messages through a link to anyone except Andy.

"Grandfather isn't here, Andy," George whispered, still scanning over the guests. Nearly forty people lined up to fill their plates with the delicious foods and eat dinner. The boys waited until most of the guests were served before they entered the food line. They didn't want Andy's mom to frown at them for eating before their guests.

"It looks good. We should be able to get dinner now," Andy said, looking at the guests and pointing at the food tables.

They piled their plates as full as they could and wandered over to an empty table to eat. Andy looked around the terrace as they ate. He only knew a few of the people from the University and only one from the Museum. George knew no one. These people we friends of Andy's parents, no one they thought interesting enough to talk with as they ate with their best manors, even putting a napkin on their laps.

The stacks of food and deserts disappeared quickly from the serving trays, filling the guests to the brim—soon everyone was full. Several of the parents left early to get the young children off to sleep. Andy and George walked up to the food table, looking for a last nibble and something to drink.

Andy grabbed two bottles of water and laughed, handing one to George. Knocking them together, they walked down the lower path towards the roaring fire Andy's older brother had made. Many of the guests followed them down to the bonfire, sipping their drinks after dinner. Sitting near the warm, blazing fire, Andy pointed out the only guests he knew to George. There was the head curator at the National museum, two Judges and their families and two University professors and their families.

"Drinking water and breathing in the fresh air is amazing," George whispered.

"Seems like a big treat," Andy signed to George in their new sign language.

"It is so important. Yet, like the Calshene people, the people of Earth don't understand its value in the universe," George signed back.

"The Calshene planet is destroyed now. It's all gone. Only a bunch of asteroids circling their sun are left," Andy replied.

"They lost what was most precious to them and now they hate the Earthers because we don't appreciate our planet," George replied, thinking of their last rotation when they were on the Calshene cadet station–a dusty, dry moon with a harsh environment.

Calshene was once a planet like Earth, full of life with water and air. The planet was destroyed by evil and now only an asteroid belt with some moon size pieces circled their sun.

"Our planet is such a jewel in the universe," George signed to Andy.

"Maybe if everyone could see it from space, they would understand how important it is," Andy replied, as the fire roared up in front of them.

Andy's older brother liked big blazing bonfires when he had the time to make them. However, for the last few years it was rare to have one as Persio was becoming busier and busier with the business of the farm. Now, the family relished the bonfires they did have even more. Persio and Malone threw a few more logs on the fire and the flames leap higher into the air, illuminating the gardens below and warming the guests in the cool evening air.

Suddenly, George grabbed his head, bending over on the wooden bench where they sat. In the bright firelight, Andy stared at George. Grabbing his shoulders, he quickly, lifted him off the bench and they backed up to the edge of the terrace.

"Are you OK?" Andy whispered, glancing around the lower terrace.

"No, someone new is here. They must have just arrived," George answered, gritting his teeth together.

Andy spun around searching for a new face they had not seen at dinner. George squeezed his head and bent over again.

"I can stop this. I can. I can do it. It's just like last year at school after you arrived. I must stop this attack," George whispered, concentrating hard.

Chapter 2

HIDDEN DANGER

Andy saw no one new sitting with the other guests around the bonfire. He lifted George up under his arm and together they walked along the edge of the terrace to the stone steps leading toward the lower gardens and a small cluster of barns at the bottom of the hill.

Across the garden path and down the hill they hurried, getting further away from the blazing bonfire and the unseen new person. They stopped and rested on a stone seat near some bushy red flowers at the lower edge of the flower garden.

Andy nudged George's shoulder and formed a weak link. Last year, their team of cadets had learned how to communicate with each other and others by thought~ a link. It was an amazing way to communicate. Links worked whether you were close together or far away from each other. Yet, there was a bad side to communicating with your mind.

Stealthy invaders could slip into your mind and read your thoughts if you were not always on guard, protecting your thoughts. And worst of all, they could send energy through the link to destroy the person on the other end of the link. Last year, stealthy invaders had attacked George each time he made a link over any kind of distance in space. Max, a being of white light, had George and Andy stay in a nearly constant link over their rotation to keep them out of trouble.

This year, hidden away in the wilds of Brazil, the team had rarely communicated through links. Now, a stealthy invader had slipped into George's mind and formed a link with him. The invader was smooth as silk, and George didn't even know the invader was reading his thoughts until it was too late.

Andy joined the link with George and the invader; however, he couldn't figure out who had made the link. In his mind, George was trying to fight the invader and stop the attack. Yet, Andy couldn't sense who the invader was; but, he was sure George was losing the battle.

Andy was the cadet team's main defender. From a young age, he had learned how to protect his family. He could form a glowing red sphere of pure energy over the palm of his hand and send it flinging through the air to disable or destroy an attacking enemy. It was one wicked defense.

On his last rotation, Andy formed and threw many glowing red energy spheres to protect their team. In reality, he had thrown more glowing red energy spheres defending the team in their third rotation than most CORE officers did in a lifetime. Their team was given special training, earlier than most cadets, to help Andy learn to control the energy spheres.

Now, he needed to form a red energy sphere and give it to George to defend against the mind invader. Andy thought of a small, glowing red sphere of energy. He concentrated on forming the energy sphere in the palm of his hand to give to George to send through the link. It was what he had done last year when an invader attacked George's mind at school. Yet now, he couldn't seem to concentrate and focus his mind enough to form any energy spheres. No dancing, red energy sphere appeared above Andy's palm like last year in the spring. He was defenseless and so was George.

"I can't make any red spheres, George. This is bad. We need to get further away," Andy whispered. "Someone with a strong mind is here, a hidden Senior Viceroy maybe and I think they are blocking me so another person can attack you," Andy added, looking quickly around the hillside.

"This is bad, bad, bad, George, something is not right. I got nothing. We are totally defenseless unless you can break the link," Andy whispered, hardly able to concentrate himself.

George only groaned, holding his arm over his stomach. Andy lifted George up under his shoulder again and turned away from the lower terrace and the guests. They walked slowly down the path towards the main barns. To someone watching them, it looked like the boys were in a secret conversation, huddled close together as they whispered.

A few of the farmhands and their families who had helped serve the guests earlier were sitting around a smaller fire in front of one of the barns finishing their desert as Andy and George walked passed.

"Can we help you with George, sir?" the eldest farmhand asked, as he sent one of his elder children to find Salo.

"Is he hurt, sir?" one of the wives asked, standing up as the boys came into view of the firelight.

"No, no, he is fine ma'am. I think he ate something that didn't agree with his stomach. Please stay by the warm fire. We will be fine. Thank you ma'am," Andy said calmly, nodding and carrying George passed the far barn to a wooden bench on the edge of one of the grazing fields.

George bent over. In the moonlight, George looked like he was sick to the farmhands watching them. Nodding, they turned back toward their warm fire, hoping Salo would arrive soon. Andy and George were not just the sons of their employer; they were nearly family to the people who worked on the farm. Out in the countryside of Brazil, the people took care of each other.

In the distance, Andy could see the first watch fire and the farmhands watching over the cattle at night. With the farmhands by the barns backs turned, Andy lifted George up and walked further from the far barns and the farmhouse down the path, leading toward the watch fires. The evening air was cool and crisp. George opened his eyes and shivered a little.

"Where are we, Andy?" he asked in a whispered.

"We are between the far barns and the watch fires. It's a good half mile from the farmhouse now. You should be getting better," Andy whispered.

A moment later, a cool breeze blew over them and they dropped to the ground, as if it was a warning sign. The breeze reminded Andy of the breeze in the caves on Jupiter station, except it couldn't leave a message here on Earth. George's head stung again and he curled up in pain on the dirt path.

"It's not a mind invasion George. This is something else or someone else. I can't get a fix on them. Can you see who it is?" Andy whispered, worried as he rolled George over on the path, lifting his head from the dirt.

"No, I, no, help Andy, I can't," George whispered, and then stopped talking mid-sentence, his body slumping down on the ground.

Andy rolled George over. He was unconscious; their weak link broke. The air was still. Andy noticed some of the farmhands walking along the path with torches. They were heading out to change places with the others at the watch stations. Andy started panicking.

If the farmhands found them on the ground so far from the barns and safety, they would bring them up to the farmhouse; and his mom would make a fuss. Then, whoever had come late to the dinner would be closer to George and Andy wouldn't be able to protect him!

In a moment of desperation, Andy rolled George's crumpled body off the path and under the small palms and bushes on the ditch side of the path, opposite the grazing fields. Together, they slid down the low bank into the ditch that kept the hillside rainwater from flooding the fields. The ditch's mossy sandy bottom was dry as Andy crouched down with George. The farmhands laughed and joked as they walked passed, not seeing the hidden boys.

The forests and rivers were filled with predators, and intentionally going into the brush in the evening when many animals fed was a dangerous choice. When the farmhands were further down the path toward the watch fires, Andy lifted George's body up over his shoulder. He walked over the mossy ground on the bottom of the ditch. As he walked, Andy tried to wake George, making one link after the next.

He carried George for half-a-mile over fallen logs and around thorn covered bushes that torn his pants. Carefully, he stepped around spots of damp sandy soil. The damp sand could be a hiding a sinkhole or very soft soil. If they got stuck, there would be no one to help get them out anytime soon.

A narrow creek bed eventually replaced the ditch. A wall of rocks was stacked on the grazing field side to stop the spring water from flooding the fields. The hillside of the creek bed was getting steeper, the further away from the farm the boys travelled. A head of them, a section of the hillside had collapsed from the spring rains and covered the sandy creek bed with sharp rocks. Andy stopped and knelt down to rest. He leaned George up against a pile of larger boulders. The boulders were still warm from the afternoon sun.

"George, you have to wakeup. We are far away from the farmhouse now. There can't be anyone in the link with you anymore. Come-on, George, you can do it. Wakeup. We have beaten worse," Andy said, as he shook George's body.

George's head drooped forward and his arms lay still at his sides. With a little groan, Andy stood up and lifted him back up over his shoulder.

"Well, George, I'll tell you a secret. Salo told me about a cave out here. He, my dad, and some others stayed in it, out of the rain, when they were young men making the ditch longer to protect more fields from the spring rains. It could be just one of his stories. Like the other stories, he has told over the years. However, right now, I'm hoping it wasn't a story at all and that the cave really exists," Andy said, stepping over another fallen tree and nearly tripping on some branches before he regained his balance.

"That was a close one," he said, talking to George as if he could hear him.

Into the night, Andy walked further and further away from the safety of the farm. In the darkness, millions of stars lit the night sky. Andy shivered in the cool night air. He scanned the wooded bank of the dry creek bed for a shelter. There were only a few fallen trees, nothing to cover over them and keep them warm from the cold night air. He had nothing to start a fire with him.

"So, how far do you think dad and Salo dug the ditch and cleaned out the creek bed, George? It must go on for miles!" he said, going around the roots of a large over turned tree.

Still no answer from George, as his body shivered in the night air. Andy stepped on a slippery tree root and fell to the ground. He grabbed George's head as they fell to keep it from hitting the rocks. However, George's body hit the ground as hard as Andy's body. For a moment, Andy laid still, checking to see if his ankle was broken or only aching from twisting it so hard when they fell. He rolled George over against some roots and reached down to rub his ankle.

"Twisted, not broken, all good," he muttered and then stared at George. "OK, so when you wake up, you're going to hurt a bit and you may have one nasty bruise on your shoulder too. On the good side, your head can't hurt anymore than it does now," Andy said, and then paused sighing a long sigh. Standing up, he groaned and shook his ankle.

"Max, grandfather, where are you? Why can't George find you? Why can't we make a link?" Andy asked into the night sky, wanting answers.

He lifted George over his shoulder and shivered in the cool night air. It was late and they were not dressed for the night air in the Brazilian countryside. In the dim light of the quarter moon, the faint outline of larger rocks and boulders appeared high above them on the hillside. Maybe it was the cave Salo told him about. Andy hoped there would be some warmth left in the rocks from the mid-day sun and some trees branches to make a shelter as he limped along, slower than before.

The ditch and creek bed were fairly even ground; however, the hillside opposite the fields was steep. When they reached the next outcrop of rocks, Andy turned to leave the ditch and climb the steep hillside to the rocky opening he saw earlier. The hillside rocks and soil slipped under their weight and made little landslides of gravel and loose dirt that slid down into the ditch. Andy didn't even try to hide their trail. His only concern was finding shelter from the cold night air.

Rock to rock, roothold to brush stalk, he pulled himself, and George higher and higher up the hillside. Halfway up, he missed his grab for a tree root and they slid almost all of the way down the steep hillside before Andy could stop their fall. He grabbed at every branch and root they passed with his free hand, all the while kicking his feet and knees into the rocks and dirt. His bleeding hand ached from grabbing at the roots and rocks.

When they stopped falling, he started up the hillside again; however, this time he kicked his feet harder into the rocky ground to get a better foothold for their climb. He was exhausted and he wasn't sure he could climb the hill a third time. Halfway up the hill, a breeze blew across his face ~ Andy froze.

"Are you our breeze from Jupiter station?" Andy asked, as if the breeze would answer him. "Can you find us help? I may have made a mistake on this one, by leaving the farmhouse so far behind. I need to be more prepared in the future. I was caught off guard this time. Man, I can't believe I'm talking to the wind. You'd think I was Emily or something. I know she can talk with you, ya know," he said to the breeze.

A few moments later, the breeze disappeared and Andy started moving up the hillside again. He was tired and thought of how strong Gus was and how good it would be to have his strength with them now or to have Sara heal whatever was wrong with George. He was shivering more now, as the night air was as cold as the mid-day sun was hot.

His link with George had slipped away. Andy could barely focus his thoughts and worry started to cloud his mind. Had he made the wrong choice in leaving the safety of the farmhouse? No, it was the right decision to leave, but maybe he should have found Salo first, his mind raced as he climbed higher and higher up the steep hillside.

Finally, he was within reach of the edge of the rocky ledge. Squinting, he could make out the shape of a small cave. Reaching up with all of his strength, he flipped George off his shoulder and pushed him up onto the ledge near some of the rocks he had seen from the ditch.

Grabbing a tree root and pulling himself up to the edge of the ledge, he was suddenly face to face with a large black puma. Andy stared into the dark eyes of the black puma. Without stopping, he pushed forward toward the large cat. He couldn't leave George alone on the ledge with the cat; so it didn't seem to matter that the puma could kill him with a single swipe of its claws across his face.

The puma backed up and grabbed onto George's shirt collar. It dragged his body toward a small cave. Andy crawled over the ledge and followed the puma, keeping close to the ground. His knees and feet ached. Andy crept quietly into the cave entrance, following the puma. The puma was waiting inside beside a man who had knelt down next to George. Andy bolted forward as he entered the cave opening to rescue George. As he leapt forward, he was caught by another man and lifted off the ground.

"Slow down child. You are safe here," the second man said calmly.

Andy flipped out of the second man's arms and landed on his feet closer to George. The puma snarled, showing its white fangs. Andy looked up at the man next to George and suddenly dropped down on one knee, lowering his head in respect. The man was dressed in an animal skin pants and wore a bone and grass collar over his shoulders.

"Forgive me," Andy whispered.

All his life he had heard stories about the medicine people of the rainforests. He had thought Salo and the other storytellers were really talking about the medicines hidden within the rainforest's plants and animals. Now in a moment of clarity, he knew Salo and the other hill people had told stories within stories and had been very careful in the words they had chosen to tell the stories. They had told a different truth within the stories. The medicine people were real and hidden from the rest of the world.

The man who had lifted Andy off the ground before, now lifted George up over his shoulder and the puma nudged Andy to stand and follow. Andy's knees melted as he tried to stand again on the flat ground. The second man lifted Andy up and he fell asleep.

In the night, Andy heard a rhythm in his sleep ~ the music of drums beating within the ground beneath him. Calm over took him as he fell back into a deep sleep.

Chapter 3

MEDICINE PEOPLE

Andy woke up in a small room swinging in a hammock with a coarsely woven brown wool blanket covering him. George swung slowly in the hammock next to Andy.

"George, are you awake?" he whispered.

Andy was hoping George was better and now only asleep. The puma from the night before had been resting in the corner of the room, the end of its long tail twitched. Andy leaned forward to see George better and fell from his hammock, landing with a thud and sending curls of dust into the air. He groaned as the big cat sneezed, shaking its head.

Standing, the puma stretched out and walked over to Andy. The cat sniffed his hair as it turned and rubbed against George's hand, leaving the small gray room. George rolled over and pulled his hand back under his heavy woolen blanket. Andy jumped forward nearly knocking George from his hammock, swinging it high into the air.

"George, you're OK? Speak to me?" Andy yelled, and then fell to the ground in pain; his shoes stained with blood, his pants covered in blood and dirt.

His hand was stinging with pain as it started to bleed again after falling out of his hammock.

"Andy, what is wrong with you? Hey, where are we?" George asked, rolling over and falling to the floor of the small room with Andy. "Awe! Man that hurts," George said, cringing and laying his head in the dirt.

His shoulder ached and as a trickle of blood slid across his forehead. He laid still in the dirt.

"I thought you were a goner. You passed out on me after your head started to hurt at the bonfire last night," Andy whispered, staring at George

"The last thing I remember was being at the bonfire after dinner. Everything else is a blur. I can't remember a thing. What happened?" George asked, rolling carefully over to sit up in the dirt. He started rubbing his head, smearing the blood on his forehead.

"You said someone came to the party late and your head started to hurt really badly. We made a link, but there wasn't anyone there. We keep walking further and further from the farm. I was looking for the cave Salo talked about for shelter when he and my dad had extended the rock wall to protect more fields from the spring rains. I think I found the cave, but when I got you to it, there was a puma in it. There were two men in the cave too. Then we ended up here," he answered.

"Where is here?" George asked, looking around from the floor of the room.

"I think these are the medicine people of the forest, but, I don't know. I thought they were only people in the stories Salo told me when I was young. Now, well, I don't know. It's like there was a story inside a story and now I have to figure out what he really meant when he and the others spoke," Andy said, shrugging his shoulders, even he was a little confused by what he said.

The puma returned to the doorway and stared at the boys on the ground.

"Rrrwww," it said and then left the door.

They locked arms and pulled each other up. George stumbled back and grabbed his shoulder as a fierce pain shot down his arm.

"Oh, ya, that, it's going to hurt for a while, sorry about that," Andy said, grinning sheepishly.

"Can't wait to find out how that happened!" George replied, gritting his teeth as they followed the puma through the doorway and into the morning light.

Andy walked on his heels as pain shot across his feet and up his legs with every step.

"What's up?" George asked, pointing toward Andy's feet.

"Must be from the rocks during our climb," he replied, as if it was not important.

"You climbed a mountain with me over your shoulder?" George asked, stunned at Andy's strength.

"More of a hillside, cliff thing," Andy replied, motioning with his hands in the form of a hill and cave, passing it off as if it was nothing big.

George frowned, but pressed no further. It would have been hard on Andy and now he was hurt. George wasn't pleased with Andy's choices and he was sure Andy was leaving stuff out so as not to worry him.

Outside the small room, they stopped and gazed. They had slept in a room carved into the side of a hill. The path in front of them connected many other houses and rooms carved into the side of the hill. The top of the cave wall towered above them as if the rooms were carved into the back of the cave. Forest trees and vines hung down over the edge, obscuring the cave from the air. Below their walkway was another row of rooms or houses carved into the hillside. Beyond the half cave, there was a valley filled with plants, the songs of birds, and a river flowing through it. The sounds of a waterfall and rushing water echoed through the valley.

"Where are we?" they asked simultaneously.

"You are in the valley of the medicine people," answered a warm voice.

An older woman stood next to them, as if, she was also marveling at the beauty of the valley. They hadn't even noticed her arrival. She was a tall woman with long brown hair that flowed in the light breeze. She wore a fluffy white shirt with a flowing brown skirt covered by a large white apron. Well-worn sandals covered her feet.

"How did we get here, ma'am?" George asked, staring at her.

"As most do, you came with the wind," she replied softly.

"I remember the breeze. It can't speak here, can it ma'am?" Andy said, guessing.

"No, not here, but elsewhere it speaks if you listen. Come, you must be hungry," she said, leading them down the path toward a cooking fire.

He boys followed her slowly, painfully down the path. Soon, she motioned them to sit down on well-worn logs that circled a cooking fire. The puma rubbed against her leg and then sat down across from George and Andy.

"My name is," George started to say; however, she raised her hand.

"I know who you are Mr. Hawkins, Mr. Penteado. I am called Tara," she said kindly.

"Please call me George, ma'am," he said kindly.

"And me Andy, ma'am," he added kindly.

"Only if you call me Tara," she said, scooping out steaming bowls of very dark brown mushy cereal with a wooden spoon from the kettle hanging over the fire. "Eat, you need to regain your strength," she said softly, as she pulled out two smaller wooden spoons from her white apron.

They took a bite. It wasn't that bad. It reminded them of the Inner Circle officer's cereal they had eaten on their last rotation on Asteria station, except there was no bitter after taste.

"I wonder if it is the same cereal as before when we were with the Inner Circle officer?" George signed and Andy nodded.

Then Andy changed the topic to find out more about where they were and whom the medicine people really were. He didn't like not knowing about his surroundings.

"Last night, Tara, there were two men that helped us. One lifted George up and carried him here. Who were they?" Andy asked, scooping a heaping spoon full of cereal into his mouth.

"They will return in the evening," she replied, not answering his question.

She smiled and ladled out two cups of water from a large wooden bucket, then brought the small wooden cups filled with water to George and Andy.

"What is this place, Tara? I feel a great calm here," George asked, looking around the valley.

"Eat more, talk less. You will know and understand soon enough," she said, ladling another scoop of very dark brown cereal into their bowls and then returned to the little table she was working at.

Andy drank down his water and held up the cup in the air, twisting it in the light.

"It's kinda blue George," he whispered, staring at the cup.

During their past rotation, each time they had been with Max, their silver cups turned blue when they shared water with him. Now, each time they saw blue cups, they wondered if Max or the beings of white light were somehow nearby, hidden so others wouldn't see him or them.

George and Andy knew of Max as a protector and teacher; however, to the rest of the universe, he and the other beings of white light commanded great respect and power.

"I know," he answered, not looking at the cup. "This place is different. We are no longer on Earth. We are somewhere else. Somewhere calm and at peace," he said cryptically, breathing deep as if to inhale the essence of the valley.

"Not on Earth, hmm, I wonder," Andy whispered and rolled his hand over, a small red sphere danced on his palm. "I can do it again. Hey, George, look!" Andy said, tossing a pointy red glowing sphere from one hand to another as if playing with a toy.

George smiled. "It is this valley. This place. I wonder...," he muttered beneath his breath so Tara wouldn't hear him.

He closed his eyes and reached out into the universe. Andy put away his red sphere and put his hand on George's shoulder, joining his link. He called out to Toma, Frank, and Pete. They answered nearly immediately.

"George you must stay hidden. We will come and get you when your school term is done," Pete said, firmly and closed the link abruptly.

"How did you do that, George? You haven't been able to do it since we started school," Andy said, gasping.

He stared at his blueish cup of water, Tara, and finally at the bowl of dark brown cereal in front of him.

"It's something in the food. The enzyme Sara talked about, maybe. We stopped being able to anything but the most basic of communications shortly after we returned to high school on Earth this year. I thought it was the Earth or maybe you had to be in space to make a link," George whispered, frowning as he thought.

"But it's not that at all, is it?" Andy asked puzzled.

"No, it's not. It's the food we have been eating. The food we freely chose to eat," George replied, staring at his bowl.

"No George. It's some sort of plot or something," Andy said, shaking his head.

"No, Andy it is the food we have been eating and the cereal Tara gave us stopped the 'something' that stopped us from making our links. Maybe it has extra enzyme like the officer's cereal and so it makes our link possible," he answered, putting together a puzzle of clues, yet, not fully understanding the answers or words he said.

"Why, George? Answer me. Why would someone do this? Why would someone try and stop you from doing your 'something' on Earth?" Tara asked, having listened to their conversation.

She poured more water into their cups as she pressed them to think.

"The Galactic council doesn't want anyone on Earth using their skills by accident?" George answered.

"Others might find out about the cadets and the officers. I'm not sure Earth, as a whole, is really ready to know they are not alone in the universe. They might see us as a threat," Andy added.

"Hmm, perhaps. However, I think there is more," Tara said, hinting.

They finished their cereal and returned the bowls and cups to Tara without answering her question.

"You are both covered in mud and dirt. I think a wash in the river would be good," she said, changing the subject.

They looked at each other and laughed. George had mud on his back and legs and more running through his hair. Andy had dirt-covering most of his arms and body, with extra clumps and smudges on his face. Odd, they hadn't noticed before.

Tara pointed out the path, and the boys hobbled down the narrow dirt path toward the river. The path wound down the steep hillside, and Andy's toes ached as his feet slid forward in his shoes. George lifted some small fallen branches covering the path and a sharp surge of pain shot down his arm from his shoulder. Instantly, he dropped the branches. He pushed them off to the side of the path with his foot.

Andy smiled and said nothing. It had been a difficult hike through the ditch and up the steep hillside. Andy wasn't going to tell George. He didn't need to know the details, only that they were safe now. He needed George focused on the future, not the past.

At the water's edge, they stopped and looked for animal tracks. If other animals used the water, it would be relatively safe. If there were no tracks, the water would be dangerous.

They scanned the river and watched a family of otters play on the far shore. A Kingfisher dove into the river, chasing fish for its breakfast. Andy nodded and they hobbled across a small sandy beach into the river. The water was clear and warm. They scrubbed their clothes and laid their shirts, shoes, and socks on some rocks to dry in the morning sun. They swam around the weeds in the river, following the fish over the river rocks. They stirred up the bottom sand and watched the smaller fish dart through the haze, catching their breakfast.

Finally, they emerged from the warm river water and sat in the sun, warming themselves and staring at the mid-day sky. The swelling in Andy's feet disappeared and George's shoulder seemed to heal. Together, they reached out into the universe again. It felt uneasy, not the calm they had been expecting.

"Odd, that everything wouldn't be calm now. Everything was pretty calm at the end of our last summer rotation," George signed, practicing their new sign language.

"We left it in good shape," Andy said, and yet... he twisted, thinking how odd it sounded; them leaving the entire universe calm and evil pushed back to its corner of the universe.

They stared at the sky and thought. They were cleaner now and perhaps a little less odiferous. Hunger over took their thoughts, and they thought of Gus and his wonderful meals and Sara and her vitamins. They got dressed and walked back up the hill path to where they had left Tara.

"You know I have always wanted to ask Gus what we were eating when he made us dinner on the cadet stations," Andy signed, also practicing the new sign language.

"And what the purple liquid is," George added. They laughed.

"Yet, I kinda don't want to know at the same time," Andy signed.

"I know what you mean, it's like you want to know, but if you did know, then you're afraid you won't like it because of what it is so then the food would be ruined for you," George said, finishing Andy's thought.

"Yup, that's it. So what is the answer?" Andy asked, staring at the banana trees lining the dirt path.

"What answer?" George asked.

"The answer to Tara's question, George," he pressed.

"Oh that. I'd say something is not right. It's not wrong. It's just not right with the energy of the universe. Well, something like that," he answered a little cryptically.

"Call grandfather and Max. Ask them," Andy suggested.

"No, we can't. Pete wasn't happy we contacted him and the others before the end of the school term. Let's think for a minute about how happy grandfather and Max might be if we call them early," he said, rubbing his chin.

The boys stopped in their tracks, on the path, with goofy-thinking grins on their faces.

"Good point, if the energy of the universe is messed up, then hearing from us before the end of school term will not go over well at all," Andy said, rubbing his chin too.

George nodded in agreement and they started walking along the path again. They gathered wood next to the path for the cooking fire and carried two arms full of wood as they walked into the outside kitchen area. Tara was scooping out bowls of very dark brown cereal for the boys when they arrived.

"Much better. I think the breeze may even return now," she said teasing, handing them they bowls of cereal.

They smiled. Laying the wood by the fire and they took the bowls from Tara.

"Thank you for the food, Tara," Andy said, smiling.

"Is there anything we can do for you? Anything you need, ma'am?" George asked politely.

"I only need the two of you to get stronger and regain your calm and focus," she said, smiling kindly.

"Yes, ma'am," George replied.

"Blue cups George, these are blue cups. It is Max, he is here somehow. Maybe they know about the beings of white light?" Andy whispered, as they sat on the wooden benches again.

"Maybe Tara is one of the beings of white light. Either way, we can't ask. It is a secret we can't betray," he signed to Andy.

Tara came back and plopped a second scoop of cereal into their bowls.

"Thanks, Tara," George said, looking up to study her face.

"Eat. You're welcome," she replied, returning to her cutting table.

"This stuff isn't so bad," Andy said.

"True, I wonder if we can do the officer's trick now?" George said, staring at his bowl.

"What trick?" Andy asked.

"You remember, you think about the food you want and then the food you're eating turns into it. It doesn't really turn into something else. You just trick yourself into it, I think," George replied, staring at his bowl harder.

"OK, I'm in. I want a stack of pancakes with maple syrup, dripping over the stack," Andy said, laughing and staring at his cereal bowl.

"I want a sandwich filled with peanut butter and jelly, oozing out around the edges," George said, as they both looked down at their bowls.

Nothing changed. The cereal still looked like dark brown cereal. Tara smiled as she cut up vegetables, knowing what the boys were doing.

"Well, maybe it takes more practice," Andy whispered.

"Is everything alright, George, Andy?" Tara asked kindly.

"Yes, everything is fine, ma'am. Thank you for the food," Andy replied.

"Are you sure there is nothing we can do for you today, Tara?" George asked again.

"Go and get some rest now. Your journey to us has been difficult," Tara said, pointing up the hill to the room they had slept in the evening before.

"Yes, ma'am," they answered together.

"So do you think she is sending us off to nap time like little kids?" Andy whispered.

"Yep, but then I don't think it's something we can argue about," George replied, pointing to the puma standing in the path looking at them as if waiting for them to follow.

Andy couldn't help but agree. Somehow crossing Tara and a puma didn't seem like the right thing to do. They followed the puma to their sleeping room and laid down on the hammocks as the puma curled up in the corner of the room.

"Is it guarding us?" Andy asked.

"I think so," George whispered.

They drifted off to sleep as calm over took their thoughts. George felt connected to the world and the universe again. No one was hurt, still, there was conflict where there should be calm and focus. It was as if the universe had suddenly realized it had stopped evolving and didn't know how to start evolving again or what to do next. It was stuck and not prepared for its next steps. The universe had been in order for more than a hundred thousand years and now it was lost in the chaos of change.

On their last rotation, their team had read the prophecy that guided the universe and all of the beings for eons. By the end of their rotation, the prophecy had changed; their team and triad had lived. The universe and Galactic councils seemed unprepared for the new challenges before them.

Had the great experiment run its course? Was it to die out, similar to the extinction of the dinosaurs on Earth? Would it now fall apart or could they change, reorder, and grow, accepting change? The beings of the universe would need to find a new way to see the future and instill the idea of change and growth again as it had eons ago. Only time would tell or the prophecy, of course.

The puma stood and stretched, rubbing up against Andy and George before leaving the small cave room. George and Andy yawned, stretched, and fell to the floor again, trying to get out of the hammocks. The rising curls of dust made them sneeze.

The puma rrrwwwd outside the room doorway as the boys dusted themselves off and walked outside. It was late afternoon and they could hear voices down by the cooking fire.

They walked silently down the path, following the puma to the cooking fire. Tara was working at the table again. She was making stacks of tortillas. Food bubbled in a second kettle over the fire. The most delicious smells wafted into the air.

"What do you think it is?" Andy whispered.

"I don't know, but it smells great," George replied, as he breathed in the air as if to taste it.

Chapter 4

STRONG AGAIN

Three men stood up from their seats, facing the boys when they got closer to the table near the fire. Andy recognized two of the men from the evening before. The third older man was new to Andy.

"Good evening, sirs. Thank you for helping us last night, sirs," Andy said, dipping his head in respect.

"You're welcome. I am pleased you are doing better," the oldest of the three men replied.

"My name is," George said, starting to introduce himself when the elder man raised his hand.

"We know who you are George and Andy. I am Aris and this Tao and Mag," the oldest of the three men said.

"Have we met before, sir?" George asked, staring at Aris.

In his mind, George was sure Aris was the eldest member of the beings of white light high council. Yet, he knew he could say nothing. Aris and the others only stared back at the boys as if studying them.

"Tara has been feeding us well, sir," Andy answered, staring at George wondering why Aris didn't answer George's question.

Tara carried two bowls of warm dark brown cereal over to the boys and smiled.

"Thank you, ma'am," George said, smiling and taking the bowls from her hands.

Andy was disappointed at not getting to taste the tortillas and the bubbling kettle of food; however, he was happy to be fed at all and so welcomed into their lives that he couldn't say anything.

"Is something wrong?" Aris asked, staring at Andy.

"No sir. The hospitality of your home is great. Thank you, sir," Andy replied, nodding his head.

George and Andy sat down on the benches around the warm fire to eat their cereal. The three men and Tara scooped the food from the bubbling kettle and placed it on the tortillas. They sat down on the wooden benches around the fire and all ate together as the boys ate cereal from their bowls.

"Andy, why were you in the ditch and the cave last night? You know it is not safe," Tao asked, as he took a bite of his tortilla.

"We were at the bonfire on the lower terrace when someone attacked George's mind. It was a stealthy attack, something like what has happened to us before. Someone was attacking his mind and I couldn't stop them. We tried to make our link stronger so I could give George a red energy sphere. But, I couldn't even make a red energy sphere. We were defenseless, so I left the farm. I thought George would get better if he was further away from whomever was trying to hurt him, sir," Andy replied and paused a long pause, looking down into his bowl. "It didn't help. It was a mistake and George got worse, sir," Andy answered, not looking up, only staring into his bowl of cereal.

Suddenly, he looked up, staring at the three men. He had told them about links and energy spheres. He was worried he had said too much. Yet, the three men and Tara didn't even seem surprised by what he had said.

"How did you find us?" Mag asked, trying to change the subject a little and keep Andy talking.

Andy grinned a little. "Salo told me a story about a cave he and dad had stayed in a long time ago when they had made the ditch to protect the fields. I was looking for the cave so we could get out of the cold night air. There was this breeze of wind when we left the farm. It kinda showed me where to go," Andy said, looking up and staring at the men, thinking his story was getting weirder by the minute; yet, the men didn't seem surprised by his words.

"It is fortunate for you the breeze looked favorably on you last night. It is not always in such a generous mood," Mag replied, as a breeze blew across the fire and then disappeared.

"Do you know where you are?" Tao asked kindly.

"Tara said we were in the valley of the medicine people," Andy answered, looking at Tara and then George.

"Yes, Andy. George, do you have a thought to add?" Tao pressed.

"No sir, we will stick with Andy's answer, sir," George replied, looking at Andy.

George knew they were somewhere else, and it wasn't the valley of the medicine people. He was sure they were no longer on Earth. He kept thinking of the tunnel hog cave on Asteria station and the beings of white light they had met there. However, he couldn't ask. He couldn't betray their secret to satisfy his own curiosity.

"The universe is a vast place, don't you think George?" Tao asked, leading George down a new path.

Aris sat quietly listening to George and Andy's words and thoughts. Aris was the leader of the beings of white light high council, and he and the other council members were taking advantage of the opportunity to learn more about George and Andy and see why Max had chosen to guide them through the universe.

"Yes sir, it is," he answered, as Tara put more cereal in his bowl.

"And what have you learned of our universe?" Tao said, questioning George.

"There is good and evil everywhere. It needs to be in balance, sir," George replied.

"Shouldn't we strive to destroy all evil?" Mag pressed firmly.

Andy signed trick and George nodded.

"No sir," he replied, taking another bite of cereal.

"Why?" Tara asked, tilting her head.

"Without evil, we would become complacent and not continue to grow and change. We wouldn't work to improve the lives of those around us and the lives of those we don't yet know, sir," George answered Mag as he stared at Aris, who had been quiet and asked few questions.

"Perhaps, without evil, you could spend more time improving the worlds around you?" Tao added, putting another log on the fire.

"No sir, without challenges and strife, we as a species don't seem to evolve and grow, sir. I can't speak for other species; however, the conflicts and necessities of life cause us to advance as a culture and society, sir," George added firmly, frowning a little, not understanding why they were asking such basic questions.

The light of the fire danced in front of them, as if trying to mesmerize them. Tara took their bowls and left them. Aris nodded and Tao opened a small leather bag he carried around his waist. He pulled out two leather patches on thin leather cords. Tao and Mag tied knots in the ends of the cords and handed them to Andy and George.

"Wear these around you necks. It will stop the affects of what is being feed to you for now," Mag said seriously.

"Do not use your abilities. Keep them hidden. Others must not know you have them back," Tao added firmly.

"Yes sir," Andy replied.

"When do we take the patches off, sir?" George asked.

"You will know. It is late now, you need to rest," Aris said and the puma stood up.

"Thank you, sir," they replied together.

They weren't going to argue with a puma. They had so many questions to ask. They would have to wait till morning.

When boys were out of sight, Aris, Tao, and Mag shimmered with a brilliant white light. They were pleased with George and Andy's answers and left.

The next morning, the boys woke up in their beds at the farmhouse. Andy glanced at George.

"What happened?" Andy signed, stunned they were at home.

They thought they would wake up in the small room with the puma and then they would have to walk back to the farmhouse. Yet, there they were in Andy and George's room.

"I don't know?" George replied, sitting up in his bed and looking around the room.

"How did we get here?" Andy asked, rolling over, his feet hitting the cool stone floor.

It was his room all right. Yet, they had no idea how they got there.

"I don't know," George replied, rubbing his neck to find the thin leather cord attached to the patch under his shirt. "It's still here," he said, tugging on the patch.

"So, it was real. We didn't dream it. Right?" Andy asked, holding his patch in his hand.

"Yes. I feel stronger today. Like I'm connected to the energy of the universe again," George replied, nodding his head and staring at his patch.

Nonetheless, he thought it sounded odd, being connected to the energy of the universe. It was a weird feeling he had and it was hard to describe.

"I wonder what day it is," George said.

"Man, we are going to be in so much trouble for leaving," Andy said, swallowing hard and George nodded.

"Boys, your driver is here. Where are you?" Andy's mom called down the hallway, getting frustrated.

"What happened to Saturday and Sunday?" Andy asked.

The boys tore out of their room, running down the hallway to the front foyer wearing the same clothes they had on Friday. It was early Monday morning, and Salo was loading their book bags and clothing bags into the car for them as they ran out through the front doors.

"You two are fortunate Salo takes such good care of you. Behave. I'll miss you both," she said, hugging them before they ran out to the car.

They were stunned. Andy's mom wasn't even mad at them for being gone for two days! What really happened? A million questions ran through their minds. Salo opened the car door and Andy clasped his other hand.

"Thanks, Salo, and I mean for everything," Andy said, thinking Salo must have been somehow covering for them.

When they returned on Friday, they would need to find out what had happened while they were gone.

"Did you find them, Andy?" Salo asked cryptically, knowing the boys had been gone all weekend.

"Yes, we did. Thank you, sir," Andy replied and let go of his arm.

"Did you find the answers you were seeking, George?" Salo asked, staring at him with a puzzled look on his face.

"No, not yet, sir," George said, shaking his head.

"In time, you will see more clearly," Salo said cryptically, adding to their puzzle.

"Thank you for your help, sir," George added, shaking his hand.

Salo patted the boys on their backs, and they slid into the car, thinking only of school and their missing homework assignments on the ride to the high school. They knew their driver was a CORE officer and accomplished at reading the thoughts of untrained minds.

An hour car ride later and they arrived at the high school. Hurriedly, they left their driver, running to their dorm room to drop off their clothes and spinning on their heels, racing to their first class.

"So, what was Salo talking about? How did he know where we were?" George asked, running up the flight of stairs.

"I don't know exactly. It's well, Salo was the one who told me the stories about the medicine people when I was very young," Andy replied, leaping around the end of the railing.

"I can't believe your mom didn't notice we were missing all weekend," George said, as they slowed in the hallway, crossing over to the classroom building from the dormitory.

"Salo must have been covering for us," Andy added, staring out the windows toward the distant hills.

"It does make you wonder if he is a CORE officer, assigned to take care of your family or something else," George said, hurrying around the last corner before their classroom.

"Perhaps, he has been with our family for as long as I can remember. We'll never make it, George," Andy said hurriedly.

He was the cryptic one now, racing down the hallway. They slid into their chairs as the first hour bell rang.

"Good morning class, open your books to chapter ten. As this is your last week of school before the summer break, we will be studying only from our books. All lab supplies are to be turned in at the end of the hour. Please review the periodic table as there will be a quiz in fifteen minutes," the chemistry teacher said, smiling with an evil grin as if pleased to see their hopeful happy faces fall at the thought of another pop quiz!

First hour chemistry ended and a second hour assembly followed instead of their regular classes. At the assembly, many of their friends and other students were honored for their accomplishments throughout the year. Andy and George weren't in the honored group of students. They preferred a lower profile as their accomplishments needed to be discrete on Earth. They thought drawing attention to themselves would most likely not be looked on favorably by the Galactic council. The assembly ended when their fourth hour classes started. Andy, George, and their friends went to the cafeteria for lunch for fourth hour. Sweet!

Unlike George's high school's cafeteria, Andy's high school's cafeteria didn't have an odor all its own. There were always fresh fruits and juices that the lunch women had prepared. They walked through the food line and sat at their usual table. A few friends sat with them and showed off their award pins and statues. George and Andy congratulated their friends on receiving their awards.

"Hey, maybe next year you'll get an award," Mika, one of Andy's friends said, trying to be encouraging.

"Of course, there is always next year!" Andy replied, smiling and toasting his friends' success with a carton of milk.

"What's with George?" Mika asked, nodding in his direction.

"Homesick I think. It's been a long year for my cousin," Andy whispered, covering for George.

George was staring at his food, lost in thought. He couldn't take even one bite. A million questions ran through his mind. His focus was gone. He had thought they were safe on Earth, hiding in Brazil. Now all of his fears from last year, when he and his dad were nearly captured by evil, came flooding back into his mind.

"George, you have to eat," Andy whispered.

"I can't eat this. I can't eat it anymore," he said, and left the table, slipping his full tray of food in front of another student as he walked out through the cafeteria doors.

The student smiled at getting extra food and gobbled it down. Andy bolted from the table, flipping his tray onto another student's back. George hadn't been out of his sight for more than a year and he wasn't going to lose him now.

"Food fight!" echoed voices in the cafeteria, as Andy raced through the double doors after George.

In the hallway, Andy grabbed George's shoulder. George winced, bending down to release himself from Andy's grasp.

"Where are you going George? You know you can't just leave!" he said firmly.

"I don't know where to go. It's as if we are suddenly lost. Someone has been trying to make us weak or we did it ourselves. Either way, we need to think and figure out what to do next," he answered, muttering on and on, rambling, lost in his thoughts.

Andy spun him into the corner, behind the trophy case as the vice-principle and principle ran passed them and into the cafeteria. Within minutes, the food fight fun in the cafeteria was over. In the hallway, the boys could hear the principle barking out orders. Classes were suspended for the rest of the day and there would be no dinner tonight if the cafeteria was not spotless in three hours! The students groaned and started cleaning up the mess.

"Hurry George, this way," Andy whispered, pulling on George's shirt to get them away from the cafeteria doors before the principal and vice-principal emerged.

Andy and George hurried quickly down the hallway.

"I need to focus Andy. I can't even think right now," George said muttered.

He was simply following Andy, running through the hallways, not knowing where they were going or why. Andy ran faster passed the school office.

"I know where to go," Andy signed.

They turned right at the first hallway corner they came to. Andy wanted to be hidden before the principal left the cafeteria and had questions for them. Down two flights of stairs they raced. Andy burst through the double doors at the bottom of the stairs, into a small room with a high ceiling and dusty white mats covering the floor. He flicked on the overhead lights and grinned from ear to ear.

"So what do you think? Am I good or what!" Andy said, beaming, hoping to cheer George up.

"What is this place?" George asked, catching his breath and jumping up and down on the soft white floor mats.

"It is the practice room for the wrestling team," he replied, happy he had distracted George.

"Andy, this may be a surprise to you, but, this high school doesn't have a wrestling team," George said, raising his eyebrows.

"Yes, I know, but, if we had one, we would have a practice room for them!" Andy answered rather matter-of-factly, grinning.

George laughed. "So what are we doing here?" he asked, distracted by Andy's humor.

"You wanted to focus and calm your thoughts. My answer is Chen Lo, of course," Andy said, bowing and spinning around.

"Thank you. You are a good friend," George said, bowing low and taking his place next to Andy.

Andy nodded and then straightened up. Chen Lo was serious business. It was more than an exercise to help focus your mind and thoughts. They knew it from their last rotation when they were given Senior Viceroy David Lu to train them. Most cadets their age had the regular instructors and most were still learning level three Chen Lo. Their team and triad were different.

They had progressed passed level ten by end of their third rotation. Andy knew there was more to Chen Lo than what the captains and other officers had said. David Lu, their Senior Viceroy teacher, had shown them the universe through Chen Lo last year. Now, all Andy had to do was understand what they had really been shown.

They stretched and started with level one, progressing through each level with ease. George opened his mind to the universe and made a link with Andy ~ something both of them could only barely do before last weekend.

With focus and control, they flipped, jumped, and rolled as if they were in fluid motion. Soon George's mind and thoughts were calm and at peace, his focus returning. In his quest to understand what had happened when they were with the medicine people, George found Max in the energy of the universe. Max started a new link with George alone.

"Max, something is not right with the universe, and we met some other beings. Salo told Andy stories of the medicine people in this part of the Earth. Yet, I don't think they were the same medicine people Salo was talking about. They said their names were Tara, Mag, Tao, and Aris. They seemed so familiar," George said in their link.

Max smiled. "Interesting names," Max replied, thinking of the meaning behind the names the beings of white light high council members had chosen. Max knew George would figure out the meaning of the names the high council members had chosen. And that he would figure out that you had to choose your path of good and to put good into action, that life was about more than just being good.

"I'm also pretty sure we weren't on Earth when we were with them either," George added.

The other beings of white light had helped George and Andy while Max was away. They were beginning to see George and his team in a new light. Still, Max worried that the high council hadn't been careful enough. George knew they had not been on Earth. Max would need to warn the beings of white light high council to be more careful in the future. This team saw the universe differently and pickup on the smallest of clues.

"Do not hide this rotation in a place of hiding. Come into the bright light and live in the open, away from fear and darkness," Max said in George's mind, not answering any of George's questions.

George smiled. Andy knew the new link George was in was a good one, not a stealthy evil invader like before. Andy held their Chen Lo motions at level ten while George talked. Without help from their Chen Lo master, David Lu, Andy couldn't go any higher, not yet at least.

Andy was sure the energy of the universe could be guided by Chen Lo. That fact alone made Chen Lo very dangerous without the focus of their triad or Senior Viceroy David Lu's, help. An hour later, the boys slowed their motions and Max's link closed.

"Who was that?" Andy asked, as they stood in the wrestling team training room, resting.

"Max," George replied, more focused and smiling.

"And he said what?" Andy pressed, as Max spoke only to George in their link.

"To hide in the light," George replied, crinkling his forehead as they walked toward the door to climb the two flights of stairs.

"He has said that before," Andy replied, not thinking much of the advice.

"Not as cryptically as this time," George said, trying to figure out what Max really meant. "And he didn't say anything about the medicine people. He didn't even seem concerned when I told him we were off of the Earth," George added, puzzled by Max's odd words.

"Maybe we were really on the beings of white light's planet," Andy said, looking for a reason why Max wouldn't have been concerned.

"Maybe, but I don't think beings of pure energy need a planet to survive. Maybe it was something they made for us. Something we could understand," George replied.

"Well, some things don't change. Max was cryptic before and he is cryptic now. The universe might be messed up, but Max hasn't changed," Andy said and they laughed, stepping on the last stair and turning into the hallway.

Chapter 5

CLEAN BREAK

At precisely 3 p.m., the principal and vice-principal rushed out of the main office doors moments ahead of George and Andy. They never saw the boys coming around the corner. Suddenly, George had a flash of the cafeteria in his mind. He frowned.

"The cafeteria isn't clean enough. It will never pass inspection by Principal Mercer and he will punish the others and no one will get fed tonight," George signed quickly.

The boys stopped in the hallway and George thought for a moment. They needed a plan.

"Think clean, Andy. I mean really clean. I mean clean like spring-cleaning day on the farm," he said placing his hand on Andy's shoulder, as Andy thought of spring-cleaning day at the farm.

Spring-cleaning day was the one day the whole farm smelled like bleach and disinfectant. Every year in the spring, Andy's mom made everyone working on the farm scrub out all of the barns, houses, gardens, tool sheds, and pool with beach and disinfectants. As a small child, Andy was sure even the bugs were cleaned. The day after spring-cleaning day there would be a big pool party for all the farmhands and their families who worked on the farm.

Right now, George wanted the school cafeteria to be as clean as Andy's mom's spring-cleaning day. George cleaned the cafeteria in the blink of an eye with Andy's thought. Last week, he would never have even thought of being able to do it. Now it seemed so easy.

The principal and vice-principal rounded the hallway corner and stopped in front of the cafeteria doors. The students were standing in the hallway in their food-covered clothing, waiting for their inspection of the cafeteria to see if they got dinner that night. The doors opened and the cafeteria nearly glowed with cleanness.

The students followed him inside and gasped, knowing it hadn't been that clean when they had finished only minutes before. The principal snapped his fingers; dinner would be served in two hours.

"Students, go get cleaned up, dismissed," the principal said firmly.

The students quickly headed for the dorms to go change out of the food-covered clothes they had been wearing when they had cleaned the cafeteria. The principal and vice-principal stood in the cafeteria, shaking their heads in disbelief. George and Andy appeared at the backstairs and left for the dorms with the others.

Minutes later, they entered their room, and George closed their dorm room door as Andy crawled under his bed.

"Andy, I don't think you fit under there, and besides, Max said to hide in the open," George whispered, laughing.

"I'm not hiding. I'm looking," he said, squeezing under the bed frame.

"I know I'm going to regret this. You're looking for what?" George asked, sitting down on his desk chair and leaning back.

"For what, what?" Andy replied, groaning as the bed frame lifted up from the floor.

"What are you looking for?" he pressed.

"These!" Andy said, twisting as he threw two ration packs at George from under the bed. Carefully, he squeezed out and sat on the floor.

"Man, how old are these? Oh, never mind I don't want to know," he said, laughing as he thought of Gus's food and Sara always adding vitamins.

They split open the stale rations and ate every piece. George rolled a bottle of water to Andy from their small refrigerator, and they sat in the dorm room, enjoying their meal.

"Did Max say anything about Tara?" Andy asked between bites.

"I didn't have time to ask. The universe is not calm and focused. Somehow, the energy that binds all things together seems to be all messed up. So it's like they are all distracted by it, and they don't quite know what to do. Even evil is distracted," George replied, thinking out-loud.

"Weird. You would think that evil would be happy for the mess up and take advantage of the situation," Andy said and laughed.

"You'd think so, but that's not the feeling I get," George said still puzzled.

George and Andy didn't fully understand the strength and focus Tara and the others had given them. The patches they wore helped them focus their thoughts, even more than the officer's enzyme did. It was similar to when Pete's dad, Viceroy Petrosky, had helped George protect his team from the anger of the Galactic council on their last rotation. The Viceroy had taught George how to focus his thoughts better and protect his team.

"Can you eat now, George?" Andy asked, checking to make sure George was OK.

"Yes, the Chen Lo helped a lot. Thanks Andy," he replied, nodding. "I can't believe there is a wrestling room here," he added with a grin.

"Oh yes, we have all the sports, just not enough players," Andy replied, laughing.

That evening in the cafeteria, dinner was meager; however, it was food so complaining would be pointless. The students ate in near silence and left in a somber mood. Four days left and each one would be a challenge.

The cooks made pancakes with maple syrup and fresh fruits for breakfast the next morning to cheer up the students. George and Andy each took two heaping bowls of dark brown cereal instead.

"Are you nuts, Andy? Why would you guys pick that stuff when there are real pancakes and maple syrup?" Ben asked, teasing them.

"I guess we are used to the taste," George replied; even though, he really didn't like it.

He was not yet strong enough to make the cereal look like something else to eat as he and the others had done on their third rotation with Toma's encouragement. Besides, if someone was watching them, then they would know the boys were regaining their strength and focus~something Tara and the others said not to do.

Their friends shook their heads and returned for pancake seconds. George looked at his brown cereal and shook his head.

"We did it to ourselves, Andy. We had a choice and we chose the pancakes instead of the dark brown cereal with the enzyme inside," George said, shaking his head again and staring at the cereal.

"Maybe? But, I think it is something more than a lack of enzyme that made us weak. Remember, we couldn't make a link with the others after the first week of school this year. I don't think the enzyme wears off that fast without help," he replied cryptically.

Andy still liked the theory of deception and mystery, not the, we did to ourselves answer. Perhaps it was really a little of both.

The last three days of school passed quickly. Andy kept thinking something else would happen, but nothing did. By the last day, the seniors were anxious to graduate and move on with their lives. The underclassmen didn't want them to leave as they would miss them in the coming year. Friday was the day of celebration at the school. The senior graduation program took up the entire day. After the afternoon party, parents and relatives moved trucks and trailers close to the dormitories to gather their student's belongings.

George's birthday got lost in the commotion.

Salo and his eldest son, Malone, came to help load Andy, George, and their accumulated treasures from the year into the back of a red pickup truck. A very clean, red pickup truck George and Andy noticed. Salo ran his finger over the paint, making a squeaking sound as the boys met him at the truck with their first load of boxes.

Yes, Salo noticed how everything was suddenly clean at the farm. He wanted the boys to know he knew. George was surprised he had cleaned the farm too when he was only trying to clean the cafeteria; it was a mystery they would need to solve later.

For now, they both nodded, acknowledging Salo's insight into the cleaning issue, and handed him their boxes. Trip after trip, they emptied their dorm room and filled the red truck. The small dorm room seemed to grow as the weight of their year's treasures were moved out. Soon, all that was left were the beds and the desks that came with the dorm room.

They all rode home in silence. The boys wanted to ask Salo about the medicine people and, yet, they didn't know where to start. George and Andy knew they would be leaving for the airport in the morning, for their fourth rotation at summer camp in space. Somehow starting a conversation they couldn't finish seemed rather wrong. The farm was quiet when they drove up the road to the farmhouse. Some of the farmhands greeted Salo, Malone, and boys by the front doors. They pushed the boys, Malone, and Salo inside the farmhouse as they started to unload the clean, red pickup truck.

"Odd, our driver wasn't here to follow us home. After all, he has been with us for the whole year," Andy whispered, as they walked through the swinging screen doors.

The house inside was as quiet as the outside. The doors to the library were closed and the people inside spoke in low whispers. George put his hand on the door and one on Andy's shoulder. Their link was made. They listened to the conversation as easily as Emily spoke to the organisms in the walls and caves.

Their cadet team was to stay hidden on Earth with the boys staying at the farm. There would be no fourth rotation for their cadet team. George rolled away from the door hardly believing what the Galactic council had decided to do with the team of the prophecy that "lived" after defeating evil.

"Well, that's wrong. That's exactly the opposite of what Max said to do," George signed, shaking his head.

"How messed up is the Galactic council in our sector of space? They don't really think this will fly do they?" Andy said in disgust.

"I'm willing to bet they think we are weak. They think we can't communicate except through the computers. If they keep us apart, then if the evil does come, they can move us around more easily," George said, walking across the living room.

He was walking, talking, and making a plan for their escape.

"Won't we be more defenseless this way? You know, less prepared and all?" Andy said, smacking his hand and fist together.

"Yes, we will. Their plan is wrong. We need to fix it," George whispered, staring out the windows along the back of the house onto the pool terrace.

"What did you have in mind?" Andy signed.

The boys walked out onto the terrace and sat down by the pool. George concentrated and made a link with their team. Their connection was weak, but it was there.

"Eat only the dark brown cereal. Just like last year, remember? Eat nothing else and eat as much as you can. Let no one see you. We'll talk in one hour," he thought to his team and then closed the link.

The boys were out of the house when dinner was served and Salo made excuses for them. He sent them to the lower barns fire pit to eat dark brown cereal and count bales of hay. Salo had a pot of warm cereal hanging over the fire pit. The more cereal they ate, the stronger they felt. They were sitting by the evening fire with the farmhands when Salo reappeared. The others left to change places with the farmhands on watch, and the boys and Salo sat alone by the fire.

"Salo, who are? I mean really? The stories of the medicine people and you always covering for us?" Andy asked directly, staring at Salo in the firelight.

There was little time left to beat around the bush for an answer.

Salo smiled. "I am a friend of the universe," he replied cryptically.

"The medicine people are real; however, we didn't see them last weekend, did we?" George asked, following Andy's lead.

"That was only a story to prepare us, wasn't it?" Andy pressed, stirring the fire with a stick.

The sparks flew up from the wood and cracked in the air.

"Yes, the medicine people are real," Salo replied, without answering George or Andy's question.

"We were in a place that was...well, is it a place like the caves of Asteria?" George asked, seeing if Salo knew of the beings of white light or if he was one himself.

"And Tara? Is she like you? I mean, you know?" Andy asked, cryptically as George set a small log on the edge of the fire.

The fire curled around the log twisting and turning.

"Think, open your minds. Inside you know the answer to all of your questions, and you know what you must do," Salo answered cryptically again.

The returning farmhands walked up to the fire to warm themselves and Salo nodded and left them, entering a small house between the barns. The boys also said goodnight and walked toward the pool terrace.

"So you think Salo is a being of white light?" Andy asked, not actually believing what he was asking.

That wasn't Salo. The being with us just now only looked like Salo. The cereal we ate was the same as what we ate last weekend. I feel stronger and move connected to the universe again. That had to be one of the people we met last weekend in disguise. He never even, flinched when we mentioned the caves of Asteria station," George signed, not wanting anyone to overhear his conversation.

"It would make more sense than Salo being anything but human," Andy replied.

"Remember, he could be Calshene, which would explain...,' George signed and suddenly stopped mid-sentence.

His head started to hurt and he bent over.

"You OK George," Andy asked, looking around for someone new.

"Not tonight, I am stronger now, and you will not stop us this way again!" he muttered, as he thought hard and sent the pain back to whoever sent it.

George straightened up and they continued up the terrace walkway, passed the swimming pool, and into the house.

"The mind invader is back," George whispered.

No one was in the living room. George wondered where the link had come from as he and Andy were half expecting to see someone they didn't know when they entered the house. Andy's parents were still in his father's library with their guests, talking in whispers.

George didn't even stop to listen to their conversation. It didn't matter now. They had their plan and they were going to follow Max's suggestion, even if the Galactic council disagreed. Inside their bedroom, George and Andy reformed the link with their team; Emily, Sara, Anna, and Gus.

"Pack your clothes. We are going to summer camp in the stars tomorrow. Emily, please order cars for everyone and smooth the CORE security computer systems to let us pass," George said calmly.

"What is going on George?" Emily asked for the others.

"The Galactic council wants us to say hidden on Earth and not go to our fourth rotation this summer," he answered seriously.

"Why?" Gus asked a little worried.

"We don't know yet. But Max said to hide in the open among friends, so that's what we are going to do," George answered calmly.

"What did Pete, Frank, and Toma say?" Sara pressed.

"Well, they weren't exactly happy when we contacted them last week. So we haven't told them about our plan," Andy said seriously.

"Besides, they didn't seem too happy about something else. Something they were hiding from us," George added, telling his team what he sensed in Pete.

"The energy in universe is all messed up right now and it's like no one can figure out what to do. Our teams not being destroyed last year seems to have changed things, and the Galactic council isn't dealing with change very well," Andy said, trying to fill the others in on what they figured out over the last school year.

"We'll meet up with everyone on the other side. Tell no one, let them think they're letting you sleep in late on Saturday morning," George said, explaining his plan to his team.

The team lowered their link; their plan was in place.

"George, how did you do that?" Andy asked, as they started packing their red suitcases.

"Do what?" he asked, as he flipped the dresser drawer over his suitcase like Frank had done a few years earlier.

"Stop the pain? I sensed no one in a link with you out on the terrace," Andy asked.

"Oh that. It wasn't a link. I was wrong last week. I think it is like a directed energy kind-of-a thing, like a point-to-point thing. I think you have to be close for it to work~ weird that there wasn't anyone in the living room. I was sure there would be," George replied puzzled as he flipped another drawer over.

"But, George, last week, it nearly destroyed you," Andy pressed.

"Last week, we were weak and didn't know it. Now we know. That's why the officers only eat the dark brown cereal every day. It keeps their links strong. Without it, you become weak," George said, lying down on his suitcase to get it to close.

"It is a weak point in their defenses against evil," Andy replied, thinking of strategies and options.

"Maybe, but I think they have more than one way of maintaining their strength, this is only one easy way," George said, as the latches on his suitcase snapped into place.

Andy sat on his suitcase and the latched snapped closed. Quietly, they rolled the two suitcases over next to the desk, out of sight.

Chapter 6
4ᵀᴴ ROTATION

Dawn came early and the boys slipped out of the farmhouse before the household was awake. Andy left a note for his mom. 'Gone to camp. See you this fall. Andy.' He slipped it under his pillow before they left.

The driver Emily had arranged was waiting for them at the entrance to the farm on the main road. One last glance after dropping their suitcases in the trunk, and they slipped into the car for the ride into town.

It was a seven-hour ride on a good day to the airport—longer if the weather was bad. Today was a good day. George thought about the last school year and all that he had learned at school and from the farmhands as they bounced along the dirt roads. The driver dropped them off at the airport terminal and said he was well paid and would take no more.

The boys pulled their red suitcases through the terminal gates and walked into the terminal beneath the open-air canopy roof. Before their eyes, patterns of colors appeared. They knew what to look for now and they were amazed they hadn't seen the parade of colors sooner. Now starting their fourth rotation, they were the older cadets, alone at the airport terminal without their parents.

"They all look so young," Andy signed, looking at the patterns of colored suitcases and the kids pulling them along.

"They are," George replied, grinning a little.

They signed back and forth as they waited in line at a security station. George showed his security card and the officer nearly fainted.

"Yes sir. This way, sir," the guard said, shuffling them around the line.

"Thank you," he replied in his most serious voice.

The guard smiled and returned to his post. They knew getting through security so easily was because of Emily's computer skills.

Andy and George walked along the corridors, turning down a less traveled hallway and stood between the rows of elevators with the sign over head 'Summer Campers Only.' Andy stepped forward and the yellow light shown down on his ID card in his palm. George followed, and they stepped through the narrow corridor together. The opposite side of the corridor opened up into an enormous spaceport with starships of every size and shape. The spaceport in Brazil was as large as in the United States and elsewhere. They watched the campers and cadets as they made their way to the different spaceships.

What had been scary and amazing before now seemed almost commonplace. Perhaps they were becoming worn-out, because of all of the challenges over the past three years, or perhaps it was because the energy of the universe was all messed up. They didn't know.

They lined up with all the other red suitcases in front of a large, saucer shaped starship and met the officer inside, holding out their hands without a second glance. Stepping into his crystalline tube, George knew the easy of their entry was because of Emily. He smiled at the thought of seeing her again and closed his eyes.

It seemed like only moments later, when they stepped out of their crystalline transport tubes and followed the line of red cadets walking down the gangplank of their spaceships onto Jupiter station on Ganymede moon.

George and Andy met the rest of their team near the dome wall where the dome and corridors met. They were all happy and grinning from ear to ear to see each other after such a long time apart. The girls hugged the boys and the boys blushed. They talked a mile a minute, trying to get caught up with what was new and all of the details as fast as they could.

Within a few minutes, the gravitational effect of Ganymede moon started to affect them. They needed to get their suits on to be protected from the effects of space and the gravity on Ganymede moon. A group of new young campers walked past George and the others, moving at a snail's pace. Anna and Emily shook their heads.

"They will never make it into the corridors," Sara said, as they walked up to the new campers.

"Follow us. It's hard to do it alone the first time," George said kindly, taking an orange suitcase strap of one of the new campers. His team each took a suitcase from the young campers and started talking and walking as they lead them along the orange corridors, two by two.

"You will all have an amazing adventure this summer," Emily said softly, as they walked.

"However, you must remember, safety first," Andy said, and then realized how much like his father he sounded.

They kept up the pace to keep the young campers moving and warned them as they had been warned years before. Quickly, they arrived at their orange cadet's sleeping room and left the new cadets with their orange captains.

"I'll tell your captain you're coming. Thank you for helping them," the younger cadet's captain said kindly.

"Yes, ma'am. Thank you, ma'am," George replied.

"I hate this part even more than being hungry all the time," Gus whispered, as they turned away toward the red cadet sector.

Everyone chuckled, too tired to laugh. Gus was hungry, he was sure he had been born early because he was hungry. They had all grown and they all looked a year older.

"Emily, how did you do all of this?" George asked, smiling weakly as he wrapped his arm around Emily's waist.

"It is a lot easier to do than you might think. It never ceases to amaze me at how few safe guards are in place at the main CORE computer centers on such important information," Emily whispered, shaking her head and wrapping her free arm around George's waist. She had missed George and the others over the school year.

"Perhaps it is something you could help the CORE officers with in a kind and understanding way without hurting them. Make it safe, even if they don't think they need it secured," George suggested kindly.

Emily was a wiz with computers and George wanted her to help them, not teach them a lesson.

"So who's our captain?" Andy asked, as they turned around the last corridor corner in the red cadet sector.

The door slid open to their sleeping room and Pete stepped out before Emily could answer. Pete didn't look happy they were there.

"Oh, this isn't good," Gus whispered to Andy.

They lowered their heads and followed Pete inside as the changing screens rose from the floor.

After they had changed into their uniforms, Pete had only one greeting, "Report!"

George explained the odd events of the year and that they weren't that tired because they had been eating the dark brown cereal. He left out the part about the medicine people and the patches that he and Andy now wore.

"The Galactic council will not be pleased you are all together and here on Jupiter station when they find out," Pete said, shaking his head.

"Is this not where normal everyday fourth rotation cadets are supposed to be, sir?" Sara asked, a little frustrated with the Galactic council's decision.

"And what fourth rotation cadets are supposed to be doing, sir?" Emily added.

"Yes, it is if you were normal cadets," Pete replied, wondering why they thought they could, in anyway, be considered normal cadets.

This team of cadets had saved an entire cadet space station, freed a slave planet, and rescued the entire Galactic council; and yet, they thought they were normal cadets. Pete was amazed. He knew CORE officers who couldn't do what they had done.

"Well, right now, we are normal cadets who need training, sir," Andy said seriously.

"Max said to hide in plain sight and this is as plain sightish as we can get, sir," George replied firmly.

"When did you speak with Max?" Pete pressed, curious that Max had spoken with George over the school year.

"On Earth, after we spoke with you, sir," George replied casually, grinning a little because he knew Pete wanted to ask more, but wouldn't.

"Rest now. The Galactic council will need to be told. They will decide what is to be done with you now," Pete said, a little ominously and left their room.

Emily locked the door as their silvery beds rose from the floor.

"Pete was a little spooky," Anna said, lying down on her bed.

"Pete, Frank, and Toma weren't happy when we called them on Earth," Andy replied.

"Something is going on. They aren't telling us something, and I think it's important," George added.

"So nothing has changed," Gus said and they all laughed.

"Emily can you do a general search on the main computer system. I don't know what we are looking for, but something isn't right," George asked.

"Stealth, Emily. Remember stealth. They can't know we're looking for information," Andy added.

"Yes, of course, they will never even know I was there," Emily replied and slipped her pad down her sleeve and into her hand. A few key strokes and she was done. "I should have something by morning," she whispered.

In the night, George felt the spaceport dome of Jupiter station lower into the deep canyons of Ganymede moon's surface.

Pete was sitting at their table when they woke up in the morning. George grinned as Pete slid a bowl of dark brown cereal to him. It was CORE officer's cereal, as grandfather had it ordered from the rotation before. However, not as full of enzyme as what George and Andy had eaten on Earth with the medicine people.

"I don't know how you did it, but, the Galactic council is going to let you stay. Apparently, they are impressed with Emily's computer expertise and want her to secure a few loopholes in the CORE computer system. I, however, am not so easily impressed and your training will be particularly grueling this rotation," Pete said firmly; yet, he seemed nearly happy to George.

"So is your team here on Jupiter station? And Frank and Toma and their teams too, sir?" Andy asked, moving quickly off the grueling topic as he sat down at the table with Gus.

Pete slid him a bowl of officer's cereal and smiled, not answering his question. Andy didn't even wince with his first bit or complain about the cereal. Gus actually asked for seconds.

"Are you really my team?" Pete asked, as they all eat their cereal without complaint.

Soon they had all eaten and left their sleeping room, heading out for the meeting with the station Commander.

"George, answer the question please?" Pete said, walking down the corridor and stopping at a wall computer terminal.

George concentrated for only a moment.

"Your team is here, sir. Frank, Toma, and their teams are on a scouting mission to ...," he said, when Pete cut him off, looking around to make sure no one had heard George.

"That will be enough, George!" Pete's captain voice returned.

George nodded, he knew their triad teams were going to the second kitchen, a Zeleion outpost, on a reconnaissance mission.

"Where are we going today, sir?" Sara asked kindly.

"Commander Leafscott wants to greet you. Then the other red cadets will have free time to get reacquainted," he said firmly.

They had disobeyed the Galactic council's orders and come to Jupiter station to start their fourth rotation. The Galactic council may have let them off easily and let them stay together; however, Pete was going to make sure their free time was well used.

"What training will we be going to, sir?" Emily asked, knowing they would have little free time.

Pete didn't answer. The door of the dining hall opened and the cadets followed him inside. George nodded to Hans and Jennifer as they walked deeper into the hall to find an empty table. George bumped into Bailey halfway into the hall.

"Hey where have you guys been? I looked for you last rotation?" Bailey asked.

"Oh, we weren't here on this station," Andy answered, grinning a little.

"OK I can accept that. So did you guys hear about the Earth team that set the new flight record on some other station? Hey wait a minute, you have been here, and then you were gone," Bailey said, staring at George and Andy.

Andy smiled. "Yup, that was us," he said grinning.

"Now you know and now you can't tell anyone," Emily said firmly.

George lowered his head to hide his grin, wrapping his arm around her waist.

"I would do what she says. She kinda scares me sometimes," Andy whispered.

"It's good to see you too, Bailey," George said, patting him on the back and walking on to an empty table.

Bailey stood in the middle of the room with his mouth hanging open like a codfish. A tap of a staff on the floor and the room fell silent as the fourth rotation cadets stood up~ so different from their first rotation.

"Be seated cadets. This is the start of your fourth rotation and I want to welcome you all to Jupiter station. For this rotation, you will have more training classes. Again, you will have Colonel Hawks for physical training and self-defense. Colonel Petrof will teach you first aid and basic survival. Major Doyle will train you in tactics and basic armaments and Major Wright will continue your flight training. Your teams will also begin assisting in the training of the younger cadets. And finally, your teams will be allowed to participate in Sport this year," the Station Commander said, grinning a little.

The cadets exploded with excitement, cheering wildly for a few minutes. Then the Station Commander raised his hand and they calmed down again.

"However, Sport training is separate from the classroom training and will be done only in your free time. Any teams missing classes for Sport training, without permission, will be disqualified for two rotations. Am I clear!" he said firmly.

"Yes sir. Clear, sir!" the cadets replied excitedly.

"Cadets dismissed," he said, smiling.

The dining hall burst into cheers and a roar of commotion as the cadets turned to greet their friends and make plans for Sport.

"Excellent! I can't wait to compete," Andy and Gus said, high fiving each other.

"I don't think we will have time to practice," George said, looking across the room at Pete standing by the door.

"We have to go," Emily added with a sigh.

"Hey, George, where are you going?" Bailey asked, making his way to George through the crowd of cadets, wanting to talk with him more about the flight record they set.

"Training," George replied, lowering his head and motioning toward their captain in the back of the room.

"See you around," Bailey said, with a low five and knuckle knock.

George and Andy nodded.

"They sure do have one tough captain. Glad he's not ours," Bailey whispered to his second, then turned around to greet more friends from their last rotation.

Out the door and down the red sector corridor they ran, following Pete. They stopped at Colonel Hawk's training dome. Inside stood Pete's team and David Lu, the Senior Viceroy Chen Lo master, from their last rotation.

George and his team stopped at the door with Pete. David Lu nodded and they entered the dome. Pete's team didn't even acknowledge them as they walked inside. George knew they wanted to; however, not with a Senior Viceroy, retired or not, in the dome.

George signed and their team lined up behind Andy. Oddly, Pete's team was now lined up behind Nick. How un-Calshene, George thought, until he caught a glance from Pete. Then he focused only on their Chen Lo training. David Lu spoke no words. He bowed to the cadets and spun around to begin.

He started them out slowly and easily walked through the first eleven levels. They flipped, spun, jumped, and rolled through the air with speed and focus. Move after move, they were in harmony with universe. George and others felt their focus and control increase. Neither the cadets nor the captains were breathing hard when David Lu slowed down for them to rest.

"You have all learned to control your energy better this year, let us start with level twelve. Begin," he said to their minds, bowing again and spinning around.

Level twelve was like level eleven. It combined more of the motions of the previous levels together into complete actions. For each move, there was a counter move. However, it was harder than level eleven, a lot harder.

They leapt, rolled, and twisted, crashing into each other more. Pete's team rose up from the ground silently each time they fell or collided with another person. However, George's team laughed and giggled each time they fell and tumbled together, enjoying the moment before returning to the motions. At the end of level twelve, the captains and cadets were both breathing hard when David Lu slowed down them to rest. He turned and bowed raising his hand in front of his chest as before, dipping his head slightly.

"Dismissed," he said kindly.

The cadets and captains returned the bow and quickly left the training dome. A shimmer of white light appeared in the dome as the door closed.

"Welcome," David Lu said, not turning around.

"Hello my friend. What do you think? Can they be taught further?" Senior Viceroy Petrosky, Pete's grandfather, asked as he walked up to David Lu.

"They are an amazingly accomplished team for being so young. Are you sure about this Alexander? They will figure out soon what they are being taught. George and his team are so very young and the others that guide them are also young, talented, however, very young as well," David Lu asked, shaking his head.

"They will need everything you can teach them to stay alive. They have escaped evil three times now and somehow they have managed to even defeat evil once. They are still alive. This has never happened before. The writings on the prophecy scroll have changed because of them," Alexander replied, a little surprised by his own words.

"An amazing feat in itself," David Lu added, nodding.

He knew the prophecy had never changed before and that no other teams or triads had all lived after meeting evil face to face~ including Alexander's triad.

"We must give them every advantage. We didn't do that in the past and the results were tragic. This time will be different. Everything we can do to help them must be done," Senior Viceroy Petrosky said confidently.

"Yes, well, they did get here without the knowledge of the Galactic council or the Senior Viceroys. I will teach them further about the raw energy of the universe and how to use it," David Lu replied, grinning.

Together, the two Senior Viceroys disappeared in a flash of white light.

The cadets walked quietly along next to the captains without saying a word. Pete led them back to their sleeping room and they all crowded inside. The door closed and their silence was broken as everyone chattered at once. Hans and Gus started passing out ration packs, from where, no one really knew as they had been with them all day. However, no one was going to complain about being fed.

Pete flipped his hand over and a small yellow sphere appeared. They sat down as a large silver circular table and chairs rose in the middle of the room. They set the rations down on the table as Pete and George made a link to join everyone together.

They reached out and found Toma, Frank, and their teams on a transport ship headed for 'somewhere'. As the last captain joined the link, calm filled the space between them. They spoke as if they were next to each other. It had been a long time and they had missed everyone's company. The events of the school year were shared, and all too soon, it was time to close their link with Rachael and Gus's help.

Pete's team and George's team finished their ration dinners and talked on with each other long after the link closed. Pete and the others left the cadets for the evening and calm over took the cadets.

"Max is here," George signed, as they all laid down on their silvery beds.

"Emily, we need to know more about Chen Lo and why we are being trained at this high of a level. Also, did your search last night find anything unusual going on here?" George whispered.

"There was nothing from the search last night George. Whatever is going on, the officers are keeping it well hidden. As to your Chen Lo question, fourth rotation cadets are trained at about level four normally," Emily said, calmly reading her pad.

"We are at level eleven and I think David Lu would have finished teaching us level twelve if we didn't get so tired," Andy added seriously.

Inside Andy was worried. What was going to happen that they would need this high of a level of Chen Lo at such a young age? Whatever it was, it must have the Senior Viceroys worried, Andy figured. Yet, he said nothing to their team, no sense in having them worry too.

"I'll have more information on Chen Lo in the morning, George," Emily whispered, making a few key strokes on her pad before sliding it back up her sleeve and falling asleep.

Emily loved her pad. When they had been given pads on their first rotation, she couldn't imagine what information she would store in its memory. Now four years later, it was her constant companion, even on Earth.

That night, George dreamed of the cave on Asteria station and of seeing Max and the other beings of white light. Calm filled the room; it wasn't an accident ~ it never was. George wanted to speak with the beings of white light and find out what they knew about their rotation and why Max had warned them not to hide.

Pete was in their room when the cadet woke up the next morning. The dark brown officer's cereal wasn't so bad this year and breakfast was over in short order.

"You will alternate your morning training every other day starting with Colonel Petrof and then with Major Dole. In the afternoon, you will alternate with Colonel Hawks and Major Wright, starting with Colonel Hawks this afternoon. In the evenings, you will rotate between your specialized training and Chen Lo training, starting with specialized training tonight. Any questions? Good. I'll be back after dinner," Pete said firmly.

He turned and left them standing in the middle of the corridor in front of their sleeping room. Pete leaving them so abruptly surprised the team. Especially, since they had all been so closely watched in the past. They stood in the corridor, staring at each other and the empty corridor.

"Emily, do you have our schedule?" George asked still surprised.

"Yes. It's on everyone's pads now too," she replied, and pushed her send button.

Some other red cadets walked past them and they followed them through the corridors to their first training class alone.

"What's with Pete?" Gus asked, wrapping his arm around Anna and hugging her.

"He's even more cryptic than usual," Andy added, holding Sara's hand.

"Remember, we weren't supposed to be here and neither were they," Sara whispered, and the team nodded.

"Yes, but, it seems like there is something more. We really need to find out what is really going on. The universe is all messed up right now," George said and Emily wrapped her arm around him.

"How do you know?" she asked curiously.

"It's like an odd feeling and I can't shake it," George replied nodding to the team.

Chapter 7

NORMAL CADET

Emily barely twisted her free hand and the doorway of Colonel Petrof training dome slid open easily. They crossed the small dome and lined up in columns with the other red cadets. Bailey nodded and George returned his nod. Colonel Petrof walked out from a small room off the side of the dome as the last red cadet team lined up in a column next to George and his team.

"Good morning, cadets," Colonel Petrof said, greeting the cadets warmly.

"Good morning, ma'am," the cadets replied, smiling and nodding, happy in an odd way to see Colonel Petrof again.

She was the quietest instructor they had; yet, they had great respect for her. George and the others had been at the Calshene and Thorean cadet stations for their last two rotations and had forgotten that Jupiter station was friendlier than the other stations ~ less protocol, more compassion, and kindness.

"In this training class, you will be taught the basics of first aid and basic survival techniques in a hostile space environment," she said with enthusiasm.

The Colonel waved her hand and small brown cots rose from the floor of the dome. One member from each team walked across the dome to pick up three medical kits from the stack of brown boxes leaning against the dome wall.

"For this training, three cadets from each team will be injured and three cadets will bandage their wounds. Then you will switch places and repeat the procedures with the opposite cadets," she said kindly as a large video screen rolled down the wall.

Andy, Gus, and George laid down first.

"No point in missing a chance for a few Z's," Andy said, grinning as he stretched out, and crossed his hands behind his head.

"I'll wrap you up while you sleep, no problem, no problem at all, Andy," Sara said, with a wild grin on her face.

"Maybe I'll watch and learn while you work, Sara," Andy said, correcting his words, a little fear creeping into his mind while he stared at Sara's wicked grin.

"A wise man indeed," George signed, to Gus as he lay back down and smiled politely to Emily.

The holographic instructor on the wall video screen displayed each wounds location, severity, and the appropriate bandage to use to bind the wound. Andy was nearly a mummy by the time Sara was done. Emily and George chuckled, as they were sure extra bandages were involved to keep his attention. Sara had also wrapped Andy's hands to keep him from his continuous onslaught of signed bad bandaging jokes.

The Colonel walked by each cadet commenting on their technique and releasing them to switch places. When she approached Sara and Andy, she turned her head away to hide her smile.

"Cadet, I see your excessive use of bandaging has silenced your victim's humor. Keep up the good work," she said kindly.

To Emily and Anna she had only said good work; however, Sara's work was exceptional. Sara had every knot perfectly tied and in straight rows. It was amazing. Now, it was George, Gus, and Andy's turn to watch and follow along with the holographic instructor. George and Gus were sure Andy had more bits of tape and bandaging on him than were covering Sara's wounds. Gus could hardly look in Andy's direction without laughing.

Andy glanced back at the screen, tied his hand to Sara's leg, and then turned around again to look at the hologram instructor for the next instruction.

He shook his hand behind his back, then shook it harder, lifting the cot and Sara into the air as he spun around, trying to free his hand. Instantly, he flipped Sara off her cot; her bandages unraveling as she flew through the air, landing in George's arms. George stumbled backwards as he had only half-caught Sara, her bandaged legs spinning around him. George's knee caught the edge of Emily's cot and he and Sara started to fall squarely onto Emily lying on the cot.

Emily bolted up from the cot as George tried to spin around the front edge of Emily's cot with Sara still in his arms. He clipped Emily's shoulder as she turned and his knee hit the cot. Instantly, his knee folded. He and Sara dropped onto Emily's cot. It collapsed, leaving them groaning in pain on the ground.

Emily twisted around the other side of the broken cot as she tried to stop her momentum. Her arms waving in the air, she fell backwards into Gus. Gus teetered and Anna jumped from the cot as he and Emily crushed the cot into the ground. Bailey caught Anna in his arms. Spinning around to stop her momentum, he crashed into his team member.

As each team members tried to stop the next person's crash, they fell like dominos falling in a pattern, one cadet after another. Soon the entire dome was littered with cadets sprawled out across the floor, intertwined in bandages and tape, all groaning and moaning from their real injuries.

Colonel Petrof stood in the center of the room speechless. What do you say to a cadet that can tie up and knock down thirty-five other cadets in a matter of seconds and still wondered what happened? Quickly, the Colonel started helping the cadets up and checking them for real injuries. Once untangled, all the cadets started clapping their hands, and Andy took a long low bow.

"Class dismissed," she said, when all of the cadets were standing and free of injury.

The cadets returned the brown boxes and headed for the door.

"So you guys are really the team that set the flight record?" Bailey asked, as they walked to the sliding door.

"No, no must be someone else," George replied quickly, rolling his eyes at Bailey.

"Like they could have ever done that," another team said, teasing as they walked out the door and headed for the dining hall.

"Maybe Andy tied everyone up before the race started!" another red cadet said, laughing as they walked down the corridor to lunch.

George and his team were the last to leave the dome.

"Sorry about that," Andy said, motioning toward the empty dome.

"Accidents happen," Sara said, wrapping her arm around Andy's waist to cheer him up.

It was hard, Andy and the others were the team that broke the race record; however, they had to keep quiet or Jupiter station would be at risk.

"It's hard to know?" George whispered, wrapping his arm over Emily's shoulder.

"You know we are just kidding, Andy, right?" Gus said, trying to cheer Andy up, as he suddenly looked sad.

"Ya. I'm fine," Andy replied.

"What's wrong?" Sara asked.

"It's not the crashing or this training class. It's the next class I'm worried about," he said, his face looking worried.

Sara twisted her head.

"Why? You know everything about blowing things up," she said, wrapping her arm over his shoulder.

Andy shook his head. "It's more than blowing things up, Sara," Andy said seriously.

He was worried about their team and whether or not, they were ready for the truth about defending a team. He hoped the class would be general and not explain what defending a team really meant.

On their last rotation, Pete's team had taught them the basics about the red energy sphere defense and offense. Gus had learned how to use the red sphere energy and feed their team the raw energy in a sphere. Yet, Andy worried. Red energy spheres weren't the only weapon they need to learn about. It was just one of many and all of them were deadly serious weapons.

Lunch came and went quickly, and soon, they were on their way to Major Doyle's training. They followed the other captains and fourth rotation red cadets to Major Doyle's classroom. It seemed so odd to see other cadets with their captains to Emily and Anna. The captains didn't seem nearly as self-assured of themselves as Pete, Frank, and Toma did; even though, they were the same age.

They entered the new classroom; however, there were no chairs or desks to sit on. Standing in team circles, the cadets waited, whispering between themselves. When Major Doyle entered, smoldering and brushing embers from his uniform, some of the cadets gasped.

"Cadets, armament training will introduce you to the basic weapons we use in defense. Tactics will teach you when to use this training," Major Doyle said, flicking his wrist and out sliding a staff weapon into the palm of his hand. The class gasped. He turned and opened a small closet and tossed out wooden sticks to the cadets.

"Hey, these look like the sticks we had when we were swinging on the vines," Bailey said.

A few of the cadets on Bailey's team nodded, remembering last year's rotation. Then Bailey turned slowly and stared at George.

"You said they were weapons last year. How did you know?" Bailey pressed, staring at George.

"My uncle had one and he showed it to us," Andy answered, quickly to keep George from speaking.

"Cadets, line up," Major Doyle said, helping them space out so they wouldn't hit each other.

The cadets stood at arm's length from each other, holding their sticks in one hand. The Major demonstrated the first simple moves on how to hold and move the stick. Then he showed them how to aim, fire, and wield the stick in defense.

Andy was in torment. Their team was so far passed this basic lesson; yet, they stayed exactly with the class. It was hard for them not to show what they knew. However, they had chosen to be fourth rotation cadets, and they were going to persist and stay. The training ended and the cadets handed in their sticks as they walked out the door.

"Cadets dismissed, except your team Cadet Hawkins," the Major said firmly.

Bailey glanced back and George shook his head. The door closed and the Major walked up to the team.

"I didn't think you could do it. I have heard you are all much more accomplished. Let me see what you know, and I'll see what I can do about getting you training more suited to your level," he said, smiling kindly.

"Thank you, sir," Andy said, answering for their team.

This was his arena. George nodded and Andy stepped forward to lead their team. The others stepped up and stood in formation behind Andy.

"Wait a minute and I'll get you staffs," Major Doyle said, hurrying to the cabinet to get the training sticks.

"No need, sir. We brought our own, sir," Andy replied, nodding to the team and the cadets shook their arms.

Silently, staffs fell from their sleeves and extended to full length. Even Gus had a staff this rotation. The Major's mouth fell open as he stepped back to watch. Andy held the staff out in front of him at arm's length and started his first thrust and spin with the staff. Silently, they followed his motions from level to level. By the sixth level, Gus rubbed his stomach and Andy stopped the team. They collapsed the staff and slid them back into their sleeves.

"Why did you stop? You're not at your highest level yet are you?" the Major asked, stunned by what they knew at such a young age.

"Gus is hungry. We need to eat, sir," Andy said, replying for the team.

"Oh yes, yes. Well, you are quite accomplished. Go eat now. I'll make new arrangements for you for the next training class," the Major said, smiling as the cadets left the classroom.

A dark figure appeared in the back of the classroom as the doors closed.

"Well?" the dark figure asked quietly.

"They are more accomplished than we were led to believe master," the Major replied, lowering his head.

"Watch them, send them to special training, and I will teach them the truth," the dark figure whispered.

The Major who was in the training room with them was not the real Major Doyle. He nodded and the dark figure disappeared into the shadows.

"Call Pete or we will be in trouble. It's late," George said, as they hurried through the corridors to the dining hall.

Andy nodded and took the assignment.

"Odd, that Pete didn't come and get us when we weren't at dinner?" Emily puzzled, turning the last corner.

"Maybe he got tied up with something?" Gus said, though he had his doubts.

"Maybe," George mumbled, agreeing with his team.

They entered the dining hall ~ it was empty!

"Gus, how late is it?" George asked, standing in the archway.

"Not that late, maybe 8 o'clock or 8:30 pm," Gus said, rubbing his stomach.

"Andy, did you call Pete?" George asked, his voice raised.

"I'm trying; however, he is not answering," Andy replied, shaking his pad.

"Try Nick or Rachael or the other captains," George said, starting to worry.

Quickly, they were all calling the triad captains. George calmed his mind and reached out searching the energy of the universe for their triad. Andy grabbed his shoulder and the others joined in the link.

"Pete, where are you, sir?" George asked when he found him.

"Right here in the room with you. Where do you think I am?" Pete replied, staring at his team of red cadets.

"Pete, we are in the red cadet dining hall and no one is here, sir," George answered.

"Stay!" Pete ordered and broke the link.

"Call security, Andy. Emily, Anna, find Pete's bio signs and send a message to Nick and the others. Tell them where Pete is and that he is in danger," George said, giving orders as fast as he could.

Emily found Pete's bio signs and location on the station computer. Emily called Nick over the station computer and told him what happened. Nick and six CORE security guards raced to Pete's classroom. The red cadets were right behind Nick and the other captains as the security guards burst into Pete's classroom. The fake red cadets in the classroom stood up slowly from their desks.

"Who are you?" Pete asked harshly.

The fake red cadets started backing away from Pete and the guards in the room.

"Pete, you know us. It's me George," the lead cadet whined.

"I don't think so," George replied, from behind Nick and the others.

"No, you're not George or my red cadets. Who are you? Why are you here?" Pete replied to the imposter.

The CORE guards raised their staffs circling the imposters. They started to twist their staffs to the horizontal position to trap the imposters. The imposters became antsy and then agitated.

"Who are you? This is the last time I'll ask!" Pete yelled, as the guards tried to invade the imposter's minds.

"It does not matter, the master has what he needs," the lead imposter said, straightening up.

In a flash of red light, six piles of gray ash were all that remained of the imposers.

"What happened?" Gus asked, staring at the piles of ash.

"We didn't do anything," Jennifer said staring at the piles of ash.

The security guards all shook their heads. Pete glanced at Nick. Instantly, he was on the computer, sending a message.

"Odd, why would Nick be on the computer? He has to know it is not secure," Gus whispered.

"Exactly, he wants whomever to know we know and that we found the imposters," Andy whispered.

Suddenly, six Inner Circle officers burst into the room and grabbed onto George and the other red cadets. In a flash of white light, they were gone.

"Noooooo!" yelled Pete.

Chapter 8

NOT AGAIN

Immediately, the cadets reappeared in the Galactic council corridor outside the council chamber.

"Protocol," George signed and lowered his head.

The others quickly followed his example.

"Man, we are in so deep now," Andy signed.

"But we didn't do anything," Gus replied, using their new sign language.

George glanced at the team and shook his head.

"Focused and calm or we will lose all of our freedom," he signed, as seriously as he could.

A Viceroy walked up behind the team and nodded. The Inner Circle officers left down the corridor. A second Viceroy walked up to the group. It was George's dad! He didn't acknowledge them other than to make an archway and a door.

Emily tripped, by accident, of course, and touched the door before he could open it. It glided open easily. He didn't even raise an eyebrow. Gus lifted Emily off the floor and touched their entire team, making a link as Emily stood up.

"Calm and focused," were the only words George kept repeating through their link.

The Viceroy entered the Galactic council chamber and the cadets followed. Before they had been bold and brash, now they were quiet and respectful, heads lowered—a full protocol test with no mistakes.

As it turned out, there were several Galactic council chambers across the known galaxies. The Galactic councils moved from council chamber to council chamber as needed to maintain the flow of galactic energy to all known sectors of the universe.

George's dad led the cadets into the council chamber and placed them in a circle around the three Senior Viceroys and the center Senior Viceroy. They stood silently in their circle, waiting for the Senior Viceroys to speak. Pete's grandfather, one of the three Senior Viceroys on the white circles, reached out and joined the team into the Senior Viceroy's link.

"George, you and the others have been discovered by evil again," Senior Viceroy Petrosky said calmly in the link.

"Yes sir," George replied, not looking up.

"Jupiter station, the cadets, and your team are now at risk," he said quietly, trying to get George and the others to accept what was about to happen.

"Yes sir," George replied again, there was little else he could say.

"Actions will need to be taken to insure your team's safety and the safety of this station," he added calmly, trying not to frighten the cadets.

"Yes sir," George repeated.

"Your team will stay in the CORE sector until a decision is made. Is that clear?" he said, a little more firmly.

"Yes sir," George answered.

"No running through the caves cadets," he added firmly, staring at Emily.

"Yes sir," they all chorused quietly.

Senior Viceroy Petrosky closed the link, and George's dad walked the cadets out of the council chamber. Andy tried to ask a question; however, George cut him off.

"Remember where we are," he thought through their link, and they lowered their heads again as they walked in silence through the Galactic council corridors.

George's dad made an archway and this time he nodded to Emily to open the door. With a flick of her wrist, the door opened. A dozen CORE officers stood in the outer corridor, waiting for the cadets to leave the Galactic council corridors.

George was last to leave the council corridors. His dad placed his hand on his shoulder.

"This will be hard on you and your team. Stay focused and keep them safe son," he whispered and then released his son. The Viceroys didn't follow them into the CORE corridor.

Pete and the other captain were frantic. They formed their link and reached out for George and the others. They found nothing, just like on their last rotation. However, this time they knew their cadets were with the Galactic council.

"Why Pete? Why did they take them? Nick asked.

"The Galactic council is afraid of them. I think they are more afraid of George and his team than they are afraid of evil. Their fear will make them put George and the others in isolation," Pete said, shaking his head.

"Then we need to be there with them," Nick said firmly, as the captains reached out to find Toma and Franks teams with their link.

The CORE officers surrounded the cadets and started marching through the CORE corridors. They stopped in front of a small archway of a small dome. The door opened and the CORE officers spread out around the edges of the small, dimly lit dome. The officers encircled the cadets in the center of the dome when the last officer entered. The cadets had not eaten since lunch. It was late and everyone was hungry and tired.

Gus pulled two ration packs from his backpack. He motioned everyone down. Emily touched the ground and small circular seats spun up a few inches for them to sit on. Gus finished slicing and dicing and handed everyone a few slices. They shared two bottles of water, one cap full at a time. It was late and they were getting tired.

"Andy, we have to stay awake," George signed.

They were uneasy and not feeling entirely safe even though, they were surrounded by CORE officers.

"Then let us begin," Andy signed, getting up as Gus slipped the wrappers and water bottles back into his backpack.

Andy stepped forward and the others lined up behind him. With the wave of Emily's hand, their seats melting back into the floor. George and the others never knew that other cadets their age couldn't control the raw energy of the universe the way they did. Opening doors, raising seats, making mind links were all things only CORE officers and above could do. The CORE officers surrounding the cadets stood in amazement, watching the young cadets.

"Chen Lo begin," Andy said quietly.

He bowed and spun around like retired Senior Viceroy David Lu. Together, they progressed through the levels and reached the eleventh level without a rest. Most of the CORE officers were watching the cadets intently now as many of the officers had only just reached level eleven themselves. Andy slowed the team and they all rested in the center of the room.

"I can't do anymore. I don't know the next level well enough," Andy said, shaking his head and breathing hard.

One of the CORE officers guarding them stepped forward. "I know the next level," the CORE officer said, boasting in front of the other CORE officers.

"Can you show us, sir?" Andy asked politely, backing up from the center of the room.

"Yes cadets," he replied seriously, straightening up and parading out in front of the cadets.

The CORE officer strutted as he walked, swinging his arms wide making a show for the others officers. He started his Chen Lo motions out slowly, repeating the eleventh level before he started the twelfth level. The CORE officer's twelfth level was different. Not like what David Lu had shown them during this rotation or last year's rotation.

"Are you sure this is correct, sir?" Andy asked kindly, not wanting to upset a CORE officer.

"Yes, of course. I know what I'm doing," the CORE officer snapped, struggling with the level twelve moves.

Yet, Andy wasn't so easily convinced. The cadets were tired and the CORE officer's motions were nearly hypnotic. Sara, Gus, Anna, and Emily dropped to the floor. Andy and George stopped, wobbling as they stood in the center of the room~ they were fighting sleep. Andy made a small red energy sphere and tossed it to George. It stung; however, it kept them awake for a few minutes longer.

George stared at Emily, Anna, Gus, and Sara lying on the floor. He looked up at Andy as he tried to sign a message. He thought of Pete, "help, something is wrong! Call gran..."

George and Andy hit the floor of the dome ~ thud, thud. They were all asleep ~ no dreams, only a deep sleep.

George woke up with a prickly burning sensation in the palm of his hand. The small red energy sphere Andy had given him earlier was still glowing in his palm. He stared at the pointy red sphere and then looked up. His head hit the inside of a crystalline status tube. It was odd to have a glowing sphere just sitting in your hand after they had been asleep. It should have dissipated. Andy wasn't awake and he wasn't sending George energy to keep the red sphere active, so who was? And why was he awake in a stasis tube?

Through the carved surface of their crystalline tubes, George could see Andy's body slumped over, his head squished against the crystalline tube's wall. He rolled his hand over and placed the glowing energy sphere on the tube wall. The tube trembled and then cracked open. Peering through the slit, he saw two officers standing by a doorway across the room.

"Wasn't this kind of how we started out our third rotation–trapped, kidnapped, and stuff into a box! This was getting tiresome. Why won't these fools give it up?" George muttered, shaking his head.

He concentrated on the two officers and wormed his way into their thoughts. The cadets were on a transport ship to somewhere; however, neither officer knew exactly where they were going. These were CORE officers and their mission was to take the cadets to somewhere safe, where they could be protected—meaning isolation.

"They are taking us somewhere to protect us. Why didn't they just ask? We would have gone willingly. Why the whole kidnapping thing? Seems like a plan meant to fail by design," George muttered, but his thoughts were too late.

Suddenly, the door burst open and two new officers rushed into the room. Two quick flashes of red sphere energy and the two CORE officers were destroyed. Only two piles of gray dust remained. The two new officers closed the door and took their places on either side of the door guarding the cadets.

George bent over in pain as the link he had made with the two CORE officers ended abruptly. Slowly, he stood up in his tube, concentrating hard to stop the pain. Then, he carefully wormed his way into the new officers' minds. These officers were different, not as controlled and focused as the first two CORE officers.

"The transport ship is ours now. The master will be pleased," the first officer said, grinning and rubbing his hands together.

"How long until we are home?" the second officer asked.

"It can't be more than one or two days with the master's help," the first officer said, smiling and rubbing his hands together again.

"What do you think we will get for capturing the team of the prophecy alive?" the second officer asked, eagerly awaiting any knowledge the first officer might have.

"I don't know. The last team that killed a prophecy team lived in luxury. We have ours alive. That has to be worth even more," he replied, chuckling and pointing toward the cadets crystalline tubes. The officers laughed and carried on.

George needed Andy awake if they were going to get free from these new captors. He thought of Andy's palm and about the small, glowing pointy red sphere Andy had given him before they were captured. Carefully, he sent a new pointy red sphere to Andy's palm.

Andy flicked his hand and the red pointy sphere went bouncing around inside his crystalline tube, stinging him. His eyes popped open. He was awake. He grabbed the red sphere and crushed it in his palm. A trickle of smoke wafted into the air from his hand as he looked around.

Andy stared at George through the crystalline tube. George grinned and signed what was going on. In a few minutes, Andy knew what George knew.

"We are going somewhere. We were guests of the Galactic council, but now, we are prisoners of the master," George signed, quickly in their new sign language.

"Seems like a Galactic council plan meant to fail and get us captured by evil again," Andy signed, frustrated with the council's decisions.

"Yes, I agree. I am getting a little tired of this too," George replied and sighed.

"Can't we just obliterate evil when we see it this time?" Andy asked, looking hopeful for something to do with large red energy spheres and knowing evil would be back.

"No. When we met the beings of white light during our last rotation, the really old being of white light, the one who I now think is Aris, asked if we should simply destroy evil. Then it wouldn't both us anymore. My answer was no and Aris seemed pleased. I think evil and the beings of white light are somehow connected. Like you can't destroy one without hurting the other," George signed before Andy abruptly cut him off.

The two officers turned around to face the computer terminal next to the door. With their backs turned, Andy silently slit open his tube. Two quick red sphere energy bursts from Andy's hand, and the two new officers fell to the ground with a thud. The boys bolted out of their crystalline tubes and dragged the two officers across the room to their tubes, sealing them inside with Andy's energy spheres.

"Hey, George isn't this exactly how we started our third rotation. I mean really, it's like déjà-vu," Andy whispered, shaking his head.

"Yes, but, I think this is worse this time. We need Emily now," George signed and Andy nodded.

They spun around and headed for Emily's tube when the door slid open.

"Hey, get back to your posts! You're not supposed to be near them! Do you understand?" an officer yelled, coming through the door.

"Yes ma'am!" George replied, as they backed up and the officer passed them to look at the sleeping cadets.

A minute later, Andy let loose with another red energy sphere and the third officer dropped to the floor with a thud. They woke Emily and placed the third officer in her crystal tube.

Emily pulled up the flight plan and started reconfiguring the computer system as George and Andy woke the rest of their team. Emily made a hologram in each tube as each cadet was removed.

"I don't know, George, this isn't good. The transport has 30 officers, not including the slaves running the transport," she said, shaking her head.

"How close are we to their destination?" George asked, needing more information.

"Looks like one or two days at most; however, I can't tell where we are by these charts. Where's Anna?" Emily asked, staring at the charts on the computer screen.

Anna stretched and walked up next to Emily. Casually, she glanced at the star charts and turned toward George to say something silly. However, as she realized what she had just causally seen, her mouth dropped open in horror. Terrified, she spun around again facing the terminal. Her hands raced over the terminal keys at an unbelievable speed.

"Well, where are we?" George pressed, growing impatient.

"In the one place we cannot go! We are very, very close. How long have we been asleep?" she asked, as her face turned white, not looking away from the computer terminal.

In an instant, she was re-scanning the navigation charts and triangulating their position again. She shook her head.

"We are so dead. This transport is nearly in the center of the expanding universe. We cannot be here!" she said frantically.

"Why?" Gus asked, not understanding as the ship seemed to be fine.

"Remember in class when Major Gote had us plotting all the courses across the known universe and he asked why we took longer transport routes than going through the center where all the lines crossed?" Anna replied.

"Yes, what about it?" Sara asked, getting interested in what Anna was saying.

"You cannot go through the center of the expanding universe and live," Anna said, staring at the navigation charts.

"Anna, you're not making any sense," Sara said, staring at the charts with Emily and Anna.

"The navigation charts say we are on the edge of the center of the universe. Think of it as if we are just entering the corona of our sun. Remember, Major Gote said how many ships were lost and that travel through the space was now forbidden. Come on! I know you were all in the training," Anna pressed.

"Anna, we were in the training; however, the discussion was about folding space," Andy said.

"No, no, it was about not going through the center of the universe and then the math for folding space," Anna said franticly~ this was bad.

They stared at Anna with vacant expressions.

"Hmm, OK try this, there is no space in the center of the universe. It is a point of expansion. Mathematically, it doesn't exist. Matter has to start from something, yet, here it is created. It is as if we are the tail of a black hole, and matter is being dumped into our universe without any of the gravitational issues involving black holes existing," Anna said.

Her voice was cracking as she spoke hurriedly, saying any idea or thought to get the others to understand. Fear was creeping into her mind. Andy twisted his head staring at Anna.

"Andy, what is the opposite of your red sphere?" Anna asked, trying a new thought direction.

"No red sphere?" he answered guessing.

"No, negative energy, a little black hole that absorbs energy. It's not nothing. It's the negative of nothing," Anna replied, thinking she was failing in her explanation.

"Anna, are we passing through nothing or are we landing on nothing?" George asked.

"Landing! We need to leave before we get to nothing," Anna said, scanning the chart for any inhabitable planets or asteroids.

George had no idea what Anna had said other than it was really, really bad and it was time to leave now.

"Emily, the holograms how long will they last?" he asked.

"Only until they open the tubes. We really need three more officers to stuff into the tubes. Small officers if you can," she replied, working with Anna.

Andy nodded with George.

"Small officers," Gus crinkled his eyebrows.

"Look here, there are two young officers in the engine room and a third in the galley," Sara said, working on a second computer terminal on the opposite side of the door. She was happy for having found the officers Emily wanted.

Gus, Andy, Sara, and George went out the door on their trip to find the small officers. Anna and Emily stayed behind and downloaded computer programs into the main transport systems. Quickly, Emily hid their bio signs from the transport ships computers and Anna plotted in an escape path.

Sara and the others made a quick stop in the hospital and picked up a couple of sleeping medicine spay canisters before they headed through the hallway to the engine room to collect their officers.

No one even questioned them as they walked through the hallways of the transport, passing by many other officers and servants. They thought only of reward and treasure for themselves ~ an oddly simple disguise.

A few more turns and they entered the engine room. Across the room were the two officers they were looking for. Gus, Andy, and George entered first, walking directly over to computer terminals and opening windows to look like they were working. Sara entered and tripped in the center of the room, her arms whirling around as she fell. The two officers came running to help her.

Andy and George spun around and tagged the two officers in the neck with the sleeping medicine. They dropped like rocks. Gus lifted one officer over his shoulder and Andy and George hung the second officer between them. They carried the officers back to the cargo room and again were surprised to get few questions.

"How oddly submissive they all are," Gus whispered, as they entered the room with the others.

"It is as if without free choice, they are simply waiting for instructions from someone else. They seem to have no thoughts of their own. Well, other than the implanted thoughts of treasures and reward for their work," Sara whispered, as they slipped the two officers into the stasis tubes.

"We have a plan," Emily whispered.

"Good. Don't tell us," George replied, and waved them off.

With the two officers in the tubes, they left again. In the galley, the team picked up the third officer as easily as they had gotten the first two officers. Quickly, Gus stuffed as many rations and bottles of water into his backpack as he could. Then he flipped the third officer up over his shoulder.

Andy picked up Gus's backpack and they hurried back to the cargo room with their last officer. Carefully, they pushed the unconscious officer into the crystal tube.

With the crystal tubes full, they walked over to Anna and Emily. Anna looked worried and Emily looked as worried as Anna. She now understood what Anna had been talking about.

George reached forward to hold their shoulders and help calm their worries and regain their focus. However, Emily pushed him away.

"No time," she said rather short, oddly annoyed.

"We are too close to nothing. We have to leave, now!" Anna whispered nearly frantic.

George nodded and they followed Emily and Anna out of the cargo room. Quickly, weaving through the ships hallways, they arrived at the transport ship's main hanger bay. They stood at the edge of a moderately sized hanger with a dozen small silver fighters lined up across the floor. A few officers pushed carts around, fixing this and that on the fighters. Another officer with a clipboard walked between the officers, checking their work.

"See that fighter. That's the only fighter ship we want. No other fighter will do," Emily signed.

Following Emily and Anna across the hanger, the team pushed tool carts, pretending to be servicing the fighters. Their thoughts focused on treasure and reward. No one questioned Emily's decisions or plan as Emily, Anna, and Sara slipped inside the little fighter she had pointed out. Anna's hand popped out of the open hatch.

"Now is good, come inside," Anna signed, with no thoughts in her mind.

They were in the open and any mistakes could foil their plan!

George, Gus, and Andy set down their tools and followed the girls inside fighter, closing the port hatch behind them. Emily, Sara, and Anna stepped up to the control console and sat down on the floor in front of the control consol. This way they would be less visible in the front view screen of the ship.

George, Andy, and Gus sat down behind them and Gus made a link with the team. Anna and Emily slid out their pads and started activating their programs. When all of the other fighter engines in the cargo bay started up, Sara started their fighter's engines. In their link, George calmed the team's fears so they could focus on their escape.

As each of Emily's programs activated, the transport ship's systems roared to life. The ship went on full alert and then stopped. The life support system flickered on and then off. The navigation array, main flight controls, and sensor systems blink off and on sending the crew racing across the transport fixing ghost problems. Emily may not have had access to the main computer controls, but the secondary computer systems access she did have was stunning to George and the others.

Finally, the transport's propulsion system misfired and exploded the fuel control system. The failed controller then dumped fuel into the storage room and ignited one section of fuel storage after another. Instantly, the transport ship was burning and the emergency sirens rang out, filling the transport ship with chaos.

"Abandon ship, abandon ship!" came the orders from Emily's computer program. The officers and crew ran for the escape pods and fighters. Emily launched some pods and fighters without anyone inside them. Then she blew up the escape pods just inside the hanger bay doors, destroying the control mechanism. The bay doors were locked open, Emily smiled.

Within minutes, the tiny fighter lifted off the hanger floor with a dozen fighters filled with officers and crew. Outside the hanger bay, Anna crashed an empty fighter into space debris from one of the exploded escape pods to make it look like some fighters were destroyed in the chaos.

Finally, Emily erased their fighter from the transport ship's logs. The transport was now crippled and the cadets were free. Anna programmed the new navigation coordinates into the fighter's navigation computer and set it on autopilot. Emily started more programs in the transport ship's computer sub-systems to prevent any clever computer programmers from regaining control of the transport ship's systems too quickly.

"How long before they recover?" George thought through their link.

"It will be at least two days. I locked the room they had us in too. That will keep them busy," Emily replied with a grin, returning to her programs.

"How about us? Why did we have to be in this particular fighter?" Andy asked, as Anna's hands slowed down over the control console.

"I had the crew load it with extra canisters of air, fuel, and supplies," Anna replied, as she and Emily smiled.

"Is it enough to get us home?" George asked softly, worried about her answer.

"Not to get to Jupiter station. I don't even know how we got this far in only two days," Anna answered.

"Perhaps evil knows how to use the raw energy of the universe like grandfather and transported us here," Gus said; however, like George, he was worried.

"Maybe, but it would take a lot of raw energy to move a whole ship," Emily replied.

"So if we traveled at normal speed, how long would it take us to get home?" Andy asked, not actually understanding where they were and thinking they were not that far away from Jupiter station.

"If we use one of the Thoreans fastest warships with Emily's engine programs then Jupiter station is about eleven or twelve months from here, Asteria station is a little closer, assuming we are folding space of, course," Anna replied seriously.

"This little fighter well, it can't make it there," Emily answered honestly.

Andy's face went white. "Where are we?" Andy gasped.

"We are a very long way from home, Andy," Anna replied, concerned Andy would freak out now that he was beginning to understand where they were in the universe.

He paused and thought for a minute. "Please tell me we are not going to Asteria station. You know they hate us. Isn't there a nice rock we can go to instead? Really you guys?" Andy said, pleading.

"Calm down, Andy. We're not going to Asteria station either. We are too far away for that too," Anna said, grinning a little.

Asteria cadet station was the one place that could put fear into Andy. Even evil couldn't do that.

"This fighter has a very limited range, even with Emily's extra air and fuel," Anna added.

Andy sighed.

"So where are we going?" Gus asked, beginning to think they were going to the Mahadean slave planet.

"Well, there is this trader's planet. It is at the limit of what this ship can reach, even with our extra fuel and air. If we conserve our energy, we should be able to make it there," Anna replied, as confidently as she could.

However, inside she was worried. There were no moons or asteroids to use to increase their speed in inner space.

"Is there anywhere else we can go?" George asked, calmly focusing on the fear that was creeping into everyone's minds.

"No, this is the closest planet. That's why we are going there. We'll need air and fuel when we land," Anna added, oddly annoyed by his question.

Anna finished setting the autopilot on the fighter, and the girls spun around facing the boys.

"And if we don't make it?" Andy asked hesitantly.

"Andy, I don't know why you ask. You know the answer," Sara said, raising her eyebrow as she scolded him.

"Oh, I see, so we are going along like always. We make it or we die. Wow! I am happy nothing has changed!" Andy said sarcastically.

His goofy face and sarcasm was funny and the cadets laughed. George formed a small yellow sphere over the palm of his hand and strengthened their link.

"Are we calling Pete?" Sara asked.

"No, I think we are on our own this time, at least for a while. Evil seems to be strong in this sector of space. I think it will know we have escaped if we try and send a message with the energy of the universe," George said, shaking his head.

"It is what would be expected," Emily added, understanding what he meant.

She thought back to their last rotation, and how each time George and Andy had tried to call grandfather with a link, using the energy of the universe, their message was intercepted and they were attacked. If evil was strong here, then they should be extra careful as they had no way home and had a long way to go to get to the traders planet.

"So it is the last thing we will do," George said, wrapping his arm around Emily's waist to comfort her.

"We will be on our own for a while," Andy said, as he and Gus followed George's lead, hugging the girls tight.

This was not the beginning of their fourth rotation that they had imagined, when, they were back on Earth. The fighter was small, like a training glider, perhaps a bit smaller inside as the entire rear of the fighter was filled with battered canisters of fuel and air. Emily's programs had the ship looking like a slow comet, streaking across the galaxies. Their life signs masked with a static feedback emitter.

Anna put life support and all others ship systems on minimum power consumption. Then Sara put everyone into a near status state with one of her medicine mixtures. The boys wrapped their arms over the girls squishing close together on the floor of the fighter to stay warm. They closed their eyes, sleeping to conserve energy. Emily's program would wake them when it was time to change the canisters of air and fuel. Silently, they traveled across the vast emptiness of inner space.

At each fuel change interval, Gus sliced and diced a ration for the team to share and poured bottle caps of water to drink. Huddled closely together for warmth, they fell asleep again.

After four days, Anna was worried. The engines were not as efficient as she had calculated and the fuel was going faster than expected. It should have been a canister of fuel each 24 hours, instead they were using one and a quarter canisters each 24 hours. Now there was only one canister left and a day and a half of distance left to travel before they got to the trader's planet. Even Emily's engine programs couldn't fix this!

Chapter 9

SHADOO

On the sixth day after their escape, the cadets awoke to the warning alarms Emily had programmed in the fighter's main computer. Through the view screen, they could see the solar system and trading planet they were headed for. However, they had only just entered the planet's solar system when the fuel alarm sounded.

Anna shook her head as she stood up at the main computer console. She didn't remember switching the last fuel canister out; however, there was no time to solve the mystery now. She brushed the frost off the control consoles, and she, Emily, and Sara's hands raced across the fighter's computer controls, looking for drops of fuel they had missed.

George rolled over and leaned his back against the hull of the ship. Gus and Andy followed George's lead. The three boys knew what they had to do. Last year, during the race through the molten core of Mahadean, the boys had feed energy into the ship's engines to win the race and set the slaves free. Now, they would do it again to get the fighter safely to the trader's planet. They also knew what would happen to them once they started feeding energy into the ship's engines.

"Emily, Anna, and Sara are strong. They will find a way to get help," George signed cryptically, and Andy and Gus nodded.

Andy made a red sphere of energy and handed it to Gus. However, he didn't use the energy of the universe this time; instead, he used his own strength. He knew it could destroy him, but he did it anyway. He couldn't let the others die in space.

Gus converted the energy and put it into their link, giving it to George to use. George sent the energy into the ship's engines. Sphere after sphere the boys fed the fighter's engines as they had done on Mahadean the year before. The boys knew they could not use the energy of the universe this time or evil's minions might find them here.

George thought of his dad as they fed the engines. At the start of his third rotation, George's dad had hidden them with a simple holographic projector. However, he fed the projector with his strength alone, as he knew the evil that hunted them would be able to locate them if they used the energy of the universe. The boys now hoped they had enough strength to save the girls and make it to the station!

Anna guided the fighter close to the trader's planet, and Emily switched off the comet disguise behind a moon. Sara called the local administrator and asked for landing instructions. She told the administrator that George was their master and that they were traders. Then she sent tribute, using their old Mahadean trader's code from the years before. It worked! The administrator accepted the code and granted them a landing port.

The girls guided the fighter through the planet's atmosphere. When they cleared the upper atmosphere, Emily and Sara gasped. It was a dry planet with nothing but rocky cliffs and sandy plains. It made the dry barren wastelands of Mahadean look like a lush green planet with its rings of green irrigated vegetable fields around the cities. Here, there was nothing but sand and rocks; miles and miles of dry sand coating the planet's surface.

Close to the city, they could see the spaceport landing fields. The landing ports were set up similar to Mahadean. Each port had a series of high circular walls that interconnected through archways that encircle the city.

"The high walls must slow the sand down and protect the spaceships during a sand storm," Sara muttered.

"Or whatever else is living in the ground," Emily replied thinking of Cal and his warnings not to sit on the ground outside of Earth.

"No nature walks here," Anna added and the girls giggled.

Soon they were hovering over their circular landing port. Carefully, Anna threaded the fighter down into the port, maneuvering on thrusters under the wings of half a dozen slightly larger ships. Emily, Sara, and Anna breathed a big sigh of relief as the fighter's landing gear touched down, and they shut off the main engine.

"We made it," Sara said thankfully.

"I still don't know how. I was sure we were one fuel canister short," Anna said, staring at the console's readouts.

"It's good and we can breathe the air. You picked a good planet Anna," Emily said kindly.

They were happy and high fiving each other that they had landed safely. Laughing and smiling they spun around to talk with the boys. Their faces dropped in horror! They didn't know.

"They were the fuel we didn't have!" Anna said, rushing over to Gus and holding his bleeding arms.

Instantly, they knew the boys had fed the engines with their own strength and energy, like they had done on Mahadean during the race. Only here, there was no one coming to help them. Andy, George, and Gus lay in a heap on the floor in the back of the fighter.

Suddenly, someone outside knocked loudly on the hull of the fighter. Panic raced through the girls minds.

"It must be the administrator or the magistrate," Emily said hurriedly, trying to focus and figure out what to do next.

"They let us land, but, I bet they don't get many outside visitors," Sara said worriedly.

"Sara can you wake George, even a little?" Anna asked, panicking.

Emily opened a storage locker and threw out cloaks, shirts, and pants for everyone to wear over their uniforms. The servant on the outside of the ship banged harder on the hull.

"George, George, listen to me. You have to talk to the Magistrate. Sara and I will help you," Emily said, as Sara made a small yellow sphere, trying to wake him.

They lifted him up between their shoulders and covered him in a long white cloak that touched the floor. As quick as they could, they dragged him to the port door and held him up in the doorway. Anna slid out on to the gangplank a little and the port door spun open. Emily and Sara staggered two steps out onto the gangplank supporting George between them to meet the local Magistrate.

"How long will your stay with us be, sir?" the Magistrate asked, staring at George and the two girls with him.

Emily pulled George's hair from behind and his head popped up. George looked at the Magistrate and Sara flipped his arm over.

"Sir, forgive us for speaking, sir. Our master is not well. He is running low on ale, sir," she said, lowering her head as if ready to be hit for speaking.

"I see," the Magistrate replied, nodding and rubbing his chin.

Sara crumpled under George's weight and he seemed to flip his head.

"Ale woman," Anna said from behind the gangplank port door.

"Yes, master," Sara replied, lowering her head ready to be hit.

"I see you have your hands full. You are forgiven for speaking. I will be back when your master has recovered," the magistrate said, then turned and left with his servants and slaves clearing his way through the port.

They backed up into the tiny fighter and closed the port door. They knew outside of the Galactic Union life was harsh and slaves were common. It would be a good cover for now.

Anna had the computer carefully collecting bits of information on the planet and filling the canisters with air when Sara, George, and Emily re-entered the ship. She had laid Gus and Andy out across the floor. Emily and Sara laid George down next to the other two. Like before when they raced on Mahadean, George's back was bleeding. Gus's hands and arms were badly burned, and Andy's skin had very little color.

While their ship's computer worked searching for information about the planet on the public computer systems, the girls formed a small healing circle around the boys. Sara focused and a small yellow sphere formed in the palm of her hand. Unlike one of George's yellow link sphere, Sara's yellow sphere was for healing. Anna and Emily placed their hands on Sara's shoulders to share their strength and energy. Sara's small yellow sphere grew.

She held her healing sphere slightly over George's back. Within half an hour, Sara sphere stopped his back from bleeding. Next, she moved to Gus. His arms and hands were blood red. She held her hand carefully over each arm moving her hand over his, her yellow healing sphere glowing between them. Within a second half hour, Gus' arms and hands also stopped bleeding.

Sara paused for a moment and rested. She used a lot of energy to heal the boys, as their injuries were more than just stopping their bleeding. She had to feed energy back into them. Their outward injuries were only the tip of the iceberg of what needed to be healed.

Andy was the last and the most difficult to heal. His strength was actually pulled out of him and they needed to feed him energy, energy the girls didn't really have. Yet, the girls would not quit. Sara ran her yellow sphere over Andy's body. Slowly, color returned to Andy's skin.

Two hours passed and Sara did as much as she could. The boys were no longer bleeding and shaking, but they were still unconscious. Emily set up sensor arrays to warn them if someone came too close to the fighter. The girls were all tired and wanted to lie down and rest, however, they knew Gus wouldn't be pleased.

Instead, they sliced open one of Gus's ration packs. Slicing and dicing they made six portions, saving three pieces for the boys. With water in the air on the planet, Emily started the ships distillers collecting the water out of the air to fill their empty water tanks and bottles using the fumes of fuel that were left in the fuel tanks.

"Is there anything about this planet that we can use to make tribute?" Emily asked, as they ate their meager meal.

"Sara can heal in the marketplace; however, without Gus to cook again, I don't know what else we can do," Anna said, looking down at her ration. "I hate rations you know. Yet, somehow, it is all we ever seem to eat," she added.

They were sad and were having a hard time fighting the fear that kept creeping into their minds.

"It is another dry planet, like Mahadean. Maybe we can distill water to sell?" Sara added.

"Maybe, however, we need fuel first. We are using the fumes in the fuel canisters now to make water for us now," Emily said seriously.

She was their leader now and she would need a plan.

"We have only half a day of fumes left at most," Sara said, tapping the computer console as if it would make a gauge move.

"To tell you the truth, I don't even know why we aren't drifting in space. I'm sure we were short one full canister of fuel you know," Anna said puzzled.

"Then someone is helping us, Anna. Remember, we are never alone even if we don't see them," Emily said, trying hard to be strong and comforting.

"I wonder if Max can help us here," Sara said hopefully.

"I don't know. But if what George said about evil being stronger here is true, then I bet good is weaker here," Emily said, trying to reason his words out.

"Well, first we need some rest," Sara said, staring at Andy.

"OK, first we rest and then we will work to make tribute for fuel," Emily said kindly.

The girls rested on the floor next to Andy, George, and Gus and closed their eyes. The ship was warm in the mid-day sun; however, they didn't want to leave the port door open without having enough energy to protect the fighter.

Late in the afternoon, when the air in the fighter had cooled, Emily, Sara, and Anna woke up. The boys were still asleep, as if, they were in a deep sleep. Sara and Anna left the ship to find a market to setup a healing location.

Emily stayed to watch the boys and search the information on the trader's planet that Anna's program had collected. The planet was called Shadoo and it had long ago fallen to evil. As she read, Emily worried they wouldn't be able to escaped and return home.

Like the Mahadean home world, the spaceship ports were setup in a circular manner with the smaller ships clustered together. The walls were tall between the ports, perhaps two stories with four high-carved archways leading between the ports on two sides and the public streets and markets on the other two sides.

Anna and Sara walked through the city and were stunned by the similarity to Mahadean. It was as if no progress had occurred since the moment evil took control over of the planet's population. Time and progress had stood still.

On a busy market corner a few ports away, Sara and Anna setup shop with an old mat and a yellow scarf. Sara sat on the mat, her legs crossed like a pretzel. She healed and Anna collected the tribute-one tribute for easy aliments, two tributes for more serious injuries. The poor of the planet came to be healed by Sara that afternoon. Anna and Sara stood up to when the crowd started to thin in the market.

A carpet merchant, near where they sat all afternoon, told them where the fuel merchant was located in the city. He had watched them all afternoon heal a steady stream of customers and offered a corner of his rug shop to Sara and Anna to heal in the next day. The deal was made and Anna and Sara would be back in the morning.

The girls threaded their way through the other markets on their way to the fuel merchant's shop. Some markets were full of brown, tan, and black clothes and furniture of similar dull colors. No reds, yellows, and vibrant oranges filled these markets. Only dull and dreary colors filled the markets.

Another market was filled with the sweet aromatic scents of spices and seasonings wafting into the air. Yet, the people looked sad and gloomy as if even the wonderful smells of the spice merchants couldn't bring joy to their lives. The vegetable and food markets were the last big markets they passed through. The prices were high for meager amount of roots and vegetables.

"It will cost a lot of tribute for Gus to cook here," Sara signed and Anna nodded.

The fuel merchant was nearly halfway across the city. Finally, they reached the building the rug merchant had described. They stood in the archway of a small stone building built into the side of one of the ports.

"My master has requested we buy fuel today, sir," Anna said, her head lowered ready to be punished for speaking.

They knew how a servants and slaves were to act from their time on Mahadean; slaves could be killed for speaking and servants beaten. Life outside the Galactic Union was harsh.

"You should be beaten for speaking; however, I have heard of your master and I understand. How much do you need?" the fuel merchant asked, not looking up from his old stone desk.

Anna laid out all of the tributes they had collected that afternoon on the fuel merchant's stone table.

"I will have ten bottles delivered to your ship," the merchant said, sweeping all of the tributes up in his hands.

"Kind, kind sir, forgive me for speaking again, but I think you are mistaken on your count. It is worth our lives that we come back with the proper amount of fuel," Anna said, cringing and lowering her head further to be hit by the merchant.

"Your master doesn't deserve slaves as good as you. Granted, sixteen bottles of fuel will be delivered," he said, clinching his fist on the desk.

"Kind, kind sir, forgive me once more," Sara pleaded.

"You try my patience slave. What is it now?" he said, looking up at Sara ready to strike her.

"Kind, kind sir I have noticed your hand is hurt. May we heal it for you? Please, sir. My master wouldn't have to know, sir," Sara said softly.

He held out his hand and Anna wrapped the yellow scarf over his wound. When she removed the scarf, the wound was healed. They lowered their heads and left the fuel merchant's shop.

"Do you think it was wise showing him we could heal? I mean he will know where our ship is," Anna asked, as they walked through the main street toward their port.

"We need fuel and sixteen canisters isn't enough for the tribute we paid," Sara answered a little harshly. "Besides, only his servants will know where we are. It is them I was really showing that we could heal," she added less harshly.

"You mean for when he beats them," Anna said, understanding Sara's decision.

They walked quickly back to their port, turning and twisting passed the dusty shops that lined the main streets.

"Look how similar this planet is to Mahadean," Anna whispered, marveling at how close it was to the other slave planet.

"It is as if they are nearly identical places," Sara replied, nodding.

"If I didn't know how close we were to the center of the universe, I'd say we were on Mahadean," Anna whispered, stepping through another port archway.

"Anna how bad is this place compared to where we were when we were captured on the transport ship? You know the place in the center of the universe?" Sara asked just above a whisper.

She had been with the boys on the transport ship and hadn't stayed with Anna and Emily on the computer system. Now she wanted to know where they really were.

"I don't know for absolute sure; however, Major Gatte made a point of telling us it was bad. It can't be good if a Major makes a point of telling you so you'll remember," Anna said, not telling the whole truth.

"More, I don't understand," Sara pressed.

"If our sun is the place where the entire universe started, then this planet is about where Venus is in our solar system and Calshene is out in the asteroid ring with Pluto," Anna replied.

She was worried if they really knew where they were, they would panic. When they had escaped, there were few options of places to go for them and this was the best place. Anna worried that evil would be able to figure out they were on Shadoo before they could get a bigger ship and escape again.

They walked up to their port archway and on through it zigzagging around the other ships in their port. Emily opened the door and lowered the gangplank as Anna and Sara walked up and slipped into the ship.

"How did you do?" Emily asked.

"We will see," Anna replied cryptically.

"We bought the fuel. We just don't know how much," Sara said, shrugging her shoulders.

A knock on the hull of the ship startled them and they spun around. Anna and Sara open the door; however, they didn't lower the gangplank. Instead, they lowered their heads.

"Please, you will disturb the master. Please be quiet," Emily whispered kindly.

"Forgive us, mistress. We are here to deliver the fuel you ordered," a servant replied softly.

"So quick, you are most kind. I will open the fuel control port for you to fill," Anna replied, and lowered her head to the servants again.

Four servants pulled up their wooden carts and started loading the fuel through a long dusty brown hose that had one end connected to a large canister on the first cart. The ships magnetic locks sealed the hose to the fighter's fuel fill port. The carts all floated above the ground and seemed to rise up as the fuel was transferred into the ship. Quickly, the second, third, and fourth carts were emptied and the servants started winding up the hoses.

"Thank you kindly," Anna said quietly and smiled a little.

"Twenty four canisters, mistress," the lead servant replied with a little smile.

"No, no kind, sir, it is more than we paid for, surely your master will beat you," she said, concerned for their lives.

"No, our master has tried to cheat you even after you healed his hand, mistress," the lead servant replied.

"Then tell me how can we repay you for your great kindness?" Anna asked kindly.

Out from behind one of the carts walked a women carrying a small boy- his leg was badly injured.

"Can you heal him, mistress?" the lead servant asked hopefully.

"We will do our best," Anna replied, and slid the gangplank out to the ground.

Sara came out of the ship and Anna covered the boy's leg with the yellow scarf. In a few minutes, the scarf was removed and Anna lifted the boy from his mother's arms and set him down on the ground. The boy jumped and circled around behind his mother, hiding. The mother was stunned and happy. She hugged Sara and Anna. Gushing on and on with many thanks.

"Please kind, sir, ma'am, tell no one where we are or we will get no rest and our master will beat us. We will be in the market each day with the rug merchant if you need us again," Anna requested.

"As you wish, mistress," the lead servant said, dipping his head.

The servants left with the little boy skipping around his mother.

"George won't be happy that so many people know where we are," Emily said, stepping out of the ship raising her eyebrow like George.

"He is in no shape to complain and we will need more fuel. At least for now we can get the ship operations up and running," Sara replied.

Emily smiled and helped Sara up the gangplank and back inside. Anna had the ship systems off the reserve power, and running on the new fuel the moment the servants had started filling the fuel tanks.

"Now we can find out more about where we are," Emily said to Anna with a little smile.

On reserve power, Emily's searches of Anna's data were short as they couldn't cover their computer path through the planets main computer system. Now with fuel, Emily had the energy to slip into the planets main systems undetected. Emily had written programs all day and quickly sent them into the main computer systems. It was a little like hacking into a government's top-secret computer system undetected~ impressive by any standards.

Sara and Anna made dinner from rations again.

"Can you wake them? They need to eat and drink," Anna asked, pointing to the boys as they sat down

"Not now, my strength is weak from healing today," Sara replied, as Anna cut up a ration and poured water into the silver cups.

"Then we will let them rest and recover, and we'll get more fuel tomorrow," Emily said, not looking up from the computer.

Chapter 10

TOO EXPOSED

Five days passed slowly as Anna and Sara healed in the market during the day and bought fuel each evening. The same servants always delivered the fuel each night. By the evening of the sixth day, Sara was getting worried.

"We must somehow start a link with them. The boys are getting weaker now and need food and water," Sara said, holding her hand over each them, after their evening meal.

The girls rested that evening regaining their strength. In the early morning of their seventh day, they sat in a circle on the floor next to the boys. They flipped the boy's palms over and placed their hands over the boy's palms creating small yellow spheres. In their minds, the girls jostled the boys and then jostled them again, and again, and again until they finally woke up.

"You need to eat and drink. It is time to get up," Emily spoke calmly in their link.

Slowly, George opened his eyes and stared at Emily. She smiled and he closed his eyes again.

"Oh no you don't, you need to wake up," Emily said, kindly as they jostled the boys' minds again.

By mid-afternoon, George, Andy, and Gus rolled over, opening their eyes. Emily spoke through their link as the girls feed them all of their missed rations. They told them everything they had missed. Shadoo was too close to the center of where they couldn't be and evil was strong here.

Emily was right about George, he wasn't happy that anyone knew where their ship was. However, he understood their desperation to obtain more fuel for the fighter.

In seven days, they had refilled the ship's fuel system, the extra canisters, and the ships water supply and air supply. What they didn't know about was the food?

"There are enough rations for thirty days total. We have used some already, so well, there will be problems if we can't eat the local food," Gus said firmly, eating his rations.

Then he paused and stared at Emily, Anna, and Sara thinking perhaps he had been too direct and honest. The girls were tired and worried. They didn't need an extra thing to scare them.

"I will teach you what you need to know about cooking. I never thought of this happening," Gus said, a little sad he hadn't thought of teaching the others the basics of cooking before.

"Perhaps we all need to share more of our skills. It is our weakness," George added, trying to distract his team and focus on the work before them.

Fear was an easy place to slip into on Shadoo, and they couldn't afford to lose their focus. They nodded and Emily locked down the fighter for the night. In the morning, they all felt better. George, Andy, and Gus were awake early.

"Let them sleep. They really are amazing, all they have accomplished in a world dominated by fear and mistrust," George said, staring at the girls in the morning light.

Gus stretched and stopped at the port door.

"I'm going to the market to see what there is on this planet I can cook with. I'm taking the extra tribute Sara and Anna collected," he said and glanced at George.

George nodded and Gus stepped out of the ship and into the bright morning light heading out for the market place to see what he could buy.

George stepped onto the gangplank and stretched in the morning sunlight. Andy stood behind him watching the people in their port come and go. The Magistrate had two servants placed in the port. They were to watch for the "master" to appear and then come and get him when he did.

The two hiding servants ran from the port when they saw George standing in the fighter's door. Andy saw the two servants run from the port and stepped in front of George pushing him back into the ship. Emily had told George and Andy the parts they were to play on this planet. George was the master here and Andy was the muscle. The rest of them were his servants and slaves.

Emily rolled over and the boys were gone. She jumped to her feet, bumping Anna and Sara. They scrambled for the port door, following Emily out onto the gangplank as the local magistrate entered the port. He had been waiting for 'the Master' to emerge from his ship. Emily, Sara, and Anna skidded to George's feet. However, Anna slipped off the gangplank and Sara followed her tumbling to the ground. From the magistrates perspective it looked like he had kicked them out of the door and thrown them to the ground below.

"Off with you two, earn your keep before I beat you for your disobedience!" George yelled, waving his hand wildly in the air.

"You go help him with preparations!" he said to Emily, raising his voice as if he was angry and pointing at Gus struggling with some new kettles.

It was a brilliant show for the magistrate and his servants. Gus had left the port early to buy kettles and wood to start cooking for the people of Shadoo planet. It would be the same as he had done for the people of Mahadean. As Gus entered their port, he began struggling with a stack of wood in his arms. A large black kettle hung over his back, making him tippy. Emily caught him and lifted some of the wood from his arms before he fell.

"Are you 'the Master' of this ship?" the magistrate asked, as he hurried up to the end of the gangplank.

"Who is asking?" George replied gruffly, turning to face the magistrate.

"I am the magistrate of the Southern ports of Shadoo," he replied firmly.

"And a fine magistrate you are, sir," George said, warming his voice as a wicked smile curled over his face.

The magistrate stepped onto gangplank and Andy appeared behind George with a staff weapon in his hand. Immediately, the magistrate stepped back and George walked down the gangplank to meet him. Andy stood inches behind George, making threatening faces. The magistrate's servants and other guards backed up the closer they got to the magistrate.

"What business do you have on Shadoo?" the magistrate pressed, his voice quivering a little.

"I am a trader and merchant, of course," George replied, nodding his head.

"Yes, we are all traders of sorts," the magistrate replied rather annoyed. "And your business here, sir?" he pressed again.

"I am in search of a larger ship, sir. We lost our last one in an unfortunate event," George said, stepping up close to the magistrate nearly whispering in his ear.

"Your ship is from the Galactic Union?" the magistrate replied, becoming interested in George's story.

"Yes, it's all that was left from our most unfortunate encounter with the Galactic Union. It seemed like a fair trade at the time," George whispered, grinning an evil little smile.

The magistrate wasn't satisfied with his answers; however, he thought he was pressing his luck to ask for more details. He nodded and left through one of the busy archways into the city market. George motioned to one of the magistrate's servants.

"Come back this afternoon and there will be food for you and your family," he whispered.

The slave curled his eyebrows and ran after the others. George walked over to Gus sitting on a small log, slicing white root vegetables into the black pot he had bought in the market. Emily scurried around, tending the fire and collecting more wood. With everyone busy, George returned to the fighter and called up Emily's programs.

Shadoo was a small planet, more the size of a large moon. The solar system was made of twenty-two small planets, with twelve of the planets in synchronous orbit and an asteroid belt. The system was old and yet with the exception of some scattered bits of technology, the inhabitants were poor and lived in fear. It was nothing but a subsistence life for the people now as the planet had long ago fallen to the evil.

The smell of Gus's stew wafted through the port and into the fighter. It distracted George and he looked up, out of the fighter's view screen. Gus and Emily had people lined up through the port.

"What do you think, Andy?" George asked, staring out the front view screen.

"I think we are exposed and careless. Gus is feeding the people right next to our ship and the magistrate is far too interested in our business. We have no way off this rock and no backup. We were safer on Mahadean," Andy said seriously.

"Actually, I was asking about the food. But, I will accept the other as your report," George replied, knowing Andy was right.

"Oh, it smells good. I hope we can eat it this time," Andy said, however, he was worried. They were too exposed!

Andy left to find out how Gus was doing. After healing for the day, Sara and Anna returned to the port with more roots, firewood, and another black kettle for Gus. Emily took the wood and kettle, while Gus stirred another kettle over the fire. Then they sat down in the dirt and started cutting up vegetables for Gus. Sara looked weak, yet, she cut on.

George knew Andy was right. The girls may have been desperate; however, now they were sloppy and exposed. They would need a plan and a destination to escape to if needed. With Emily's program, George scanned the planets computer system looking for an opportunity, anything to give them hope. As Gus had said, they had only thirty days of rations!

"What's this little tidbit? A race. When is it?" he said, talking to himself when the others entered the fighter.

Emily stood in front of the ships other control panel and started locking the ship up for the evening.

"What? What's going on?" George asked, looking up from the computer.

"George, it's late," Emily replied kindly, wrapping her arm over his shoulder. "We need to rest," she said and kissed him on his check.

"No, no it's only mid-afternoon," George replied, spinning around, staring at his team and hugging Emily.

"What have you been doing all day?" Anna asked, as she sat down on the floor to help Gus with their evening meal.

"Looking for opportunities," George replied, walking over to the team with Emily and sitting on the floor with them.

"On the planet's computer system?" Emily pressed, shaking her head and giggling as she sat next to George on the floor.

"Ya, ya and the whole day is gone. I hate when that happens," George replied, as he realized he had lost the entire day.

Gus sliced and diced another ration and Anna poured full cups of water.

"Gus, you need to move the cooking into the market and get some local help. Sara you must limit your healing time to eight hours. You are too weak to keep this up," George said, more captain like in the tone of his voice.

Gus and Andy smiled, nodding to each other. George had made a plan and they knew it.

"So what's the plan George?" Andy asked, grinning.

"There is talk of a race and a prize in the magistrate's personal computer database. Emily your access program is amazing. I would never have discovered there was a race without it," he said, giving her a hug.

"Nothing fancy," she replied and blushed.

"For the race, we will need a bit more information and most likely another ship. Anna, is there another traders outpost or planet in this solar system that we can get to in this ship?" George asked, taking a bite of his ration.

Anna laughed hard and spit her meager ration across the room.

"We're lucky we even got here. Technically we should be dead," she replied, stunned he had even asked.

The difficulty of their situation had made them all tense. Anna was still amazed they had made it to Shadoo and now George wanted to go to another planet!

"OK, so everything is looking up from here on out," George said, frowning. "We are making a plan to get home."

He paused. This was serious business and he needed the team to focus on the goal. They were running out of rations and Gus wasn't feeding them any of his food. George knew that meant they couldn't eat it.

"First we need to know how big a ship we will need to leave Shadoo and make it to the nearest Galactic Union station or make it to any other planets in this system. Anna, please?" he asked kindly.

Anna nodded as Gus gave her a piece of ration.

"Why, George?" Andy asked cryptically.

"Just in case, Andy, just in case. I got a bad feeling about this place," George replied.

He had read a lot about Shadoo on the Magistrates personal computer system, using one of Emily's computer programs and none of it was good. Andy was right, they were too exposed. George worried they may need to leave in a hurry, and they would need to find somewhere to go to and soon.

"Gus can we eat the food on this planet?" George asked, hopefully for the rest of the team; yet, he rather knew the answer already.

All eyes turned and stared at Gus.

"Yes, but not for very long," Gus replied cryptically.

This time, they knew to ask why.

"And this means what in non-cryptic communication?" Andy pressed.

"We came with thirty days of rations. After the rations are gone, we will be forced to eat the local food to stay alive," Gus said, shaking his head.

"You mean, we die like if we ate the food on Mahadean?" Anna asked.

"No, worse, we become drones and minions. There is something is in the soil and water. It's not natural, it was added and it controls them, all of them. It seems to make them compliant and good slaves," Gus said, sipping his water.

"It is probably why evil is so strong here," Emily added.

"What about the food you're feeding the people now?" George asked.

"I'm boiling off as much as I can. It will lessen the drone effect, but it is still in the food," Gus replied. "The people have eaten the food here all their lives. The drone effect is strong in them," he added.

The cadets paused~ a silent gasp perhaps. The very thought of becoming drones and minions of evil shocked them. They had fought against it for four years. Now, by a twist of fate, they were trapped on a planet controlled by evil.

"We need to stay focused," George said, and paused to get their attention. "Our plan will be two-fold, first to gain enough tribute to enter whatever this race is that is listed in the planet's main computer system, and second, we will use our winnings to get a ship big enough to leave this solar system. Our backup plan is to call home with the energy of the universe in our link. We will only use our link in our most desperate hour as the evil here will know where we are the moment we make the link," George said in his most captain like voice.

They smiled. They had a plan. A plan needing details, nonetheless, a plan and a goal. They laid down on the floor side by side and went to sleep. George slipped up by the front console and watched his team. He calmed their fears and thought of Max.

"What have I done, Max? We hid in plain sight on Jupiter station and evil found us. Now, I may have doomed my team to a life of servitude," he thought.

He knew there would be no answer~ no breeze, no answer. They were on their own. Max couldn't interfere on Shadoo.

Back on Jupiter station, the Galactic council had decided any missions to find the lost team, prophecy or not, was too risky. Pete, Toma, and Frank had no thoughts of accepting the Galactic council's orders. The three teams took on the most risky missions, searching for their lost cadets. Max didn't answer their call and grandfather warned the captains not to reach out with their link and find the cadets as it may jeopardize their cover, if they were still alive. Their triad searched, galaxy after galaxy following even the remotest of leads and bits of information. They would find them or die trying!

George planned for the entire next day. Andy helped Gus move his feeding area into the main market street. As before, the lines started small and then grew. Gus trained as many workers as he could on how to feed the people. He also had the recipe written on the walls of the ports. The similarities to Mahadean were striking, yet, this time instead of saving the Galactic council, they were saving themselves.

Again, they were alone. George fought the feelings of despair and fear and kept his team focused. He thought of the old center Senior Viceroy on Calshene and how he had cut them off from everyone else and how they had fallen into despair. It seemed like a training lesson now, as if he was preparing them for their current isolation. Could the old center Senior Viceroy have known they would end up on Shadoo? Did he set up the whole isolation plan to prepare them before they were lost on a planet controlled by evil? It did seem a little too coincidental. It would be a masterful plan if it were true.

George continued his search for information on the race in the magistrate's personal computer files. Late at night, he found the files he was looking for. The prize was not as large as on Mahadean; however, the tribute could buy the bigger spaceship they needed to escape. They were further away from any Galactic Union stations than they had been on Mahadean and only slightly beyond the edge of the space they couldn't be in.

"What was it Anna had said, the sun's corona," George muttered.

He had thought the space where the lines all crossed was where the beings of white light lived. However, he was beginning to think he was wrong.

The next morning they awoke to shouts of people and someone beating on the hull of their ship. It had been twelve days since they had landed on Shadoo and the magistrate was standing waiting in the port as the gangplank extended from the fighter. George walked out of the port door and stood at the top of the gangplank yelling as he walked forward.

"Kill who ever has ordered us to be disturbed!" George said, motioning to Andy.

The slaves and servants parted and the magistrate stood alone. Gus and Emily were pushed off the ship and Andy walked in front of George halfway down the gangplank. Emily had her hands on the ground and Gus had his arm over her shoulder. Sara had put drops in Andy's eyes and they glowed red.

With a sudden thrust of Andy's staff onto the gangplank the ground rumbled. He stepped forward his arms raised. One of the servants fired an energy sphere and he caught it with his bare hand hurling it back at the magistrate, narrowly missing him.

"Why have you disturbed my master?" he yelled, his voice booming.

"Tribute, sir. A simple matter of tribute for the port," the magistrate said, cowering behind a few servants.

"Why have you come as if we are criminals. We have broken no laws and willing pay you the tribute you request. Transfer the tribute slave, and be quick about it," George yelled, pushing Anna back into the ship.

"Yes, master," Anna whispered, disappearing into ship.

The magistrate nodded and left the port with his servants and slaves. The fuel merchant's slave who's child Sara had healed lingered behind.

"You are not safe now, you must leave," he whispered to Sara.

She nodded, flipping a tribute high into the air. The slave left catching a tribute behind his back with one hand, not turning around.

"Collect all of our tribute and fill the tanks, we leave this morning," George ordered.

Everyone nodded. Gus set up the feeding system for the people of Shadoo and Sara healed only a few people in the morning. Emily had the fuel tanks topped off and Andy topped off the air and water tanks. At mid-day, they lifted off not knowing exactly where they were going. They sent more tributes to the magistrate with their Mahadean traders account from years ago and left Shadoo's orbit.

"Where are we going now?" Sara asked as Anna guided the fighter out of orbit.

"There is another planet in this solar system where we can go; however, it is far less hospitable than this one. We have enough fuel to make it there now," Anna said, crinkling her face.

"Less hospitable! How can you get less hospitable?" Andy asked, grinning.

However, Andy spoke too soon. The planet was another of the twelve planets in synchronies orbit with Shadoo in this solar system. However, it was slightly smaller than Shadoo.

"These planets all look like moons," Sara said, as they flew through what looked like an asteroid belt. "I mean the twelve plants in synchronous orbit kind of look like they could have been one planet, right?" she added, puzzled.

"You're right! Why didn't I see it? This is not like Mahadean, it's like Calshene where the people fought back and evil destroyed their planet!" Anna exclaimed, as her hands raced across the controls, rebuilding the small planets into one virtual hologram of one large planet.

The computer reassembled all of the planet fragments into one planet. It spun in front of them.

"And the chemical in the soil was put there to keep them from rising up against evil," Gus added, finally understanding why it was there.

"It is so sad," Emily said, as if she could feel the sadness of all the people and organisms on the planets. "No more lush green planets, only barren rocks."

"They are lucky there was enough left to have planets. Calshene wasn't that lucky," Andy said, suddenly feeling sorry for the Calshene people.

Everyone stared at Andy. They were too close to the place in space they couldn't be and it was affecting their thoughts and focus.

Within an hour, they were circling the other trader's outpost. As they circled the new planet, the regional administrator appeared on the viewer. Emily transferred the tribute from their Mahadean account. It worked again.

The administrator gave them very specific landing instructions. Anna followed the instructions precisely and began her decent on the far side of the planet. As they descended, all they could see was sand and more sand, blowing across the planet's desolate surface. No cliffs or rocky outcrops dotted the land, only rolling sand dunes.

"You had to say something, Andy," Sara muttered and Emily shook her head.

"I think a planet of all sand is worse," Gus said agreeing with the others.

"OK, you have a point," Andy replied, conceding to their comments.

"So what is this place called, Anna?" George asked.

"Sandue," Andy said joking.

"I really don't know why you ask any more. Sandue is correct," Anna replied, staring at Andy.

Andy shook his head.

Chapter 11

SANDUE

"We must be more careful here. No more careless mistakes," George said seriously, sounding more and more like a captain every day.

They all nodded. Andy's earlier report to George was right. They had been far too careless on Shadoo, and it had cost them their port.

At the coordinates the magistrate specified, the sand spun beneath their hovering fighter reveling an opening into a spaceport below the surface of the planet. The fighter dropped down into a port filled with a dozen small fighters of similar size. They landed gently this time as the sand spilled in over the edges of the port opening.

Within a few minutes, they turned off the flight systems and Anna opened the fighter's port door, extending the dusty gangplank as the roof closed overhead. The loud locking thud echoed through the port. At the bottom of the fighter's gangplank stood a tall thin man with half a dozen servants.

"Welcome strangers, what business do you have with us here on Sandue?" the regional magistrate asked.

"We have come to trade and race," George answered, stepping onto the gangplank.

"In that heap, you'll be lucky if you make the first turn. Where did you come from?" the magistrate laughed.

"Shadoo," George replied, as Andy stood behind him with glowing red eyes.

"Why did you leave?" the magistrate pressed.

"I'm not sure the Southern magistrate liked us. So to spare his feelings, we left," George replied, nodding his head and walking to the bottom of the gangplank.

"Most thoughtful of you," the magistrate replied, however, curious as to why the southern magistrate didn't like them.

"We will of course be in need of many supplies and will be paying most handsomely for them. If you have a suggestion as to the shops my slaves should use...," George said slyly, nearly bribing the magistrate ~ it was working.

The magistrate smiled greedily and warmed up to George. He pointed out a few shops they could favor and then left with his servants.

Emily tapped into the local computer network to see what they were dealing with on Sandue.

Gus, Sara, and Anna went foraging for foods and heating elements as Gus doubted there would be any wood in a subterranean city. Gus tested many of the local foods with a makeshift chemistry kit that he and Sara had made from bits and pieces of the fighter's medical kit and a root from Shadoo Sara had brought with her. In time, Gus found the right chemical combinations for his food. He smiled.

"I can cook here too. Besides, I'm sure we will need more tribute to get another ship on this planet," Gus muttered, a little annoyed.

Sara and Anna set up a healing shop on a market corner and collected enough tribute to buy Gus his supplies to get started. Gus was in business and cooking up a storm in no time at one of the merchant's shops. He offered free food to those that would help him and soon he had eight volunteers, slicing and dicing the white roots and mashing brown fungi into a paste.

He feed only a hundred people that first day, but the word spread like wildfire of the man that made food for the poor. Leaving Gus's pots and pans with the kettle merchant who was willing to share his space in exchange for food and kettle sales, they returned to the ship in the early evening. The three cadets took the long way back to the fighter to cover their trail.

Gus never stopped or acknowledged George and Andy when they arrived at the fighter. Instead, he marched right up the gangplank and into the fighter without saying a word.

"What's wrong with him?" George asked, twisting his head and wondering why Gus didn't stop to tell him how the cooking went and if he was successful on Sandue.

"He's tired and his spirit is low," Anna replied, covering for Gus's odd mood.

She followed him into the ship. She was also tired and the planet seemed to suck the joy out of life. In the fighter's small galley area, Gus was cooking with food from the planet for his team to eat. He was using the fungi paste and a few other ingredients.

"So is it safe to eat? I mean, it's not a ration," Andy asked, staring at Gus; confused because they had never before been able to eat the local food.

"We have only a few rations left and I need to save those. The food here doesn't have the same chemicals as on Shadoo. You can only eat what I give you and it will not be tasty," Gus said abruptly, nearly angry.

The cadets sat inside the fighter, resting from their work that day. Emily had refueled all of the tanks, using the tribute they had collected on Shadoo. She had also started a bank account for Gus's cooking so the money they earned could be used by them and the workers.

George and Andy read the magistrates main computer database all day, looking for more information about the race. George had a plan; however, it was still a plan with lots of holes.

Quietly, Gus stood in the back of the fighter and rolled the fungi paste between his hands making little cookie shaped pieces. Setting them on a silver plate, he suddenly collapsed! He hit the floor hard and the silver plate clanged loudly on the floor. The fungi paste flew through the air, sticking to the walls and floor of the fighter.

Sara and the others jumped to their feet and ran to Gus. Sara grabbed his hand first. It was as cold as ice and beads of sweat were trickling across his forehead. Gus was wrong, the results from their simple chemistry set gave him a false reading. The root from Shadoo they had used to build the chemistry test kit had traces of the bad chemicals hidden within it.

When Gus tested the local foods for the chemicals, he was looking for the difference between the test chemicals and the new foods. However, because the test chemicals he was using were contaminated with trace amounts of the bad chemical, he was really testing the difference between the same chemicals. The test results made the contaminate food look like it was safe to eat, when it really wasn't safe.

The result was worst than even Gus thought. Because he thought he was testing one food without the chemical and one with the chemical, his results showed less chemical in the ingredients, as he had only measured the difference of the two chemicals. Instead, the food was twice as contaminated on Sandue as it had been on Shadoo.

Sara made a small yellow healing sphere and held it over Gus. The palms his hands were stained white, and he had dark blue streaks running through his veins from the roots he had peeled earlier that day. The team joined Sara and placed their hands on her shoulders to share their energy and strength. Her yellow healing sphere grew.

"The stuff Gus was talking about on Shadoo must be in the roots here too," Emily said, gathering up Gus's root paste balls with an empty cup.

"Somehow, it must be stronger here. It never did this to us when we peeled the roots on Shadoo," Anna added, staring at the paste in the cup.

"The sunlight must destroy some of the chemical in the vegetables on Shadoo, but here the vegetables are all grown underground and the chemical stays really strong," Emily said, trying to figure out what was different between the two planets.

"Well, it really doesn't matter how. Right now, it has a strong hold on Gus's mind," Sara whispered.

"Sara do you have any medicine that can destroy only the bad chemical in Gus?" George asked.

"This chemical doesn't exactly work like that, but I will try," Sara said, loosening her hold on Gus.

She reached back for the fighter's medical kit. She filled a medicine dispenser with several different kinds of medicines and shot it into Gus's arm. Gus's body twitched and then twisted, spinning away from the team as if it was trying to prevent Sara and the others from destroying the chemical in his body. Sara rolled over and reconnected with Gus. Again, his body shook and trembled, fighting Sara at every turn.

"What is going on? He only touched the roots and fungi for a little while," Andy asked, puzzled by Gus's severe reaction.

"Only one short exposure to the chemical and look at the hold it has on his mind," Anna said amazed.

"Imagine the hold the chemical has on the people who grew up eating this stuff," Emily added sadly.

"Maybe someday there will be enough energy in the galaxies to set them free," George added solemnly.

"Yes, but, right now I am worried about clearing the chemical from Gus, and whether or not we can keep him off the chemical in the future," Sara answered seriously.

The others hadn't even thought of that. They had assumed, once the chemical was gone from his body, everything would return to normal, well at least, normal for them. Not that Gus would want more of the chemical; even crave it.

After a few hours passed, Gus's body stopped shaking and Sara lowered her yellow sphere. Emily locked the fighter and changed the codes so Gus couldn't leave while they slept. Andy sliced and diced a ration pack and they ate their meal in silence. They laid down to rest as George and Andy slid to the front of the ship.

"So what do you think?" George asked.

"I think the magistrate didn't act like a drone," Andy whispered, rubbing his chin.

"It is either his food or he has an antidote for the chemical in the food," George whispered back.

"I'm going with antidote and we need to find it," Andy whispered, oddly serious and left George alone to think.

Andy knew what he would have to do; one way or another, he would get the antidote. He and George had read the magistrates database all day and the time of the race was now.

Doubt filled George's mind as he sat alone in the front of the fighter. He could hardly concentrate. What had he done? Why was he having these thoughts? Did the evil know they were there and was simply toying with them, giving them bits of hope only to destroy their hope and make them weaker? He wanted to reach out into the galaxies and call for grandfather. However, it would mean certain death for his team if evil found them on the planet so close to where they could not be.

Morning came early their second day on Sandue. Andy was gone before the others were even awake. George slipped out after Andy and set up Gus's cooking without actually touching any of the roots or fungi.

Soon the people, Gus had taught to cook the day before, were cooking kettle after kettle of food. The sweet smells wafted through the air and soon there was a line of people waiting to eat Gus's soup. By late afternoon, they had fed more than a thousand hungry people. George distributed the remaining food and paid for the raw ingredients. The cooks stayed and cleaned up when George left to deposit the remaining tribute in the crude banking system, before taking the long way back to their little fighter.

Andy hadn't yet returned when George entered their port in the late afternoon. Sara and Anna were away healing in the market. George wasn't happy they were not back yet, and that Sara was healing so many people. She needed to save her strength.

Gus was awake and agitated when George walked up the gangplank in the late afternoon. He peered inside the ship to find Gus hog-tied on the floor of the fighter with Emily standing over him like a guard.

"Let me go. Untie me. I have work to do. Make them let me go, George. I'm fine, you can see that, right?" Gus said, pleading and squirming to break free from the gauze ropes.

Emily shook her head out of Gus's view.

"It's a kind of withdrawal or something. You can't trust him," she signed, standing behind Gus.

"Who made the gauze rope?" George asked, trying to be positive.

"Sara. She is very clever, you know," Emily replied and hugged George.

George sat and guarded Gus while Emily went back to searching the planet's computer system. Within an hour, Anna and Sara returned from their corner healing station. Sara looked tired, as if healing on Sandue was harder than on Shadoo.

"You are healing for too long, Sara," George said quietly, yet seriously.

"There are so many sick here," she replied, with great sadness in her words.

"Perhaps, but you can't help them if you get too weak," he said, a little captain like.

Anna sliced open a ration and cut it up. George fed Gus and made him drink water. All the while, Gus pleaded to be released. Emily had spent the day on the magistrate's computer system network and she had learned a lot about the planet and the people that lived here.

"There is a lot of talk about the upcoming quarter race and a brutal fight the day before the race starts. The chatter is favoring a well know champion; however, there are some new contenders in this quarter's challenge," she told George, as he looked around their small ship.

"What about the race? When is it?" he asked, leaving Gus and walking over to the computer and Emily.

He wrapped his arm over her shoulder softly and stared at the computer screen. She always looked so neat and clean. Now, her hair fell over her face, covering smudges of dirt. Like the rest of them, her uniform was dirty under the clothes they had on and her hands were dirty. The powder like dust of the underground city coated everything in the little fighter.

"The race in this solar system is in space. The course weaves in and out around the small planets and asteroids that orbit the two suns of this solar system. There have been no winners for the last eight quarters," Emily said, shaking her head.

"Why?" George asked, confused about how could there be no winners.

"Only the fighters can race and many of them die in the competition. Those that have made it to the race have crashed into the asteroids or other planets as they fly alone and most are badly injured during the competition," she said, still shaking her head.

The hatch door of the ship opened and Andy quietly slipped inside.

"Sara, give him two drops now, and one drop every six hours after that until it's all gone," Andy said gruffly.

He tossed her a small vial of blue liquid wrapped in a dirty brown cloth as he walked by. Sara put two drops on part of her ration and forced Gus to eat it. Andy walked to the back of the fighter and slid down the wall, streaking it with blood as he slumped over to rest.

"I thought I heard Andy return?" George said, turning around.

He walked away from the little control area of the fighter back toward to Sara, Anna, and Gus.

"You did. He gave me this vial of blue liquid and said to give it to Gus. Then he left for the back of the ship," Sara said, holding up the vial to show George.

George crinkled his face and rushed to the back storage compartment of the ship. He knelt down.

"Andy what happened? What did you do? Sara, come, quick!" he yelled.

Anna held Gus and Sara hurried to George. In the evening light, she could see the blood streaked wall and Andy slumped down on the floor of the ship. Her yellow sphere glowed bright in her shaking hand before she reached him. Immediately, she started to heal his wounds.

"Andy, you look like you were in a fight?" Sara spoke quietly and calmly, as George placed his hand on Sara's shoulder to share his energy.

"I was," Andy whispered gruffly.

"Emily, tell me more about this fight!" George yelled to the front of the ship.

Emily came running, grabbing onto Sara's shoulder when she saw Andy.

"What did he do?" she asked worriedly.

"You tell me. When are the fight and the race through space you were talking about? When is it, exactly?" George asked pressing for details.

Emily's face went white as she realized what Andy had done.

"There was no time listed in the computer system. It must be now! He must have entered the race and the fight, didn't he?" Emily said, staring at George.

"Yes, he did," George replied, piecing together what Andy had done.

"I'm here, you know. Stop talking about me like I'm dead. I made it through the fight. I'm in the race now. However, I will need the fighter tomorrow and you can't come along," Andy said, his voice was low and firm.

"The competition is a brutal fight. It is held in a large arena much like in the ancient days of Rome on Earth. The fighters are like gladiators. George, the fight is to the death. Only twelve competitors can advance!" Emily said and then paused, afraid Andy had killed to win his place in the race.

"I didn't kill anyone one, well, much at least," Andy replied, sitting up straighter and holding Sara's free hand as she healed his wounds with her other hand.

"Why Andy?" George asked in disbelief. "Why did you do this?"

"George, it is the plan and we need to get off this rock. The medicine for Gus will not last long and it is really expensive. I'm the only one who could have entered the competition and lived, and you know it. I can win this space race and we can get a ship big enough to leave this pile of sand. Don't even say it, George. I know what you're thinking," Andy said harshly over his cut lip.

George lowered his head. Andy was right; he was the only one who could have survived a competition where the fight was to the death. Now he would need to fly their tiny fighter alone, as if he had Anna's navigation and flight skills.

"Emily, when is the race?" George asked.

"If the competition was today, then Andy has to be in the race arena by noon tomorrow," Emily replied, remembering what she had read.

Now she would need to come up with some programs for the race quickly.

"Then we have until noon tomorrow to find a new ship, heal Andy, and teach him to fly," George said firmly, and stood up walking over to get Gus.

Anna had untied Gus and he sat on the floor in the middle of the fighter.

"Gus, are you OK?" he asked, kneeling down next to him.

"Better George, but this medicine must have cost a lot and I'm not talking about tribute alone," Gus said, sliding a drop of the blue liquid into the ships crude chemical analyzer.

"Gus, we need to strengthen our link, like when we were on Jupiter station, and the Viceroys slipped the enzyme into our rations. Something like your red liquid, maybe," George said, staring at Gus hoping he was well enough to make his red liquid again.

When they had rescued the Thorean cadets and officers from the Mahadean invaders, Gus had made a red liquid that had strengthened their link. Now he would need to do it again to save their team. However, this time he didn't have the amazing hospital chemicals that had been on-board the Thorean Galaxy class cruiser.

"I will have to leave the ship," Gus said, lifting his eyebrow.

"Take Emily with you. Emily watch him, you know what to do if anything happens. Also, we will need another ship," he said seriously staring at Emily.

The time to lead had come and they were counting on him and his plan. It was only by working together that would they be successful and leave Sandue.

Emily and Gus left in a hurry, slipping out of the fighter into the evening light. The underground city was illuminated by mirrors reflecting the sunlight down long shafts from the wind sweep surface of the planet above. With the light diminishing from the setting sun, they would have to hurry. They didn't have much time left to find the correct ingredients before all the shops closed for the night.

"Anna can you use Emily's information and create a safe course around the planets for the race? See if you can find the winning time of the last race winner and find out what the flight path was?" George asked, giving commands, as their opportunity to leave this solar system was quickly approaching, and they weren't ready.

Anna searched the magistrate's files using Emily's programs. They would never know Anna was even in their computer system. She plotted course after course. Refining each move and yet, she knew none of the courses she plotted would win. All of her simulations ended with crash and burn or a second place finish. There had to be a way for Andy to win, Anna was sure of it.

"What am I missing?" she muttered. "He will need different advantages here than on Mahadean. Something the others will not expect. He can't out fly them and he certainly isn't the fastest ship racing. So what can we give him that is the edge he needs to win?" Anna muttered, trying to sort out a strategy that was more than just flying the fighter.

Gus and Emily ran through the market, stopping for a few minutes at the cooking place he had started. The people working smiled and nodded. The merchant had changed business in two days. He handed Gus some extra tribute and said the rest would be placed in the bank. Gus explained how to use the tribute they collected and what to do for the other people of the planet before they hurried away.

Ten minutes later, they were running onto an apothecary shop to look for native spices they could eat. George and Sara stayed with Andy in the back of the ship.

"Andy, we will make our link strong and then as the race begins, I will call our triad for help," George said, explaining the whole plan to Andy.

"George, if you do, evil will find us and kill us," Andy said, shaking his head.

"If I don't do it, we will die anyway. So, it really doesn't matter now," George said seriously, and pressed on with his plan.

Gus found the spices and herbs he needed and paid with the tribute the merchant had handed him. On their way back to the fighter, Emily made a little detour to buy the largest spaceship she found when she had scanned the magistrate's private computer database. Gus's mouth dropped when he saw the ship she wanted to buy.

"Emily, are you kidding? It looks worse than the one we have now. It has cannon fire marks on it, Emily!" Gus said stunned.

"Yes, yes it does. That is precisely why I want it. It is the one that got away, besides it's the biggest one I could find!" Emily whispered and smiled, pleased with her find.

Emily and Gus talked and traded with the merchant until the price for the ship was reasonable. She used the money in the bank as collateral on the loan. It made them look wealthy, even though Emily knew she could never use the money ~ it was money for the people of Sandue. By the end of her negotiations, the merchant was exhausted, and Emily had him throw in extra fuel tanks for free. The spaceship would be loaded with fuel and ready in a few hours.

They stepped out of the merchant's office and into a tavern across the narrow dusty street to hire a pilot to move their new spaceship. She wanted it moved to the space the fighter would leave open when fighter flew to the race arena. Gus was sure Emily knew what she was doing; however, he was worried there wouldn't be enough time left for them to complete all of their work.

Four hours later, Andy was standing in the back of the fighter drinking a cup of Sara's vitamin water when Emily and Gus returned. Sara gave Gus another dose of the medicine Andy had brought back earlier the moment she saw him. She was worried the effects would wear off before he could finish his new liquid.

Gus stopped, drank down his cup of water with the medicine, and hurried into the tiny galley area to create his red liquid. Anna pulled Emily to the control console and showed her what Andy needed to do to win the race. It was more than speed and skill! Emily gasped and turned to stare at Andy for a moment.

Chapter 12

FIGHT, RACE, OR DRONE

With only a few hours left before the race, Andy, Sara, Emily, and Anna assembled the canisters and firing mechanisms Anna had created to help Andy win. Gus and George had worked through the night too, mixing and heating the red liquid-like scientists in a lab. Every bit of bad chemical, that was in the spices and roots, had to be baked and boiled away or the liquid wouldn't be safe for them to drink.

It was early in the morning, when Anna and Emily reconfigured the fighter's engines as Andy and Sara attached a canister launcher to the side of the fighter. It would launch fuel canisters, as if they were cannon balls from an ancient sailing ship. If the fuel canisters hit their target, the canister would burst and the fuel would eat through the hull of an attacking ship or through a small asteroid.

They also built attached computer control canisters that could be fired at another ship. If the canister stuck to the other ship, it would interface with other ships computer systems. Andy fighter could then disappear from the others ship senses.

George and Gus emerged from the galley area on the ship as the sun was rising in the reflecting mirrors the morning of the race.

"This will taste really awful; however, it will strengthen our link to each other," Gus said, carrying a small pitcher of red liquid.

Anna reached over and gave Gus another drop of the blue medicine as they all sat down on the floor in the command deck to eat their ration and drink their water.

"Andy, you can't fly this ship and win," Anna said, sipping her water.

"Anna, you can't come. There are rules and they will know," Andy said sadly.

"I know; however, Emily and I have a plan," Anna said and glanced at George.

Leaning back, George smiled. He was yielding command of their team to Emily and Anna.

"The basic flight course is stored on the fighter's computers in two places. The first location is in the main control computer up here. The second location is on the galley computer. The galley computer isn't connected to the main computer, so if the main computer is damaged, you can connect the power system cables and engine controls to the galley computer," Emily said, pointing out the roll of cable on the floor and the path to use to connect to the galley computer system for Andy.

"Now as to flying, well, Andy, this isn't about flying the course well or fast. The past winners were neither fast nor efficient, they were, well, they were, ah," Anna said hesitating.

"What? They were what?" Andy asked, twisting his face.

"The only ones left alive when they passed over the finish line marker," Emily said, finishing Anna's words.

Andy paused and stared at Emily and Anna "Why?" he asked, crinkling his forehead.

"They avoided all of the explosions and weapons fire from the other competitors," Anna answered directly.

"You and I both know no one can avoid everyone. Someone will notice and then go after you," Andy said, pressing them further for more answers.

"Yes, Emily wrote a program for that. You can load it into anyone's computer system, and it will project your holographic imagine with their computer system. They will be confused, however, most likely, not for long. It is only a little advantage, but, it is something," Anna said, concerned it would not be enough.

"So how do I win?" Andy asked, his voice low and deadly serious.

He knew the stakes were high and understood the risk was all of their lives.

"Anna will fly the ship through our link. It will be hard for you, Andy. Anna has been preparing herself to destroy obstacles. You must prepare yourself to glide, flow, and fly without effort," Emily replied seriously.

"What kind of gobbly guck are you talking about?" Andy said and laughed uncomfortably.

"It's not gobbly guck, Andy! It's the ebb and flow of the universe around us. You need to feel the rhythm of nature around you," Emily said, motioning with her hands and Anna nodded.

"We are on a dead planet of sand, Emily. There is no ebb and flow here, other than the shifting sand," Andy replied, not convinced they had a good plan.

Emily glanced at George. He placed his hand on Andy's shoulder and then on Anna's shoulder.

"See passed where you are and look to the spaces between spaces. Life is all around you," George thought to Andy.

Andy stared deep into Anna's eyes, focusing solely on her and her thoughts. They connected. Through her eyes, Anna showed him the flow of life around them on this little sand sweep planet far from home. In Andy's mind, the rhythm of life came into focus with Anna's help. An hour later, George slipped his hands off Anna and Andy's shoulders and the images faded in Andy's mind.

Andy stared at Anna as if for the first time, seeing her for who she really was. Anna was not as physically strong as the others were, but, she had an inner strength and calm he hadn't sensed before. She was amazing.

"I can do this," Andy whispered, staring at Anna. "I can learn."

"We know," Anna answered, staring deep into Andy eyes.

"It is time," Emily said calmly. "We can't be late."

Gus poured the red liquid into the six silver cups and mixed in a little water so it wouldn't be as thick. They toasted in silence and gulped it down, barely tasting it. It was bitter; however, no one said a word. Then Gus poured a second round of red liquid and water into everyone's silver cups. George raised his eyebrow at Gus.

"No, it is not safe; however, it is the only way to maintain our link over the greatest of distances," Gus said firmly.

They all gulped down the second cup and formed their link. Sara opened the port door and lowered the gangplank. Gus, Emily, and Anna left the tiny fighter, walking to the edge of the port as George, Andy, and Sara lifted off, heading for the Starting Arena. Sara's glowing yellow sphere continued, healing Andy's wounds as they flew over the city.

The underground city ceiling was low. Weaving in and out among the buildings, Andy could sense the ebb and flow of life Anna and Emily had spoke of earlier.

Their ship was the last one to arrive in the Start Arena. The Start Arena was no bigger than a football arena on Earth and all twelve competitor's ships were crammed into it together. Some smaller ships even had their wings under the larger ships' wings.

As Andy set the fighter down on the only empty landing pad, the magistrate's security guards stepped forward to scan the tiny ship.

"You know the rules, you have to pilot the ship alone!" the magistrate's lead security guard yelled into the ship's communication system, shaking his arm wildly in the air from his alcove under the magistrate's box.

The magistrate nodded toward the lead security guard for having yelled the warning well. The port door opened and George and Sara slipped out of the fighter, without sliding out the gangplank.

"No need to invite unwanted visitors," George thought, the game was on.

"We are never alone," Andy thought into their link and closed the port door.

Two mechanics fitted a small transmitter device to the underside of the fighter's hull. It would transmit the location of each competitor's ship as they flew around the racecourse to make sure each competitor passed by the all of the course markers. The markers would prevent the competitors from cheating, by forcing them to fly the whole course.

With the transmitter in place, George and Sara were walked off the dusty arena ground between two guards dressed in black robes. The guards were scanners, however, not strong ones like on Mahadean. They tried to read the cadets minds as they lead them away from the racers. George brushed their weak mind invasions off with little difficulty.

As they walked, George focused on each of the other competitors and Sara sensed their relative health through him. She nodded and he picked up the pace, she had the information she needed to send through their link. Outside of the Start Arena, they stood in a crowded archway filled with servants and slaves.

"Focus and concentrate, calm are we," George thought through their link.

A few minutes after their fighter left for the Start Arena, their new larger spaceship arrived at their old port. Quickly, Emily, Gus, and Anna went to work to secure the large ship's cargo before Andy needed them for the race. Gus counted the cargo~ all of the extra fuel and air tanks were on-board. Emily had bought the biggest spaceship she could find and filled it with as much air and fuel as she could.

Yet, Gus worried. He alone knew there would be no food going with them on their long journey home as he had fed them nothing today except the red liquid and water.

"I still don't understand why we have to race? We have the big spaceship and the supplies. Why can't we just leave?" Anna asked looking around the ship.

"We only made a down payment on the ship using the tribute in the bank. To fly it off this planet, we will have to totally pay for the ship or they won't let us leave," Emily replied.

"To pay off this spaceship, Andy has to win the race," Gus added somberly holding Anna's hand softly.

Anna nodded her head, understanding the problem now.

"Racers ready!" the magistrate yelled into a microphone, his voice booming through the Start Arena and the city beyond.

The crowd in the small arena went wild, yelling, and cheering. The first boulder fell from a platform similar to the one on Mahadean and the ships lifted off the arena floor, hovering in place in the arena.

'Screech, crunch, scrape.' The sounds of the city roof moving open over the arena were deafening to the people in the arena. Slowly, the roof panels folded and slid back into the supporting beams, reveling the noontime sky above.

The blowing winds above the city on the planet's surface swirled fine sand into the city below. The sand lofted high into the air, coating everything it touched with a thin coating of brown flour like dust. The servants and slaves ran from the arena arches, covering their mouths, coughing, and sneezing.

The fleeing crowds pushed Sara and George back from the archway entrance. The magistrate waved his arm and a second bolder was pushed off its platform. The huge bolder sent a shudder through the ground when it hit and raised a thicker fog-like plume of fine dust high into the air. Andy landed the fighter and shut down the engine to prevent the fine dust from choking the engine's atmospheric air intakes. They had learned that lesson before when they had raced on Mahadean.

"No reason to relearn a lesson," Andy thought and grinned a little.

Three other pilots were not as quick and their ships choked and sputtered, sending billowing black smoke out of their thrust ports and filling the arena with foul smelling exhaust.

A spark from one of the sputtering ships engine's ignited the dust. In a bright flash, everything in the arena was on fire and burning. George and Sara rolled back onto the outer wall of the archway as the flames from the burning dust raced through the archway.

A fourth pilot gunned his engines to shoot through the flames and raised even more dust into the air. The ships engines exhaust fanned the flames and the fire leapt over the walls of the Start Arena into the city. Another pilot missed the opening in the dust fog and hit a large support pillar for the dome over the city. Suddenly, tons of sand fell in on the city as sections of the supporting pillars collapsed under the stress and weight of the shifting sand.

The magistrate had saved his precious money by not having the sand above the city domes removed for months. It was a mistake. He didn't understand the dome's structure and that supporting pillars could buckle and fail from the weight of the shifting sands above.

Chaos ran through the city as more and more sand poured onto the buildings, merchants, and people below. Within a few minutes, the air thinned, and Andy restarted the fighter's engines. He shot straight up out of the collapsing dome. As he cleared the dome's edge, the tiny fighter was caught by the planet's fierce surface winds and spun wildly in the air.

Two of the other racer's ships lay on the sandy surface, burning. Andy's hands raced across the control panel, fighting to stop the fighter's wild spin in the raging sand storm. Finally, Andy regained control of the fighter and headed across the planet for the first race marker. Up, up, higher and higher, he flew out of the wild winds of the planet's surface.

Six racers were already lost and the race had only just begun! He focused his thoughts now; there were six markers in the race and all of them had to be crossed.

Andy was in fourth place when he crossed over the first marker. Immediately, he shot up out of the planet's atmosphere and into space following the beacon for the second marker. Anna concentrated and Andy started to move as fluidly as Anna, his hands gliding across the controls, changing the engine configuration to match the new conditions.

As fast as they could, George and Sara raced back to the new ship, weaving in and out around the burning buildings. Their link was strong as they slipped into the command deck of the new ship. An hour passed and the cadets stayed focused.

Outside their new ship, the city was in chaos as the dome support pillars were failing one after another in a cascade effect. As each new group of pillars was stressed, baring the load of the failed pillars next to it, the new pillars started to buckle and fail too. If the magistrate and people couldn't stop the cascading failures, soon the entire city would be buried in sand and twisted metal from the domes above.

Within two hours, half of the city was exposed to the fierce winds of the surface above. The sounds of buckling pillars filled the air, screeching and banging. Loud crashes and the screeching twisting of metal droned out the sounds of the screaming people.

The cascade of failing pillars had made it to the cadet's port in only four hours. The dome section next to their new ship buckled and collapsed crushing four other spaceships next to theirs. They were no longer safe!

The tons of sand that had piled up on the domes poured into the port, burying everything not crushed by the buckling pillars. Soon their new ship was buried in sand. The air in the ship got warm and filled with a fine dust. George leaned back and focus his mind on strengthening the hull of their new ship. Without the engines running, the ship was venerable. Somehow, George held their new ship together, keeping it from collapsing under the weight of the falling sand. The others were oblivious to what was going on around them. They were absorbed in their mission, keeping their link strong and guiding Andy's flight.

Out in space, Andy's speed started to increase and soon the tiny fighter was neck and neck with the third racer. The third racer swerved his ship at Andy's fighter. Andy and Anna veered right and rolled gently over a small asteroid. The attacking ship clipped the asteroid with its wing sending debris into space and into the ship in fifth place. The fifth ship exploded, sending hull fragments flinging through space.

Andy was safe; however, the ship in third place was hit by the hull fragments near its rear engine. Fuel spewed out, crippling the ship. Andy rolled again, keeping clear of the spewing fuel. A fuel leak or spill in space was as dangerous as a fuel spill on the planet. It may not be able to ignite in space; however, it could eat through even the most formable hull plating. Andy was now in third place as he rounded the second marker. With a new fourth ship close on his tail, Andy and their team focused again. His speed increased and he raced passed the second place ship.

"Odd, that the racer would be slowing down. Why?" Andy thought.

"Focus!" George thought through their link, straining to maintain his focus.

The roof of their new spaceship was collapsing under the weight of the sand and he was now splitting his energy between the new ship and his team~ not quite the turn of events, he had imagined.

The third marker was the halfway point in the race. Ahead of the racers was a rolling, moving asteroid field. Smaller blinking red markers laid out the path they were to follow. The racer in first place was fluid and smooth as he passed by each of the small markers.

Anna had Andy using the gravity of each asteroid and small moon he passed to propel the fighter faster. The pilot in first place may have been fluid in his motion, but he was losing ground the longer they stayed in the asteroid field. Slowly, Andy gained on the lead ship. A little bit longer, only a few more asteroids and they would be neck and neck.

The first place ship burst through the asteroid field, knocking loose fragments from the last asteroid. Andy dove to miss the fragments, skimming over the hull of the ship that had been in fourth place. He, too, had used the gravity of the asteroid field to decrease the distance between them. Andy jerked up hard and squeezed between two spinning boulders, narrowly missing a third asteroid crossing his path.

The other ship passed by the little fighter as Andy fought to regain control. The passing ship fired on the lead ship as he approached. The lead ship fired back, missing the second racer, however, striking an asteroid close to Andy's fighter.

Again, Andy rolled and dove, then raced forward faster as the two ships started to exchange a volley of weapons fire. Andy fired a small canister at the second ship and then a second canister at the first ship. Both canisters hit their targets. No explosions occurred and both racers wrote the blasts off as duds, laughing at the tiny fighters weak weapons.

However, the other pilots were wrong. The canisters weren't exploding weapons; they were computer viruses. Soon both ships sensors showed the tiny fighter falling further and further behind as the two ships raced on, shooting their cannons at each other. In reality, Andy was now far ahead of the two ships and racing by the fourth marker. Two markers left to go as the tiny fighter raced across space toward the fifth marker, nothing was in his way, only open space.

Suddenly, Gus grabbed his stomach and rolled over on the floor of the new ship. Sara put a drop of medicine in a silver cup of water and made him drink it, however, not before they saw the image in Gus's mind.

"Andy stop!" Anna screamed in their link.

In an instant, the two fighting ships blew over the tiny fighter into the open space. Space mines exploded off the wings of the first and second ships.

The second ship hit one of the tiny mines and fuel started spewing out the rear engine. The fuel set off a chain reaction of a hundred space mines.

The shock wave flipped the second ship, landing it in a field of new mines. Suddenly, the second ship imploded, sending a bigger shock wave through the minefield. Hundreds of mines exploded and their tiny fighter was pushed off course on the wave of energy.

The captain of large lead ship was now blasting his way through the minefield. However, he had underestimated the size of the field and quickly ran out of dispersion weapons. With his weapons depleted, the lead racer slowed his speed and crept forward, inching his way around the mines. Andy slowed the tiny fighter's roll and scanned for mines. The open space was filled with tiny mines no bigger than a football. The field was too wide to go around, over or under.

Andy would have to go through the field; however, at a different angle than the lead ship. Emily scanned and Anna plotted the new course. Andy pushed the engines forward and the ship moved ahead, slowly at first and then to half speed. The little mines spun and twisted in space from the exhaust of Andy's engines. Andy was gaining on the lead ship again and soon he would pass the lead ship for the second time.

At the edge of the minefield floated the fifth marker. He could see its blinking red light and it's shiny silver hull, glistening in the sunlight. Suddenly, out of the corner of his eye he caught a glimpse of a bright flash of light. It was headed right for him. He gunned the engine as cannon fire grazed the fighter's hull, flipping the tiny ship over in a perfect loop.

He landed in the thermal wake of a new ship. It was one of the racers that had clogged his engine in the Start Arena. The new ship had used the lead ships path through the minefield and was now blasting his way through the remaining field. Andy gunned the fighter's engines again and stayed close to the thermal wake of the bigger ship. He was going to ride the wake~like a surfer catching the big wave. The old lead ship tried desperately to get to the path the new ship was making.

Before reaching the fifth marker, the bigger ship, now in the lead, blasted it from space. Without the marker, there would be no heading given for the last leg of the race.

Andy launched a computer canister at the ship. Again, it hit its target. Emily down loaded the directions from the new lead ships computer just before the canister was struck by space debris from the fifth marker. It wasn't much information; nonetheless, they knew where to go now, and Andy took off like a bolt of lightening the moment he cleared the minefield.

In their new spaceship, George had shifted the fuel canisters into the room. He made a circle around the team to help support the collapsing roof of the new spaceship. The air inside the ship was getting stale and warm. With the ship covered by sand and the engines not running, their only air was the air that filled the room. George knew there wasn't much time left before the air would be gone and the ship completely crushed by the sand.

Anna and Andy raced across the open space chasing the bigger ship. Yet, once again, it wasn't really open space at all. It was a trick!

Emily made corrections to the course, seeming to turn around invisible objects. She was watching the gravitational pull of the space. It was as if the space had been fractured and tiny singularity type gravity wells dotted the open space. Any one well contained enough gravity to crush a Thorean Galaxy class cruiser, let alone a tiny little fighter. The large ship in front of Andy touched the edge of a singularity and spun around wildly, fighting to free itself from the immense gravity.

Andy slipped by, veering left to avoid the spinning ship. He leaned left further and the fighter's wing tipped a smaller singularity, sending the tiny ship spinning out of control backwards through space. Frantically, Andy and Anna worked to regain control of the ship before it touched another singularity.

The larger ship regained control and raced on through the rest of the field, it's thermal wake drawing the singularities in like moths to a bright light. With new open space in front of him, Andy pushed the engines power to maximum, bolting the fighter forward away from the singularities. In open space, Andy pressed the engines even harder to catch the larger ship. He was not yet close enough to launch one of their cannons.

In their new spaceship, George's strength of will was the only thing keeping them alive. Emily, Anna, Sara, and Gus were firmly locked in their link and didn't notice the seriousness of the events going on around them.

George's strength was weakening; he could feel it. Someone had found their link and was trying hard to break in. He needed help or they would all die and Andy would be left alone; a drone far from home on a planet shattered by evil.

"Max, help us!" George yelled, out into space with the raw energy of the universe. He collapsed.

Instantly, evil found them. Their link broke suddenly. Sara, Gus, Emily, Anna, and Andy collapsed in pain and agony, holding their heads, screaming.

Gus couldn't help them fix the link as he had done many times before, as he was directly part of link. Without George holding the ship together, the hull started to split, and the sand covering the outside of the ship started to pour in through the tears in the ship's hull.

George's message was loud and heard by more than just Max. Within minutes, guards dressed in black robes were racing to the port to find the spaceship. In his mind's eye, George could hear the shouts from the people outside the buried spaceship.

"Max, is that you?" George whispered, through the searing pain.

"Why have you called?" Max replied, knowing evil would find them now, as secrecy had been their only protection.

"We are dying," George whispered, twisting on the floor of the ship in agony.

"You know I can't help you in the place evil controls," Max replied seriously.

"Then evil has won," George replied, angrily.

"Only, if it is your choice." Max said, with a grain of hope.

"Help us, don't let us die like grandfather's team of the prophecy did before us," George said, pleading, trying any angle to save his team as tears ran from his eyes in pain.

"You know not what you say young one," Max replied, his voice filled with sadness.

"I know it to be true, as it is the only thing that grandfather can't forgive you for and now it is repeating," George pressed, hoping Max was weakening and would help them.

His focus faded. They all lay in the ship unconscious.

"Your wisdom is astonishing, all is not lost George," Max whispered, yet George and Max were no longer connected.

With sand still pouring in from the dome above and covering the top of the ship deeper, the street people and merchants Gus had fed dug a path to the side port door of the ship. Quietly, they worked scooping the sand away, one bucket at a time. Reaching the ship two hours after they had started, the people broke open the ship's smaller side escape hatch. With a snap of the last hinge, they were inside the ship.

The roof of the ship had collapsed and the merchant who had first helped Gus with his cooking crawled inside on his belly. He found the team sprawled out between the fuel canisters on the main command deck. The merchant grabbed onto George and then the others and dragged them out of the ship one at a time, handing them off to the others who were waiting next to the ship in the port.

At the port archway, the team was passed off to another group of people. They covered the team with brown cloaks and hurried away, while the merchant and others reburied their side of the ship and then disappeared into the city.

Evil, through the magistrate, sent guards and scanners in black cloaks to tunnel in toward the ship from the other side. However, with the team gone, the scanners couldn't tell if they were in the correct port and soon left.

Out of the singularity field and headed for the sixth marker, Andy struggled to regain control of the fighter. His head ached as if it was on fire. He leaned into the controls of the ship, pushing them passed their limits. With nothing left to lose, he converted the life support and all internal systems into energy for the engines. Finally, he converted their only weapon into an engine booster. The tiny fighter barreled ahead at an enormous speed. Its hull plating barely holding together from the impacts of the small pea sized asteroids covering the open space.

The larger ship was insight again. The race wasn't over yet. He flew passed the wing of the large ship, causing only a slight disturbance with his thermal wake, aiming for the planet, the sixth marker, and victory. The large ship was caught off guard and launched a barrage of cannon fire at the little fighter.

Andy leaned this way and that, dodging the energy blasts ~ sensing the ebb and flow of the energy of the universe. Down, down, down to the surface of the planet he dove the fighter. He careened across the planet's sandy surface with the larger ship hot on his tail.

He dipped low and raised a cloud of dust; however, the engines did not clog on the larger ship. A great valley opened up below him as the large ship overtook the fighter. The pilot crashed down on the fighter's outer hull, forcing him to the floor of the valley into the steep sand dunes below. The wing of the fighter clipped a high sandy peak, spinning the ship helplessly toward the valley floor.

With the engines still running, Andy recovered inches above the canyon floor and bolted up over the steep sand mound. Ahead, the larger ship was dodging cannon fire from the surface of the planet. The fighter caught up again. It was too small a target to be hit by the ground cannons. The two ships raced, neck and neck, across the dusty plains, causing tornadoes of dust in their wake.

The red lights of the sixth marker blinked above the underground port. Andy pressed on the controls hard and got to the sixth marker first; however, the larger ship dove down through open port into the city below before Andy. Andy followed. Now he was playing catch up. The larger ship reached the Start Arena before Andy and the pilot set his ship down quickly. Andy entered the arena a second later. Skidding to a stop across the arena floor, his ship cutting off the other pilot before he could reach the magistrates box. The arena and city were in chaos, and yet, both pilots remained fixed on the prize and the prize alone.

"I have reached the arena first!" the pilot of the larger ship yelled, as he approached the magistrate's box.

"I have reached the sixth marker first!" Andy yelled, running and catching up to the first pilot.

Andy knew this man, he hadn't faced him in the fight arena, however, his fighting style hadn't gone unnoticed by Andy. He was a ruthless killer, having no mercy for his victims.

"You, I should have known. The only man I know who can disable an entire arena full of competitors and kill no one," the pilot yelled, trying to distract Andy.

"Killing by flailing about is easy, any hired fool can do that," Andy yelled harshly.

"I am here to claim the prize!" the pilot yelled, at the magistrate when they stopped in front of the magistrate's box.

The magistrate turned and stared at the other pilot and Andy.

"I am here to claim the prize!" Andy said, as wildly as the other pilot.

"My city is nearly destroyed and the prize is all you care about? You will split the prize this quarter!" the magistrate replied harshly.

"NO!" the first pilot yelled, raising his fist in the air.

The magistrate spun around facing the first pilot. "Press me no further or I will have you killed where you stand," the magistrate threatened, snapping his fingers, and four guards and two beings in black cloaks closed in.

The pilot backed down. A servant stepped forward and snapped the gold medallion in half, handing one piece to each of the pilots.

Andy spun around away from the view of the other pilot, and slipped the servant his medallion piece and a few tribute he had left in his pocket. The servant understood, he knew Andy was one of the strangers that healed and feed the people of the city. The servant would bring the medallion to the bank for Andy. The servant hurried away following the magistrate, who was now leaving the arena to attend to the affairs of his struggling city.

"I will kill you where you stand and take what is mine. There is no one here to stop me and your tricks in the fight arena will not fool me, child," the pilot yelled, spinning around toward Andy.

"I have no time for you. Leave while you still have some honor left, sir," Andy replied, trying to walk around the pilot.

"I have killed for less, child!" he said, circling Andy.

"I believe you. You have your prize. Leave now. I have business to attend to," Andy replied, moving away from the pilot and trying to get to the archway.

The pilot jumped at Andy, trying to grab his shoulders. Andy ducked and rolled, landing on his feet.

"Chen Lo," he whispered. David Lu would certainly smile for a well-executed move he thought.

"Come here, you little sand worm," the pilot yelled angrily.

Again, the pilot dove at Andy and again he rolled and flipped out of the way. The pilot hit the ground hard. His face covered in sandy dust, he coughed, and ran at Andy a third time. Andy dropped to the ground a moment before the pilot reached him. The pilot crashed head long into the wall of the magistrate's box. He lay motionless.

Andy nodded to a few people who had gathered around to watch the fight. He tossed a tribute in the air and a servant caught it.

"Take him to a tavern to recover. Make sure his prize is well guarded as I will know if it is not," Andy said, nodding to the servant.

"As you wish, master," the servant answered lowering his head.

Andy reached forward and shook the servant's hand.

"I am not your master. I am but a traveler. Also, take care not to be too close when this pilot awakes," Andy said, sliding a second tribute into the servants hand as he left the arena.

Chapter 13

TAKEN AGAIN

Out into the main street Andy ran toward their port. The city was devastated by the race. The air was thick with smoke and entire sections of the domes over head had collapsed, exposing the city to the sand and fierce winds on the planet's surface. He pulled his shirt up over his face, trying to block some of the dust and smoke.

As he looked around, he saw the people running from building to building, digging others out of the rubble. Quickly, he came to the place where Gus had been cooking. The heaters were out and the kettles were over turned. Andy knelt down, restarted the heaters, and set the kettles back in place.

He filled them with water from the merchant's well and started looking for the roots and fungi Gus had been using. On the wall, above the merchant's tent, was scrawled Gus's recipe. Using some of the merchant's rug hooks as squires, he lifted the roots up and dropped them into the kettles of boiling water. He scooped the fungi into the kettles with a ladle and added the spices he found in another merchant's shop. Soon the smell of Gus's food wafted through the city.

The people came and lined up. They tried to pay Andy the customary one tribute; however, he wouldn't accept their tributes. Instead, he set them to work, cutting more roots and finding more fungi to feed more people. He slipped away when they were organized and promised to accept their tribute the next day for the food.

He turned a few more corners and hurried into their port, his face fell. Their new ship was crushed beneath mounds of sand and rubble from the dome pillars. His heart raced as he ran into the mound of sand and started digging as fast as he could.

From behind, a hand grabbed onto his arm, catching him by surprise. He spun around, a red energy sphere already formed in the palm of his hand to defend. Beneath a brown cloak, a man's hand met his hand and absorbed the energy from Andy.

"We must leave now," he whispered and held Andy's shoulder, Andy collapsed.

A second man in a brown cloak stepped up and lifted Andy over his shoulder in one motion. Together, they hurried away from the ship as guards and scanners black cloaks swarmed in surrounding the ship again, having sense Andy's energy sphere.

They had escaped detection and had their last missing cadet. A third figure in a brown cloak ran up, joining the other two and threw a brown cloak over Andy as they ran, hiding him from view. They ran at speed through the crowded streets, ducking down alleys and then back out onto other main streets in the city. Far from the section of city that had collapsed, the three figures slowed and slipped down a narrow alley. It opened up into a larger port with larger ships.

The gangplank of one of the larger ship unrolled, as the group ran across the open port with Andy bouncing over one man's shoulder. Hurriedly, the group ran up the gangplank and entered the transport ship. Its port door spinning closed as the last person entered. Moments later, two guards and a scanner in a black cloak walked through the port on their standard patrol. Andy was handed off to the team waiting inside the transport ship the moment the group entered. Still asleep, Andy was rushed to the hospital room.

The three figures sat down in the hallway as the captain's voice echoed through the hallways of the transport ship. He was requesting departure for the ship and paying the tribute required to the city's port administrator. Departure was granted, and the transport ship rose out of the port and headed slowly for the dome opening. They slipped through as the section dome was still opening~not wanting to wait for someone to change their mind and not let them leave.

In the ship's hospital, Andy was slipped into a yellow stasis tube next to George, Emily, Anna, Sara, and Gus.

"We have them all," an officer whispered.

"Did you really think we would not find you?" a second officer added, as if the cadets could hear her.

"You used the tribute from Mahadean, it was only time until we got to you," the first officer whispered.

The transport ship left orbit and disappeared under their cloak. Their trip home would be longer, however, they would be harder to track cloaked. Silently, they slipped along through open space, not a thought or stray link was made. On the fifth day after they had left Sandue, George's stasis tube was opened. One by one, the cadets were laid on the cots in the hospital room.

"Are we clear of the inner space?" Jennifer signed as Frank entered the hospital room on board their transport ship.

Frank nodded. The cadets had been found by their triad! Soon Pete and Frank's teams were standing in the hospital room, circling George and the others.

"It is time. Let us begin," Pete signed, and the captains formed a link hand over hand.

Glowing yellow spheres danced over their palms. The captains circled each cadet and focused solely on him or her. One by one, the captains revived each of the cadets.

George was last. When they revived him, he weakly opened his eyes and smiled; it was Frank and Pete. They were safe. He flipped over his hand, revealing a small yellow sphere glowing above his palm.

"How is that possible?" Frank asked, amazed that George had the strength to form a link.

"I don't know, it's just them," Pete signed, pleased they had found them alive and safe.

All of the captains reformed their link and then joined the link with George and the other cadets.

Kindly, Pete said his familiar word in their link, "report."

George told of their capture and the evil that possessed the officers they encountered. Andy joined in with Gus and the others and told of the evil on Shadoo and the race on Sandue.

"Anna raced the race through our link, it was amazing," Andy whispered.

"Rest now. There will be time later for more. Know now that you are safe," Pete replied kindly.

The cadets laid down on the soft comfy pillows and fell back to sleep. Rachael turned on the yellow beams in the ceiling. The hospital's yellow healing beams pushed nutrients into the cadets as they slept. Another ten days passed and the cadets woke up again. This time they were hungry.

Hans and Sven brought bowls of dark brown officer cereal into the hospital room from the kitchen. George focused on his team and the cereal like Toma, the leader of their triad, had taught him last year. He made the cereal look like a feast was set before them. The cadets ate until they could eat no more.

Hans and Sven stared at each other and then at the cadets, not knowing what George had done for his team. In the command deck of the transport ship, Pete and Frank glanced at each other. They knew what George was doing; they could sense it in the ebb and flow of energy of the universe.

"He is learning," Frank whispered.

"Perhaps too fast. It is a lot of responsibility," Pete replied seriously, worried George had more strength than brains to focus it.

Back in the hospital, Andy looked up at Hans between bowls full of cereal.

"When did you get to Sandue, sir?" he asked, his mouth half-full of food.

"When you were at the second marker Andy," Hans replied kindly.

"We saw nearly the whole race. We couldn't believe you would even race in that tiny fighter," Sven added, handing Gus another bowl of food.

"Where did you get that fighter anyway? It looked like one of the Galactic Unions fighters?" Hans asked carefully.

"It was a Galactic Union fighter, sir," Gus replied rather matter-of-factly.

"It was all that was left flying from the transport ship that captured us after Emily's programs, well, you know, sir," Andy replied, teasing Emily.

"All I did was make them abandon ship and eject all of the escape pods and fighters, sir. That's all, no biggie sir," Emily answered, rolling her eyes at Andy.

"And disable their primary drive system," Gus added between mouth full's.

The captains sat with their mouth hanging open. They were stunned. How could fourth year cadets do so much damage and not be terrified? Their courage was amazing to the captains. Yet, the cadets thought nothing of it. To save their lives, they had to make a plan and follow through. They had worked together and had saved the lives of hundreds of other people on two planets in the process.

"But I still don't understand. How did you end up on Shadoo?" Jennifer asked, knowing the math didn't work out right for the fuel consumption on the fighter.

"We don't really know. The math doesn't work out sir," Anna answered still puzzled.

"It was the closest trader's planet Anna could find on the star charts sir," Gus answered.

"And we barely made it there as it was sir," Andy said, as if it was no big deal; even though, he knew that he and the other two boys had been the fuel to get to the planet.

"Where were you when you escaped?" Hans started to ask, when Niels waved him off in their link.

Pete and Franks teams had been careful in exactly what questions they had asked George and the others. They had been in the space between, where good and evil cross and can't interfere with each other.

Evil had long ago won over the space around Shadoo and Sandue, entrapping the inhabitants of those worlds. It was the reason Max couldn't help them on the planet. They had to be helped by others of their kind that had made the choice to enter that region of space by their own freewill. However, the captains didn't know Max had walked a very narrow line, helping them out in open space.

The cadets were found in the solar system nearest the point where all of the lines crossed in Colonel Gote's stellar navigation class; the one place they could not go and live!

When they had finished their meal, the cadets stretched and stood up with a little help from the captains. George and the others walked around the hospital room for a few minutes, showing Lucita and Rachael they were OK to leave the hospital room.

"So where are we, sir?" George asked, leaning on the edge of his cot.

"On our way home," Niels replied with a smile, knowing he had not answered George's question.

"You mean back to Jupiter station. Right, sir?" Andy said anxiously.

"Sure, that's the closest cadet station to here," Niels said grinning.

"Oh ya, that's it," Hans added, joking with him.

Andy stared at the captains and sat down on the edge of his bed with his hands between his head. Slowly he looked up.

"Please, sir, not there. Anywhere but there, sir," Andy whined, and Gus shook his head. "Anywhere but there, sir. You know they hate us, sir," Andy said, trying to get the captains to change their direction.

"Andy that's not true. Asteria station simply doesn't understand you," Hans replied, grinning.

"You say that now, but every time we go to Asteria, there are issues, sir," Gus said in a matter of fact way, as if the trouble was already in the works, just waiting for them to arrive.

Hans and Niels laughed hard as Nick, Sven, Karmen, Kate, Maria, and Jennifer slipped into the hospital room.

"What's so funny?" Nick asked, wrapping his arm around Andy.

"Andy was expressing his delight in going to Asteria station for training," Niels answered.

Nick smiled and then burst into laughter. Sven grabbed Gus's shoulder and laughed louder, nearly toppling them to the ground. Soon everyone was laughing. A bump from the ships propulsion sent the captains and cadets to the floor of the hospital room, laughing even harder.

"You all laugh now, but ya know, sir...," Andy whined again, sitting on the floor.

"Andy, we know something will happen, that seems to be inevitable," Nick replied, grinning.

"We are laughing, cause it's the only thing left to do," Sven added, laughing again.

"Taking it too seriously will put us in a bad mood, and we need to be happy right now," Niels said and laughed some more.

"We have found you and you are all alive," Jennifer added kindly.

They laughed harder as they leaned against the hospital room walls, sitting on the floor. Moments later, the door burst open and Frank and Pete came rushing in out of breath. They all looked up and laughed again, their sides and cheeks hurting.

"Are you all right?" Frank asked, out of breath.

They laughed again, Emily, Rachael, Kate, and Sara were nearly crying from laughing too hard.

"I can't take it, my sides hurt!" Emily said, grabbing her ribs.

Pete and Frank shook their heads.

"When you are all done with your frivolity, there is work to do," Pete said rather officer like.

The two lead captains left and everyone in the room burst into laughter again. In reality, Pete and Frank were happy to see them all laugh again. The search for their lost cadets had been hard on their teams, too focused for too many weeks.

Eventually, everyone in the hospital stood up and regained their presence. Together they all left the hospital room for their stations to catch up on what had been happening since they had been gone.

Each cadet left with two captains. Both captains focused on calming the cadet's mind. Oddly, they no longer needed to wrap their arms over the cadet's shoulders to help them maintain their focus and calm. The captains were growing up too.

George chuckled and wandered up to the command deck of the transport ship alone. He stopped at the door. It slid open and Pete nodded him inside.

"So this is the size of ship you borrow. I must remember that, sir," George said, teasing the captains as he walked onto the command deck of the transport ship.

"George, you and your team are a site for sore eyes. We knew you were alive. Pete and I could tell," Frank said, grinning and grabbing his little brother's hand, pulling him in close for a bear hug.

"How did you find us, sir?" George asked kindly.

"You used the tribute account numbers from Mahadean last year," Frank replied, pulling him in tight to hold his brother's shoulder.

"It took us some time to get the coordinates. After that, it was simply a matter of time for us to get to you," Frank said, happy his little brother was alive.

"Where were we really, sir?" George asked seriously, his smile fading away.

"What can you tell us?" Pete asked, his voice low and quiet.

"There was a point in space that when we crossed it in the CORE transport, the officers seemed happier. Like, we had passed something important, some coordinates they were marking in space. Anna may know the coordinates better. She was the one who knew it was really bad where ever we were, exactly. She said it was like being in the corona of the sun sir," George said, and then paused as he thought about the details of their capture.

"Are you OK, George?" Frank asked, worried they had brought up bad memories too soon.

Pete focused on George's mind, as Frank talked on about nothing, distracting him. Slowly, George's mind calmed and refocused. Pete waved his hand over the floor and three silver sitting columns rose from the floor. They sat down and George's voice became low and quiet, like Pete's, as he continued.

"Then we escaped from the transport ship in the fighter and made it to Shadoo. We should have died, sir. We were one canister of fuel short, even with Emily and Anna's modifications, yet, we didn't, sir," George said, more talking to, than reporting out, for Pete.

"George, when you were passed the 'point' as you say, the corona, what did you think of?" Pete asked cautiously.

Grandfather had warned the captains not to ask too many questions. Somehow, these cadets had escaped from the one place no one else ever had and the captains wanted to know how.

"Home, only about getting my team home, sir," he said. His voice was shaking.

"Nothing else?" Pete pressed, needing to know more.

"No, nothing. I had to get them home. Why, sir?" George said, then paused and stared at Pete and Frank.

"You are the only people who have ever gone to the center of the universe and lived. Colonel Gatte wasn't joking about it being a forbidden place," Pete answered seriously.

"Everyone else who has gone there has died, George," Frank added compassionately.

"But you were there, with us on Sandue, sir," George added quickly.

"Sandue is an outpost far from the center of where all the lines of the universe cross. Far from Anna's corona example. It's like being on Mercury and traveling twice the distance to Pluto," Frank said, trying to explain the distance in words George would understand.

George nodded his head. Twice the distance to Pluto from Mercury was still really close to the center of the universe.

"And like you, we also don't know how your tiny fighter made it to Shadoo," Pete said, shaking his head.

"Maybe the fighter was too small to be seen, sir," George replied still puzzled.

"No, it must have been something else," Frank said puzzled, too, thinking, trying to understand how the impossible was possible.

"Emily made us look like a comet and we were nearly comatose for most of the trip on minimal life support, sir," George added, looking for a reason.

"Perhaps; however, you are too important to evil to just let you escape," Pete said, thinking more cunningly like Nick and Niels.

"Evil's minions thought we died with the transport. Emily does excellent computer effects you know, sir," George added.

"Perhaps," Frank said, shaking his head.

"Max or grandfather will know. We can call and ask them, sir," George said, starting to make a link.

"No, it is not safe yet," Frank said, quickly cutting off George before he could start a link.

George stared at Frank and Pete. This wasn't like them. They were always connected and reported to the Viceroy's, their dads, what was going on. Now, out in the middle of space close to evil, they told no one George and the others had been found. Something was wrong and George needed to find out what was really going on with the captains and the Galactic council.

"How long will it be until we get to Asteria station, sir?" George asked, changing the subject.

"It will take at least three or four weeks at our present speed. We don't know how you got to the forbidden space so fast or how we have either," Pete replied, still puzzling.

"The officers said the master was helping them. Maybe someone has been helping you, pushing you faster than the ship can go. Maybe bending time and space, sir, like us," George said and then added, "Calshene is the closest galaxy to the evil. Right, sir?"

"Yes." Pete replied, saddened by the thought.

"That's why they were attacked so long ago," George pressed, to see if what his team had suspected was true.

"Yes," Pete answered solemnly.

"And Mahadean, they were next. They relented to evil so they would not suffer the same fate as Calshene, sir," George added, connecting the dots.

"Yes," Pete answered.

"Earth and the Thoreans, we are further away, so it is taking more time to get there. However, it will happen, evil will get there, sir," George said, stopping staring at Pete and Frank.

"Yes, now you are beginning to see the universe for what it is and how it is evolving," Pete answered slowly, deliberately choosing his words.

"It is all so sad, so fatal, as if no matter what we do, nothing will change and stop the spread of evil and hatred, sir," George said, looking down and not knowing what else to say.

"The universe is filled with conflict George, good and evil. What is that thing the people of Earth say, I can't think of it?" Pete asked, pausing and staring out the front view screen of the transport ship.

"The cup is half-full or the cup is half-empty," Frank whispered.

"Thanks, Frank. On Asteria, most people will say the cup is half-empty. However, on Earth, most will say the cup is half-full. Earth is notoriously optimistic. I think it is what fascinates the universe. No matter what happens, the people of Earth always seem to work hard make something good happen. It puzzles us to no end," Pete replied, trying to lighten their thoughts.

"We Earthers are too naive to know any better, sir," George said, shrugging his shoulders.

"Perhaps, but, I think it is in your very nature and it is what scares evil the most," Pete added. "It fears you and your team most of all."

Chapter 14

OPEN SPACE

"Sirs, dinner is ready," Gus said, standing outside the command deck door, waiting to be let in, another bit of protocol far away from home.

They nodded and followed Gus to the galley, everyone else was already there waiting for them before they began.

"You have missed a lot of training. We will pick up where you left off tomorrow in the cargo bay," Frank said, sitting down next to George.

"Training, don't you mean relaxxinngg, sir, oohh," Andy said, waving his hands around as if trying to hypnotize the captains.

"Are you feeling OK, Andy?" Rachael asked, concerned Andy was slurring his words.

She and Lucita looked like they were going to pounce on Andy and fix whatever was possessing him.

"Oh, he'll be OK, ma'am. He has missed training and can't wait to get started again," George said, crinkling his eyebrows at Andy to stop.

"It was going to work," he muttered.

"And Asteria likes us and will welcome us with open arms, Andy," Sara whispered, bumping Andy's arm gently.

They ate and talked late into the night, catching up on all they had missed while they were away. Morning came early and Pete was sitting at a silver table in their cargo bay sleeping room when they awoke. George smiled as Pete slid a bowl of officers brown cereal toward him. George sat down and spun around, looking at the others. They all looked tired and thinner, even Gus had lost weight. It had been a difficult ordeal for his team.

"Pete, Gus was almost an evil drone back on Shadoo. He didn't actually eat the food. He got infected with the chemical in the ground that controls the people by cutting up the roots and fungus for his stew, sir," George said, scooping cereal into his mouth. Then he paused. "Andy got some medicine for Gus. I don't know where it came from. I don't think he actually destroyed anyone to get it. But, it was strong stuff, and Andy... well, it cost him something too, and I don't mean tribute, sir."

"Rachael and Lucita will mix some ahh..., vitamins to help Gus for now. The Galactic council will remove the remaining elements from all of you when we arrive at Asteria station. Nick and Niels will help Andy come to terms with what he did to save his team," Pete replied, now worried about Gus and Andy.

Within half an hour, Andy, Sara, Emily, Gus, and Anna were awake and sitting at the table eating.

"So what training do we have today, sir?" Andy asked, swallowing hard.

"Major Doyle has prepared a few lessons on tactics and armaments for the morning and Colonel Petrof has a few lessons on basic survival for this afternoon," Pete answered.

"We could have used that a week ago, sir," Andy said, scooping more cereal onto his spoon, the extra clumps flopping back into his bowl.

The cadets finished quickly and followed Pete out of their sleeping room. As they walked, George signed behind his back instructions to his team in their new sign language. They were in training again, they had to remember their protocol training and act like cadets again. Pete glanced back once and George instantly changed to signing in their original sign language. A language he knew Pete could read, keeping their new sign language a secret for now.

Niels and Nick had transformed the large cargo bay into a tactical arena. They had boxes piled high for the cadets to climb over and vines hanging down on one side for them to swing on. Scraps of metal were scattered across the floor and large green cargo nets hung over the walls. The two seconds had done well.

The cadets lined up in the center of the room and Pete started a 3-D holographic projector of Major Doyle. Nick and Niels tossed staff weapons to the cadets from a closet and left the room. The Major's holographic image began talking on and on about the different types of weapons used for personal defense and offense.

Soon George and the others were running and leaping over the obstacles Nick and Niels had placed around the room. Quickly, they climbed the cargo nets and swung through the air on the vines. It reminded George of the first time they had swung on the vines at the end of their first rotation in the Sport arena. Slowly, over the next four hours, his team started to relax. It had been a difficult, grueling escape and they needed a safe place to rest.

As he swung on the vines, George was sure Emily was talking with the vines. However, she hadn't talked with anything in a very long time so he said nothing, leaving her to spin on the vines as they carefully swung her from place to place.

Andy and Gus were less acrobatic in the air than the others. Rather more bullish in their swinging, crashing into the walls and cargo nets more often. Anna and Sara, following Emily, had little issue in quickly navigating the course. By the end of training, Andy and Gus were tired and Anna, Sara, and Emily were happy and only a little tired. Pete wasn't in the hallway when they emerged from the cargo bay.

In the hallway, Gus rubbed his stomach. It was time to eat. George nodded and Gus led the way. They found the captains in the galley, eating lunch.

"What are you doing here?" Nick asked, surprised when the cadets walked into the room.

"We're hungry and the training class ended, sir," Gus replied.

"Early, odd," Niels said and got up, leaving the galley with Nick carrying their sandwiches with them as they left the galley.

"How was the training?" Frank asked, as he slid sandwiches in front of the cadets and Hans handed them purple drinks.

"I like this stuff," Andy said smiling, holding the cup up in the air, and swirling the purple liquid around.

"You do? Its...," Sven started to say, when Gus waved him off and then made it look like he was only brushing back his hair when Andy glanced up.

"What was that?" Andy asked, eyeing Gus oddly.

"Oh, nothing, Andy. Nothing at all," Gus replied, trying to be causal.

"So you never answered. How was training cadet?" Frank repeated, distracting them.

"Oh, not too bad, of course Emily, Sara, and Anna did have an advantage, sir," Andy said, crinkling his eyebrows.

"Not really, sir," Emily said, blushing.

"What advantage did they have?" Jennifer asked kindly.

"The vines like them, ma'am," Gus grumbled.

"Gus, vines neither like nor dislike you," Jennifer replied, raising her eyebrow.

"Hump, they like Emily, Anna, and Sara, ma'am," Andy added, grumpily too.

"So the girls found a tactical advantage and used it," Kate replied, smiling.

"Well, yes. Yes they did, ma'am," Andy answered, looking confused, and yet he knew he had been beat at his own game.

Niels and Nick ran back into the room and whispered to Pete and Frank. Picking up more sandwiches, they plopped down on their seats to finish their lunches.

"You need to go to your next training class. It is ready now," Pete said, as the cadets finished their lunch.

Pete nodded to Maria and Katie. They stood up and walked with the cadets back to the cargo bay.

When the galley door closed, Frank turned toward Pete, Nick, and Niels. "What do you mean?" he asked cryptically.

"George and the others went through an entire week's worth of training from Major Doyle in four hours," Nick reported, stunned by his own words.

"The whole week?" Frank repeated and the two seconds nodded.

"We will need to step them up to the next level and slow them down a little," Pete said, making a new plan.

"They will be passed us," Nick said, a little concerned.

"Then we will need to work harder to keep up with them, Nick," Pete replied, grinning knowing it was going to be harder for the captains now.

Niels and Nick shook their heads.

In the cargo bay, Nick and Niels had reconfigured the room to fit the needs of Colonel Petrof and basic survival techniques. As the cadets entered, Pete, Frank, and the others ran through the hallways and entered the cargo bay, sitting down next to the cadets. The Colonel started discussing liquids and purification methods. An hour past, and soon the Colonel was discussing foods and chemical combination.

Gus, Sven, and Hans were in heaven. Andy was making a rocket launcher from bits and pieces he had picked up from the floor as they sat listening to the Colonel talk on and on. Sara asked about some of the herbal combinations her grandmother had taught her when she was very young.

The Colonel explained how the chemicals interacted and caused the desired effects. It was not any one herb alone, but, a combination of herbs acting together. Chemistry was about combinations of chemicals, compounds, and elements coming together.

"Like our teams," George thought.

"Yes, like our teams," Pete answered, reading his thoughts.

George had not been shielding their thoughts, he had forgotten. He had done it for so long on Shadoo and Sandue that it felt good to be among friends where he didn't have to worry about stray thoughts. Pete and Frank both nodded. He smiled. The training ended and they all stood up stretching.

"Anyone up for some Chen Lo, sirs?" Andy quizzed.

The cadets lined up behind Andy. Frank and Pete's team stood on either side. Andy began before Niels could call up David Lu's program. He started them out on level one and progressed up through level eleven before slowing them down to rest. Pete and Frank nodded and they ended their training.

"It is time to eat," Pete said, motioning to the door.

"If you are going to go galaxy hopping, you need to eat more," Sven said kindly.

"Galaxy hopping?" Andy and Gus whispered between each other, walking across the cargo bay.

Nick and Niels stood back, staring as the cadet left the room. They were in awe of the cadets.

"How can they possibly know through level eleven so well?" Nick asked.

"They may know how to do the moves, however, they do not know it's meaning," Niels replied.

"No, surely they know," Nick said, crinkling his forehead. "I mean they have figured nearly everything else out."

"You forget how young they are," Frank said, nodding toward the door.

"But they are so talented. I know a bunch of CORE officers who can't do what they just did," Niels added.

"True, yet, they don't know its meaning nor are they to be told," Pete said firmly, repeating the words the Senior Viceroy had said to him.

"As you wish, sir," the seconds chorused seriously.

In the galley, everyone was busy with the evening meal.

"What's up for tomorrow, sir?" George asked, flipping plates out to Pete and Frank as they sat down.

"Colonel Hawks thinks you may have become lazy so he has special training devised for your team," Pete answered seriously, even captain like.

"No really, sir?" Andy pressed, whining a little.

"I think he's serious, Andy," Sara whispered, half grinning.

"It's OK, we'll do it with you," Nick reassured, sitting down next to Andy.

"Why, sir?" Andy asked, puzzled as to why captains would want to train with cadets.

"Because we are a triad and we need to practice together more," Pete said, before Niels could answer.

Dinner lasted late into the night again as they talked and laughed. It was hard to be social on the cadet training stations, as protocol always seemed to get in their way. So they enjoyed the precious time they had together to learn more about each other and the bonds they had made. Reaching out to Toma was still forbidden, as was any contact with the CORE or the Galactic council. George didn't like it; however, it was an order so it would stand.

On their way to the cargo bay for Colonel Hawks training the next morning, George signed instructions to his team. They needed to know where in space they were. More than six weeks had passed since their capture and they needed to know how close they were to Calshene space. The captains had been far too careful with their words and George knew it.

Again, Pete and Frank's teams joined the cadets for training in the cargo bay. The training was hard on the cadets, and yet, Pete, Frank and their teams looked like it had been a mild training day.

"Why, sir?" Andy asked again.

"Why what?" Niels asked.

"Why are you here with us? It looks like light training for your teams. We think we are holding you back, sirs," George said, clarifying Andy question.

Nick choked and coughed, "Holding us back?"

"George, we are holding you back," Niels answered.

"Not from our perspective, sirs," Gus said.

"Chen Lo tonight, sir?" Andy asked, in the late afternoon.

"You go ahead. We need to check our course," Pete said, nodding.

The captains left the cargo bay as Andy and the cadets lined up for Chen Lo training. The moment the door closed, Emily had it locked and the cadets started accessing the computer terminals around the bay. Emily hacked in first and rerouted the other computers to keep them from being traced.

Anna plotted their speed and stellar location. Gus and Sara ran a review of their ships stores. In a few minutes, Emily had the ship looking like a comet and had increased their speed one and a half times. Andy found a small armory locker and gave everyone a real staff weapon to slip inside their sleeves again. George blocked their thoughts and prevented any interruptions.

In ten minutes, they all had the information they needed. With a glance from George, Emily changed the computers in the cargo bay back to their original configurations; and Andy started Chen Lo at level four. As they practiced, they shared the information they had each learned.

"We are in Calshene space now, George," Anna reported, flipping over Gus. "It looks like we are about two days away from Asteria station. But, I don't know how we got here so fast. Someone has to be helping us," she added.

"The weapons on this transport are for training. Nothing of any consequence. Our captains are either stupid or brave for going across the universe after us in this training transport ship," Andy said, shaking his head and rolling under Sara.

"The odd thing is there isn't enough fuel or supplies on a training transport for them to have been gone for more than four weeks and there aren't any extra fuel canisters in the logs," Emily said, flipping passed George.

"Perhaps it was the only ship they could get," Sara said, thinking of why they captains were in a training transport. "I mean, you know, without someone missing it," she added, thinking back to their escape last year and having used a training ship to do it.

"The original stores are meant for only a three or four week mission. They were out here for at least six weeks, looking for us. And now, another three and a half weeks after they found us to get us home. And I agree, someone is helping us with the distance problem," Gus added, puzzling as much as Emily.

"Does seem odd that we are so close to Calshene now, when Shadoo is eleven or twelve months away from Calshene," Anna said, talking in circles.

"Someone has been helping them. Has to be," Gus said, thinking.

"So that leaves us where?" George asked, getting everyone thinking.

"I'd say our captains didn't give up when everyone else did," Emily replied.

"And for some reason, they don't trust the Galactic council anymore," Andy said and the others nodded.

"No communication with the CORE or the Galactic council for nearly ten weeks. That has to be a big breach in protocol," George said, frowning as Emily flipped over him.

"There is no chatter on the sub space communications. No communications at all," Anna said, shaking her head as she flipped over Gus.

"Odd," Emily added.

"Odd, indeed," George said, puzzling.

"George, can you call Max or grandfather?" Emily asked.

"No, not without being found out. Pete and Frank will know instantly. They have been very careful with their thoughts and words and have been blocking the energy of the universe as best they can. I know that doesn't sound right, but trust me. They will know and I don't think they will be happy. Especially, if our message gets intercepted," he said and shook his head.

"Well, something is weird, and I don't mean in a good way," Andy said.

"And then there is the hold time and distance problem," Anna added and they all nodded.

Something odd was going on in this training transport ship.

"Emily what did you find out about Chen Lo? Remember when we were on Jupiter station," George asked.

"Ah yes, day one of our fourth rotation, such a fond memory," Emily said whimsically.

"Emily!" they all chorused.

"Fine. Almost everyone in the CORE learns up to level ten. Some like David Lu become masters. I suspect the entire Galactic council or at least the Senior Viceroys, Inner Circle officers, and Viceroys are all masters of varying levels. No one our age or Pete or Frank's age has in a millennium mastered level twelve or beyond," Emily reported.

"Again most unusual," George said, thinking as he flipped over Andy and rolled under Emily in one fluid move.

"What is Chen Lo and please don't say to help focus and regain control. It may help us do that; however, I don't think that's what it's really for," Andy asked.

"There is something about it, familiar and yet, not familiar," George agreed.

"You are both right. Eons ago, Chen Lo was started as training for the warriors of the galaxies. It was a way of controlling and focusing their thoughts. Then overtime the galaxies became complacent and Chen Lo was only used to calm and focus ones individual thoughts," Emily replied.

"Nothing else? I mean it's like we are missing something," Andy said shaking his head.

"Well, there are some bit and pieces of information that says they used it to hold back the evil somehow, and now there are only a handful of true masters left," Emily said a little sad.

"So without them holding back evil, evil is growing," Andy said, creating a web of deception and espionage.

"A reasonable conclusion, Andy," Emily said, sliding over next to Anna and Sara.

"Did it say how Chen Lo holds back the evil? Did it say what they actually did?" Andy pressed, flipping off the cargo bay wall. "You know, like put these moves together and evil is banished from the galaxies?" he asked.

"No, Andy. There wasn't a cookbook, only a lot of odd bits and pieces left in the database," Emily said, and stopped in her tracks as she realized someone had erased the information and she knew it.

"So like the prophecy, someone has been there before us and erased the good stuff," Sara added, spinning over Andy.

"Sounds like a trip to the officer's library on Asteria station to me," Anna added, grinning as she leapt over Gus and hugged him as she turned.

"Well, maybe we can ask and see what we can find in the CORE database first. Our captains have changed, maybe, they will not stop us this time," George said, wanting to trust their triad and get help this time, before they raided the officer's library.

They all nodded slowly, accepting George's request. They were at level nine and George knew Pete and Frank could sense the Chen Lo energy they now knew they were using. He motioned and Emily twisted her wrist to unlocked the cargo bay doors. At level ten, they were all getting tired, so Andy slowed the team down to rest. No eleventh level today.

Chapter 15

MORE QUESTIONS

Nick and Niels entered the cargo bay the moment the team stopped to rest. Andy glanced at George. He was right, the captains may not have been in the cargo bay; however, they were still watching them in their links.

"Hungry cadets?" Nick asked, trying to hide a smile.

Gus spun around in a flash. Andy and George smiled and lowered their heads.

"What, I'm hungry. I know you're all hungry. I simply want to get to dinner before Nick and Niels, that's all," Gus said, sending the two captains down a different path.

"Good point," Andy said, racing Gus to the door and out into the hallway.

Anna and Sara laughed as all you could hear were Andy and Gus's footsteps, racing down the hallway. A sudden 'thud' of crashing bodies echoed in the hallway after the two rounded another corner.

"They knocked someone to the ground," Anna said concerned.

"It's Pete and Frank," Emily said, gasping.

"No, they're in the command deck," Nick replied.

"Fast running feet, it was Pete and Frank, sir," George said, lowering his head.

"Oh, that will be bad," Niels added, nodding slowly.

The cadets spun on their feet and everyone ran from the cargo bay into the hallway and around the corner towards the galley. Skidding to a stop, the captains, and cadets gasped and then turned away to hide smiles. In front of them, Pete and Frank laid flattened on the floor!

Gus and Andy were apologizing as fast as they could. George and the others turned away to hide their grins as Niels and Nick reached down to pull the two lead captains up from the floor.

Pete and Frank had been extremely protective of the cadets, not a stray thought or issue had gone unnoticed. However, shear wild behavior was not in their plan. They wanted the cadets to relax and heal after being, well, being where they were. However, total chaos and tom-foolery was their limit.

As they stood up from the floor of the hallway, Pete started yelling commands. The cadets stopped smiling and lowered their heads. Even Andy and Gus knew they had crossed the imaginary line. There would be excessive cleaning chores to use the extra accumulated energy in the cadets that evening after dinner. No more light training with Colonel Hawks. The cadets would now train only at Pete and Frank's teams captain level of training!

That evening, the cadets all sat in silence eating their dinner. Pete and Frank seemed oddly happy to George. They had found a way of increasing the cadets training level without giving away the plan.

After dinner, Nick and Niels led the cadets to the engine room to clean the ship's filters and air systems. Normally, these would be cleaned automatically; however, the ship systems were having problems keeping up on such a long voyage. Andy and Gus took the worst jobs of cleaning the filters as Anna, Emily, and Sara crawled into the air system ducts to fix some broken controllers.

George handed tools up to them from the maintenance cart. Andy and Gus loaded the filters into the plasma shoot and ran them, one after the next, through the engine exhaust, burning the filters clean.

Emily crawled further and further up into the air system to find the broken controllers; however, each control system she tested functioned correctly, nothing was broken. Yet, something was not right.

"I need George," Emily whispered, wiggling back out of a long side duct to the main air duct.

George climbed up the stack of boxes and helped Anna and Sara down from the main duct inlet on the side of the cargo bay wall. Then he lifted himself up and slipped inside the main duct. Sara ran back from Andy with a small red sphere dancing in the palm of her hand. She reached inside and passed it to George.

Emily spoke no words. Instead, she signed her message in their new sign language. George curled his eyebrows, frowning in disbelief. He slipped passed her in silence, into the smaller duct, holding Andy's sphere out in front of him. The light shimmered and seemed to bend as it reflected inside the duct. He reached forward with his free hand.

"Let me see what my eyes hide from me," he whispered, and the sphere grew brighter in his hand.

A man lay crumpled in the smaller air duct, his skin nearly translucent.

"Max, how could you?" he gasped.

George folded his hand closed and the red sphere was gone. Reaching forward, he pulled Max free of the duct and dragged him along through the main air system. Carefully, he handed Max down to Andy and Gus below. Sara had a yellow healing sphere on Max before he touched the floor. For a moment, Max was in mid-air and the transport ship lurched and bucked. It stopped when they laid him on the engine room floor.

"Well, that explains a lot, now doesn't it," Andy said, shaking his head.

"You're right Andy, Max is the reason this ship has been able to do what it did," George said, knowing Max had held the transport ship together so they could be found.

"Eight, ten weeks and no refueling, no extra supplies. And then there is the distance time traveled issue and all to find us," Emily said, stunned.

"Andy, go get our captains, we have work to do. Emily, stop the engines and make us look like a rock, drifting in space. Anna, I want to know how bad of shape this transport ship is really in. Gus, I need a link with you and the others. We will try and keep the ship together while we heal Max," George said, giving out orders like a captain as his team took off running.

Pete, Frank, and the others came racing to the cargo bay, the moment Andy sent the message. They gasped as their eyes met Max's eyes. George lifted Max up in his arms and Pete, Frank, and Gus formed an inner circle around them. Next was a circle of Sara, Anna, Maria, Lucita, Karmen, Rachael, and Jennifer. Around them in another circle were Nick, Niels, Emily, Andy, Sven, and Han.

"You're going to find out what Chen Lo is really all about," Niels whispered to Andy.

"It's OK, we already knew, sir," Andy whispered, lying through his teeth hoping Niels would say more as they knew only bits and pieces about Chen Lo's true meaning.

"We just don't know which moves do what yet, sir," Gus added, whispering.

"You will now," Nick said seriously.

"How do you know, sir?" Andy asked, looking for more information.

"I cannot say," Niels whispered, oddly seriously.

Andy nodded, he knew there were things they could not tell them~ someday they would know.

Max was nearly dead. His skin was as translucent as the librarian's on Asteria station. Sara's yellow sphere grew as the captains and cadets circled Max and George; however, he did not get stronger.

"Will Max's kind help him?" Sara asked, worried for Max's life.

"No, I think he is on his own~ like us. I'm pretty sure he broke a lot of rules on a cosmic level, and they will not help now," George replied seriously.

"Sara's healing sphere is not helping," Andy said, looking at George.

"Remember when you asked about Chen Lo and then went searching for answers when I told you not to," Pete said to George.

"Yes, we remember, sir," Emily replied, rather matter of factly.

"Well, I now wish I had told you the answers as you are about to have a crash course in the power and energy of the universe," Pete said, seriously worried.

"I thought the Galactic councils controlled the power of the universe in each galactic sector sir?" Andy asked, looking for more information.

"They do in a sense; they make the raw energy of the universe useable for everyone. They change it from its chaotic random form into a form the galaxies can use," Pete said, deadly serious.

"Like last year, remember?" George said and the cadets nodded.

Pete was about to tell them things they had been told not to say.

"Chen Lo harnesses the raw energy of the universe itself. That is why there are only a few Chen Lo masters," Frank added seriously.

"It is the only real power evil cannot withstand," George said, finally understanding their words.

Nick, Niels, and Andy, started Chen Lo at level one in their minds, tracing each jump, roll, and flip with their arms only, never moving their feet from where they were standing. Emily, Sven, and Han started at level one when Nick, Niels, and Andy started level two. At the start of level three for Nick, Niels, and Andy; Emily, Sven, and Han started level two and Sara, Anna, and Maria started level one. With the next level change Lucita, Karmen, Rachael, and Jennifer joined in.

It was the sequence of motions and when they each started the Chen Lo levels that was important! Pete, Frank, and Gus focused only on George and Max. This time when they did Chen Lo, the room vibrated with their motions. Each motion added to their rhythm.

As Nick, Niels, and Andy reached the eleventh level, the energy in the air around them seemed to come alive. As if, you could see the electrons, neutrons, and protons dancing in the air between them. Pete, Frank, and Gus focused the raw energy and fed it to George and Max.

One by one, the groups progressed to the twelfth level. As each group joined the others at the twelfth level, the room they stood in started to bend and warp as if the sub-atomic elements were losing their cohesion; and all that were left were dancing strings of pure energy, changing dimensions as easily as someone walking through a door.

Each Chen Lo motion focused the raw energy and streams of white light sped through the spaces between them, impacting Pete, Frank, and Gus before streaming on inward to George and Max. George and Andy had seen this before on their last rotation. However, now they knew what they had seen was the focused raw energy of the universe.

In and out of space, they were joined by Toma, Cal, Sheta, Darri, Tillie, and Gabe. It was as if their energy and physical beings were in two places at the same time. Toma took Gus's place with Pete and Frank and Gus stepped back into the Chen Lo motions with Sara, Anna, and Maria. Their power and control increased. The engine room was gone, their bodies a mere blur in the cosmic space.

"George, what are you doing?" Max asked, weakly lifting his head.

"We are saving your life, Max," George replied seriously.

"How do you know it is a life that should be saved? Perhaps, I am evil in disguise and you will have saved your enemy," Max said, weakly trying to push George away.

"Perhaps, but, even my enemy does not deserve to die in this way. All of our lives have become intertwined, Max. Good cannot exist without evil; yin and yang, ebb and flow, that is what the beings of white light are trying to teach. The universe is a little out of balance right now and, it needs balance--equal and opposite forces, pushing and pulling, always together," George replied, suddenly understanding the nature of the universe's energy.

"They will not be happy with what you have done," Max whispered, seriously as he grew stronger.

George squinted and stared at Max, he understood. Max meant high council of the beings of white light, he wasn't talking about the Galactic council this time.

"It is not their choice to make. We have freely chosen this path," George replied seriously.

George understood that life and existence was about freewill, the right to choose your own path. They hurt no one else, they disrupted no other lives, they chose this path to help others, and it was their will, work, and determination that would set them free from evil.

An hour later, Max breathed deep and straightened up. His strength had returned to his body. He spread his arms wide; a brilliant white light washing over the triad. Over the next hour, Toma, Pete, and Frank slowed their Chen Lo motions. Finally, they knelt down on one knee to rest. Max pulled his arms in and their bright white aura faded away, as did Toma and his team. The energy of the universe in their sector was released and returned to the ebb and flow of life. Max sat down on the floor with them.

"Why did you come with us?" Pete asked calmly.

"Why did you hide from us?" Frank asked.

"You couldn't know I was here or you would have been killed for knowing. It was my choice, not yours. Imposing myself, my will, upon you and having you suffer the consequences would have been wrong," Max replied calmly.

Again, George knew Max was talking about the high council of the beings of white light, so he changed Max's focus.

"Does the Galactic council know about this type of raw energy of the universe in this way?" George asked, choosing his words carefully.

"Only if you choose to tell them," Max replied, cryptically focusing solely on George.

"But they should have noticed the shift in energy and that something changed, right?" George said, pressing for more information and finishing his thoughts.

"The level of energy you are dealing with is only truly known to a very few," Max said, hinting.

"Only by the Chen Lo masters, right? David Lu knows, doesn't he?" George asked eagerly.

"You will have to ask him. For now, you all need to rest," Max said, lifting his hand into the air.

The captains and cadets gently slipped to the floor, falling asleep to the peaceful hum of the transport ship's thermal engines starting again. White lights shimmered near the doorway.

"What power do you have over these young ones?" Aris, the eldest of beings of white lights asked, taking human form and walking into the cargo bay next to the captains.

"I have no power over them. It is they who have power over me as I have said before," Max replied, standing up, his strength restored.

"It nearly cost you your existence this time. Most inhabitances of these galaxies would have let you die instead of risking their lives to save another," Aris pressed, looking for more understanding.

"These young ones and those around them that care for them are not like the others you speak of. No matter how beaten down they are, they never lose their truth, hope, or the strength that lies within them," Max replied, kindly motioning toward the sleeping captains and cadets.

"They controlled the raw energy of this universe well," Aris said, nearly complementing the cadets and captains.

"They are very young to hold such power," Max replied more seriously. "However, it is not their control of the power or raw energy that worries me," he added.

"Then what?" Mag asked, taking human form.

"Their curiosity of the space between the raw energy," Max said, looking worried.

"I don't even think they noticed," Mag replied.

"They did, they simply can't see it or define it yet. George knew it on Earth when you helped them. He knew they were no longer on Earth, but somewhere in between," Max said, noting that he has seen Mag, Aris, and Tao help the cadets.

"They are most clever, indeed," Tao said, thinking they would need to be more careful in dealing with these beings.

The white lights all faded away. The transport ship's systems were restored and no longer needed Max to hold it together. Emily's comet disguise was running and their course set for Asteria station again.

The transport was nearly at the asteroid field round Asteria station when Emily's alarms sounded two days later. Pete and Frank woke up first and woke the teams still sleeping on the floor of the cargo bay. Quickly, they all set out on their tasks to check out the ships systems and to find out where they were.

Gus, Hans, and Sven went to make a meal for everyone, while Pete, Frank, and George hurried to the command deck. The others ran to the armory, navigation, computer system, and the hospital before going to the galley. Pete, Frank, and George were the last to arrive in the galley for lunch.

"We are nearly at Asteria station," Anna reported, as the three entered the galley.

"Everything on this transport ship has been restored," Emily added.

"You know, now that the transport is better, perhaps we could go visit Toma and the rest of our triad, sir?" Andy suggested.

"Andy!" they all chorused.

"It won't be that bad on Asteria station," Niels added, sitting next to Andy with his plate of food.

"OK, but if I have to light up one more red energy sphere, I'm not going to hold back this time, sir," Andy said, muttering biting into his sandwich.

Quickly, Nick and Niels glanced at each other and lifted Andy from his seat, dragging him out of the galley as he struggled to free himself from their grasp.

"We need Andy for a minute," Nick said seriously.

"Yes, yes we forgot something," Niels said seriously, firming up his grip on Andy's arm.

"What, sir?" George asked, confused by what was suddenly going on.

"I don't know, we need Andy for something," Niels said, as he and Nick dragged Andy down the hallway, still struggling to get free.

"What was that all about, sir?" Sara asked, biting into her apple.

"Sometimes lessons need to be relearned, Sara?" Frank said, lowering his head.

"Oh, that can't be good, sir," Anna said, looking a little worried.

"What is it you said, with great power comes...," Pete said, starting the phase.

"Great responsibility, sir," Sara said, finishing his phrase.

"All things have checks and balances. Nick and Niels are Andy's check and balance, right now. I'm not sure Cal would be as kind. It is best not to say anything," Lucita whispered.

"OK," Sara replied slowly.

With Sara now distracted by Lucita, Pete and Frank turned their attention to George.

"Asteria station is better than before; even so, you will need to guard your thoughts carefully as you know more than most," Pete said seriously.

"We want to read about Chen Lo in the officer's library, before it is erased, sir," George said boldly.

He was taking a big risk, telling Pete and Frank their intentions. They could lose their opportunity if they couldn't trust them. However, George figured the captains no longer trusted the Galactic council, so maybe it was worth the risk.

"So you finally trust us with your team's inner most thoughts?" Pete replied, leaning back and staring at George.

"Your duty has been to the Galactic council and to protect us. All of that has changed, sir," George said, staring at Pete. "I think you and Frank no longer blindly follow the Galactic council's directions, or you wouldn't have found us, sir," he added.

"The more things change the more they are the same," Pete said, grinning a little.

"No, it is different now. I can sense it. Something is different here sir," George whispered.

"Then you will have to teach us, George. I can't sense any difference," Frank said, lifting his head.

"Finally, something I can teach you two, sirs," George said and laughed.

The two lead captains shook their heads; their cadets had changed entire worlds. Did they not see what they had done?

"What did Max say to you?" Pete asked kindly.

"You heard him, sir," George replied, biting into a sweet date.

"No, he spoke only to you. Now you have to choose," Pete replied.

"Man, I hate that. Why can't Max just tell everyone, sir," George whined.

"You have to decide who knows what and when. You must learn to be judicious in the knowledge you share," Pete said, his voice serious and low.

"Just as we must be judicious in the knowledge we share," Frank said, raising an eyebrow.

He was reminding George there were some things they couldn't tell them. George's face crinkled. His brain twisting in thought.

"Less cryptic, sir?" George asked and shook his head.

"George, if we had told you about the Thoreans, the Mahadean and the evil in the universe on your first day as a cadet, what do you think would have happened?" Pete asked, raising an eyebrow.

"We would have thought you were all crazy or lying, sir," George replied, his mouth falling open.

"So you must regulate the kind of information that is distributed and to whom," Frank said calmly and quietly.

"Like the Galactic council, the raw energy of the universe and the knowledge of Max, right sirs?" George said, beginning to understand.

"Yes, so Max gave you information and he wants you to learn how to make choices with that information. Starting with easy information that is interesting and yet, can have more than one meaning if properly understood," Pete said, staring at George, hoping he would understand.

The information Max had given him was meant to be shared with his triad leaders, but, only his triad. George smiled and flipped his hand over reveling a small yellow sphere. Frank and Pete joined in the link and George told him the words Max had said. They nodded and Gus ended the link from across the room.

"How did you know, Gus?" Rachael asked, not looking up from her plate.

"It was like you said, you just sense it in them," Gus replied and Rachael smiled.

A warning alarm sounded and the captains sprang from their chairs.

"Get them into the stasis tubes, quickly! No one can know they are with us," Pete and Frank yelled, running to the command deck and the front viewer.

Rachael, Lucita, and the others ran to the stasis tubes in the hospital room with the cadets. Nick and Niels came running, carrying Andy between them. All three looked badly beaten.

"Don't ask!" Nick said gruffly.

They slipped Andy into the last tube and Lucita hid their life signs.

Jennifer and Kate turned off Emily's computer programs and locked them away from the command deck as Maria and Karmen flew the transport behind a large moon on the edge of the Calshene solar system. The comet ship became a transport ship again.

Mid-way across the solar system, Pete called the station administrator. Quickly, a dozen fighters from Asteria station were on their way to meet them. Pete and Frank answered the administrator's questions as fast as they could. Soon, permission to land was granted. The fighters circled the transport and waved their wings when they were told it was Pete and Frank's team returning home.

Chapter 16

HOME ON ASTERIA

The administrator closed the viewer and Pete and Frank made a link. They thought only of Senior Viceroy Petrosky, Pete's grandfather. They needed him and him alone.

"They are safe. We are all home," they said in their cryptic message once their link was made.

An instant later, the station administrator was calling them.

"You have been redirected by the station Viceroy to new landing coordinates. I don't know what you did captains, but, the Viceroy didn't seem very happy with you," the administrator said, shaking his head and turning off his screen.

Maria and Karmen entered the new coordinates into the navigational computer as the fighters broke off their escort. They were ordered away.

The captains knew the Senior Viceroy was pleased with them as they could sense it when they were in their link. Yet, there was an uneasiness too. Pete's grandfather had been short in his communication with them and not just because he didn't want the cadets discovered by any evil infected officers on Calshene. It was something else, Pete and Frank would need to figure it out and soon. They had to keep George and the others safe. They hadn't worked so hard to rescue them, only to lose them now.

Maria and Karmen landed the transport in a small hanger bay on Asteria station. Quickly, two dozen CORE guards surrounded the transport. A few moments later, in flashes of white light, Pete's grandfather, a Senior Viceroy, and two Viceroys appeared in the command deck of the ship.

"Report!" Pete's grandfather said firmly, not kind and welcoming as they had expected.

"They are safe. We are all home, sir," Pete answered formally stepping forward.

The two Viceroys behind the Senior Viceroy were Pete and Franks fathers. They said nothing, yet, looked like they were straining to control their thoughts.

"Bring me to them, captains," he ordered, his voice strained, seeming to hardly recognizing them.

They left the command deck and headed for the hospital in the back of the transport ship. The captains kept their minds closed as they walked, not a word or thought was shared. In the hospital room, Rachael and Lucita had the cadets out of the stasis tubes and lined up by the time Senior Viceroy Petrosky arrived. A third and fourth Viceroy entered behind their fathers. The four Viceroys surrounded the cadets, raised their hands and in a flash of white light they were gone.

"Good work, captains," Senior Viceroy Petrosky said formally, without acknowledging the captains as grandsons, even though they were now alone.

In a second flash of white light, the Senior Viceroy was gone.

Pete, Frank, and the others were stunned. They had not expected great fanfare when they returned home; nonetheless, they had expected a little bit more after having been gone for more than eight weeks.

Kate and Jennifer locked down the transport with some of Emily's more special computer programs and left the small spaceport, not sure, where they were going. In the main corridor, Major Gatte stepped out in front of them from a classroom. He looked both ways down the corridor and stepped back into the classroom, motioning the captains to hurry inside. The door slid closed and Colonel Moawk quickly locked the door behind them. Major Pannelo, Colonel Payate, and Major Dozel were also inside, waiting for them.

"Welcome home, captains," Major Gatte whispered, clasping all of their arms in greetings.

The other four officers said nothing, instead they stood silent in a circle, focused and concentrating, blocking any thoughts.

"Greetings are sent through us from your families," Major Gatte continued. "They are all please you have returned and found the lost cargo," he said, choosing his words very carefully.

Something was very, very wrong. The four senior officers were blocking their thoughts and the Major was picking his words very carefully. This was not the Calshene station they knew.

"We thank you for your kind regards on our behalf sir," Pete replied for the teams.

He was as careful with his words as they were being careful with theirs.

"You have been gone a long time and will need nourishment," Major Gatte added and smiled slowly. Major Gatte was being obvious in his use of specific words.

It was as if they were fighting against something, and yet, there was nothing there.

"Yes, you will need nourishment before you rest. Your training will begin in the morning," he added, straining.

Colonel Gatte held out his hand and motioned toward the door. The captains left following Colonel Gatte down the corridor to the dining hall. The dining hall was quiet, even though, it was filled with captains and cadets. It was hardly the noisy corridors and dining halls of a cadet station. The Colonel nodded and shook their hands before leaving them inside the dining hall. Shaking Pete's hand last, he left him a small scrap of paper. Quickly, Pete folded his hand around it. Patting Pete on the back, Colonel Gatte spun around and left in a hurry.

The captains recognized nearly everyone in the dining hall, and yet, no one said hello or asked where they had been for the last eight weeks. The room was quiet except for the sound of spoons bumping their bowls. All around them, the captains ate bowls of orange mush.

Pete looked at his hand. 'Eat nothing' was scratched on the scrap of paper. The captains made their way to an empty wooden table and sat down on wooden stools. Officers working as waiters and waitresses, brought bowls of orange food to them. Odd, since the food normally flowed up from the silvery tables.

Pete signed the Colonel's message to the teams and they all spilled their food, in one way or another. Nick and Niels actually threw their bowls across the room, hitting a picture of old Calshene. Quickly, two officers brought new bowls and placed them in front of the boys. They said nothing, turned, and left. The captains were stunned.

George, Andy, Gus, Sara, Emily, and Anna woke up in the Asteria station brig. Each cadet was held in a separate cell.

"It is for your own safety," the CORE guards said, placing bowls of orange cereal on the floor in front of them to eat.

"Eat nothing. Something is wrong. I can sense it in Pete and Frank," George thought through their link.

Andy couldn't see George. He could only see Emily and she could only see Gus and Gus could only see Anna and Anna could only see Sara and Sara could only see Andy.

"Emily, Anna, open the cave doorways and get us out of here," George thought.

Emily nodded as George focused his mind and made the CORE guards sleepy. Anna made archways into the caves behind each cell and Emily opened the doors with a twist of her wrist. The cadets stepped backwards through the cave doors and into the caves. When the doors closed, they disappeared from the brig.

Moment later, Emily, Anna, and Sara came running around through the cave, grabbing onto Andy, George, and Gus's arms spinning them as they ran by.

"We are not alone," Emily yelled.

The boys started running after the girls. They could hear the footsteps from guards behind them, gaining on them, getting closer and closer. Emily touched a crevice along the side of the cave wall and it opened up a little. Andy and Gus pushed everyone into the crevice before Emily could make it bigger. She held the wall and it covered over Andy as the guards ran passed. Emily expanded the crevice. The dust filled the air as Gus dug Andy free from inside the wall.

"Call Sid and Mid," George signed.

In few a moments, the wall rumbled and the tunnel hog's side slit opened. Once inside, the tunnel hog took off like a bolt of lightning. They fell to the back. It was Sid. Emily hugged Sid for a long time and he seemed to hug her back, telling her about the happening on Asteria station.

Sid came to a gentle stop in the tunnel hog, sleeping cavern. As they slipped out of Sid, Emily could feel the sadness well up in the dull looking fungi. Gus slipped out his purple liquid, sprinkling it around over the fungi to feed it. It glowed a warm bright green. Gus stroked its soft green coat.

"Careful, Gus," George warned.

"I know, it's just so sad," Gus replied.

"It should be. The food here has been contaminated and they are all starving to death," Sara said, scanning the soil with her pad.

"Contaminated with what, Sara?" George asked, looking around.

"I don't know, Sid said everything is contaminated. That is why everyone is acting oddly," Sara replied. "He said it started a few weeks ago and now everyone is infected."

"Gus, any ideas?" George asked, thinking about Shadoo and Sandue and the stuff in the soil there.

"Give me a minute," Gus replied.

He and Emily were bent over, collecting samples of soil the moss had brought him.

"How is he talking with the moss?" George whispered.

"He's not, Emily is helping him, see," Andy said, pointing and George nodded.

"Gus knows what to ask for and Emily can do the asking," Sara added, quietly analyzing more soil.

A few minutes passed and Emily and Gus stood up.

"Well, it's like the drone chemical on Shadoo and Sandue. But, the organisms on the station are fighting it here. So, the drone chemical has had only limited success in controlling the station. However, they can't keep fighting for much longer though as they are all starving," Gus said and paused.

"Somehow we need to clean the Calshene station and any other stations and planets that have been infected with this drone chemical," Emily added.

"This is bad George, someone planted this here recently and a lot of it," Gus said staring at George.

"Is it alive Gus?" George asked seriously.

"No, the drone chemical is just a chemical created to conquer races for evil long ago," Gus replied.

"So how did it get here?" Anna asked as the cadets walked toward the other cave.

"A mystery we will need to solve," George replied, and patted Mid's side.

Mid was lying in the entrance blocking their way into the next cave.

"What's wrong Mid? We are here to help," Emily asked.

Mid seemed to be crying on the inside as she slid forward. On the floor of the other cave, in the place they first met the beings of white light, laid two dimly glowing beings of white light.

"Mid says they came to help them and somehow became infected. She says they are dying and the tunnel hogs can't get them home," Emily said, sadness filling her words.

The cadets went to the center of the second cavern and surrounded the two beings of white light.

"We can help. We know how to use the raw energy of the universe now. We can do this. First, this drone chemical must be gone so it does not infect anyone else. Then we will rescue them like we rescued Max," George said, making a plan.

"George are you sure? It was a lot of energy and we aren't the best at focus and control," Anna said with sadness in her voice.

"We have to try. We can't do nothing and just let them die," George replied.

"Yes, it is a good day to die. Besides we have been here and conscious for nearly one day, seems almost like things are slowing down on Asteria station," Andy said sarcastically, and they all laughed a little.

"Think of the drone chemical and think of spring cleaning. Use a lot of disinfectant Andy. We want sparkling clean, like spring cleaning day on the farm," George said to Andy.

Andy laughed.

"Inside joke?" Sara asked.

"Oh ya, we have done this before. It's just that we didn't know what we were doing then," Andy said and grinned.

George stood in the middle of their small circle. Anna, Gus, Andy, Sara, and Emily surrounded him.

"Are you sure we can control this?" Gus asked seriously.

"No. This time, it will most likely kill us as we really can't regulate this much energy, but we have to try. Even with the odds against us, to do nothing is worse," George said and laughed like Andy.

"Chen Lo begin," Andy said, and started with Sara at level one moving only his arms, not his feet.

Then Anna and Emily started level one when the first three started level two. Last to start was Gus. It was the way to build up slowly to use of the raw energy of the universe. By the third level change, all of the cadets had begun and entered the growing rhythm.

George stood alone in the center of the circle, focusing and concentrating. He held up the two beings of white light, hanging one arm over his right and left shoulders. Andy reached Chen Lo level eleven and the cavern walls and floor began to vibrate with their motions, each motion adding to their rhythm.

When Gus started level eleven, the energy in the air around them seemed to come alive. It was as if you could see the electrons, neutrons, and protons, dancing in the air between them.

Gus stepped out of the Chen Lo rhythm and focused a few rays of brilliant white energy, streaming through space. The light streams slowly joined together at Gus and then, burst into George and the two beings of white light. Gus was shaking, focusing the energy all by himself. George was having a difficult time holding the two white light beings up and keeping his concentration.

The raw energy of the universe was wild and focusing and controlling it was way passed their abilities. Their faces showed the strain. Yet, they wouldn't stop. They couldn't.

Somehow, Andy progressed them to the twelfth level. The cavern they stood in started to bend and warp as if the sub-atomic elements were losing their cohesion, and all that was left were the dancing strings of pure energy, changing dimensions as easily as they walked through a door. Each motion focused the raw energy better and little by little, more rays of brilliant white light sped through the spaces between them, impacting Gus, then bursting onward to George and the two glowing beings of white light.

In and out of space, they were joined by Pete, Frank, Toma, and the other captains in their triad. They were neither, here nor there. They existed only in the energy between the space. Gus stepped back and Frank, Pete, and Toma stepped inside to the inner circle to regulate the stream of raw energy. Their power and control increased again.

George now focused his thoughts on spring-cleaning. On cleaning away all of the drone chemical. Wave after wave of raw energy spread across the station, their galaxy, and then the next galaxy, and so on until all that was left was the dark place Max had once warned George about. He left the dark galaxies alone, not cleaning them.

Instead, he moved his focus to another galaxy and cleaned it of the drone chemical. Their cleaning completed, the triad focused their thoughts on the two beings of white light. Another hour passed and the two beings straighten up, glowing a brilliant white.

The drone chemical was gone, evil was stopped, the galaxies would be free of evil again. They slowed their Chen Lo rhythm and Toma, Pete, Frank, and the others faded away. Again, they knelt down on the ground, resting on one knee. The glowing beings of white light dimmed and solidified.

"Why?" Mag asked, hiding his appearance from George and Andy.

"Why have you risked your very existence to save us?" Tara asked hiding her face as Mag had done.

"Why what, sir, ma'am?" George asked from the floor of the cavern.

"Why have you saved us?" Tara pressed.

"You needed our help, just as we have needed your help from time to time. Doing nothing is not in our nature, sir," George replied, lowering his head respectfully.

These beings were not Max. The cadets had watched the reactions of the other Viceroys when the beings of white light appeared. The beings of white light were greatly respected in the universe. George and the others showed them the proper protocol and respect. Only with Max were they less formal.

"And the universe?" Tara asked cryptically.

"Perhaps a little more in balance now, ma'am," George replied, hoping the beings of white light would understand.

"Why did you not destroy the place of great darkness and evil when you came upon it?" Mag asked.

"It would not hesitate to destroy you," Tara added.

George smiled. "That is what separates us, sir, ma'am," George replied.

"And what is that you speak of child?" Tara asked kindly.

"Compassion, ma'am. Compassion," Andy answered, understanding the true meaning of the word.

"Sleep now children. You need your rest," Mag whispered.

The cadets slipped softly to the ground, the bright green moss swirled beneath them lifting them up on a soft, velvety cushion.

"A wise answer from ones so very young," Mag said as they faded away.

They woke the next day, sleeping on Sid, next to Kid and Bid. As if a replay of the rotation before, Andy fell off Sid and Kid and Bid bounced him onto the ground. George nearly slipped off himself, laughing. The ground rumble hard and Sid wiggled over blocking the view of the other cavern. Pete, Frank, Niels, and Nick stepped out of Mid with six CORE officers.

"Cadets report! What are you doing here?" Pete yelled.

He was the distraction as the CORE officers circled the cadets. This was so familiar now. They knew immediately what to do.

George signed; "frightened, hiding," in their new sign language.

It was a mistake! Niels saw the new sign language but said nothing. He would keep the secret for now.

The cadets focused on being afraid and begging for forgiveness for running away. The CORE officers were buying it. However, Pete never stopped yelling as they stepped into Sid and Mid. Inside, Sid and Mid, Pete yelled at one group and Frank yelled at the others. The tunnel hogs stopped at the main tunnel hog terminal and let the cadets, captains, and CORE officers out.

"They are truly sorry. They were frightened, that's all. Remember, they are only Earthers and they frighten easily," the lead CORE officer said.

"Thank you sir for helping us find our lost cadets," Pete replied formally.

The CORE officers left; but Pete and Frank didn't stop yelling, only a little less loudly. Walking though one of the main corridors towards the Sport arena, the wall rumbled. Nick and Niels threw the cadets through the open slit with Frank and Pete slipping in last. Inside, Sid, the tunnel hog glowed a warm red as the cadet hugged him and he started to move.

"Report cadet," Pete said, facing George.

Using thought in the tunnel hog, George told the captains what had happened to them, starting with when they were taken off the transport ship by the Viceroys and placed in the station brig. He thought about what he had learned from Max on the transport ship about choices and information sharing. George told the captains about the entire day's events, leaving out the part about saving the beings of white light.

"So you're saying, our triad cleaned away all of the drone chemical across the universe? It's all is gone?" Pete replied, stunned at the distances across the universe they had reached with the raw energy.

"No sir, there is one place, a group of galaxies that are very dark, where evil is strong. We did not go there, sir," George said cryptically.

Pete didn't press for further explanation.

"I wonder how the drone chemical got here and everywhere else while we were gone?" Frank asked, changing the subject.

"We will need to investigate," Pete thought only to Frank and the captains.

Sid bumped and they all thanked him for the ride, stepping out exactly where they had entered one hour earlier.

"So where do we go from here," Anna asked, standing in the corridor.

"First, you will be getting newly cleaned food and then off to rest," Pete said kindly.

"Your training on Asteria station will begin early tomorrow morning," Frank added.

"What, no welcome back party, sir?" Andy said, looking sad.

"Don't worry, you can blow something up tomorrow," Frank said, teasing him.

Chapter 17

CHEN LO AND ENERGY

Some things had changed on Asteria station and some things had not. Everything was cleaner now and few people had any memory of the events on Asteria station over the last few weeks.

George was a little surprised that they hadn't gone to the hospital the moment they arrived. Perhaps, it was a mistake caused by the drone chemical. Either way, they weren't going to say anything; after all, they had already spent too much time in station hospitals.

The red cadets were talking in the dining hall when George's team entered that evening. The room fell silent.

"We heard you were dead," a cadet said as they sat down.

"Not yet," Andy answered.

A quiet murmur ran through the hall.

"So anything happen while we were gone?" he asked.

The murmur grew and several cadets told unusual stories of the last few weeks and the odd behavior of the officers. However, now, everything seemed to be back to normal. Well, except for Colonel Moawk. He was especially grueling this rotation. Food rose from the table and the cadets all started eating. They knew it wasn't real food, but at least it didn't look like cereal.

"George, I think Niels saw you use our new sign language in the tunnel hog cave," Andy whispered.

"No, I didn't sense anything in him," George replied; still, he wondered; if Andy was right, the captains would know they had a new more complex sign language. Something, the cadets really didn't want to share yet.

Dinner ended and Pete dropped the cadets off at their sleeping room instead of going to another classroom for more training. A quiet week passed and the cadets were getting used to being on Asteria station and training at their captain's level.

The morning of their second week, Pete picked up George and the others early from their cadet sleeping room.

"We're late," he said, running through the corridors after breakfast.

He pointed to his sleeve as they ran, and Emily turned everyone's stripe color from red to blue as they entered the blue sector. They bunched up so they looked like captains running to training instead of cadets following a captain.

Pete stopped at Colonel Moawk's training dome. Inside, Pete's team and a dozen other blue, green, and yellow teams were lined up in columns.

"Hot shots today, take your positions," Colonel Moawk said kindly, grinning a little.

"Odd, it wasn't an order," Andy signed to George, and Nick shook his head.

The blue captains, cadets, and half the yellow captains gathered on one side of the dome. The green captains and the other half of the yellow captains gathered on the other side of the dome.

Nick grabbed Andy's arm and placed a medium sized red energy sphere in his hand.

"The energy spheres are to be only strong enough to sting your opponent. If they are any stronger, your whole team will be doing laps," he said seriously.

"Yes sir," Andy whispered.

Gus touched the cadet's shoulders and linked them together. Andy shared Nick's warning with the team.

"Dodge ball with red energy spheres?" George asked shaking his head.

"Red hot energy spheres," Andy said and winced.

"Oh, this can't be good," Gus added.

"You feed us, Gus. We'll do the rest," George said, trying to reassure his team.

He wasn't sure they were really ready to be in training with energy spheres as their control wasn't the best and it had been a difficult fourth rotation. However, he was sure something had made the Galactic Union council change their minds a little. After all, the cadets were in a captains training class.

"Andy, aim for the captains feeding energy to the other teams," Gus whispered.

"Gus, you're wicked. You have been hanging around Emily too much," Andy replied, patting Gus on the back and smiling.

"What's up?" George asked.

"Oh nothing, just a little strategy Gus and I worked out," Andy replied, nodding towards Gus.

"Are you going to tell me?" George pressed, feeling left out of a good plan.

"No, I don't think you will approve of the strategy right now. Maybe later," Andy said.

Andy was the cryptic one this time, and he was having fun leaving George in the dark.

"Centar, comen!" Colonel Moawk yelled.

The game was on. The green captains spun around and hailed the blue and yellow captains with fiery hot red spheres. Nick, and Niels caught the spheres passing them to Rachael, Maria, and Gus to feed their teams the energy as Pete, Frank, and the others returned with a volley of red spheres of their own.

Emily, George, and the cadets lobbed red spheres high into the air. The opposing teams of green and yellow captains laughed, looking up and easily stepping out of the way. Nick, Niels, and the others took the opening and hailed the green and yellow captains with red energy spheres, hitting the other captains.

"Hey, that's not fair!" one of the lead captains yelled.

"You're welcome!" Frank yelled back.

The angry captains returned the volley, hotter than the first.

"Coming in hot, Andy. Let them pass!" Nick yelled.

However, he was too late. Andy caught one right in front of Gus and a second next to Emily. He dropped one into Gus's hands and returned the hot sphere, aiming for the closest captain sharing energy. Andy's aim was excellent, and he dropped the other yellow team's energy sharing captain to the ground.

"That's not fair," the lead yellow captain yelled.

"That sphere was too hot!" another yellow captain whined.

"It was a returned sphere, the yellow captain that threw it is disqualified!" the Colonel yelled.

A yellow captain fell out of the group and started his laps as two of the yellow captains carried off their injured team member.

"Their cheating," the yellow captain yelled again. "No one could have caught that and returned it.

"Centar, comen," Colonel Moawk yelled again.

Without their source of energy, the yellow captains were sitting ducks. The green team retaliated and soon both yellow teams were out of the game.

Now it was three blue teams against three green teams. Oddly, Frank's team was blue. Next, George, Emily, Sara, and Anna intentionally threw smaller, weak spheres only slightly above the ground. They rolled to a stop in the middle of the dome fizzing. The opposing captains laughed again. Pete and the other hailed them with hot red spheres hitting their marks.

George, Anna, and Sara lobbed their spheres high into the air, raining down on the green team, making them dodge this way and that. Their spheres didn't have nearly the same energy as Andy, Pete, or Frank's did; nonetheless, they were annoying and stung if they hit you. It was an excellent distraction!

Both sides returned volley after volley of red spheres. Neither team giving an inch. Andy waited for an opportunity.

"Nick, can I collect the energy spheres?" he asked.

"Sure as long as you don't join the energy in the spheres together," Nick replied, wondering what Andy had in mind.

Andy smiled. He caught one and kept it while George, Emily, Sara, and Anna fed Gus and returned the others as best they could. Soon Andy was juggling the energy spheres like a juggler in a circus. Nick smiled and started his own collection. Niels joined in too. Pete and the others were now the defenders.

They needed a distraction. Andy nodded to Sara and she flipped over into the center of the dome seemingly unprotected reaching for an energy sphere fizzling on the ground. The green captains attacked and Sara flipped backwards as if suspended in mid-air gracefully landing behind Pete. The green captains were mesmerized by her grace and poise.

At that moment, Andy let fly his collection of energy spheres in rapid succession, like a Gatling gun of the old West on Earth. Any one sphere wouldn't have stopped the green team's energy captain, however, ten in a row was another story. Nick and Niels followed Andy's lead. The three green team energy captains fell to the floor of the dome. Emily dropped to the ground and asked the ground to help the captains.

George leaned over holding her shoulder, "Emily, you OK?"

"Yes, I asked the ground to help them," she replied.

"A kind thought, Emily. Thanks," George whispered, holding her shoulder.

A few of the green captains went to help their energy captains and the three lead green captains dropped their hands to their sides and stepped forward with their seconds.

"Excellent game, captains," the lead green captain said.

Then they turned, lifted their fallen team members up, and left the dome.

George turned toward Andy. "You're right, I would never have agreed with your strategy. I'm glad you didn't tell me," he said.

George helped Emily up and she turned toward Pete.

"Sir, they were officers and I don't mean the junior ones either, sir?" she whispered to their triad.

"Yes, Emily, they were officers," Pete replied grinning a little.

"I'd say CORE officers," Frank added.

"Excellent deduction, you are all correct. Dismissed," Colonel Moawk replied.

The captains were beaming.

"George, Andy, Emily, Sara, Anna, and Gus, we would never have beat them without your wild distractions," Niels said.

"I would never have thought of lobbing small red spheres over their heads to rain down on them. It really annoyed them," Nick said, bumping Emily.

"Go with your strengths, I say," Emily said and winced.

"What do you mean?" Frank jumped in grinning.

"Hmm," Pete paused and then nodded to Frank in their cryptic captain way.

"Nooooo!" Andy whined. "But, sir, we won!" he added.

"They will not be so easily fooled next time," Nick added.

"What, what did I miss?" Gus stammered.

"More training, Gus," Anna said and shook her head, hanging it low and wrapping her arm over Gus's shoulder.

"How come every time we do something good, we get more training sir?" Andy said bewildered.

"Cause that's how it works, cadet," Niels said and laughed, bumping Andy's shoulder as they turned into the captain's dining hall.

Two weeks passed and their training was becoming routine. All was quiet and calm—translation, boring. Nothing out of the ordinary happened. Yet, each evening, Pete, Toma, or Frank said nearly the same thing.

"Get some rest. I don't know why I even say that. OK, just don't cause any trouble," they each said, leaving as Emily locked the doors and scanned for bugs.

"It's clean," Emily signed, when the door closed.

"Emily and Anna, did you find anything more about Chen Lo? Gus and Sara, I'm sure we need rations," George signed.

Emily twisted her wrist, unlocking the door. Quietly, Gus and Sara slipped out and disappeared. Emily had two computer terminals running in their sleeping room. Most sleeping rooms only had one terminal, a point not lost on George and Andy.

George reached out with Andy in a link and found grandfather. In a blink, grandfather was there in the sleeping room with them. He raised his arms and chairs rose from the floor. Moments later, Gus and Sara crashed through the door, landing on the Senior Viceroy's lap and scattering the ration packs and bottles of water across the room. Little bottles of purple liquid fell to the ground from Gus's sleeves.

"Oh, sir. Sorry, sir," Gus apologized as fast as he could, standing up and moving the purple bottles away from the Senior Viceroy with his foot.

"Report, cadets!" the Senior Viceroy said firmly, standing up and staring at Gus and Sara.

They glanced at George and he nodded.

"We were just gathering a few supplies, sir," Gus answered meekly.

"Planning another trip, cadets?" Senior Viceroy Petrosky asked firmly.

"Oh no, sir. We never know where our next meal is coming from so we want to be prepared. That's all, sir," Sara added.

"And the purple liquid, do you know what it is?" he asked, staring at Gus.

"Ah yes, sir. I'd rather you not say it out loud, sir. It is highly nutritious, sir," Gus said quietly and smiled a little.

"Why are there so many bottles cadet?" he questioned frowning.

"They're for a sick friend who needs us, sir," Gus said, hoping grandfather would stop asking questions.

Senior Viceroy Petrosky raised his eyebrow and smiled. "I have never seen fungi and moss wrap cadets around their little green tentacles, except to nibble on them before. Get some rest," he said, turning to face George and the other cadets. He smiled; "good work, cadets, I am proud of all of you." In a flash of white light, he was gone.

They hurried to put the rations, water, and purple liquid away and then slipped onto their beds. Suddenly, the door burst open before Emily could get it locked. Red sector officers shined their lights in onto the cadet's faces. All breathed in and held their breath.

"They're all here, keep looking," one of the officers whispered and they left the sleeping room.

They all sighed when the door closed. Quickly, Emily locked the door with her program.

"Stealth, Gus, Sara. Do you remember what the word stealth means?" Andy whispered.

"Andy, it's getting harder to break in around here," Sara whispered.

"Pretty soon they are actually going to take security seriously and you will be going hungry," Gus replied and they all chuckled as if any security system could really keep them out.

"Emily, Anna, what did you find out?" George asked, shaking his head.

"There is no upper limit to Chen Lo. It numbers to level twenty and then well, the information is well...," Anna said and stumbled, looking for new words.

"Wacked, George, it's wacked," Emily replied.

"Do you mean someone has removed the information?" George asked, questioning their choice of words.

"No, it's wacked. It doesn't make any sense. The level of master is well...," Anna said and paused; she had no words to describe what they found out.

"It is a transcending of our reality and dimensional shifting kind-of-status," Emily said with a smirk on her face.

"Not too many beings make it that far," Anna added.

"Ya think!" Andy said and laughed.

The cadets' mouths dropped open – stunned, not actually understanding Emily's words.

"So I know I'm going to regret this, but, what happens if they don't make it?" Andy asked.

"Nothing, making it to Chen Lo level twenty is awesome and amazing," Emily replied.

"Not too much information on Chen Lo after that. Transcending reality must make them less chatty," Anna said, giggling.

"OK, so let's concentrate on our next level of Chen Lo and leave the transcending for later," George said, grinning a little too.

"I hate to say this, but, I think we may have done the transcending thing already," Anna replied.

"Twice!" Emily added, staring at her pad.

"We skipped the stuff in the middle and went right to the end," Anna added, still giggling.

"So, how much trouble do you think we are in for that one?" George pressed.

"I don't think we are. I don't think the Galactic council knows. Our triad did it alone, with Max and then with the two other beings of white light, to save their lives and stop the drone chemicals. Remember what Max said. 'The raw energy was different, coming directly from the universe, a different kind of energy'," Emily answered.

"Maybe, he was only using words that we could understand," Andy suggested.

"Maybe, maybe not. I think he told us the truth and we didn't hear what he said," Anna added.

One by one, they fell asleep not wanting their thoughts and discussion to end. Pete was in their room the next morning with bowls of brown officer's cereal.

"So what are you still doing here, sir? Shouldn't your team be out on a mission?" George asked, only half-kidding Pete.

"Yes, however, Frank's and my team have been granted some time off after our last mission. We'll be here for a while. Besides, I hear you weren't caught at anything last night. All was calm," Pete said, pleased as the others cadets sat down at the table to eat their cereal.

"A chatty Senior Viceroy, for sure," Emily muttered, sitting down next to George.

"What! I was kidding. Report, cadet!" he said stunned, suddenly getting worried.

"We walked into that one," Andy said, shaking his head and Sara patted him on the back.

"Well, sir, we didn't exactly get caught by any of the guards last night sir," George said, wincing.

"Then who, George? Who caught you and what did you do? I know I'm going to regret this. Who caught you?" Pete asked, cringing.

"Well, sir, grandfather was here last night and well," George said, waffling when Pete cut him off.

Pete dropped his head onto the table, beating it up and down.

"You don't get caught by a simple guard on Asteria station. Instead, you get caught by a Senior Viceroy on the Galactic council. Our lives are over, just send me to isolation on a deserted outpost now. You have only been back for three weeks!" Pete yelled and whined.

"Sir, he wasn't angry, sir," Emily said kindly.

"You'll see, he was, he just didn't say it in so many words. How many rules did you break here, on Asteria station, last night?" Pete asked, shaking his head.

"Well, we did save everyone from being drones of evil on our second night here, sir," Sara piped in.

"They don't know that," Pete said, staring at his cadets.

The cadets faces drop. Pete was right.

"Oh man, we are so dead," Andy answered, looking sad.

"Yes, yes we are," Pete replied, and lowered his head.

"Are you going to tell Frank, Niels, and the others, sir?" Anna asked.

"No, they should have a few more moments of peace before, well...," Pete said, sighing a heavy sigh. "It's time to go," he added and stood up.

Slowly, they followed him out into the corridor.

"Where are we going today, sir?" Sara asked.

"Colonel Moawk's training again, cadet," Pete said, his voice had become more formal, not a good sign.

"But I thought," Emily started to say when Pete cut her off.

"The schedule changed this morning," he said and shook his head.

"We are so, so dead," Andy whispered.

They entered a training dome filled with blue and green captains. Frank turned and glanced at Pete as they walked into the dome. In an instant, he knew George and the others had done something the night before. Niels, Nick, and Andy were still beat from the hot sphere's game the day before and a particularly grueling workout wasn't what they wanted.

Andy had underestimated Colonel Moawk's ability to teach life lessons about rules and behavior. Today, Colonel Moawk was without mercy. The captains and cadets ran at top speed across the dome, jumping, flipping, and rolling, while Colonel Moawk and Major Gatte hurled hot red energy spheres at them. Hit after hit, they stung the captains and cadets. By mid-morning, the Colonel dropped the Sport vines down in the center of the dome. The captains and cadets swung with one hand while holding a staff weapon with their other hand.

Again, the Colonel and Major hurled hot red spheres at the cadets. They dodged and swung, flipping over, and rolling down the vines, catching themselves in mid-air. By noon only George, Pete, and Frank's teams hadn't been taken to the hospital wing. The Colonel and Major were tired and called the captains and cadets down.

"You are dismissed for lunch; however, you will return immediately after lunch for additional training," Colonel Moawk ordered firmly.

"Yes sir," Pete and Frank replied formally.

The captains and cadet hurried out of the dome, nearly collapsing in the corridor the moment the doors closed.

"George, what did you do last night?" Frank asked, wincing as he leaned against the wall.

"And who caught you?" Nick added, rubbing his back.

"The Senior Viceroy of the Galactic council caught them," Pete answered, before the cadets could say a word.

"We are so dead," Niels said, rubbing his neck.

"Or at least we'll wish we were," Lucita said, leaning on Niels.

They sat in the blue captains dining hall, nearly alone. Most of the other blue and green captains were out on missions or now in the hospital, recovering. All that came for lunch was more officer cereal. They ate every scoop. Gus, Han, and Sven even had seconds. They limped back to Colonel Moawk's dome. At the door, the captains straightened up and entered the dome, as if they were not in pain.

Master level, Senior Viceroy David Lu was standing inside, waiting for them. The captains and cadets lined up for Chen Lo training. However, David Lu didn't start. He turned around and stared at them as if they were different. He stepped forward, motioning them to sit down and rest. He stared at Pete, Frank, Nick, and Niels crinkling his forehead. Then he turned to George and Andy and lowered his head.

"Stay here!" he ordered firmly in their minds.

He turned away and in a flash of white light, he disappeared. Sara slid over next to Nick and ran her little yellow sphere over his face and arms, healing his burns.

"He knows," Andy whispered to George.

"Of course, he knows," George answered.

"The question is what level of master is he?" Emily puzzled.

"The records list him as master above twenty," Anna answered, flicking through her pad.

"Oh, well that's not good," Sara said, shaking her head.

The captains stared at the cadets, listening to their cryptic conversation.

"Report cadet, what do you know?" Pete ordered.

George motioned to Emily and Anna and they repeated their discussion from last night.

"Level eleven Chen Lo to transcending dimensions with massive amounts of raw energy from the universe at our control, sir," Emily whispered.

"What?" Frank asked.

"We used the raw energy of the universe, and David Lu somehow knows we did it, sir," Anna replied.

"Great," Niels added with sarcasm.

"And the Galactic council doesn't know, sir," Emily added.

"So how bad can it be?" Andy added, sarcastically laughing, knowing this was really bad.

"Andy, stop saying that. You know what happens every time you do," Sara said, as she moved closer to Niels.

Emily was playing with the swirling ground on the dome floor, listening to the conversations.

"The ground! We need to get up!" Han said urgently, staring at Emily's whirlwind of dirt.

"Sit, sir. I asked it not to hurt us, but to protect us for a while. It is tired like us and happy for the rest, sir," Emily said, playing with her swirl of soil.

"Emily what level of master is grandfather?" George asked.

"Don't forget your dads, they were there with him last year," Andy added.

Emily stood up and the ground swirled around her legs, wanting her to play more. Jennifer and Kate followed Emily to the computer terminals in the training dome. In a few minutes, they were nodding and whispering. They turned and Jennifer motioned for Emily to speak.

"Grandfather is listed as master above twenty, George," Emily replied with a smile.

"He knew too," George whispered.

"That's what he meant," Andy added, finishing George's thought.

"George, Andy, what? What exactly did he say last night?" Pete asked firmly.

"Oh, I guess we left that part out, sir," Andy replied, grinning a little.

"And that was what cadet?" Frank pressed firmly.

"Well, last night, when we got caught by grandfather he said, 'good work, I am proud of you.' It seemed odd at the time; however, it makes sense now, sir," George said.

"He knew what we had done," Andy added.

"He knew about the whole-transcending-energy-thing to save Max and the drone chemical cleaning of the universe, sir," George said, nodding to Andy.

"Now what?" Frank asked worried.

"I'm sure it was unexpected," Pete added, equally worried.

This wasn't in the captain's training. The triad's captains had been handpicked and trained since they were new cadets. Never in their training had they trained for transcending time and space.

"Well, I can't just sit here anymore, sirs," Andy said and stretched. "Emily can you bring up a Chen Lo instructor, level ten? We need to do something."

Quickly, Emily's holographic instructor projection appeared in the center of the dome and bowed.

"Level ten. Begin," Pete ordered, and the cadets and captains assembled into position.

The instructor bowed and began at level ten. Quickly, they progressed to level eleven. It seemed easier this time and their motions were more fluid. Level twelve started and the combinations were difficult. They flipped, fell, and crashed into each other, yet they did not give up. They repeated the moves, over and over, until Gus rubbed his stomach. George signed for a rest with their old sign language.

"We can't leave, George," Pete said, staring at the cadets.

"We don't need to leave, sirs," he said, motioning to Gus. "We got caught getting supplies last night, sir. Rations aren't the best, but it is food."

Gus slid out three ration packs and three bottles of water from his backpack that he had left on the floor near the door when they had entered. Soon, Hans and Sven were helping pour caps of water and handing out Gus's ration slices to everyone. From the small room off the main training dome, Senior Viceroy Petrosky and Senior Viceroy David Lu stood, watching the cadets and captains.

"Even now, they could order up anything to eat, and yet, they pull out rations and share a meager meal," David whispered.

"The question is can you train them enough to protect them from the raw energy of the universe?" he asked, no longer as concerned about the evil that hunted them.

"Their abilities will kill them, if their talents are not controlled soon," David said, as worried about the teams as Senior Viceroy Petrosky.

"Twice now they have used the raw energy of the universe and George was in the center. Pete, Toma, and Frank guided it; however, George alone focused and controlled it," Senior Viceroy Petrosky said, still in amazement by what they had done.

"I don't think they really know what they have accomplished or the power and energy that they now wield," David Lu replied seriously.

"Then we must let them discover that on their own. Who else knows of their accomplishment?" Senior Viceroy Petrosky asked.

"Each galaxy sector Galactic council has at least one true master within their council. Most are Senior Viceroys. Very few are young and none, I know of, can control the raw power and energy of the universe like this triad," David answered. "Very few will know what they have accomplished."

"Indeed, they would be a formidable adversary," Senior Viceroy Petrosky said. "No wonder evil wants them so much."

"No, Alexander," David Lu said and paused. "You don't understand the depth of the issue. They can wipe all of us out of existence with only an accidental thought!"

"Then we must do a good job of training them so we can stay around a little longer. Help them now, before they hurt themselves following that holographic instructor," Senior Viceroy Petrosky said, backing into the shadow.

Chapter 18

OFFICER'S LIBRARY

David Lu stepped out into the main dome and with a wave of his hand, the paused holographic Chen Lo instructor faded away. The captains and cadets spun around and stared at David Lu. He stepped up in front of them, bowing low as they scrambled to their feet re-forming their lines for Chen Lo. Turning around, he started them out on level twelve again. Following his every move, they spun, rolled, and flipped. David Lu spoke only to them through their thoughts. No verbal words were spoken.

"Only a few know of your recent accomplishments. Yes, Senior Viceroy Petrosky is one of them. We will increase your practice time, as you need improvement on your focus and control. Additionally, you will need to spend time in the officer's library. I am told you are well acquainted with it here on Asteria station," David said in their minds.

The cadets lowered their heads. The last time they had been there, they had made quite an uproar.

"The librarians will assist you as well. Listen to them. From this moment on, you will learn Chen Lo from the lower levels to the higher levels. No more skipping levels. Is that understood?" he said seriously.

His voice was firm, yet kind, trying to impart value to learning each step.

"Yes sir," they replied together.

He didn't know they had stumbled upon the raw energy of the universe by accident, out of pure desperation. They would say nothing; they weren't going to miss an opportunity to grow and learn from a true master.

The twelfth level wasn't as hard with David Lu teaching it. They fell less often and joined their motions together more fluidly.

"Do you think Toma and his team will mind coming to Asteria for training this rotation?" David Lu asked kindly, knowing their answer.

"No sir. Their delay in coming has only been in waiting for an invitation, sir," Pete replied for their triad.

The cadets were excited and found it hard to contain their enthusiasm. Rarely had their entire triad been together for very long and now the Senior Viceroy was offering to have Toma's team brought to them.

"Arrangements will be made," David Lu said with a little grin.

"Thank you, sir," Pete answered gratefully.

He slowed their Chen Lo motions and stopped.

"Dismissed. Except you, George, Pete, and Frank may stay a while," David Lu said, motioning with his hand toward the archway.

The others left the dome, lingering on the other side of the door ~ listening through their team link. Senior Viceroy Petrosky, grandfather, appeared in the corridor behind them with two of his Inner Circle officers.

"Cadets, captains?" he said firmly.

Their link dropped as they turned around to face the Senior Viceroy. Nick dipped his head in respect and the others followed. They were in public now and protocols needed to be followed.

"Walk with me," Senior Viceroy Petrosky said kindly, holding out his arm and distracting the teams.

Inside the dome, David Lu stood before George. "George, when you focused the raw energy of the universe recently, what did you think of?" he asked kindly.

"Cleaning, sir. However, it's really not me that has the thought, sir. It's Andy. His emotions are much stronger than mine. He and I talk about what needs to be done and then he thinks strongly on the topic. I use his emotion and focus on that. It's stronger that way, I can tell the difference, sir," George answered honestly, as if talking with Pete's grandfather.

"Hmm, again your team twists our perceptions and traditions. We never thought of that," he said, thinking on George's answer.

"That's OK, sir, you probably haven't broken as many rules in your entire life as we did in our first rotation, sir," George said, a little sheepishly.

"Probably not, George, probably not," he said and then turned toward Frank and Pete.

"You have all done very well. Keep up your concentration and focus. You are dismissed to go dinner as I think Senior Viceroy Petrosky has them all quite worried by now," he said, looking off into the air and nodding.

They left David Lu standing in the dome and ran out the doors, turning right toward the dining hall. Senior Viceroy Petrosky was pretending to enter the dining hall. The cadets and captains were doing their best to discourage him from entering and scaring the other captains. Most captains were not used to seeing CORE officers and certainly not a Senior Viceroy and two Inner Circle officers in person.

"George, Pete, stop him, he wants to," Sara said, pleading.

"I will leave you now," he said, smiling.

Instantly, he was gone in a flash of white light with his two Inner Circle officers.

"What was that all about, sir?" Emily asked.

Pete and Frank glanced at each other then started to laugh so hard their sides hurt.

"I am certainly glad to see it still works on you," Pete said through his laughter.

"What, sir?" Andy asked, turning to stare at Pete and Frank.

"Grandfather was the distraction!" George said, smiling.

"Man, he's good, sir, ah, he's good!" Andy said, shaking his head.

They all laughed as they entered the busy dining hall. No one even noticed them coming in late for dinner. Unlike the cadet dining hall with circular tables set up for one team at each table, in the captains dining hall the silver tables were long, like picnic tables at a family reunion, and there were individual chairs that the captains moved around. The cadets red stripes turned blue as they entered the room.

"We've been promoted again George," Gus said, beaming as he started walking taller.

"Emily," George whispered and crinkled his eyebrow.

"I didn't do it. I thought about it, but I didn't do it," she whispered, holding George arm.

"It must be grandfather," George whispered back.

"From now on you will eat in here with our teams," Pete signed.

The cadets all nodded; however, they missed their friends in the red sector.

"This whole growing-older, getting-more-responsibility thing is bumming me out," Andy signed.

"We can do this," Sara whispered, leaning in close to Andy and holding his hand.

George covered their thoughts. They liked Pete, Frank, and the others; they just wanted some independent time with cadets their own age, even if they couldn't talk about where they had been or what they had done.

"Pete, where have you been?" one of the other captain's asked.

"Training of course," Nick replied quickly, covering for their team.

"For Sport again? No wonder you're champions!" another captain said enthusiastically.

"Yes, we're training hard. We heard there was some strong competition this rotation," Nick added, rubbing his shoulder for effect.

After dinner, they all walked to the blue alcove.

"Anna, how do you get to the officer's library?" Frank asked quietly, when the door closed.

Anna blushed. "You mean by which way, sir?" she asked, giggling.

"By walking?" Frank pressed, crinkling his forehead.

Anna blushed again. "I don't actually know how to get there that way, sir. It's not exactly on anyone's pad map, sir," she replied, giggling again.

The cadets all grinned.

"OK, so how do you know how to get there?" Frank asked further, a little frustrated by their odd humor.

"Like this," she replied and leaned over, touching the floor with her finger.

A spiral port door spun into place. Emily twisted her hand and the port spun open. The captains were surprised. They had never thought of looking in the floors for doorways to other levels of the station.

Andy was the first one through the door. Niels and Nick followed quickly behind Andy. They helped the others onto the dome supports on the small dome below the alcove. On the dome floor, Anna made a second spiral port and Emily opened it. Through it, the cadets and captains dropped onto the upper balcony of the officer's library once again.

George motioned forward and they followed him around the carved wooden balcony and down the spiral wooden stairs to the main reading floor.

"Cadet Hawkins, I see you brought company with you this time," their translucent librarian said, smiling as she glided up to them on the main floor of the officer's library.

"Yes, ma'am. This is part of our triad, ma'am," George said and paused. "Ma'am, our last visit was less than honest. Please, forgive us our error in judgment," he added, lowering his head and the other cadets followed his lead.

"Apology accepted, Cadet Hawkins. Please sit here," she said kindly, her translucent robes turning a reddish color.

Her graceful hand motioned in the air as if floating through liquid toward the long wooden table in the center of the library. Soft blue leather chairs lined the sides of the long table.

"Every other evening, you will come here. Your books will be placed out for you. When you are done, you may leave. However, there will be no stray thoughts or reading of unapproved materials. Am I clear?" she said firmly, her robes shimmering white to red as the cadets and captains passed by her.

"Yes, ma'am," they answered in chorus.

"Cadet Jhang, Cadet Millar, in the future, I would prefer you use the library doors instead of the ceilings," she added, raising an eye at the girls.

"Yes, ma'am," they replied, lowering their heads again.

"Your pads will now show you how to properly enter the officer's library," she said, looking serious.

Under their uniform sleeve, their pads glowed a warm red.

"Thank you, ma'am," Anna and Emily replied, dipping their heads again.

The librarian's head twisted up, then, she looked at the captains and cadets again.

"The others have arrived. Please sit and I will bring them to you," she said and left them.

Their mouths were still hanging open as they sat down on the soft blue leather and wooden chairs. Books rose in front of them from the top of the long wooden table.

"Nothing is every what it seems, sir," George said, staring at the books on the table.

"No, George, it's not," Frank agreed.

"Do you really think she'd hurt us if we read something else, sir?" Gus asked, a little curious about what they were reading.

"Worse, she'd make us leave the library!" Emily whispered emphatically.

George stared at Emily. "You really need to get out more, Emily," he replied, sliding his arm over her shoulder.

A high whistle whispered through the air. The captains and cadets jumped up. Toma, Cal, Tillie, Sheta, Darri, and Gabe came walking in behind their librarian. Everyone smiled and spoke not a word.

"Please be seated and do try and remember this is a library," she said firmly.

She left them all sitting along the long wooden table. George, Pete, Frank, and Toma had a link the moment their librarian was out of view. In a few minutes, Toma, Cal, and the others understood what had been going on.

"We were warned not to contact you when you were missing," Toma said seriously.

"It's the hardest thing we have ever had to do," Sheta whispered to the cadets.

"We missed you all so much," Darri added as she sat down next to Cal.

"We were afraid you would be in danger if we created a link," Cal added, and then twisted his head staring at Andy, Nick, and Niels.

Nick waved him off and Cal nodded. Their explanation of their odd injuries would have to wait for later. However, Cal was sure it had something to do with Andy's more specialized training.

"We are happy Frank and Pete were able to find you," Tillie added.

"We never thought of following your tribute markers," Darri said, pleased they were all together.

Soon Gus and Rachael closed their link and they all set about the business of reading the books the librarian had set out for them. They weren't half bad. Andy read about armaments with Cal, Nick, and Niels and about the red energy spheres.

Andy had not said what really happened the evening Niels and Nick had dragged him off on the transport ship, but whatever it was Andy had changed. It wasn't from the cuts and bruises either, it was something else, something significant, maybe a defining moment, maybe not. Now, they were in it together that was for sure.

Niels and Nick were the only ones who could have separated Andy from George and they did. Andy changed and grew. Andy could never tell George about the anger inside of him. George would never be able to understand. Nick and Niels knew, and they knew how to make him face his fear and come to terms with his past and his present responsibilities.

Sara, Gus, Han, and the others had books that captured their imaginations too. Sara read about mixing herbs and chemicals with Rachael, Lucita, and Darri. While Gus, Han, Sven, and Gabe read about ingredients to add energy to foods to prevent harm and strengthen their focus. Gus finally understood the chemicals that made the drones and how it controlled them. He shared what he knew with the captains and together they searched for a way to cook it out of the food so it could not hurt them again.

The books were captivating each captain and cadet. The words were alive and told them stories of the universe, of how it had existed for millions of years. George looked around. The others were happy and intrigued.

However, he was bored as his book was the history of the known galaxies. Information he already knew. He had read it in the book of the prophecy. His head hit the table. Pete bumped him on one side and Toma bumped him on the other. Frank glared at him across the table.

"I have read all of this before. I need something new I haven't read, sir," George muttered to himself.

"It's OK to reread a good book," Pete whispered.

"This is the history of the universe. I have it memorized from, well let's say, from before. It didn't change from the last time I read it, sir," George signed.

"Patience is a virtue," Toma whistled.

"It's overrated if you ask me, sir," George muttered.

"Is there a problem, Cadet Hawkins?" the translucent librarian asked, standing behind him.

They all jumped ~ a little startled. They didn't even notice her arrival.

"Is the book incorrect?" she asked.

"No, ma'am. The book is fine. It's well, I have read all of this before, ma'am," George said, looking up sadly.

"Hmm, and you remember it from before?" she asked.

"Yes, ma'am," he said, hopeful for something new.

"Odd, that you would remember it. I would have thought, hmm. Let me get you another and the rest of you, do you remember the contents of your books as well?" she asked kindly, looking at all the captains and cadets.

"No, ma'am. We are all fine. Thank you," Toma answered for the others.

When they were all together, Toma was their leader. George never asked why. Once they had become a triad, it was that way from the beginning. It didn't bother him. It was more of a curiosity thing; a mystery to solve another day.

"As you wish," their librarian replied, and George's book sank into the tabletop.

A moment later, their librarian slipped a book onto the table in front of George. The book was older than the first and written in a character language. He turned back the worn, red-leather cover and started reading it as if it was his native tongue. It was the history of Chen Lo, of how the ancient art was discovered and brought to life. It told how Chen Lo brought balance to the universe. Yin and yang, good and evil always in balance was all George could think of.

An hour passed and then another. He read of how the ancient peoples of many worlds had discovered the power and strength within the motions. Some had learned to control it and some had nearly destroyed themselves with it. He came to a narrow passage only one paragraph long. He couldn't quite read the words as his head hit the book with a thud.

"They lasted longer than most," their librarian said, gliding up to the captains and cadets.

"It is their strength of will within them, Madam Librarian," Senior Viceroy Petrosky said kindly.

"Yes, you are right," she said, smiling.

"It has not been seen it in many centuries," Senior Viceroy Petrosky added, nodding.

"Yes, they are most unique. Will they be back?" she asked.

"Yes, however, I think George has read enough in this book for now," he whispered, sliding the Chen Lo book George had been reading from his hand.

"You should know he remembered his first book's contents," the librarian said kindly.

"Hmm, interesting that he should remember the history of the universe. Nonetheless, no more of this book. They are still too young," he replied seriously, and a little concerned that George could recall the words of the prophecy.

"As you wish," the librarian replied.

In a flash of white light, the captains and cadets were gone.

Chapter 19

GREATEST FEAR

Pete was sitting at the silver table in their sleeping room the next morning. Andy rolled over and collided heads with George as they stood up.

"Hey, what are you doing up?" George asked.

"Wouldn't want to miss cereal for breakfast, you know," Andy said, smiling his fake smile.

Pete slid two bowls toward the cadets.

"What did you learn about in your second book, George?" Pete asked casually.

"You made it through two books. Man, I barely made it halfway through my first book!" Andy said surprised.

"Oh, not exactly two books. I traded my first book for something I hadn't yet read," George replied, scooping up his cereal.

"What was your first book?" Andy asked.

"The history of the universe from the prophecy scroll," George replied, as if it was no big deal.

"How did you know you had read the history of the universe before? I thought that information was taken from us?" Emily asked, sitting next to George.

"Perhaps it was only hidden until you were older and could understand the information better," Pete replied, looking for an answer for the overly curious cadets.

"How'd we get here, sir?" Andy asked, scooping more cereal into his mouth.

"The usual way," Pete replied, grinning.

"Cereal, I presume, for breakfast, sir?" Emily said, swallowing hard.

"As you request," Pete said, sliding a bowl to Emily.

The others sat down in their usual seats.

"Where are we going today, sir?" Anna asked.

"Colonel Payate's training, Anna," Pete replied, not actually saying what Colonel Payate taught.

"What type of training are we going to be taught in Colonel Payate class, sir?" Emily asked.

"Well stated, cadet," Pete said and Emily smiled.

"Colonel Payate will instruct you in first aid and basic survival of sorts," he answered.

After a breakfast of officer's cereal, they left the sleeping room and quietly followed Pete down the corridor. However, it wasn't the red cadet corridor they had been expecting. Instead of red cadets, the corridor was filled with blue, yellow, and green captains. The stripe on their sleeves were still blue. They hadn't even noticed.

"Why are we here?" Andy signed; however, George shook his head.

"Observe, watch, know where we are," George signed behind his back.

George slipped up next to Pete. "Chen Lo, sir."

"What?" Pete asked.

"You asked what I had been reading. I read the history of Chen Lo, sir," George answered.

"What do you think?" he pressed.

"It is a great power placed in the hands of very few. I think it has destroyed a great many civilizations, sir," George said somberly.

"Perhaps, it is the only thing keeping us free from the evil," Pete said.

George didn't hear Pete. He was lost in thought again. Pete turned and walked into a classroom and motioned for George and the others to sit at an empty table between Niels and Nick. Pete sat with his team as Colonel Payate entered the room. The captains all stood up and Andy lifted up George.

"Be seated, captains," Colonel Payate said.

With their holographic projector bars on, Toma and his team looked like Calshene captains and sat behind George. They were once again surrounded by their captains ~ yes, very safe.

"Captains, you will be entering the station caves for training today. There will be three challenges within the caves. You will need to solve all three challenges to be allowed to return to the sector corridors. The challenges for each team are designed to confront your team's weaknesses and for you to overcome them," Colonel Payate said firmly.

Toma, Pete, and Frank weren't happy with this challenge. They didn't want their cadets wandering around in the caves of Asteria alone and especially with a challenge designed to confront their weaknesses.

The Colonel waved her hand over the computer terminal and two archways opened into the caves on the back wall of the classroom. She motioned team after team through the archways. She motioned Toma's team, then Frank's team, then George's team, and finally Pete's team. Pete turned to say something to Colonel Payate; however, she raised her hand before he could utter a word.

"The play is in motion. Fulfill your rolls," she said firmly.

Nick pulled Pete into the cave and the door closed, vanishing into the wall.

"What was that about?" Kate asked.

"I don't know. Colonels aren't usually cryptic. Actually, anything but cryptic," Nick replied.

"We need to find them," Pete said.

"What about the challenges?" Karmen asked.

"I'm sure this is one of our greatest fears for us," Pete said.

Jennifer and Karmen laid out a standard search pattern for their team. Nick tried to form a link with Niels and Cal but couldn't.

"They're blocking us," Nick signed.

"Can they do that?" Jennifer asked.

"Apparently, they can," Nick replied.

"What does our standard training say we should do?" Pete asked.

Rachael slid out her pad and recited protocol to the team as they started to run.

"Then that is the last thing we should do?" Pete signed.

Andy half-carried George into the cave, expecting another team to follow right behind them. No one entered after them as the archway in the cave wall closed.

"Something is wrong with George," Andy said, setting him down on the ground.

"Maybe it is one of our weaknesses," Emily said, kneeling next to George with Sara.

"Yes, Emily, I agree. We do all depend on each other's strengths and so haven't developed those strengths within ourselves," Andy said, taking over leading their team.

"There is nothing that says we can't switch rolls and practice each other's skills," Gus suggested.

"You're right, Gus, there isn't," Andy replied.

"However, I'm not sure we are prepared enough since we're not actually captains, you know," Sara added.

"I don't think we will ever be prepared enough, captains or not," Emily answered.

"OK, so who needs to practice what?" Andy asked, looking at everyone. "Anna, you need to lead and make the team decisions," Andy said.

"Me!" Anna gasped, as her face went blank.

"Oh ya, you!" the cadets replied together and laughed.

"Gus, how about the navigation thing; and Emily, you can feed us and practice healing. Sara, you can defend, and I'll talk with the walls and the wind until we find a computer. So Emily, how do you talk with the walls?" Andy asked with a grin.

They laughed out loud again. It was funny and yet, rather serious, they did need to practice each other's skills.

"Sara, I mean, Emily, how is George doing?" Anna asked, as her first leader task.

"It is like he is asleep," Emily answered.

"Andy make a link with George, Gus can get you out for now," Anna said, giving her team orders.

"Sure Anna," Andy said, forming a small yellow sphere in his hand and Emily lifted up George's palm. Their link was made.

"Nothing, I get nothing," Andy said, shaking his head.

Sara placed her hand over Emily's and then over George's forehead.

"He's there. He's in a deep sleep of some sort," she said.

"What is our first greatest fear, Andy?" Anna asked.

"That one of us will be taken or destroyed before their time," Andy replied.

"So we have found our first challenge," Anna said.

"How do we solve it?" Gus asked.

"We already did, we changed places," Sara replied.

"Now we need to finish the other two challenges before Pete, Frank, and Toma burst arteries looking for us. Which way, Gus or Andy?" Anna asked, shaking her head.

Emily and Anna knew; however, they had to let the others figure it out for themselves.

"This way," Gus said, twisting his pad in his hand and pointing the wrong way through the cave.

Andy hugged the cave wall. "Thanks."

Emily lowered her head, giggling. They took off running with Gus reading Anna the directions from his pad. Andy carried George slung over his shoulder and Sara watched their backs.

"Emily, what is our second greatest fear?" Anna asked, as they ran.

"Losing our triad, Anna?" Emily said sadly.

"But we have already done that. Do you remember what happened?" Anna asked.

"Yes," George answered, and the cadets skidded to a stop.

"Hey, how long have you been awake?" Andy asked, setting George down.

"Only a few moments; however, I could hear all of your decisions. Excellent and no, we aren't changing back. I'll learn to talk to walls too," George said, laughing and hugging the cave wall with Andy.

Emily smiled, the cave wall creatures were happy, confused, but happy.

"OK, so let's go back to losing our triad," Anna said, trying to lead and refocus their team again.

"Anna, can you find our triad?" Sara asked. "I mean like George does in his mind with his thoughts."

"I don't know how, Sara," Anna replied and then stared at George.

"Ground, we are going to sit down now. Please don't cover over us," George said, staring at the ground.

"George, what are you doing?" Emily asked.

"I'm doing what you do so we are safe, Emily," George said, and sat down on the ground next to Anna, placing his hands on her shoulder and Sara's shoulder as the dust swirled around them.

"Anna, clear your mind, use Sara's strength to help reach out and find our triad in the energy of the universe. Their thoughts are there, sometimes they are a little hidden. Focus now," George said calmly, encouraging her.

Anna cleared her mind and Sara shared her strength, placing her hand on Anna's other shoulder.

"I can sense them, I can. Oh dear, Pete is going to... It's gone. I could sense them. They 're OK; although, Pete really needs to calm down," Anna said, a little worried.

"What is our third challenge, Anna?" Andy asked, gently lifting Anna and Sara from the ground.

"Well, our first challenge was losing our team and our second was losing our triad," Anna said, and then stopped, thinking.

"So our third must be losing something else, right?" Gus asked.

"Yes, but losing what?" Emily asked.

"How about losing to the evil?" Andy suggested.

"No, we did that and overcame that already," Anna replied, as if it was no big deal.

George lowered his head, he knew the answer and couldn't bear to tell them for fear it would come true as their other two fears already had come true.

"Perhaps it is losing of our innocence because we now know," Sara suggested.

They were stuck. They couldn't imagine a third challenge they hadn't already overcome. Andy stared at George and Anna saw the stare.

"George, what do you know?" Anna asked softly.

"The answer, Anna, the answer," George replied sadly.

"Will you tell us?" she asked kindly.

"No," he said firmly.

"Then we are lost," Anna said, sighing.

"Are we really?" Gus said puzzling. "I mean no one said we all had to discover the answers, only that we had to find the challenges and resolve them," Gus added.

"Gus is right. George knows this challenge and has resolved it. He doesn't have to tell us," Anna said, agreeing with Gus's logic.

"This means we are done," Sara added, smiling, happy to be done.

"Which way is out, Gus?" she asked.

"Ah-oh yes, I forgot," Gus said and blushed.

"Andy, are you hungry?" she asked.

"How did you know?" Andy answered and his stomach rumbled.

Anna smiled. Gus pointed and they ran through the caves again following Gus.

"Will you ever tell us?" Andy asked George as they ran.

"No," George replied firmly.

"I can live with that," Andy replied.

George knew he could never tell his team the truth. Max was right, some information shouldn't be shared. Their greatest fear was the destruction of everyone they knew and loved and that it would be an accident. It was what David Lu had told grandfather.

Gus stopped running and Andy and George made a shaky archway and door. Emily stabilized it with a little twist of her wrist. Anna raised an eyebrow.

"We don't want to get hurt going through," she replied, stepping into the classroom they had been in earlier.

"Welcome back. You are the first and I must say you have finished in record time," Colonel Payate said, smiling.

"Thank you, sir," Anna replied.

"Is dinner ready, ma'am?" Andy asked, thinking it was late in the afternoon.

"Not yet, cadet. I will make the arrangements. You can wait in the blue alcove," she said; nonetheless, she had an odd look on her face.

"Thank you, ma'am," Anna replied.

They left the classroom; however, they knew they couldn't enter the blue alcove without Pete or his team. They were neither blue nor captains.

In a flash of white light, the Senior Viceroy appeared in the classroom after the door had closed.

"They traded places, sir," Colonel Payate said, nodding her head.

"It seems to work for them," the Senior Viceroy replied.

"Will they be safe now, sir?" she asked.

"Yes, they will be safer now," he replied, thinking about what the cadets had done.

"George knew the team's third fear and wouldn't tell the others. Why? Why didn't he share the burden, sir?" Colonel Payate pressed.

"It is not time," the Senior Viceroy replied cryptically.

"But I thought this training was to give them time to prepare," she pressed, worried they wouldn't be prepared if their greatest fear occurred.

"Their greatest fear must be must be something you do not prepare for," he replied, trying to be comforting.

"What fear could it be that you wouldn't prepare for?" she puzzled.

The Senior Viceroy disappeared without answering the question, only he and David Lu knew the truth about the power and energy this team could control.

"So where are we going?" George asked.

"What time is it?" Anna asked.

"It's only 30 minutes after we entered the classroom this morning!" Emily answered stunned.

"It sure seemed like a lot longer," Gus said, rubbing his stomach.

"We have the whole day free!" Sara said, spinning around in the corridor.

Andy reached out and stopped her spin, shaking his head. "Not here," he whispered then held her close around her waist.

"A day free on a station that hates us. This can't be good," Gus added pessimistically.

It will be OK, Gus," Anna whispered and he wrapped his arm around her.

"What about Sport. Maybe we can get in some practice time? After all, we are captains," Andy suggested, pointing to his blue sleeve.

"Who do we ask?" Sara asked, looking at George.

"Anna, who do we ask?" George asked.

"I thought we were done with that game," Anna replied.

"Anna?" George said, his voice suddenly turning serious.

"Yes, yes, of course, practice, practice. Colonel Moawk?" Anna replied, really wanting the 'change roles' game to end.

"Gus leave a message for Pete, Frank, and Toma. When they get out of the caves so they will know where we are," Anna said. "Sara, please call Colonel Moawk and ask if we can practice Sport somewhere," Anna ordered and George smiled.

"You smile now. What happens if the vines don't like us?" Andy quipped.

"I didn't think of that," George signed back to Andy.

"Colonel Moawk said the only thing open is the main Sport arena and we have permission to use it," Sara replied with a smile.

Gus guided them through the corridors and only ended up at dead ends twice. When they made it to the food court, they knew they were close.

"This whole guiding thing is harder than it looks," Gus said, sighing.

Chapter 20

SPORT PRACTICE

The cadets entered the empty Sport arena, descending the steep steps to the Slugamie floor below.

The cadets stood at the edge of the Slugamie ground cover and stared up at the field of hanging vines. An automatic ball launcher hung from the ceiling, and a second launcher rose up from the floor in the center of the arena.

"The arena looks so enormous from down here," Andy said, looking around the Sport arena.

"All three of our triad teams have competed here and won," George said in awe, pausing for a few minutes as if seeing the Sport arena for the first time.

"Our triad teams really are amazing," Emily whispered and the other nodded.

"George, please talk to the Slugamie so we can get to the vines," Anna asked, kindly looking at the ground.

"Slugamie we want to walk to the vines," he said, standing on the edge of the field.

"George, you will need to touch the Slugamie to communicate with it," Emily whispered.

He reached down and the Slugamie swirled up and grab onto his arm, pulling him under the surface of the ground. A moment later, his head popped up through the Slugamie. His arms failing around as he bounced along in the Slugamie.

"Help, it's tickling me!" he yelled, laughing as he submerged again.

Andy ran in after him and started laughing as the Slugamie swallowed him whole.

"Emily, save us, it won't stop! George will laugh to death!" he yelled, laughing before submerging again with George.

"There are worse ways to die, oh honestly," Emily said, laughing.

Emily glanced at Anna and she nodded like George. Emily didn't even touch the Slugamie as it swirled around her legs. A rumble of the ground and George and Andy popped up like Daisies!

"Took you long enough," Andy said, coughing a little.

However, one glance from George and Andy apologized.

"Thanks, Emily, guess it's not so easy," he said kindly.

"Learning something new never is easy, not really," she said nodding.

The Slugamie hardened and pushed George and Andy onto a small path it formed for them. The cadets walked over to the vines and climb up. They swung around getting a sense of the vines and the arena and then divided into teams.

"No help from the vines, Emily," Gus said, watching Emily twist graceful around on the vines.

"Only an honest game, Gus," Emily replied, nodding.

Anna, Emily, and Sara wanted to face George, Andy, and Gus with only two rules. Gus and Andy can't throw from more than half the field and not at their maximum strength.

They started out at different heights on the vines as the ball was launched. Emily and George both dove from their vines, racing for the ball. George nabbed it as Emily flipped over, skimming the top of the Slugamie. For anyone else, the Slugamie would have reached up; however, it seemed to dip and bend, preventing Emily from coming out of play.

George threw a wobbly under handed ball to Gus. Sara swung by as if she were a trapeze artist, snagging the ball and flipping it to Anna before Gus knew he had missed the ball. Anna tossed the ball to Emily as she scrambled up another vine. She spun and threw the ball to Sara.

She caught the ball and let loose with her hardest shot for the goal. Andy dropped down from the rafters of the dome and caught the ball mid swing with a thud in his chest. He flipped over, throwing the ball to Gus, while hanging by his feet upside down. Gus wound up and batted the ball toward the goal. Anna swung gracefully across in front of Gus. With one arm, she grabbed and tossed the ball to Emily for an easy score, behind George's back.

Gus hooted and hollered. "I didn't think you could do it," he said.

"I guess we have been schooled," Andy said, laughing.

"Hey, what are you captains doing here?" came a yell from the floor of the arena.

George stared at Anna. She shook her head. He raised his eyebrows and nodded toward the purple cadets or captains or officers? Anna rolled her eyes and slid down her vine with the rest of their team following.

"What are you doing here? Captains?" the team leader asked, strutting onto the Sport field.

"Practicing Sport. What are you doing here?" Anna asked kindly.

"That's junior officer, sir, to you, captain," he said, pressing back and raising his voice.

"Yes sir. Practicing Sport, sir," Anna said, with more sarcasm in her voice than actual respect.

"It's time for you to leave now. We've come to practice," the junior officer said, arrogantly motioning his team onto the field.

"No sir. We have the Sport arena scheduled with Colonel Moawk, sir," Anna replied, trying to be kind and remain calm.

"Well, I've just unscheduled it, captain. Now leave," the junior officer said firmly, his face pressed up to Anna's face.

Not a hair separated them ~ nose to nose. He towered over Anna, trying to intimidate her. Oddly, she didn't seem to care. He didn't intimidate her one bit. She knew intimidation from the scanners on Mahadean on their last rotation and this junior officer wasn't even close.

George leaned back and smiled. She was growing and learning to lead. He knew inside she was terrified, and yet, on the outside, she was as cool as could be. He helped her calm her fear so she could remain focused and not lose track of the goal.

"I don't suppose you will leave so we can finish our practice, sir?" Anna asked nicely.

"You have that right, little lady," he said, trying to insult her and rattle her into making a mistake.

"Then how about if we play you for the arena. First team to score a point gets to stay and practice," Anna proposed, looking for a compromise.

"You play us," the junior officer second said, laughing.

"You're nothing but a bunch of scrawny captains and young looking ones at that," another junior officer said, laughing.

"You're no match for junior officers," the lead junior office said, stepping back to stare at the captains.

"Then maybe we can learn a thing or two on tactics and technique. Automatic ball launcher OK for you?" Anna said, waving her hand as the cadets took to their vines. She turned and stared at George. "This has gone on long enough," she signed.

"OK," he signed.

A quick glance and the team knew they were back to their standard roles.

"And Gus and Andy, throw as hard as you want," Anna added.

They grinned.

"Honest game everyone," Gus added, and yet, inside he was worried.

This team of junior officers was brutes; not at all what they had imagined junior officers to be like. The junior officers took their places on the vines.

"I see you favor starting at different levels too, sir," Andy said, poking fun at the junior officer across from him.

"Ya, I'm going to different level you, captain," the other team's second said angrily.

"Yes sir. As you wish, sir," Andy replied, mocking the junior officer.

The ball launched and Andy and a junior officer dove for the ball. Andy got there first and accidently bounced the ball off the junior officer's head and into Gus's arms. The junior officer took a swing at Andy; however, Emily snapped Andy's vine away and the junior officer spun on his vine. Gus threw the ball behind him to Sara and she wound up and threw the ball across the arena to Anna.

The lead junior officer dove at Anna, clipping her in the shoulder and knocking the ball free. Andy rolled and caught it inches from the floor of the arena. He was sure the Slugamie had dipped to keep him from touching. He threw the ball hard, straight up to the top of the dome. George was hanging from the arena's supports and caught it. Quickly, he threw it to Sara. Again, she threw the ball to Anna.

This time Anna was ready for the hit from the junior officer and flicked the ball away with her vine. The junior officer turned to see the ball fly by and crashed into another junior officer. The thud echoed through the dome as the two junior officers fought to regain their control as they slide down their vines. Emily threw the ball as hard as she could, swooshing the ball through the other goal, passed one of the junior officer defenders.

"You'll pay for that, captain!" one of the junior officers yelled, threatening the cadets.

"That's a game, sir and I believe we have won. Now, please leave, sir," Anna said firmly.

"We will leave when we decide to leave, captain," the lead junior officer said angrily.

A new ball dropped from the ceiling launcher, and Gus dove for it spinning his vine as he dropped. He caught the ball as a junior officer rammed into his shoulder. Gus cringed on his vine as he climbed back up with the ball. Each hand grab sending a burst of pain through his arm and shoulder. With a short toss, he handed the ball off to Andy.

Andy took off like a shot with the ball, leaping from vine to vine towards the opposing goal. One of the junior officers grabbed Andy's foot and snapped him loose from his vine. Sara grabbed the ball from Andy's hand and tossed it to Anna for the goal.

"You little worm!" one of the junior officers yelled, as he twisted Andy's foot harder, trying to rip him from his vine.

Andy broke free from the junior officers grasp as another junior officers lost his temper and swung at Anna. This time he connected with her back and she fell from her vine. Gus swooped in at incredible speed, catching her mid-fall with his good arm.

"I don't know how you do it. That really hurts," Anna whispered.

"You'll be OK, Anna," Gus whispered.

"Been better. I guess we aren't done yet," Anna said and flipped over, hanging on the vine next to Gus trying to catch her breath.

"George, where are you?" Pete thought in their new link.

"Main Sport arena," he replied, and closed the link with help from Gus.

"It's Pete, they made it out. I told him where we were so they won't worry," George relayed to his team in their link.

A third ball launched; this time from the ground launcher. The leader of the junior officers caught the ball, knocking Emily off her vine in the process. George grabbed her arm and swung her around in mid-air to a new vine. Quickly, they hurried up the vines to help the others.

The junior officers were trying to hit the captains more than make a goal this time. They tossed the ball back and forth, trying to set the captains up for a hit. George and the others knew the game and backed out as the junior officers swooped and dove at them. A junior officer flipped over and slammed directly into George. George took the full impact of the junior officer's body. On his return swing, the junior officer half kicked the ball from George's his hand. It hit his chest hard and then raced upward, gashing George's forehead. He spun on his vine, gasping for air as a second junior office kicked at the ball as it fell next to George. The officer missed the ball and connected with George's leg, gashing him above the knee.

Emily caught the falling ball. Two junior officers were waiting for the opportunity for another captain to catch the ball. They collided with her the instant she touched the ball, crushing her between them. The cracking of her ribs echoed through the arena. Emily fell back letting go as George free fell down vine to vine from nearly the top of the vines to catch her. His hands started bleeding from the friction as he dropped. He caught her barely ten feet above the floor of the arena. He held her in his arms, his hands crushing the vine to slow their decent.

"Let me rest, George, I can't help you now," she whispered, a few feet about the Slugamie covered floor.

He laid her gently in the Slugamie. It curled gently around her body not knowing what to do as there were no medics below to care for her wounds. George climbed the vine with amazing speed. He was angry and struggling to control his rage. He hardly noticed the blisters on his hands or the blood running down his leg and forehead.

One of the junior officers threw the ball near Gus and Andy. Without thinking, Andy dove in front of a throw to stop it from hitting Sara while her back was turned. The ball handle gashed Andy's face and ricocheted across the arena to Anna. Blood ran down one side of his face, dripping onto his shoulder. Gus turned and leap from vine to vine toward Anna and the ball. Anna grabbed the fly ball and flip off her vine onto the next vine, tossing the ball into the goal.

A junior office slammed into Anna the moment she let go of the ball. She screamed, her ribs crushing as she let go of her vine. Gus dove from his vine and caught her mid-air. He swooped to a new vine and Anna grabbed onto the vine trying to regain her breath. The junior officer who had knocked Anna from the other vine was still angry. He free fell from his vine and landed on Gus's back, stripping Gus from his vine. Gus spun wildly around trying to grab another vine. His hand caught a vine and his body twisted and snapped with his momentum. His body rolled and another vine twisted around his leg. "Snap" the vine tightened around Gus, his leg fractured as he dangled in the air. He was a sitting duck!

"STOP! We are up by three points, sir?" Anna yelled, at the lead junior officer three vines from her. "We won, get out!"

The junior officer only yelled at the captains.

Another ball launched and they were in play again. The lead junior officer swung in for the ball, using all of his weight. George flew back. Still on his vine, Gus reached down and pulled George up to another vine as the junior officer tried to plant his fist into George's body on his return swing. Sara skated down the vine next to the junior officer and stripped the ball from him, kicking it high into the dome ceiling and Andy's waiting arm.

Gus flipped over and hoisted himself up by his arms alone, his muscle straining on the vine as he climbed into position, avoiding the junior officers. George rolled around the lead junior officer as Andy threw his rocket ball across the arena. The second junior officer dove on Andy's out stretched arm. He crushed Andy's shoulder, twisting his arm nearly around. The cracking sound echoed around the arena as Andy crumpled on his vine in pain. A quick second hit and Andy's collarbone was broken. Like Gus's leg, Andy could no longer use his arm.

The pain was excruciating, and yet, for some reason they played on. Someone had to be influencing them to play, even though they were badly hurt. However, the cadets didn't know it.

A junior officer pushed Gus forward and the ball hit him squarely in the chest knocking the breath from him. George grabbed for Gus again, sliding the length of the vines to catch him, his hands cover in blood from friction burns on the vines a second time.

Another junior officer drove after George and knocked off his vine. George scrambled to grab onto another vine as Gus hit the Slugamie hard. The Slugamie rose to meet Gus and tried to cushion his fall.

Pete, Frank, Toma, and their teams entered the Sport arena expecting to see their cadets having fun on the vines as Colonel Moawk had granted them practice time. To their horror, they saw their cadets crushed and beaten by older stronger junior officers ~ blood covering their once white uniforms. The teams raced down the steep arena stairs hardly touching every third step. Cal called for security as the other Thoreans flew down to Emily and Gus on the Slugamie.

"Friend, friend," Emily whispered to the Slugamie, as it swirled around Toma, Cal, Sheta, Tillie, and Darri's feet.

Pete, Frank, Nick, and Niels climbed the vines with remarkable speed, blocking the junior officer's attacks. High in the dome the junior officer threw the ball and Niels intercepted it as two junior officers swung in for the hit. Toma and Cal flicked their vines from below and the junior officers flew from the vines, landing on the clear roof over hangs that protected the crowds from falling dome and players. Gabe, Niels, and Nick pulled the junior officers off the ceiling supports, dropped them into the Slugamie.

"What's wrong, need your captain buddy's to come to your rescue?" the lead junior officer yelled, and jeered at the captains.

"Stand down, sir!" Toma yelled at the junior officer leader, his voice echoing around the arena.

"Back off, captain," the lead junior officer yelled at Toma.

"Stand down, sir!" Toma whistled in Thorean, so loud some of the wall behind the dome supports crumbled.

"Why? Did you come for the same treatment as your little captain buddies," said the second junior officer, jeering at the new captains.

"They are not captains, they're cadets, and they have the rights to the Sport arena, sir," Frank yelled back angrily.

"Only if I say so, captain," the lead junior officer yelled back.

"Stand down, sir!" Toma repeated again, as the others hurried around, picking up the bleeding cadets.

"Who do you think you are?" their second asked, taunting the new captains.

"Stand down, Officer Kershj!" boomed a voice from the Viceroy's box.

They all looked up to see a Viceroy standing in the box, motioning them to the ground. Security officers came rushing into the Sport arena and the Slugamie released the two junior officers it had trapped. Quickly, the other junior officers were captured and taken away.

However, the cadets paid an awful price for standing their ground. Medics ran into the arena to get Emily and Gus, lying on the Slugamie. High in the air, Niels unwrapped Sara from the vines and carefully carried her to the ground. Her arm was broken and blood was dripping from her sleeve. Somehow, she had continued to play using her feet and her good arm.

Andy flipped over and Anna caught him with her legs. Her shoulders were badly bruised and she could only slow their decent. Cal and Toma caught them above the Slugamie, handing them to the waiting arms of the medics.

George flipped over and started to descend. As his vine untwisted, his leg became visible. Blood stained his right leg as if it had been stabbed with a sharp object. His arms were covered blood from his hands, and blood dripped from the gash on his forehead. Medics whisked the last cadets away the instant George was in their hands. The security guards took the junior officers away as the captains raced to the CORE hospital wing, following the medics.

"Why not the cadet hospital wing? Cal signed as they ran.

"Because of who they are. They are not like other cadets," Frank whispered.

"True enough," Cal signed.

The CORE hospital archway wouldn't open for Pete and the others.

"Not this time!" Pete said, frustrated as he slid out his pad.

"What's up?" Niels asked, staring at Pete's pad.

"One of Emily's homemade specials," Pete said, raising his pad.

Instantly, the archway appeared and the door opened with ease. They took off running again, the thunder of their run filling the quiet corridors of the CORE hospital.

"In here," Toma whistled, loudly as the teams skidded by the cadet's room.

Toma and Cal had gone with the medic and were now standing at the entrance of the cadet's room. The doctors were slipping the cadets into the yellow healing tubes when Pete and the others entered the room.

"All of you out," a CORE doctor ordered.

However, they didn't move. Instead, they sat down, circling the cadet's healing tubes.

"And so our worst fears comes to life," Niels muttered.

"We leave them alone and they get hurt," Nick answered.

"Again," Cal added.

Pete, Frank, and Toma were in a link, talking with one of the station's Viceroys, not their fathers.

"How are the cadets?" the Viceroy asked worried.

"Not good, sir. Their spirits are strong; however, their bodies were beaten badly sir," Pete answered.

"What about the junior officers, sir?" Frank asked, trying to contain his anger.

"The junior officers will be severely reprimanded, captain," the Viceroy replied firmly.

"Reprimanded! What are you talking about? They nearly kill the cadets, sir!" Pete shouted in their link.

"A reprimand, that's nothing. It's hardly a slap on the wrist, sir," Toma added, yelling.

"It will stop them from being promoted with their class and send them to retraining. It is the most we can do, captains," the Viceroy answered sternly.

"Yes sir. We understand. Thank you, sir," Pete replied, lowering his voice.

They closed their link. The three captains sat in disbelief.

"How could junior officers nearly kill cadets and get away with only reprimands," Pete whispered, his anger welling inside him.

In the mean time, Lucita, Maria, Rachael, Karmen, Darri, Han, Sven, Jennifer, and Tillie sat on the floor weaving in and out between the cadets. They formed a healing link, while Kate distracted the medics, and Sheta and Gabe hid the thoughts from any others.

Pete, Frank, and Toma were angry; inside their rage was out of control. They may not have had as much power over the raw energy of the universe as George, but they were formidable opponents in their own right. Nick, Cal, and Niels felt the rage within their team leaders. The three seconds had matured and grown up knowing the rage and having to control it when protecting their teams. However, the three leaders had often been shielded from the truth of anger and rage. It clouds a person's judgment and can cause one to lose focus on the goal.

The three seconds circled their three lead captains and silently slid out staff weapons from their sleeves. Quickly, the seconds lengthened the staffs. Out of the corner of Pete's eye, he saw the movement and the three leaders spun around, facing their seconds. Instantly, the seconds twisted the staffs from vertical to horizontal. The ends touched and they all disappeared. The lead captains were out of control, screaming at Nick, Niels, and Cal for taking them away from the cadet's room. They didn't even notice they were in a room with glowing white walls.

"Nick, Niels, Cal, you have done well to bring them here. Lower your staffs and step back, out of the cube," the Senior Viceroy said calmly.

The seconds twisted their staffs to the vertical position and slid them back up their sleeves. Slowly, they backed out of the glowing white cube. Cal, Nick, and Niels remembered the glowing cube room from their previous rotation. They weren't actually sure how they got there, but, they knew they were in the Galactic council sector of the station.

The three lead captains raged and yelled ~ trapped within the glowing white cube. They wanted revenge and retribution against the junior officers that had hurt their cadets. This was one of their greatest fears and only hours after admitting it, their fear came true. It was too close to home for the lead captains.

"It is time for you to leave Cal, Nick, and Niels. We will take care of them now," the Senior Viceroy spoke, quietly from the outer edge of the all white room.

"No sir. They are our leaders and so they are our responsibility, sir," Cal said quietly.

"We need to know how to help them, sir," Niels added, nodding to Cal.

"We can't always depend on you being here or us being able to get to you sir," Nick answered, adding to their determination to stay with their leaders and help.

"You are all growing up so fast. You may stay," the Senior Viceroy replied kindly.

Two days later in the hospital room, George rolled over and bumped his head on the healing tube. Han stepped forward and helped the medic removed the glowing yellow tube.

"You are going to be alright, George, the others too," Han whispered.

He smiled weakly, as sharp pains reminding him of the wound in his leg and the vine burns on his hands.

"Maybe next time an older group of officers challenges you, you should back down until you can get some help," Gabe spoke quietly, yet sternly.

Chapter 21

RIGHT AND WRONG

George looked around the room. Many members of their triad were missing. He started to concentrate on his triad, especially Pete, Frank, and Toma.

"Now we'll have none of that, cadet," Viceroy Petrosky, Pete's dad, said, appearing in the room in a flash of white light.

The CORE medics and CORE doctors hurriedly backed out of the room.

"Your triad needs to rest," he said firmly.

The junior officers had ruthlessly beaten the cadets. The Viceroy was stunned by how badly the cadets looked, even after two days in the healing tubes.

"Sir, do you need us? Is something wrong, sir?" George whispered, trying to sit up.

"Calm yourself, cadet. Everything is fine. I am concerned for the welfare of you and your team. Can you walk with me?" he asked, his voice was still serious but softened a little.

George rolled over and Han helped him to his feet. The Viceroy motion for Gabe to get Andy out of his bed too. Senior Viceroy Petrosky, grandfather, had given the four seconds one primary rule. Andy, Nick, Niels, and Cal would never leave their firsts alone and unprotected, and Andy, like the others, wouldn't intentionally break this rule.

"Let's take Andy with us so he will not worry," the Viceroy said, staring at the other cadets.

"Yes sir," George whispered.

Gabe helped Andy to his feet and the Viceroy wrapped his arms around both boys. They seemed to limp less as they hobbled across the room to the smaller room off in the corner.

"Amazing," Gabe signed. Sven and Han nodded.

They entered a small room off the main hospital room and the Viceroy raised silver stools for them to rest on.

"George, what happened in the Sport arena two days ago?" the Viceroy asked firmly, yet, his voice was kind and calm.

"We finished our training early with Colonel Payate and got permission to go and practice Sport. The arena was the only place open, so Colonel Moawk scheduled it for us. Then these junior officers showed up and tried to intimidate us into leaving, sir," George said and then paused, he saw the error in their decision to stay.

"Why didn't you leave? You knew they were stronger than you. Your team was put in a position of unnecessary risk," Pete's dad said calmly.

George knew he wasn't pleased with their choices.

"We were right, sir. We had the Sport arena scheduled in our name, sir," Andy added, still a little angry.

"Yes, Andy, you were right. However, the question still remains, why didn't you leave and go get help from another officer or a Viceroy? You know many of them and you know they will come to you as quick as they can, if you call," Pete's dad asked, giving them alternative solutions that would not have put their team in danger.

"Yes sir," they replied in unison, lowering their heads.

"Sometimes, even if you're right, you need to back down. Being right didn't prevent the beating your team has taken?" he said, a little more firmly.

"No sir," they replied sheepishly.

"You're team is not the only one to have suffered from this unfortunate event," he said, changing the subject.

George snapped his head up, his eyes widened.

"Where are they? Why can't I sense them," George replied, panic in his voice.

"None of that, they must learn to deal with their anger and rage," the Viceroy replied firmly.

"We are the cause of that anger, our arrogance," George replied, lowering his head. Saddened by the trouble they had caused.

"We thought if we beat the junior officers they would back down and leave. They didn't. It just made them madder, more angry," Andy added, shaking his fist.

"George, Andy, you must learn that there are times to stand your ground and there are times when you need to get help. You must learn the difference," the Viceroy said, his voice calm and focused.

"Yes sir," they replied together, not knowing what else to say.

"Will they be OK?" George asked, worried about Toma, Pete, Frank, Cal, Nick, and Niels.

George couldn't sense them and only knew that all six of them were missing.

"It depends on them. This was ones of their greatest fears coming true. Their defense of you and your team is strong. They will need to come to terms with their rage in order to be released. They are still very angry. For now, let us return. The rest of your team is waiting for you," Pete's dad said and paused. "Remember, no more beatings, ask for help," he said, reinforcing his words.

Whether they realized it or not, George's team could control the raw energy of the universe and could have easily have destroyed the junior officers by mistake. Pete's dad was trying to make sure this incident didn't happen again. As sometimes, accidents do happen.

The teams were gathered around the cadets' beds when the boys returned to the main hospital room. Gabe and Han took George and Andy from the Viceroy and helped them into the room.

"We're sorry. We didn't mean to cause so much trouble for everyone," George and Andy said, lowering their heads to their triad captains, asking for forgiveness.

The other cadets followed. Here the team of the prophecy, the team that had saved the entire sector Galactic council and Thorean cadet station was apologizing to them. It amazed the captains, they stood around the cadets beds still focused on healing and calming their triad's minds.

"We need to help Pete, Frank, and Toma," George said, joining the captain's link as Gabe set him down on the chair next to his bed.

"No! Not yet, they're not ready," Gabe ordered firmly, surprising everyone with his forcefulness.

"They must deal with their rage or it will tear them apart," Han added more kindly, and yet, still serious.

"It is time to leave. I think everyone is hungry," Sheta said, changing the subject.

In the absence of the first and the second, Sheta took the lead for the triad with Jennifer and Kate as her seconds.

"Han, Sven, Gabe, any kitchen we might visit on our way back to the captains sector would be highly appreciated," she said kindly.

Han smiled as the captains lifted up the cadets. With cadets hanging between them, the triad aimed for the hospital room door.

"They are not ready to leave, captains," the CORE doctor ordered.

"Yes sir, they are. We will keep them safe while they finish healing, sir," Sheta ordered firmly and Jennifer and Kate nodded.

The CORE doctor shook his head, however, allowed them to leave handing Sheta bottles of medicine at the door. Out the door and down the corridor they went carrying the cadets between them. Sheta, Jennifer, and Kate opened archways and doors with twists of their wrists. Emily and Anna had never noticed before.

Gabe found a kitchen at the first captain sector they passed through. He, Han, and Sven had a meal fit for a king laid out before them in a short time. The captains set everything up while the cadets rested on the silver benches Sheta had raised from the floor. They ate every delicious bite. The guys were amazing cooks.

"I was hungrier than I thought I was," Gus said, leaning back and stretching.

"Gus, you're always hungry," Emily said, giggling weakly.

"Yes, but this was great food," Gus said and then his face twisted. "Food, oh ah, I need a tunnel hog. I forgot to feed someone, sir," he said, staring at Emily.

"Yes, yes that's right, Gus needs a tunnel hog, sir," Emily said, nodding her head.

"Maybe we could do it for you," Jennifer offered.

"No sir. Sid can do it. He knows what to do, sir," Gus said, making a quick decision.

"OK, our cryptic cadets. We'll get Sid to feed someone for you," Sheta said smirking oddly.

"It's a them, not a who, ma'am," Gus said, correcting her.

"As you wish, Gus," Rachael added, trying to keep Gus calm.

"We don't want anyone to go hungry," Darri added, with a funny look on her face.

The kitchen wall rumbled and Jennifer opened the slit in Sid's side. Gus laid six bottles of purple liquid inside Sid.

"You know what to do. Tell them not to drink it all at once," he whispered.

Sid bumped and left the cadets. Han, Gabe, and Sven stared at Gus and then at the bottles of purple liquid. Who could Gus possibly be feeding that would need that much purple liquid?

The captains cleaned up and nearly carried the cadets to their sleeping room in the captains sector. The captains dropped the cadets off and Jennifer raised a large silver easy chair and sat down, locking the doors after the others left. The cadets laid down to rest.

George couldn't sleep. His foolishness had caused his triad great pain. He thought of Max, and grandfather, and the beings of white light. Of all they had tried to teach them and how poorly they listened, so many teachers, so little listening. Each time there had been a price to pay when they reacted poorly or made poor choices.

It would be much easier if there was a list of do's and don'ts, when to do this and when to do that. Instead, they were learning some by listening and some by acting. When they were under attack, everything seemed so straightforward. Now, everything was different and oddly more difficult to make the right choices.

Grandfather was right. They needed to listen more and learn from others mistakes so they wouldn't repeat them. Still, it was so dull and boring most of the time. Don't adults understand that young people today get bored with just listening to instructors talk on and on about different subjects? George was sure the information they were teaching was good and that it was what they would need it to grow and survive in the changing galaxies. However, George didn't know how to stop making mistakes that put others in danger.

"Why Max? We hid in the open and I nearly got my team turned into drones. We returned to Asteria and our triad is hurt by our own stubbornness," George muttered.

Beads of sweat formed on George's head. He had to understand. Andy reached over to George and they were gone. As if in a dream, Andy and George were standing in the tunnel hog cave.

"What are you doing here child?" a being of white light asked, walking toward George and Andy, however, not fully solidifying so George wouldn't recognize her.

"We are looking for Max. Is he here?" George asked, lowering his head in respect.

"No child. You will find him among you," Tara said, kindly.

"Why?" George pressed.

"Why what, child?" Tara asked softly.

"Why is he among us, shouldn't he be here with you, healing? The evil is still strong," George asked, worried he could be easily hurt if he was weak.

"He makes his own choices, child. As do you?" Tara replied kindly.

"And if he dies because of us, how do we go on without him?" George asked sadly.

"You will adapt, you always do," Tara replied.

"I need to stop making mistakes, ma'am! I have to," George said, his voice falling off into a whisper.

"Making mistakes are a part of life. It often teaches strong lessons you will not forget," Tara replied, trying to comfort him.

"Why?" George asked; however, Tara did not answer his question.

"You must leave, child. The time is late for you," she said, motioning them toward the other cave.

"Can we come again?" George asked, searching for more answers.

"If it is your choice, child," Tara said and blew a white mist across them.

They awoke the next morning in their sleeping room with Gabe sitting at the table. All of their broken bones and gashes had been healed by healing medical tubes and their triads healing circle; however, the cadets were still weak and needed easier training for a few days, while they recovered.

"Where's Pete, sir?" Andy asked, standing up and gently moving his shoulder. It was sore but no longer broken.

"Not back yet," Gabe said, making circles in his bowl of cereal with his spoon.

He slid a bowl of cereal to each of them as George and Andy sat down.

"They're not going to make it out, are they, sir?" George asked.

"I don't know. They are still really angry. Maybe Andy can explain it better," Gabe said, glancing at Andy.

"It doesn't matter. It is our fault they are there," George said, flopping his spoon into his bowl.

Andy knew about the rage and anger. Nick and Niels had taught him a good lesson onboard the transport ship. He knew it was something George would never understand. The others slipped up to the table and ate their cereal in silence, staring at Gabe. He looked worried.

"Colonel Moawk wants us early today. We need to leave," he said quietly.

They finished and followed Gabe out into the corridor. The other captains were in Colonel Moawk's training dome when they arrived. David Lu stepped out of the small side room and walked over in front of the captains and cadets.

"Today's study is about focus and calm," he spoke directly to their minds, blocking all other thoughts of the captains.

All except George that is, who pushed the block away as easily as he pushed away the scanners on Mahadean. He couldn't help worrying about Pete, Frank, and Toma. They should be here learning with them, not trapped within themselves.

David Lu started the captains and cadets out on Chen Lo, level one, slowly, deliberately walking them through each level at an excruciatingly slow pace. At level five, Colonel Moawk entered taking over the training. David Lu walked over to George.

"You and Andy were there last night. Did you get the answer you were looking for?" he asked, staring at George as if he saw something no one else could see.

George looked up bewildered at first as he stepped out of the Chen Lo. How did David Lu know where he and Andy had been in a dream, unless it wasn't a dream at all.

"You know them, the beings of white light, sir?" George whispered.

"Yes, George. Worry not your team has kept their secret well. We all search for answers to questions we have. Most often, we know the answer before the question is asked and we only need time to find the answer hidden within us," he said cryptically.

"That's what everyone keeps saying. That we already know the answer to the questions we ask," George replied, twisting his head as if it would make David Lu's words less cryptic.

"Yes, they are right. What question did you need to answer?" David Lu asked, staring at George, not reading his thoughts.

"Thank you, sir, I understand now. I know what I need to do, sir," George said, suddenly figuring out David Lu's meaning.

David Lu had given George time to think and discover the truth about his triad's leaders. Time to find a way to help them release their rage and return to their teams. David Lu backed away and George reached over and grabbed Andy's shoulder. In a flash of white light, Andy and George were gone. David Lu smiled, nodding to an empty wall. Not even concerned that George could now travel on the energy of the universe like the Senior Viceroys!

Their triad stepped out of Colonel Moawk's Chen Lo. Standing in their now familiar circles, Jennifer started a link, ready for when they were needed.

George and Andy appeared in the glowing white room. They stepped forward and Nick, Cal, and Niels crossed over in front of them, shaking their heads.

"They didn't get there alone, and they can't get back without our help, sirs," George said firmly.

"No, George, we need to wait," Nick said, shaking his head.

"They're not ready yet. They have a lot of rage to come to terms with," Niels added.

They held George and Andy back. Suddenly, George glowed a bright white and walked through them, as if they were not solid matter, and stepped into the glowing white cube that held Pete, Frank, and Toma captive.

"How'd he do that glowing white thing?" Nick whispered.

"Only Senior Viceroy's can do that," Cal added stunned.

"It is how we arrived, sirs," Andy replied, not answering the question or taking his eyes off George.

"It is time to leave, sirs," George said, his voice calm and low.

"No, we will kill the junior officers that hurt you," Pete answered, gritting his teeth.

"It is our fault for not finishing soon enough and being there to guide you," Frank added, straining against his anger.

"You know that is not true. Our first two fears came to life and we lived through them. They were easier to see and admit than your fears, as yours have not come true. They truly are only fears," George said firmly.

"Our deepest fear is the destruction of our triad, and leaving you and your team alone again and the consequences for the universe," Pete said and lowered his head and Toma nodded.

"Our second is that we now carry within our triad the power to control the raw energy of the universe. To create and destroy at will," Frank added.

"Our third is not being able to protect your team and you all die because of it," Toma whistled.

"My team's first two fears have already come true and our triad was destroyed when we were separated by evil. Still, you found us and we are whole again. We all lived through that fear. Now, our third fear can't be spoken, for fear it will also come true as the other two already have. So, I am the only one who carries the information for our team. And no, it isn't something our team can prepare for, sirs," George said, lowering his head.

Silence filled the air between them as George thought.

"We cannot live in fear of what may happen, Pete, Frank, Toma. We must live in the light of what will happen if we work together. The beings of white light say to look within; the answer is there. They say that it is only hiding inside you because you might not be ready to hear it. We all make mistakes. Our fault lies in not learning from those mistakes and then repeating them. For that we are truly sorry, sirs," George said, dropping to one knee, sad that their arrogance had led them to this point.

They all stared at George for a long time. There George was, a member of the team of the prophecy, kneeling before them, asking for forgiveness. Pete, Toma, and Frank reached out and held his shoulder. George stood up straight.

"You are right, George, you are right. It is time to come out and release our anger," Pete replied, staring at George.

"We have also made many mistakes, and we need to learn from them as well," Frank added.

"What was it we were reminded of, oh yes: the very young do not always do as they are told," Toma said, moving across from George.

George stood in the center and the captains circled around him. They reached out with their minds to the universe. Calm filled the air and the white cube faded away. The Senior Viceroys smiled, stepping back out of the small room as the light in the room turned a warm yellow.

"How did George do that?" Nick asked, puzzled as to what George said to get the lead captains to release their anger.

"Nothing we said did a thing," Cal added equally puzzled.

"We each have our talents," Andy whispered.

"Well, right now we need Emily and Anna to get out of this room," Cal said and the seconds chuckled.

Pete, Frank, Toma, and George broke their circle and stared at their seconds.

"She would be so disappointed in us that we have learned so little," Andy whispered.

As if on cue an archway and door appeared. George, Pete, Frank, and Toma smiled.

"Thanks, Anna. Thanks, Emily," Pete thought to their team.

They walked out into the sector Galactic council corridors. Two Viceroys were waiting for them. They followed Pete's dad in single file with their heads down. Frank and George's dad was the last in their line. They cleared their minds and thought of nothing. Being in the Galactic council corridors was not ever a good thing, even if you were escorted. Any stray thoughts could be punished; especially by their fathers.

An archway and door opened as they approached the end of a corridor. Pete's father nodded at each captain and cadet as they walked through. The door closed and the archway vanished. They were standing in Colonel Moawk's training dome.

"Training will begin again, if you are ready, captains," David Lu said, turning around.

They all turned, smiling and lined up again. Gus, Han, Sven, and Gabe joined them in their new link. This time, David Lu raced through the first eleven levels at lightning speed. The twelfth level started and the captains and cadets were combining moves easily. They moved as a fluid team, smiling and laughing together again.

At level thirteen, Niels and Nick spun around and sent an energy wave thundering across the dome. The dome supports buckled and the dome's sidewall started to collapse. Pete, Frank, and Toma spun back around. With their hands stretched out, they held a constant wave of energy against the wall. Straining under the weight of the wall, they held the soil and rocks back until Niels, Cal, Nick, and Andy could get everyone free from the fallen rocks and boulders.

As if one person, the three captains stepped one-step back, lowering their hands to their sides. Instantly, the energy wave stopped and the dome wall crashed down. Emily calmed the ground and lowered the dust until other officers arrived to help.

"What happened?" Cal asked stunned.

"How did you hold the wall back?" George asked, staring at the three captains.

"I don't know. It was what had to be done," Pete replied, as stunned as the others.

"Most unexpected. A level eighteen move. Don't do it again until we get to that training level!" David Lu's said sternly. "Dismissed."

They faced David Lu and bowed, raising their arm to their chest.

In the corridor, Nick and Niels shook their heads.

"Level eighteen, who knew!" Niels said.

"Don't even know how we did it," Nick said still stunned.

"What is going on?" Pete asked, in the corridor, for the bewildered three leaders.

"You, Frank, Toma, Niels, Cal, and Nick disappear two days ago, sir, right out of the hospital room, sir," Gus answered.

"Then George and Andy disappear today in a flash of white light from David Lu's Chen Lo training class, sir," Emily added.

"A moment later, you all walk into the dome though an archway and door--as if from thin air, sir," Emily replied and smiled.

"And finally, Nick and Niels destroyed the wall of the training dome and you three held it in place with a massive wave of energy; however, you saw that, sirs," Sara answered happily.

"Yes, sounds about right, cadet," Sheta added with a grin.

"And worst of all, Andy and Cal are sad because they didn't get to blow up the wall with Nick and Niels!" Anna said, hanging her arms hands on their shoulders.

"Well, there could be some truth to that," Jennifer replied, hiding her smile.

Pete, Frank, and Toma stood in the corridor with their mouths hanging open. For most cadets and captains the events of the last few days would have been terrifying. However, for these teams it seemed to be business as usual. They were getting use to the unusual and took it all in stride. Pete nodded and Nick was on his pad with Niels and Cal.

"Where are we going, sirs?" Gus asked a little worried.

"Lunch Gus," Frank said. "Just lunch."

"For real, you mean real lunch, sir?" Gus repeated.

"Calm yourself, cadet. It's only lunch," Toma replied.

"No sir, there is no such thing as just lunch. We don't usually make it to lunch, sir," Gus said anxiously.

The cadets had the most unusual looks on their faces as if lunch was a rare treat. It made Cal, Nick, and Niels uneasy--truth be told. They walked through the corridors and entered the captain's dining hall. Toma was right, no catastrophes or dire emergencies happened, just lunch.

Lunch with the captains was dull, not quite as dull as with their parents, although, it was a close second. Only a low mumble filled the air. No exciting tales of crashes or boring lectures. No one even clicked their spoon on their plates.

"How do you eat without making any noise," Andy whispered.

George frowned and Andy rolled his eyes. A few captains who had read his thought shook their heads at another table.

"We are caught between two worlds," Emily signed.

The cadets looked sad. They were too experienced for their own class, too inexperienced for the captains. The silence was deafening. Gus wondered if it had always been so quiet; if there had been a time when the captains actually spoke to each other and worked as a class team.

"This is all I have ever seen," Kate signed, to Gus in the cadets sign language.

"Too bad, seems to me like they are missing the point of eating together," Gus signed back.

She nodded and took a most un-Calshene risk; she spoke. "So, Gus, how did you like that Sport training?"

Gus smiled. He knew the risk she was taking and he took the opportunity she offered.

"Sport looks easier than it is. Until you have swung on the vines in the main Sport arena, you haven't lived," he replied politely.

"Hey, what do you mean? You got to swing on the vines in the main Sport arena?" asked, a captain who was ease dropping on their conversation as he leaned back on his chair.

"We finished early and it was the only place open to practice," Gus said spinning around, leaving out the part about the junior offices.

"So, do you think you're any good for the competition this rotation?" he asked eagerly.

"We sit with three championship teams. We not at their level, however, we are learning fast," Gus said, nodding to his triad.

Within a few minutes, all of the captains' tables were talking about Sport. It wasn't anything of importance, like the fate of the universe. However, they were talking. Kate nodded to Gus. He was happy.

Chapter 22

HELP, NOT AGAIN

After lunch, the captains went to the Sport arena for training with Colonel Moawk again. The other captains were still talking when they entered the Sport arena. Quietly, Emily asked the Slugamie to tolerate the intrusion.

"I heard the dome collapsed during Colonel Moawk's training," a captain whispered to Pete as he chose a vine.

"Must have been a grueling workout to cause the supports to collapse," another captain added and Pete smiled.

"Captains, ascend your vines!" said Colonel Moawk, his voice booming around the arena, however, he was nowhere to be seen.

George's team's wounds from three days before may have been mended by technology, but, their muscles were still weak and sore. George couldn't use his leg and could barely close his hands around the vine. Anna couldn't use her arm, and a vine was actually pushing Emily up as her lungs still hurt as she reached up. Another vine lifted Sara into place. Gus and Andy couldn't pull and raise their arms over their head. George closed his eyes, if he could hold a ship together through the molten core of a planet, he had to be able to help is team. He pictured them well, without their wounds.

"Stop that, stop that right now! Ask for help!" was the thought that popped into his mind.

Pete's dad, Viceroy Petrosky, had been watching the cadets and listening to their thoughts from time to time when George used the energy of the universe in a link. George may not have realized that he was doing it on a regular basis now, but, the Viceroy did.

George opened his eyes, looking around for the person who had spoken to him. He slid down his vine and motioned his team to the ground with him. Colonel Moawk was standing in an archway.

"Sir, my team is still badly injured. We can't lift our own weight today, sir," George said, walking toward the archway.

"Your team will be watchers today," Colonel Moawk said kindly, pointing to the high seats.

"Thank you, sir," George replied, and motioned his team to the stairs.

They took up a watching position, halfway up the arena. Six sets of teams were now perched on the vines in the arena. Frank and Pete's teams were the opposing group captains. Quickly, they each chose two more sets of captains for their teams.

"Rule one: all captains on your team must touch the ball before a goal can be made. Rule two: any contact between players whether intentional or unintentional will remove both players from the field. Teams ready?" boomed the Colonel's voice.

Each team replied with a single clap of their hands in unison. It echoed through the arena.

"Centar, Comen," boomed the Colonels voice again and the cadets cheered.

The ball was thrown high into the air. Toma was on Frank's team and what would have been an advantage on Indus station was a distinct disadvantage on Asteria station. The vines were closer together on Asteria station and Toma, Cal, and the others' hidden wings kept hanging them up.

Pete's teams dove for the ball. However, without time to discuss a strategy, they crashed into each other and knocked each other out of play. Toma flipped and hit Darri. She screamed and brought four other captains to the ground with her. The ball thudded on the ground between the captain's bodies, covering the arena ground and the Slugamie.

George, Andy, and the others were having a hard time~not laughing. It was like watching a comedy of errors.

"What is their problem, George?" a voice asked in his mind.

"They have no strategy. They are not working together," he replied muttering out loud.

"Yes, George. I agree," Andy answered; however, he wasn't the one who asked the question in the first place.

George looked around and saw only his team.

"Everything OK, George?" Emily asked, sliding in close to his side.

"I'm fine, Emily. Just tired I guess," he replied, sliding his arm over her shoulder. "Thanks for asking," he whispered.

"I'm not sure I could have swung today," Emily replied, leaning against his warm side.

"I know what you mean," he replied softly.

The Colonel yelled and all the captains slid down their vines. The Slugamie curled around their feet, yet, didn't rise up. Emily had asked it to behave and not play with the captains.

"What are you all doing?" the Colonel asked loudly.

"We didn't have enough time to make a strategy, sir," Pete replied for his team.

"Then why did you answer, 'yes' when I asked if you were ready?" the Colonel asked looking perplexed.

The captains stood staring at the Colonel with blank expressions of their faces.

"Because we didn't think to say no, sir," Frank said.

"Excellent. Ascend you vines and this time answer, 'yes' only when you really are ready," the Colonel ordered.

The captains ran to their vines. They got it! They may have been playing Sport, but what they were learning had nothing to do with the game. The teams huddled high in the vines.

Almost immediately, the Colonels voice boomed, "Teams ready?"

This time the teams yelled a resounding, 'No!'

The Colonel smiled and waited a few more minutes.

Again, his voice boomed, "Teams ready!"

The captains nodded to each other and then replied with a single clap of their hands in unison. It echoed through the arena.

"Centar, Comen!" boomed the Colonels voice again and the cadets cheered.

Again, the ball was thrown high into the air. Toma was first to catch the ball and threw to Cal in his new repositioned place. The plays were smoother and the captains didn't collide. Frank to Darri and so on the captains played, trying for their first goal.

Mid-way through the game, George, Andy, and the others were grabbed from behind and dragged out of the Sport arena before they could call for help.

The junior officers were back and wanting to practice; however, seeing the Colonel, they backed down and chose an easier target. They threw the cadets into a classroom and locked the door. The cadets helped each other up from the floor and George stepped forward.

"Why do you continue to bully us?" George asked, while signing behind his back to Emily and Andy to call for help. They wouldn't make the same mistake again.

"Because we can," the second junior officer said, taunting the cadets.

"So you're cadets in captains clothing," another junior officer mocked.

"Who would have guessed. No wonder you're so scrawny," a third junior officer chimed in.

"What are they hiding you from?" the lead junior officer Kershj asked, pressing for information.

"You don't have the correct clearance level to be told," George answered.

"You will address us as, sir," the second said, stepping into George's face.

"No, I don't think so. That means you have attained a level of maturity and respect from those around you," George said calmly.

George was the distraction, the yelling officer, and he had to keep them talking and focusing on him. All the while, he signed behind his back for Anna, Sara, and Gus to worm their way into their thoughts and find out what was really going on?

"Our rank means you will give us respect, cadet!" junior officer Kershj yelled.

"Respect is earned every day by our actions toward our fellow cadets and officers," George said firmly. "It is not given easily; yet, it is easily lost by our mistakes," he pressed back, coming nose to nose with the junior officer Kershj.

"What would you know about that?" their second asked.

Emily lifted her arm up with great fanfare and rolled her hand over motioning to each of the cadets. As she passed her hand by each person, the two awards they had earned on their first and third rotations appeared on their uniforms.

"We know a lot about it," Emily said, her eyes squinted.

"We are equally familiar with courage, compassion, and honor," Andy said, facing off with the second junior officer.

The junior officer's mouths dropped open. Emily rolled her hand again and the awards disappeared. She collapsed to the floor, her strength gone, she was breathing hard again. Sara knelt down, made a small yellow sphere in the palm of her hand, and placed it over Emily's right lung.

"What is she doing?" junior officer Kershj asked rudely.

"Sara is a healer. Judging by the look on Sara's face, I'd say Emily is hurt again," George answered harshly.

George was in junior officer Kershj's face. He had to buy time for help to arrive.

"That's just a trick of some sort," the second junior office said gruffly.

"No, you crushed her lungs three days ago. Now you have hurt her again. My second thinks we should destroy you where you stand. A strong emotion for sure. However, I am more of the diplomat and believe you can be rehabilitated," George replied, turning the junior officer's focus toward him so the others could help Sara and Emily.

"Destroy us. You're nothing but a bunch of scrawny cadets in captains clothing, hiding from something," their second jeered.

"Then it is a good disguise," Andy added, kneeling next to Sara, although, not turning his back on the junior officers.

"Be warned, if you try to hurt us again, I will not stop those who protect us. Leave now while you still can," George said firmly.

The junior officer Kershj raised his hand to strike George. Gus lunged forward pushing George out of the way, as Andy met the junior officer's hand with a burning red energy sphere.

"Without George, you would all be destroyed for what you have done. I don't even care about the paperwork on this station," he whispered, stepping back to help George up from the floor not taking his eyes off junior officer Kershj.

His second raised his foot to trip Andy, George lifted his hand and the second flipped backwards, landing hard against the wall as the door burst open. It wasn't the guards. It was Pete, Frank, and the others. Tillie, Darri, Kate, Maria, Jennifer, and Karmen lifted the cadets into their arms and left the classroom at a run.

Pete, Frank, Toma, Cal, Nick, and Niels stayed behind. The other captains who had been in the Sport dome watched the door outside the classroom, while more captains helped get the cadets to the CORE hospital wing again.

"Violence is not the way," George signed.

"You warned them, George. They chose not to listen," Andy replied harshly.

Yet, he knew George wouldn't understand. George had done what he had been told to do and still his team was being rushed to the CORE hospital again. Protocol protected the bullies and they knew it. The first time had been a chance meeting. The second time was kidnapping.

The captains were protecting one of their own. As the captains ran with the cadets to the hospital, they passed CORE officers walking casually toward the classroom with some of the captains from the Sport arena. They were in no hurry to get there. The bullies had to be stopped, and if protocol prevented the CORE officers from acting, then it was up to the captains to show their displeasure with the junior officer's actions.

The CORE officers would assign them to some outpost far out of harm's way. George didn't understand, but Gus and Andy did. Andy knew the anger and rage within. Nick and Niels had taught Andy how to control the anger and rage and use it to his advantage. They had all been badly beaten in the process of teaching the lesson, but Andy now understood.

"They won't destroy them. Remember where we are and the huge amount of forms that would have to be filled out. It would be a nightmare. However, the junior officers will wish they were. Of that I am sure," Andy thought to George in their link.

Andy thought about the lesson Nick and Niels had taught him. Cal would have been less forgiving!

The medics and doctors in the CORE hospital slipped the cadets into the yellow healing again as Tillie and the others circled the cadets. A few hours later, Pete, Frank, Toma, Nick, Niels, and Cal appeared at the CORE hospital doorway beaten and bruised, yet standing.

"Not this time, captains. They need to heal," the CORE doctor said, firmly facing off in front of Pete.

Pete, Toma, and Frank lowered their heads and the doctor let them enter. They surrounded the cadets, adding to the strength of the healing tubes. Late the next day, the medics disappeared from the hospital room. Pete looked up to see his grandfather, Senior Viceroy Petrosky.

"The three of you walk with me," said the Senior Viceroy sternly.

Toma, Frank, and Pete left the circle with Nick, Cal, and Niels tagging along behind. Like George, Pete, Frank, and Toma were never to be left alone.

"You can't guard them all of the time. You must let them live," he said firmly.

He wasn't their kind understanding grandfather at this moment; instead, he was a seasoned veteran Senior Viceroy with harsh firm words.

"Grandfather, if you knew almost all of your triad was going to die when they did, wouldn't you work to prevent it. To change what was, sir," Pete pleaded, trying to get the Senior Viceroy to soften and see their point of view.

"How can you know these events happened? It was long before your time and I know you were never told," he replied, abruptly stopping in the hospital corridor.

"George and the others figured it out, sir. They pieced it together from fragments we never even looked for sir," Pete whispered.

"They understand about you and Max in a way I'm not sure we will ever fully understand. Yet, they knew and they told us sir," Frank added quietly.

"So our teams pieced together other fragments of what we have been able to find, sir," Toma whispered.

The three captains paused and looked at their grandfather. He looked old and greatly troubled.

"Sir, we know what the prophecy scroll says. 'In the fourth rotation the team of the prophecy dies and hope is lost for a millennia of time until a new team emerges strong enough to face the challenges'," Pete said, repeating Nick's words.

It was Nick's family who had brought to the prophecy scroll to the Galactic Union eons ago and Nick had told them what it said so they could protect their cadets better.

The Senior Viceroy waved his hand gently through the air and a door opened in the corridor wall. He stepped through into a small office and sat down on an old comfy desk chair.

"Have your seconds come in, too, before they hurt themselves in casual stealth mode," he said, motioning to an old couch on the far side of the room.

The six young men entered the small office and sat on the edge of their seats. They knew the Senior Viceroy was angry, but, it was his disappointment with their actions and choices that worried them the most.

"Pete, Toma, Frank, your triad has already changed the prophecy as it was originally written. We don't know how. It has never changed before, nothing written in the past had even suggest it was possible. Yet, there it is and each day the events change. Everything that was written, has changed," grandfather said, ominously to Pete and the others.

"So why are there all the guards around them, sir?" Frank asked directly.

"David Lu, a retired master Senior Viceroy, you, and Toma's grandfather, all of you hardly a whisper away? I have seen my dad and Frank's dad more since our triad was formed then in all my years growing up, sir," Pete asked as bluntly.

"And Max, a being of white light, that's unbelievable sir. What is it that you all know that you are protecting them and us from sir?" Toma asked bluntly, as the others listened intently for his answer.

They needed answers for their triad.

"Your triad needs David Lu, you need focus and control. In the classroom, George flipped the junior officer away with a simple flick of his wrist as easily as Emily now opens locked doors at a run. The raw energy of the universe is real and it is very dangerous. It can save, as easily as it can kill. The energy doesn't care. The control comes from those that focus and use the raw energy of the universe. You must learn control or it will destroy you and all that you value," grandfather said sternly, his voice deadly serious.

"What are you talking about, sir?" Frank pressed, not understanding his meaning and wanting his answer spelled out.

"From my perspective, all of the raw energy of the universe now lies in the hands of a sixteen year old child and his young teachers," he answered bluntly, raising his voice.

The captain's faces dropped. Grandfather leaned back against the desk with his chair- it creaked.

"But, sir," Toma started and grandfather cut him off.

"No buts! You all need to learn control as acting out your anger and rage is unacceptable. Your teams must show George and the others the path of focus and control and lead by example. What example have you shown them now? Andy can destroy the junior officers from where he now lies inside a healing tube! And he knows it! Only George prevents it from happening! His humanity alone!" the Senior Viceroy said, raising his voice sternly.

He wanted them to clearly see the damage they had done.

"Yes sir," they answered in unison.

In a flash of white light, the captains were back in the hospital room, their heads low. They were in misery as they now understood what grandfather had meant. They had acted out of anger and retribution to payback the junior officers for the beating they had given to George and the others. Now, their grandfather was greatly disappointed in their actions. They had been handpicked and specially trained to be members of this triad. How could they have made such a bad choice?

"We all make errors in our decisions. It doesn't mean we are bad people, only that we made a bad decision or action. As long as you understand why it was a bad choice and learn from it, all is not lost. As a child, we make good and bad choices that affect only a few. We build a solid ground from those decisions. In this way, when a difficult decision needs to be made, we each have a strong base to make a good decision and to have a positive effect on those around us," Max said, only to Toma, Frank, and Pete's minds.

Toma, Frank, and Pete looked around the room. No one was there.

"Max is that you?" they thought in their link.

There was no answer; however, they were sure it was Max. He was always close by and he would know what had happened.

Chapter 23

PEACE IS NOT FREE

Another day passed and the doctors and medics slid the cadets out of their yellow healing tubes slowly waking the cadets up. Gently, the medics moved each cadet to a white hospital bed to rest. Pete, Frank, Toma, and the others sat in their circle not moving, focused only on healing the cadets. George could sense Toma, Frank, and Pete's sadness and the weariness of the other captains.

He thought of the tunnel hog cavern and Max. He focused his mind on the second cavern and what it really was. Slowly, he opened his mind and thought of all of the possibilities. An instant later, he knew the second cavern was a portal from their physical space to the home of the beings of white light. How he knew no longer mattered to George, he needed answers to protect his triad—it was his only focus.

In a flash of white light, he, Andy, Emily, Sara, Anna, and Gus stood in the tunnel hog's sleeping cavern. They walked into the cavern with the symbols carved into the walls. Studying in the library had paid off as they could now clearly read and understand the markings on the walls. The purpose of the cavern was clear. It was a portal to the beings of white light and other portal caverns. George was right!

"We are always being told to find the answers to our questions ourselves," Gus said, standing in the center of the cavern.

"Then perhaps we should focus, here in this portal cavern and find the beings of white light. Then we will search for the answers to our questions," Emily replied, a little afraid of what they might discover.

The team formed a tight circle in the center of the room and thought only of the beings of white light. They needed answers and they thought they needed to go to the beings of white light to find their answers.

The fungi and moss glowed a warm green and the walls of the cavern faded away. They felt the pull of good and the pull of evil in their minds. George focused on the raw power and energy of the universe that his team could now use at will. He worried about Andy, and the others and their abilities growing faster than their focus and control. It was an enormous responsibility for cadets so very young.

They opened their eyes and before them lay the universe. Enormous galaxies spun before their eyes with glowing nebula of brilliant colored gasses and rings of dust and rock spinning around, all circling gravity wells, and creating budding galaxies. Cosmic dust swirled in great loops, connecting all the galaxies in the enormous expanse of twinkling stars and black holes.

"We found them," Sara whispered, holding back tears of joy, as if, a great weight was lifted from their minds.

"I know where we are," Anna whispered, nearly in tears herself and holding Gus's hand.

They stood on a cloud of swirling galactic dust and gases, dancing and twisting beneath their feet.

"It's so beautiful, look there and there. It's as if we know all that is known," Emily said, a tear running down her rosy check as she spun around to see the whole universe.

"We are where the beings of white light live. But I thought they were pure energy?" Gus whispered, thinking they should be in a place where the energy of the universe spun and twisted before their eyes.

"Yes, they are pure energy. This place must be for us," Sara replied, her mind a blaze with a million questions and a million answers.

"We are in the one place we cannot be," Anna answered, not understanding how she knew; only that she did.

"You mean in the center of the universe?" Andy asked, his mouth hanging open.

"No, not there. This is the space between space. Like the space between the molecules of the energy of the universe," Anna whispered a little cryptically, turning to see it all.

In an instant, they knew the answers to all of their questions. It was all so easy, so simple. They wondered why the answers had been hidden from them before. George knew what he had to do as he looked at his team and the universe around them.

A being of white light shimmered and solidified before the cadets. The cadets glowed with a reddish white aura surrounding them as they walked around on the cloud of sparkling galactic dust.

"Why are you here, children?" Tao asked kindly hiding his appearance.

"We have come to see the high council," George whispered, lowering his head.

"How can a mere child know of this?" Tao questioned.

"We have come to see the high council," George repeated, dropping to one knee.

"No child, you must leave now. It is not your time. Your kind cannot stay here and live," Tao said, encouraging them to leave.

"We have come to see the high council," George said, again and the others lowered to one knee.

He had only one answer for the being of white light. The glowing white being raised an arm and a white mist clouded their vision of the universe. Out of the mist came a familiar voice.

"George, why have you come? You can't be here. It is not your time," the voice said.

"Max, so they have sent you to speak with us?" George spoke quietly, not lifting his head or standing up.

"Yes, George. What is not right?" he asked, clasping their hands and lifting each of them up in greeting.

"The power and energy of the universe belongs to the universe. It is wrong for us to posses it and to hold it captive. The knowledge of it must be taken from us before we destroy all that is important to us," George said, with great thought and emotion in his words.

"This request is most unexpected," Max said, stepping back to stare at the young cadets glowing with a white and red aura.

"Why, Max? We have asked for information to be hidden from us before. Absolute power corrupts absolutely. We need checks and balances in our lives to teach us our path towards the truth. As you and the other beings of white light have said, we aren't ready to be here, and yet, here we are," George said firmly, yet with sadness in his voice.

In his mind, he knew he would plead for help if that is what the high council wanted.

"What do you know of this place?" Max asked, kindly wanting to know the depth of their knowledge.

"It is where good and evil come together," Anna replied softly.

"Both energy's emanate from this place, and yet, neither can affect the other here," George said, clearing the white fog away with the wave of his hand.

"And how do you know this?" Max asked gently, to find their true thoughts.

George glanced around at the others. They simply smiled as if all was a matter of fact.

"We thought the question and so we know the answer?" Emily replied politely.

"The answers were inside us all along, like you said," Sara added gently.

"We thought it, and now we know everything," Anna added; even though, she was sad because nothing was left to discover.

"You must leave, now! Think of the cavern. All of you, quickly now!" Max said, glancing back as if listening to another conversation and rushing his words.

They closed their eyes and reappeared in the cavern. Max pushed them out into the tunnel hog-sleeping cavern.

"Remember, when you first came to this place and it made you feel sick. Well, it still does. Only you can't sense it now. It hurts your bodies when you go to the place of the beings of white light. You must not go again," Max said, making each one look him in the eye to get their agreement. "Return to your hospital room and rest. Decisions about your request will need to be made."

They disappeared in a flash of light, reappearing in the hospital room sitting on their beds. Pete, Frank, and the others spun around at the flash of white light in the room. One moment, they were in the lying on their white beds, then they were gone and now they were back again.

"Where were you, cadet?" Pete asked, relieved they had returned, however, concerned they had left.

"I can't say. You can't know. The time is not right," George replied cryptically, his thoughts a million miles away.

"What did you ask of Max?" Toma whistled quietly.

"How do you know we asked Max a question, sir?" George asked, staring at Toma.

"Because you always ask Max when you're trying to go around the Galactic council," Jennifer replied with concern.

The cadets had used the raw energy of the universe, like the Senior Viceroys, and traveled with the white light. Then they had gone to a place where their triad couldn't sense them. The only other time that had happened was when evil had taken them!

"We're not going around the Galactic council, if that's what you're asking," Andy answered abruptly, losing his patience.

"You shouldn't lie, you're not good at it," Rachael said, scolding Andy.

"And even if you were good at it, you shouldn't," Sheta added, raising her eyebrow.

"Rachael, Sheta, we're not lying," Sara said firmly, yet her thoughts trailed off impatient with their questions.

"Yes, we did talk with Max, but, not for the reason you think, sirs," Emily said, looking at Pete, Frank, and Toma.

The cadets stared at George and then at their triad. George needed to explain and stop their questions.

"Look at what we have done, sirs. We are destroying you, all of you. We can't let this go on. Even grandfather is disappointed with us, sir," George said, holding his hands out showing the blisters and pointing to the cuts on Nick and Cal's faces.

"He is disappointed with us, George, not you," Nick replied, pushing George's hands back.

"You acted on our account. Your rage and anger is our fault. We are connected, so he is disappointed with us, sirs," Andy added, raising his voice-why didn't the captains understand what they were saying?

"We should leave," Toma said suddenly, trying to change the topic.

He was staring at George; something was wrong, and maybe, George couldn't tell them what it was out in the open with so many ears listening.

"Yes sir," the cadets answered, standing up.

The captains surrounded the cadets and pushed through the medics and doctors out into the corridor. Something was wrong, more wrong than normal, and the captains had to find out what it was and quickly.

Sheta and Kate called for Sid and Mid as they walked through the CORE hospital corridors. When they crossed over into the captains sector, the corridor wall quivered. Sid appeared. The George, Pete, Frank, and Toma stepped into Sid, while the others waited in the corridor.

"Please sit and rest, Sid. We only need a place to talk without interruption," Pete said calmly.

"Pete, Frank, Toma, there is something about the raw power and energy of the universe. It is so easy to use and we seem to have so little control," George said his voice low and quiet.

"That's what we are learning from David Lu. He is teaching us focus and control, George," Frank said kindly.

"Pete, I know your team's greatest fear is not your deaths, but what would happen to us if you died. And Frank, your team's greatest fear is our deaths and the deep sorrow within. Toma, your team's greatest fear is the end of hope for the universe that would come with our death," George said, boldly facing each captain in turn.

The three captains had little memory of the happenings from the white cube when rage and anger clouded their judgment. However, George retained the memory of it all.

"George, these are very dark and morbid thoughts and fears. They are buried deep within us. How can you know these things?" Pete asked, staring at George.

The three captains were confused by how George knew so much.

"Pete, there is nothing we don't know. If we think the question, the answer is there. We are too young to hold this kind of power over the universe. We don't possess the wisdom to use it nor the control to focus it," George said, trying hard to get them to understand his cryptic words.

"George, what is your team's greatest fear? The one you will not tell the others," Toma asked seriously.

"That we will destroy the universe and everything inside it and it will be an accident, a simple uncontrolled thought," he answered honestly, his voice cold and unfeeling.

"What is preventing you right now from doing that?" Frank asked in astonishment.

How could George's team hold so much power that they could destroy the universe? Frank couldn't even imagine the energy needed to do it. What made George think they could do it? Frank, Toma, and Pete were stunned. It was nearly too much to absorb and understand.

"I think grandfather or David Lu or maybe Max is helping us with our control. Somehow, they are preventing us from using all of the energy right now. However, it is tiring them out. I don't know if they can sustain their focus much longer and keep the energy of the universe away from us. They are strong; however, they were badly hurt during last year's rotation and have taken longer than expected to recover," George answered, as if a Senior Viceroy of many years.

"So when you spoke with Max, what did he say?" Toma pressed, wanting to keep George talking.

"They would consider our request," George answered sadly.

"What request?" Frank asked puzzled, thinking George was now taking about something else.

"What do you need? Whatever it is; we can help," Pete said, becoming frantic.

He was worried, George was getting more and more cryptic the longer they spoke. The captains were trying to understand George's words. It would take more time and patience to explain again. Toma stared at George and guessed – an extremely un-Thorean thing to do.

"Won't the universe be more vulnerable to evil if Max takes the knowledge of the power and raw energy of the universe from you and the others?" Toma asked and then paused, wondering if he guessed right.

"The beings of the universe will not be in any more danger than before we discovered how to use the raw energy of the universe. Don't you understand, we need time! We don't know enough yet! It is too much to ask of us. We aren't ready for this responsibility!" George said firmly, his body shaking as he tried to control his emotions.

He sat down on the inside of Sid to think. Toma had guessed right, but he was too late. George's patience had run out. He flicked his hand and Frank, Toma, and Pete were suddenly standing in the corridor with the others.

Sid slipped off with George inside, alone ~ his sadness was deepening. His triad didn't seem to understand and the beings of white light were silent. He felt alone in the universe. Sid speed along for a long while, giving George time to think. At last, Sid needed to eat. He stopped and wiggled. He hugged Sid's inside, thanking him for the ride and stepped out into Asteria City ~ not where he was expecting to be.

He made his way to Max's café and walked up the stairs without making a sound. No one even looked up when he entered the café' and made his way across the room to a small table near the back wall.

Max was nowhere in sight. He asked for a cup of water and a ration pack from the waitress. Her long brown hair flowed from side to side as she moved across the floor to pick up George's order from the far counter. She brought him a silver cup with a small bottle of water. With a little smile, she laid a ration pack on the table and left him to tend another group of people entering the café.

In the sector corridor, Andy was in a near panic. George was gone and alone. Only twice had George been out of his sight or sensing in the last two years, once on the transport ship from Sandue with Nick and Niels and then when George had gone inside the white cube to release Pete, Frank, and Toma from the council chamber.

Now Andy couldn't sense George's presence anywhere and he was not allowing a link to be made with him. Andy was getting angry, his mind racing uncontrolled. George was taking a risk, an uncalled for risk!

"He knows better! Why is he doing this? I know how to give George his space and still watch him," Andy said out loud in the corridor, not caring who was listening. "I just want George safe, is that too much to ask, a little consideration!" Andy added angrily, his mind on fire.

His emotions were raging within him and they were clouding his judgment. He punched his fist into the corridor wall and huge sections of wall exploded sending fragments flying through the air crashing to the floor around them. He would soon lose control.

Snap! Pete, Frank, and Toma suddenly understood what grandfather had warned them about.

"All the power and energy of the universe in their hands and no focus or control!" Toma signed in the captain's sign language.

"How could grandfather and George have known this would happen?" Frank asked.

"A momentary loss of control and everything around them could be destroyed," Toma added.

Grandfather may have been helping George focus, but George had been helping his team stay focused. Without him there, the cadet's emotions were clouding their judgment and they each had far too much power to lose control.

The six captain's finally understood grandfathers cryptic words; 'the power of the universe was in the hands of a sixteen year old boy and his team.' George's greatest fear was coming true. Now!

Chapter 24

NO CONTROL

"We need to focus!" Toma yelled, loudly trying to get everyone's attention.

He didn't care who heard them. He was loud, yelling to get the cadet's attention. He motioned and the captains wrapped their arms over the cadet's shoulders. The cadet's minds were racing and their confusion was nearly more than the captains could handle.

"Focus and control!" they all repeated over and over, shouting it louder and louder.

"We will find George!" Frank yelled.

"Focus now!" Pete yelled.

"Where would he go to think?" Toma yelled, staring at the cadets, giving them a place to focus their thoughts.

"The library, sir," Emily said, gritting her teeth together tightly as she strained to focus her thoughts.

"Or maybe our sleeping room, sir," Anna added, straining for control as the corridor lights flickered.

"Which one? The captain's or cadet's sleeping room?" Frank asked loudly.

"Or the tunnel hog cave," Gus added, twisting his hands as the floor bent and twisted upward.

"Or the little spaceport perhaps, sir," Andy said, fighting for control of his fears.

Toma nodded and started giving orders loudly.

"Nick, Cal, and Niels, take Andy to the spaceport. Rachael, Sheta, and Kate take Emily to the library. Karmen, Darri, and Maria take Anna to the captain's sleeping room. Jennifer, Lucita, and Tillie take Sara to the cadet's sleeping room; and Han, Gabe, and Sven take Gus to the tunnel hog cave," Toma yelled firmly, forcing each group to focus on a mission and a place.

"Stay together! Don't let go of each other, not even for a moment," Toma whistled loudly to the captains. "Or their minds will tear us apart," he signed in their captain's language.

Frank rolled his hand and a small yellow sphere appeared on each of their hands; they all joined the new link.

"We'll meet back at the Sport arena in one hour," Toma whistled loudly, hurting everyone's ears a little to maintain their focus.

The cadets and captains took off running, each group focusing on their assignment. Pete, Toma, and Frank stood in the middle of the corridor and called Senior Viceroy Petrosky, grandfather, they needed help!

An older man in a CORE officer's uniform entered Max's café. He walked straight across the room, headed for George's table along the back wall.

"Mind if I sit down, son?" he asked quietly.

"As you wish; however, I am not your son," George replied coldly.

"Just an expression George," he said kindly.

"You know my name?" George replied a little surprised.

"Everyone knows your name, George," he answered, taunting him. "The great hero's of the galaxies! Defeating the great and all powerful evil," he added, mocking George and his team.

"They are your words, not mine," George replied, spinning his cup on the table, not looking up at the man.

It spun to a stop and George sighed a heavy sigh.

"So you have come to me in this form this time. Will you not relent and stop your attacks on my team?" George asked solemnly.

"My master only seeks to offer you good wishes," the man replied slyly.

"Don't play me for the fool. You are the evil master in a form I can understand. You have come directly to me to negotiate a deal, haven't you?" George pressed back, still staring at his cup.

"How can you know this child?" the man said, surprised George knew who he really was.

"It isn't important how I know. You have already lost before you have even begun. Go home and bother us no more," George said, with sadness in his voice.

"Don't you want to listen to what I have to say, son?" the man asked, trying to lead George into his trap.

"I know what you will offer and we have no interest in serving you," George replied coldly, shaking his head slowly as he slid his ration back and forth across the table.

"Again, I ask, how can you know this, child?" the man asked, confused.

"It isn't important. Return to your home as you are trying my patience now," George said, impatiently, flicking his fingers toward the man as if trying to shoe him away.

"You are not the same child I meet but one year before on the warship," the man said, crinkling his forehead and staring at George.

"I am and you yourself have made me stronger by your attacks and enslavement of multitudes of planets and galaxies," George replied harshly.

"They will worship you as they worship me, if you join me, son," the man said kindly, trying to entice George with reward and riches.

"Go home and bother us no more. I will not ask again," George said firmly.

"You wound me, child. You will not listen and you warn me to leave. Who do you think you are, child?" the man asked; his voice hardening.

"The stronger of the two. I don't want to argue and fight with you. Go home and you will live to conquer another day," George replied calmly.

"Now you threaten me, child!" he said stunned, surprised by George's words.

"No, I am simply putting my words into statements you can understand," George whispered.

The man in CORE officer's uniform stood up and walked across the room, fading away before reaching the doorway. George lowered his head, sipping his water as his cup turned blue.

"Where have you been, Max?" George asked into the blue cup.

"Waiting for you, George," Max replied, walking up with a second cup of water.

"You knew evil would come for us," George said, sliding a new chair out to Max with a twist of his wrist.

"Yes," Max replied, and sat down at the little table in the back of the cafe on the new chair not wanting to sit where pure evil had sat.

"Why didn't you destroy him? Surely, you know he would have destroyed you if he was the stronger of the two of you," Max asked, pressing for an answer for the high council of beings of white light.

George knew he was answering questions for the high council and Max was only their voice.

"Compassion, it is what separates good and evil," he replied, sipping his water.

"And if he comes back and you are not the stronger one, then what?" Max pressed firmly.

"There is no need, he will not be back. Not directly, and even if evil does come back, we know what to do, now. Evil can no longer win," George answered, smiling to himself.

"How do you know?" Max asked, worried by what George might have done.

"I gave him a simple thought~to think twice before expanding across the galaxies and attacking us again," George replied, and looked up at Max.

"So you have won," Max replied, trying to be happy for George to see his reaction.

"No, we have lost our innocence. Nothing will ever be the same, sir," George said, with great sadness in his voice, and lowering his head again.

"You can't know this," Max said, staring at George.

He shook his head, not wanting to believe George knew the answer to all questions, and that these cadets really did control all of the raw energy in their universe.

"You said to ask the question and we would know the answer. So we did. Now we know. I know there is great fear within the Galactic council. Grandfather knows it, as do you. I can't read the thoughts of high council of elders of the beings of white light yet, but, it will happen in time. As the vacuum of space is expanding, so is our power. You know we lack both the wisdom to focus the energy of the universe and the knowledge to control it. It is only time now before we destroy ourselves and everyone else," he said, staring into his cup as he swirled the water around the edges.

Max could feel his great sadness, and George's growing panic that their greatest fear was coming true.

"Has the high council of elders made a decision?" George asked in a whisper.

"Yes; however, I don't think you will like their answer," Max said kindly.

"Tell me please," George said, nearly begging.

"Can't you sense their answer?" Max pressed, testing George.

"No, I told you that before. Their thoughts are still hidden from me," George replied, straining to focus and hold his thoughts together.

"The council said the power to change is within you," Max pressed again.

Max was trying to test George to see how strong he had really become. It was a very dangerous game.

"No. I need help. I can't keep blocking everyone's thoughts. Keeping the raw energy of the universe from them and helping focus their minds is too much, Max. I told you that before," George said, raising his voice above a whisper.

"Are you losing your patience with me as you did with Pete, Frank, and Toma?" Max pressed even harder.

"Yes, I, yes. I can't do this, Max. I'm not the strong, focused one you all think I am! Please, I'm begging for your help," George said, his voice shaking from the strain to maintain control of his thoughts.

"Then stop trying to satisfy everyone else's expectations and focus on the needs of your team. What is right for you and your team at this moment," Max said firmly.

George stared at Max and the room seemed to spin around; as if, their lives were passing backwards and forwards in time. The room was gone and George and Max stood in a swirl of spinning colored gasses. In a blink of an eye, Max and George had left Asteria station. Max knew George was losing control, and he had to protect the station and save George if he could.

"Where are we?" he asked, his mind a whirl of color and space as if they were with the beings of white light again.

"You tell me?" Max asked quietly.

"I can't. I don't know exactly, but, we have been here before, and it isn't the place we can't go. It is somewhere else. I feel free here. As if, the universe has been lifted from us; and we can be cadets again. Everything here is good and at peace," George said, breathing in deep, and inhaling the sweet smells of peace and harmony in the air.

"Is that what you want?" Max asked, his voice an echo carried in the waves of energy bouncing off George's face.

It was warm and comforting as the breeze in the caves of Jupiter station.

"What is the breeze, Max?" George asked, his thoughts drifting in the space without focus.

"I don't know. It speaks only to you and your team. What do you think it is?" Max whispered.

"Somehow, here, right now, I don't know. Max, there is something about this place. I don't know what it is, but, it is good here," George whispered, relaxing for a few moments.

"You can't stay here long, George," Max whispered again.

"I know, but, it is so calm and focused. It is a place as good as good can be," George said, his thoughts calming and clearing.

"Perhaps, however, we need to leave. George, think back before you and your triad used the raw energy of the universe to heal me. Think of then, George, think of before, concentrate," Max whispered.

Anna, Karmen, Darri, and Maria reached the captains sleeping room first.

"Nothing!" Anna screamed. "The room is empty!"

Anna's fears raised and the walls shook. Darri, Karmen, and Maria held her close, focusing only on Anna and calming her thoughts.

"We will find him," Karmen whispered.

They spoke to the others through their link and continued their search, opening the surrounding rooms.

Emily, Rachael, Sheta, and Kate were next to reach their destination. They burst through the library door onto the first floor, running to their usual place in the library. Two translucent librarians came running to see what the commotion was.

"You are the first for your teams to enter the library today. Will the others be coming?" their regular librarian asked.

"No, ma'am. We can't find Cadet Hawkins, ma'am," Emily said gritting her teeth.

"He has not been here today," the librarian whispered.

"How about the reading rooms, ma'am?" Emily pressed frantically.

The librarian twisted her head, staring off in the direction of the reading rooms for a few moments. She twisted gracefully back around to Emily and the captains. She didn't have to say anything. They knew from the look on her face that George wasn't there.

"If I see him, I will call you immediately," she said, trying to help.

Inside Emily was panicking. Sheta and Jennifer held her close, focus on calming her mind.

"Thank you, ma'am," Kate said, as they ran out the library door.

When they left the library, they entered the CORE hospital instead of the cadet corridors.

"Wrong door," Sheta said surprised.

"Well, we haven't looked here yet," Kate said hopefully.

They started a new search while Rachael opened their link and transmitted their news.

"Emily, can't the station computers find him?" Sheta asked, looking for other ways to look for George than running from place to place.

"I'll try, but I'll bet he can stop the station sensors from finding him too, sir," she said, as she opened a computer terminal near an archway.

The door opened as they stood, searching the station sensor files on the computer. There was no log of George on the sensors. Emily hit her fist on the wall crushing it as a desk and chair crumpled in the doctor's office near them. She was losing control.

The medics came, running thinking there were injuries as the captains raced on through the hospital. No one had seen Cadet Hawkins. They left the CORE hospital, running to the cadet hospital next.

Andy, Nick, Cal, and Niels were the next team to check in through their link. George wasn't in the little spaceport. They were heading for the training port now and then they were going to go to Colonel Moawk's training dome. Perhaps he or David Lu had seen George. Two fighters crumpled, bursting into flames as they left the first port. Andy was struggling to maintain control and he was losing the battle.

Sara, Jennifer, Lucita, and Darri reported in right after Andy. The cadet sleeping quarters were empty. They were continuing their search in the surrounding classrooms. The beakers and containers were bursting with each empty classroom Sara looked into. Jennifer and the others had their arms wrapped over her shoulders as they ran. It was barely enough. Her focus was slipping away.

Finally, Gus, Han, Gabe, and Sven arrived at the tunnel hog sleeping caves in Mid. Gus didn't really want to show the captains the second cavern; however, he had to look and find the beings of white light. Gus knew the captains wouldn't let him go into the second cavern alone.

As they walked into the second cavern, Han, Gabe, and Sven's mouths dropped open, staring at the carvings on the walls. Instantly, they started to feel sick.

"So this is where you really were when we couldn't find you?" Gabe asked stunned by the carvings.

"It kind of makes me sick to be in here," Han added, holding his stomach.

"Yes sir. Gabe and Sven can you help Han to the other cave? I'll be safe here alone, sir," Gus said firmly.

"What is this place?" Gabe asked, lifting up Han.

"I can't say. I said I would keep the secret, sir," Gus replied, lowering his head.

"Well, it's one good secret," Sven said, nodding his head.

"Sirs, you have to leave quickly. Han is getting sicker. Please, sir, I will be safe," Gus pressed, his hands shaking.

"We're not letting you out of our sight cadet," Gabe replied, staring at Gus.

"Han can't stay, please, sirs," Gus said nearly begging, the walls crumbling with each word Gus spoke.

"We will be in the next cavern, don't go far," Gabe said firmly, somehow knowing that Gus was leaving.

"Thank you, sirs," Gus replied, holding his hands behind his back.

The captains left Gus in the cavern alone, yet, they wanted to know more about the cavern. At this moment, they needed to trusted him and his judgment. Gus stood in the center of the room. Focusing his mind, he thought of the beings of white light.

"Please, I know you are there, I need your help. I'm not George or Andy, but I know Max and he said you would help us, please," Gus asked, nearly begging in his mind.

A shimmer of white light appeared in the cavern.

"Why have you come here, child?" Tao asked kindly as he solidified.

"Please help us. We have lost George and we fear for his life," Gus said, shaking.

Tao clasped Gus's arms and focused on his mind.

"Your George is safe, child. He is with the one you call Max," Tao whispered, calming his fear.

"Where is he? Please, we must find him," Gus pleaded.

"He is safe, child. You all need to rest now," Tao said calmly.

"No wait, you don't...," Gus said and stepped back; however, it was too late.

His outstretched body fell to the cavern floor; a swirl of dust wafting into the air around him. Sven, Han, and Gabe followed landing on the ground in quiet thuds in the other cavern. Emily, Anna, Andy, and Sara fell to the floor where they stood. The captains staggered, trying to stay awake then fell to the floor in the classroom and corridors. Only George was left awake.

"They are frantically searching for you, George," Max said kindly, nodding to the air.

"I know, yet, now they sleep. Why Max?" George asked calmly.

"They were losing control and focus. Panic was overcoming their good judgment. They will need time to adjust," Max replied, even more cryptic than usual.

Max wasn't making any sense to George. Max was doing it on purpose, forcing George to focus on random bits and pieces. He knew George could no longer control his thoughts and a simple slip could make George's worst fear come true.

"George, think back again. Back before you and your triad used the energy of the universe to heal me. Think of then, George. Think of before, concentrate, and focus on that moment," Max said, his voice soothing and calm.

"Why?" George asked, but Max changed the subject instantly.

"Tell me what happened this rotation in the library, George, with the book you were reading," Max whispered, calmly distracting George again.

"I remembered the history that I had read in the prophecy scroll when I read the new history book," George replied quietly.

"Why did you remember it?" Max asked, encouraging George to reason out his thoughts.

"I don't know, Max, maybe because we were in the library when we read the prophecy scroll the first time," George said, guessing and getting impatient again.

Max changed the topic again~this time back to the past.

"Within each of us is the power to create and change our own lives. Concentrate on the time before you first used the energy of the universe. Think of your training from David Lu. Think of the fluid energy that surrounds you. Your triad posses the strength to return to a time before you all used the energy of the universe," Max spoke quietly, his voice strong and calm.

"You would have died if we didn't use the raw energy of the universe to save your life. I can' take back that moment in time, sir," George replied, only half understanding what Max had asked him to do.

"No, George. You are not going back in time physically. You are only going back with your thoughts. Everything that has happened will be as it is. However, your memory of how to use the raw energy of the universe will simply be hidden from your view," Max said, encouraging George to think passed the moment.

"When will our memory of the raw energy of the universe return, sir?" George asked, thinking on the words Max had said.

"When you can better understand, focus, and control it," Max replied calmly.

"How can this be, sir?" George questioned.

"If you ask the question, don't you already know the answer?" Max asked, tilting his head as his forehead crinkled, now understanding the depth of George's control over the energy of the universe.

"Yes," he said replying slowly, then turned his head. "Yes, I understand now. When we learn to control the energy, we will remember it is there. The information will stay in the back of our minds. We will not even need to concentrate to keep it there. Will we, sir?" George said, finally understanding Max's cryptic words.

"You will be safe for now. The evil has retreated. Think back George," Max whispered.

George paused and focused on the memories, and they slipped back deep into the cadet's thoughts–hidden in all of their minds. Max smiled.

"Rest now. Rest with your triad. Know you have all done well," Max whispered in George's mind.

Max caught George as he slipped out of his chair onto the floor of the café. Max lifted him up over his shoulder. Walking toward the café doorway, they faded away. They reappeared in the cadets' sleeping room. The other cadets were already sleeping when Max laid George down on the empty bed. In a shimmer of light, Max was gone from their room.

Senior Viceroy Petrosky was seated in George's chair, waiting for Max's return to the cafe. He sipped water from a silver cup while he waited. Max appeared at the entrance of the café, looking around as if seeing who needed to be served next, he saw the Senior Viceroy sitting in the back of the café. Max shook his head and walked to the counter. The waitress handed him a silver cup and a small bottle of water. As he walked to the Senior Viceroy's table, the cup turned blue. Max set the bottle of water on the table, then swung his leg over the back of the chair and sat down.

"Why are you here, old man?" Max asked gruffly.

"What decision has been made?" the Senior Viceroy asked, knowing George had asked the beings of white light a question.

"You don't know?" Max poked.

"You know I don't, so I must ask," he replied, a little impatiently.

Max looked down and a yellow sphere danced across the table to the Senior Viceroy. He slowly closed his hand around the sphere and accepted Max's link.

"George and the others have buried the knowledge of the raw energy of the universe deep within their minds. They and the universe will be safe. The council has granted their request~in a manner of speaking," Max said in their link.

"The prophecy has changed again, Max," the Senior Viceroy whispered in their link.

"So the prophecy was wrong and they live another day," Max replied, matter of factly.

"This is the third time the prophecy has been wrong about them," the Senior Viceroy said, raising his eyebrow.

"It will be wrong again. They have already become more than the original prophecy has said," Max added, with a little worry still showing on his face.

The cadets may have hidden the knowledge of the raw energy of the universe deep within their minds, but they still possessed the knowledge of it.

"And what of the evil that hunts them?" the Senior Viceroy pressed.

"George has sent it on an odd path. One we would never have thought of. It will not hunt them for a while. You have your time to train them. Use it well, as it will not last long," Max said ominously.

"Why, Max?" the Senior Viceroy asked, changing the topic.

"Why what?" Max asked, staring at the Senior Viceroy.

"Why the interest in this triad? Weren't the other triads as important?" he pressed.

"I am haunted by their deaths every day old man," Max replied, looking down, spinning his cup on the table.

"I too. This triad IS different from the last," the Senior Viceroy said cryptically.

"Yes, perhaps because they are so young and so unconventional. They are the generation that can change the universe if they work at it. They have the ability and are beginning to understand how to use it," Max said, staring at the Senior Viceroy.

He closed the link and stood up, leaving Max seated at the table. He stopped and turned, staring at Max.

"And the memories of the others?" the Senior Viceroy asked.

"All will be reset, except for a few, when they sleep tonight," Max replied.

"Thank you," the Senior Viceroy replied.

He walked across the floor, vanishing in flash of white light. Senior Viceroy Petrosky and Senior Viceroy David Lu would be the only two left who knew the truth.

Chapter 25

NEW DAY

They woke up in the red cadet sleeping room the next day. The events of last few weeks were hidden from their memories and all seemed good with the universe.

"Hey, what's up?" Andy asked, rolling over as the edge of his bed dipped down.

He landed with a thud on the floor. Emily rolled over and giggled.

"Andy, your bed will hold you in if you ask it," Emily whispered softly.

Andy shook his head. "It's harder than you think, Emily," Andy said, crawling up slowly off the floor.

Sara and Anna giggled and slipped off their beds to join Pete, George, and Gus at the table. Pete slid bowls of officer cereal toward them as they sat down.

"I really do hate this stuff more than the cadet cereal," Andy said, staring at his bowl, frowning.

"Grandfather's orders," Pete said, smiling.

"Yep, don't want to cross him. Bad idea," Andy said and made a weird grin.

Pete stood up and went to the computer terminal in the room. He looked like he was having a wild conversation with someone as his hands waved through the air.

"What's up, sir?" George asked, curious as to what was going on.

"A compromise has been reached. You can sleep and eat with the red cadets; however, you will train with the blue, yellow, and green captains. Today you will train with Frank's team in the morning and afternoon. We will join Senior Viceroy David Lu in the evening with our triad," Pete replied formally.

A few minutes passed and Frank appeared at the cadet's door.

"Time to leave cadets," Frank said kindly.

Frank's stripe was red. He motioned to the cadets to follow him. They had never gotten up with one captain and then switched to another captain other than when something bad was going on. It was like tag team captains.

"Is everything alright, sir?" George asked for the cadets.

It always seemed odd to George to call his brother, sir; although, Pete did call his dad, sir.

"Yes, George. Pete and his team need training time together so you will be with us today and for the next week," Frank replied, casually as they walked through the cadet corridors.

"Where are they going sir?" Anna asked, assuming Frank's answer was somehow captain's code for they were on a mission to somewhere.

"Don't ask and don't look for them," Frank replied firmly, frowning.

"Yes sir," the cadets replied disappointed.

"Where are we going, sir?" Gus asked, changing the subject.

"Read the walls and look around you. You know this place. You have all been here before," Frank answered cryptically.

The cadets crinkled their faces and strained to read the walls. Their stripes turned green as they walked out of the red cadet sector and into the green captains sector. George glanced at Emily.

"I didn't do it, George," she signed in their old sign language.

They had decided as a team, it would be better if they used their old sign language around their captains so the captains could easily ease drop on their conversations and think they were informed about what was really going on.

"I did it," Frank signed back.

One more corridor turn and the cadets followed Frank into a classroom. He motioned the cadets to sit at the table next to Niels and the rest of his team. Colonel Payate entered the classroom and the captains jumped up. Niels pulled George up and the others followed.

"Be seated. Today we will be continuing our discussion of basic survival techniques," she said, and the captains slid their pads together in the center of the tables.

Niels and Kate motioned for the cadets to follow along.

"We need to learn all of their motions," Anna signed.

"Yes, you do," Colonel Payate whispered, as she walked around the room.

Frank spun around and faced the cadets. With a glance, they knew he wasn't happy.

"Focus!" was his only hand sign.

A training hologram appeared in front of them. The character before them began with a quick refresher of the editable foods that grow on various asteroids and minimal environment planets. The speaker droned on hour after hour. Gus rubbed his stomach without thinking a stray thought. George nodded and glanced around the room at the captains mesmerized by the training.

The Colonel worked on a computer terminal in the front of the room. Quietly, Gus sliced and diced a ration pack into six slices and slid them across the table. The cadets ate the rations as the holographic speaker droned on.

A few more hours passed. Sara and Gus seemed happy about getting the information. However, they were bored by the way the information was being presented. All in all, they were enjoying themselves. Andy was sure protocol lessons were less painful as he tossed a small red sphere to George to keep them awake.

Anna and Emily were studying the captains in the classroom. They had seen many of them before. They were all about the same age. Oddly, some appeared a little older than Frank and his team. No, they were all older than Frank and his team. Emily and Anna were intrigued.

Why would Frank and his team be in a training class with older captains? More importantly, why were they there with them? The afternoon passed slowly as hiding your thoughts, concentrating on the hologram, and watching the captains was harder than one might have guessed. Eventually, the hologram training ended. The Colonel turned and faced the captains.

"Dismissed," she said kindly.

Silently, they slipped their pads back up their sleeves and filed out of the room in silence. The captains said almost nothing in the corridor, no chatter or murmurs. Only more dull silence.

In the corridor, they followed Frank to the left, while the rest of his team went right. Twisting and turning they came to the red cadet corridors. Frank smiled as they walked; they had not one stray thought. He stopped at their cadets dining hall doors.

"Do you know how to get to Colonel Moawk's training dome?" Frank asked, giving them a little breathing space.

"Yes sir. We can meet you there after dinner, sir," George replied eagerly.

"Very good, cadets," Frank replied formally, and then bolted, running down the corridor they had come through.

They entered the dining hall and walked to their table. How odd it seemed to be there, how young the others all looked. The cadets were noisy and full of talk on the day's events. The food rose from the table.

"Gus, the captains didn't eat lunch?" Emily asked, hoping he might know why.

"I know, it did seem a little odd," Gus whispered, sliding his pad down to look for some information on Colonel Payate and her training.

"The other captains in the room were all older too," Anna said, adding to the mystery.

"I suppose the captains their age are out on training missions, not guarding a bunch of cadets," Andy said guessing, however, they all wondered.

After dinner, they made their way to Colonel Moawk's training dome. Frank and Toma's teams were already there when they lined up. Odd, they thought Toma and Pete's teams were on a mission somewhere, perhaps it is only Pete's team. It must have been a diversion of Frank's and it worked. Andy kicked the ground for being fooled so easily.

Cal turned his head and the cadets straightened up and cleared their thoughts, focusing only on the moment.

Not a word was spoken. David Lu appeared at the door of the small dome off the side of the main dome and walked over to the captains and cadets. He bowed and spun around. Quickly, he progressed though the first twelve levels. At the thirteenth level, he stopped suddenly before beginning.

"Dismissed," he said abruptly.

He bowed raising his right hand to the left side of his chest. They returned the bow and watched as he left the dome thru the small dome doorway he had entered. The cadets turned back around, their captains were gone.

The captains were called out of the dome by Viceroy Petrosky and they followed him through the corridor talking. He had intentionally distracted the captains. George, Andy, Emily, Sara, Anna, and Gus stood in the empty dome, their mouths hanging open.

"Now, we will see how much control they really have," David Lu whispered, to Senior Viceroy Petrosky hidden within the small dome.

George motioned to Andy to step forward. Andy swung his arms wide, stretching and being at level twelve. The cadets weren't as graceful, however, they completed the level and called up a holographic instructor to continue onto level thirteen. The thirteenth level was harder. The holographic instructor's moves made no sense to the cadets, nor did they understand the combination of moves he showed them.

"What is he trying to teach us?" Emily asked, twisting her head sideways to see if it made more sense.

"Only how fast we can fall?" Anna said, rubbing her leg.

"This holographic instructor teaches the thirteenth level different than David Lu does," Anna replied, staring at the instructor's combination moves.

"Yes, but there is something else here," Andy replied, staring at the holographic instructor.

"Like something is hidden within the moves," Sara said, twisting her head.

"It's not about the combinations anymore is it?" Gus asked, twisting his head too.

"Both instructors seem to be teaching the same thing, only they are each using different moves," Emily added, putting the pieces together with Anna.

"It's as if there is something more to each of the moves. It's how the motions are connected, and yet, not how they are connected," George said, stopping and staring at the instructor too.

"Cadets are you dismissed," David Lu called from the small dome.

"Yes sir," they chorused as they stood, staring at the instructor.

They shut down the projector and left for their sleeping room; all the while, knowing they were missing the lesson.

For the next two weeks, the cadet's schedule never varied. On the fourteenth day, Andy was going to burst. Even Anna and Emily were having a hard time concentrating during their day class and in Chen Lo training with David Lu.

"We need some variety," Anna said, spinning on her chair during class.

"This stuff is so safe," Emily added, playing with bits of dust the filters had missed.

"We are going to die of boredom!" Andy said, dropping his face to the tabletop.

On the morning of their fifteenth safe day, Pete was in their room at breakfast.

"Sir, what are you doing here?" George asked, sitting down at the table.

"We are back from, well, from something. Now Frank's team will be gone for a while. Did I miss anything?" Pete asked, trying to change the topic.

"No sir, everyone is wonderfully safe, sir," Andy said, his head hitting the table with a quiet thud.

"We were wondering if we could have another training class, perhaps a little variety, sir?" Sara asked looking hopeful.

"Yes, we are going to Major Doyzel's classroom today. He teaches tactics and armaments," Pete replied kindly.

"And the library, sir, could we go to the officer's library again? Please, sir" Emily asked, nearly begging.

"I'll make the arrangements," Pete said, with a smile and nodded toward the door.

Smiles covered Emily, Anna and Sara's faces. Andy needed to blow something up and the rest wanted any change of scenery. Their stripes turned blue as Pete led them to a classroom in the blue captain sector. Pete sat with his team and the cadets sat down next to them. Major Doyzel entered and the captains stood up.

"Be seated. Pull out your pads," he said kindly.

The Major ran his hands across the classroom computer terminal and a 3D holographic instructor appeared at each team's table. The topic may have changed; however, the instruction didn't.

Andy's head hit the table; the cadets were bored. Hour after hour, the instructor droned on discussing one strategy after the next. Andy was numb and it was his favorite topic!

This time Major Doyzel stopped the lesson at noon so they could all eat lunch. George and the others were nearly comatose as they walked through the corridors surrounded by Pete's team. There was safe and then there was this. Their minds wandered.

"Was isolation on some deserted outpost really all that bad?" George wondered, not hiding his thoughts for a moment.

"Yes, cadet, it is," Pete replied firmly out loud.

George snapped his head up, meeting Pete's eyes as he raised his eyebrow. The doors slid open to the captain's dining hall and they walked in unnoticed by anyone. Bowls of officer cereal appeared in front of them as they sat down.

"How does it know we are here?" Gus asked, plopping down on his chair.

"Gus, it's a computer program. It reads who you are and then materialized the correct foods for you," Sara whispered.

"Oh," he replied slowly.

Even Gus was falling into a malaise from the tedium of their training.

"Is training for captains always like this, Nick?" Andy asked, his brain no longer thinking.

"What do you mean, Andy?" Nick asked, raising an eyebrow.

"I mean, it's all bookwork, sir?" Andy asked, stuffing cereal into his mouth.

"It does seem to be a lot of bookwork, lately. However, you get to go to, well, you know where tonight. That will be a good change of scenery," Nick said with a little smile.

"Yes, it will. Thank you, sir," Andy replied kindly.

Andy was in misery. How was going to the officer's library to read books different from the bookwork they had been doing!

"Be happy. We get to go at all," Emily signed.

The others nodded. It was a small little treat; however, at least it would be interesting.

The afternoon's training matched the mornings training in both boredom and tedium. Dinner was a welcome relief from the droning hologram. The dinner hall was nearly silent when they entered. Only quiet whispers lofted in the air. There were no stray thoughts to be ease dropped on or odd comments to be overheard. Nothing was wrong, but, nothing seemed right. Pete let the cadets sit by themselves. He thought they were acting odd and needed a little space. After all, a dining hall filled with captains was as safe as it was going to get.

They sat down and huddled together, as if trying to keep others from seeing what they were saying, even though no one was trying to invade their minds or listen to their conversation.

"Something is wrong here," Andy signed, looking at the captains in the room.

"No, not wrong, but definitely something is not right," George signed back.

"It's like we know something is going to happen, and yet, it doesn't. Like something is slowly changing over time," Emily added, puzzling.

Standing up, Pete motioned for the cadets to follow him and the others out of the hall. The walk through the corridors was methodical, orderly, uninteresting, and downright dull. Even their hopes for a more interesting evening of reading in the library were quickly squashed as they entered the library.

The translucent librarian that had helped them in the past was not in the library when they arrived. Another translucent librarian was in her place. Now for most officers, which translucent librarian they had helped them wasn't much of an issue; however, the cadets had become attached to their librarian and to the way she moved around them.

Something was not right, perhaps it was because they had been so bored that they had even noticed the new librarian or perhaps because the books she had chosen for them were as dull as their training had been over the few two week. The cadets didn't really know what it was, but, there was something just not right in the library too.

"Ma'am, where is our regular librarian?" George asked politely.

"Cadet Hawkins, I am your regular librarian," the librarian replied, as she glided up to them on the main floor.

"No ,ma'am, you're not. Is she alright? Is there anything we can do to help?" George whispered a little concerned.

"Cadet Hawkins, everything is fine. I am your regular librarian," she replied a little irritated.

"Yes, ma'am. My mistake, ma'am," George said, lowering his head.

The librarian glided away to greet another new arrivals to the library. George was signing to his team with incredible speed the moment she was out of sight.

"Emily, check the main computer network with Anna. We need to know about our librarian," he signed.

She opened her pad to the size of a computer terminal on top of the desk in front of her while Anna held up a book and pointed to passages on the pages.

"Gus and Sara, find information on the translucent race of beings. Andy, watch so we aren't discovered," he added quickly.

Gus stretched and tipped his chair back while Sara rolled around pretending to catch him. She leaned back and picked up two new books from one of the shelves behind them.

Pete and Nick crinkled their foreheads. What were their cadets up to?

"Report," Pete signed when he caught George's eye.

He turned and stared at Pete and Nick.

"This isn't our librarian, sir," George signed.

"What are you talking about? Of course she is," Pete signed back.

"No sir. She isn't. She maybe of the same race; however, she isn't our librarian, sir," George signed insistently.

"George your mind is creating a mystery where none exists," Nick signed, raising his eyebrow.

"Yes sirs, as you wish, sirs," he signed, lowering his head to concentrate on his book, focusing his thoughts.

An hour passed and Andy coughed. Sara, Anna, Emily, and Gus dove into their books. The librarian returned with a Viceroy following her into a section of scrolls on the far wall. It was Pete's dad!

"Why is your dad here, sir?" Sara signed to Pete.

"Perhaps he is trying to read a scroll or a book," Pete signed as his face crinkled.

"Oh, yes, that would be a good reason, sir," she replied.

"Perhaps we could all read our books in the library," Rachael added.

"Yes, yes, that would be good, sir," Sara replied, continuing on with her nonsense.

She was their distraction. Her conversation kept Pete and the others busy ease- dropping on their conversation while Emily, Anna, and Gus reported what they had found to George.

"The translucent librarian is from a race of information technologists," Emily whispered.

"What?" Andy signed.

"The business of their planet is information~past, present, future~all kinds of information," Anna signed.

"You mean an entire planet of librarians?" Andy asked.

"Yes and they take it very seriously," Anna added.

"So when one of the librarians goes missing," George signed, for them to continued their thoughts.

"Something bad has happened to her, George. They don't change jobs. This library is our librarian's life's work. Her duty is to the information within it and making sure everyone who enters is properly served," Emily signed beneath Gus's book.

"How far away is their solar system or galaxy from Asteria station?" George asked.

Andy coughed. Again, they dove into their books.

"Good evening, cadets, captains," the Viceroy said, stopping near the end of their table.

"Good evening, sir," Pete replied as the cadets and captains stood up.

The Viceroy motioned them down.

"How is training progressing?" he asked politely.

"Very well, sir," Pete replied formally.

"Very good. Carry on captains, cadets," he said formally.

"Thank you, sir," Pete replied.

The Viceroy nodded and followed the librarian to a different section of the library.

"What was that?" Andy asked.

"Andy, not everything is a mystery. Perhaps, he is as pleased to see us as we are to see him," Jennifer whispered.

"Yes, ma'am, that could happen, ma'am," Andy whispered. "When pigs fly," he muttered under his breath.

Nick raised his eyebrow at Andy's answer. Now Andy was the distraction.

"Everything is fine, sir," he signed to Nick.

"Why did you question his discussion?" Nick pressed.

"Because someone was trying to read our minds when he was with us, sir," Andy signed back.

"No, Andy, I would have known," Nick signed and shook his head.

"Yes sir, as you wish, sir," Andy signed, returning to his book.

He poked at Nicks thoughts ~ there was nothing there!

"Well that's odd," Andy signed and glanced at George. "Read Pete's thoughts."

George stared at Pete. There were no blocking thoughts, there was nothing in his mind at all. George shook his head. This was odd, very odd. He stood up, stretching.

"It's late, sir. We need to rest, sir," George said out loud.

"Yes, of course," Pete replied, smiling.

They stood up to leave. The librarian didn't appear and their books didn't slip back into the tables. Anna picked up her book and slipped it into Gus's backpack. Sara held her book in her hands and carried it out of the library, not even trying to hide the book. No one stopped her. Emily reached up and pulled the red Chen Lo book from the shelf as she reached forward and held George's hand.

"For later," she whispered.

Chapter 26

SOMETHING NOT...

On the opposite side of the library archway, the cadets and captains reappeared near the red cadet sector sleeping rooms. Pete and his team said goodnight and left them, standing in the red sector corridor alone.

"How weird is that?" Gus signed.

"They haven't let us out of their sight for weeks," Anna added.

"Now suddenly they leave us in the corridor!" Sara added.

"They weren't our captains. Were they, George?" Emily signed and stared at him.

"They were, but they weren't. So what else did everyone find out?" George asked.

"To get to the librarian's home planet we will need a transport size ship. Our standard fighter size is definitely too small," Anna signed.

"Good! I'm tired of nearly dying every time we go into space," Andy signed.

They laughed as they walked along. The rumble of running footsteps echoed through the corridor. The cadets leaned back against the corridor wall to get out of the way and the corridor wall collapsed. The cadets tumbled onto the ground in a cave.

"Emily!" they chorused.

"I didn't do it," she said, shaking her head.

"Then who did?" George asked.

Emily hugged the wall. "Nothing, nothing at all."

The cadets started to run through the cave.

"Where to?" Gus asked.

"The transport ship Pete and Frank brought us here on," George signed.

"I thought it was locked up?" Andy asked.

"Yes, with one of Emily's programs," George signed.

"Good point," Andy signed.

By the time they had finished talking, Anna had their team guided through the caves and nearly to the transport ship's port. Andy slowed the team at the entrance to the small spaceport. As Toma had done before, Andy raised a cloud of dust into the air. Red beams of light crisscrossed the periphery of the spaceport.

"Emily these beams are lower than before. Can you have the ground help us?" George signed, motioning with his hands.

Emily sat on the ground. The dust didn't swirl around her.

"No," she signed, then dropped to the ground.

The others followed by instinct. Silently, two CORE officers passed by the cave entrance not 20 feet away.

"Surely they saw us," Gus signed.

Andy shook his head looking around again. The CORE officers were gone.

"Holograms," Andy signed, and raised the dust in the spaceport again.

They laid back down and the same two CORE officers reappeared walking across the same path, then disappearing at the next turn of the spaceport. While they watched the holograms disappear again, Anna plotted a path through the red energy beams. It would be tight; however, it could be done.

They would step over the first two beams and crawl under the third. The fourth would be the hardest as it was a standing leap over three crossing beams. Then, they would need to step over the last two beams, one high and one low. Andy was first to try Anna's path. The first two beams were easy. Crawling under the third was a tight fit, even for Andy. He worried about Gus.

The standing leap over the next three was not a problem for Andy; however, Emily was going to have difficulty as a standing leap was not her strength. He landed with a thump on the ground raising another cloud of dust into the air. Inches from the back of his ankles was the low red beam.

Gus yelled, "Stop!" It echoed through the spaceport.

Andy froze as the two holographic CORE officers passed through him. He thought that was what Gus had yelled about.

Andy stepped back as Gus yelled again. "No!"

Andy fell to the ground the back of his calf split open from the red beam cutting through his skin. Blood poured from his calf above his ankle. Sara bolted over the first two beams and slid under the third with amazing agility. She leapt over the last three beams before she had even fully stood up. Landing on the other side of the last low red beam, she placed her hand directly on Andy leg. The bleeding stopped instantly as his entire leg glowed a bright yellow. Andy grabbed her shoulders and pulled her hand off his calf. She collapsed.

"Sara, why do you do this?" Andy whispered and lifted her off the ground--his leg healed.

"Emily, you and Anna go with Gus," George ordered. "Someone has to have heard us. Gus, you will need to toss Emily and Anna over the standing jump. I'll help you."

Together the four cadets stepped over the first two beams. Emily and Anna started digging a ditch for Gus to slide under the third beam. Since it was it was a tight fit for Andy, Gus wouldn't make it at all. The ground was hard and didn't want to move, even for Emily.

"It is as if there is nothing here," Emily said, digging her dip.

"What do you mean?" George pressed, staring at the ground.

"All soil has microorganisms living inside, well except soil that has been sterilized of course, but this soil has nothing. It's not sterilized. It's just nothing," Emily said, with an odd look on her face.

"That doesn't make any sense, Emily," George replied with a little smiled.

"I know, it doesn't. It's like what you said, 'It's not wrong, but, it's just not right either. Odd though," Emily whispered.

"Very odd indeed," George whispered, puzzled by the idea.

It took ten minutes for them to dig deep enough for Gus to pass under without burning his body on the red energy beam. All the while, they were exposed in the spaceport. At the next set of beams, Gus lifted Anna and Emily over easily, George knelt down as Gus stepped up on his knee.

He launched Gus up and over. He bent down, then raised up as quickly as he could. He flipped himself up and over the beam like a high jumper on the highest mark. He couldn't stop himself and he crashed into the hard ground rolling forward. Emily screamed. When he stopped, his face was an inch from the low beam.

Anna kicked up a little cloud of dust. Gus pulled back on George's collar and they stepped across the low beam together.

"All this commotion and no one has noticed us?" Andy whispered.

"This is a Calshene station, you'd think someone would have noticed our noisy entrance into the spaceport," George said, adding to Andy's thought.

Andy wasn't comfortable. It seemed too easy, to convenient, an escape. Sara was standing again with Emily and Anna around her, sharing their energy.

"Someone wants us to leave?" Andy whispered looking around the port.

"Then we have to go back," George replied. "Whatever is wrong is wrong here and we are being driven out," he added.

"And we took the bait," Andy said and shook his head.

"An easy distraction again," Emily added.

They turned to leave and suddenly real CORE officers appeared on the outer edges of the spaceport. The red energy beams flickered and turned off. The officers started yelling and running toward the transport ship. The cadets turned around, this time running up the gangplank of the ship. Emily retracted the gangplank as George's foot hit the port door. She was typing as fast as Andy had ever seen her type.

"One more command. Now run!" she yelled, the instant she pushed the execute key.

"Where to?" Andy asked.

"To the transport ship's rear port exit. We have to get out now!" Emily yelled franticly.

They ran as fast as they could through the transport ship as the engines rumbled preparing for takeoff. Emily touched the hallway computer keypad and the rear port door slid open.

They ran through the port door air lock and out the other side, leaping from the ship to the ground below. The moment Emily's hand left the ships wall, the port doors began to close. George and Andy narrowly escaped as the door rolled closed on George's shoe. Only Andy's falling weight pulled him free.

"I thought the port doors wouldn't open when you are taking off?" Gus asked.

"Technically true, Gus," Emily replied.

The ship's engines roared and the thrusters kicked up the dust on the spaceport ground obscuring the fleeing cadets from the CORE officers. Ducking into a different small cave, they stopped at the first corner to rest. The exhaust from the ships engines filled the spaceport and drove the CORE officers out.

The air was getting bad in the caves, too, as the ship lifted off empty of human cargo. They ran further into the cave, climbing higher and higher to reach cleaner air.

"We need the tunnel hogs?" Gus signed.

"No, they may be affected by whatever is going on too," Sara replied.

"How did you know it was a trap, Andy?" Anna asked.

"It was too easy, even for us," Andy signed, grinning.

"Where to George?" Anna asked.

"We need someplace safe. Someplace they would not look for us," George signed.

"Then it can't be Max's or any of the coolers," Gus signed.

"There is another place, where we were safe?" he said, tilting his head as he raised an eyebrow.

Andy grinned. "To hide in the open among friends," Andy whispered.

"Where?" Gus asked.

"Pete's family's house," Sara answered.

"Anna can you find it? It was down one of the corridors on Asteria station, not in the city like on Jupiter station," George signed.

"I remember. We can find it," she replied.

"Who?" Gus asked.

"My pad and I. We can find it together," Anna whispered.

"Anna you need more friends," Gus said, teasing.

"Silence!" George signed, dropping to the ground.

Gus reached out and touched everyone making a link. They rolled over to the edge of the cave wall. Emily thought of the ground covering them over, it rose a little as if struggling against something; however, nothing was there. George thought of nothing and they disappear as six CORE officers marched through the cave.

"What are we looking for?" a CORE officer asked, as they walked by the hidden cadets.

"The last of their resistance," another officer replied calmly.

"Some of them escaped on a transport; however, it's only a matter of time before we find them," a third answered with no emotion.

"So are there any others left on the station?" a fourth officer asked.

"It doesn't look like it. I think we have them all," the first CORE officer replied.

The CORE officers disappeared and the cadets became visible again.

"We must run now!" George signed, struggling to get to his feet.

Andy and Gus lifted George off the ground as they stood up. Emily and Anna lead while Sara followed behind watching their back. Anna turned left and right through the cave at unusual intervals.

"What's up?" Andy signed, wiggling his hand in the air.

"There are lots of life signs in the caves. I'm trying to avoid them all. I can't tell if their good or bad, only that they are there," Anna signed.

At a dead run Anna pointed forward making an archway. Emily twisted her wrist and the door slid open, as if trying it's hardest to help them. It quivered, pulling back until the cadets made it through safely. Then it slammed shut, absorbing the impact, and making no sound. They were in the guest bedroom of Pete's parent's house, or perhaps apartment would be a better description on Asteria station.

They skidded across the floor and ducked under the bed as someone entered the room. George thought of nothing and again they turned invisible.

"I told you there was no one here," Pete's mom said loudly, answering the CORE officer's questions.

"Yes, ma'am; however, we have our orders, ma'am," the CORE officer replied politely.

"Well, you looked now you can leave before my pie spoils in the oven," Pete's mom said loudly.

The CORE officers left and Gus broke the link. George was unconscious. Andy readied a red energy sphere for Gus to feed to Sara to heal George when Mrs. Petrosky skidded around the doorway, landing on the bed with a bounce as she grabbed Andy's hand.

"No!" she signed. "They will be able to trace the energy here," she ordered, absorbing the red sphere from Andy's hand.

The cadets sat on the floor, their mouths gaping open. She knew, somehow she knew they were there. George laid limp over Sara's lap. Mrs. Petrosky placed her hand over his forehead.

"He will be alright, he needs to rest. Lay him here. You all need to rest, however, you must eat first," she whispered.

Andy tilled his head and stared at Pete's mom. He read her thoughts.

"Yes, Andy, I am really here. I have not yet been discovered," she replied.

Andy shook his head. Her mind was strong. He nodded.

"Forgive me, ma'am, I had to know, to keep them safe, ma'am," Andy signed, lowering his head.

"Nothing to forgive, Andy. You have all done well," she replied.

Her words were comforting and warm. She had said very little in the past few years when they had been in her home. More often than not, she was cooking for them and making sure they were well fed and safe. At this moment, she seemed to be so much more. Odd, they had never noticed before.

"You all need to focus and concentrate on nothing and I mean absolutely nothing. As if all you have in your mind is air. No brains, only air. No worries, no stray thoughts only air, lots and lots of mindless air," she ordered.

"Why, ma'am?" Gus asked.

"No, Gus, no thoughts. Only air," Andy signed, raising his eyebrow and looking rather Viceroyish.

Gus lowered his head as Mrs. Petrosky left the room. In a few minutes, she returned with six rations and six bottles of water. Gus sliced and diced two of the rations and slipped the others into his backpack. She didn't even question him. Instead, she held her hand over George's forehead again.

"It's time to wake up and eat George," she whispered.

He stirred and opened his eyes. Sara's mouth dropped open, was Pete's mom a healer like Sara? She helped him sit up to eat his ration. As they ate their ration in silence, Gus poured the water into little silver cups saving four bottles for later. Suddenly, the cadets leaned back and slipped to the floor asleep.

"We need to get them out of here Martha. The station is lost. There are very few of us left," Pete's dad said walking around the corner and staring at the sleeping cadets.

"Pete and the others?" she asked.

"There is nothing we can do, we have to leave, it is only time before we, too, are discovered," he answered.

"They will not leave Pete and the others behind," she whispered.

"This time, there is no other choice. We don't even know what is attacking us. We can't fight, what we can't identify," he whispered, holding his wife close.

"Perhaps we can't fight it, but they can," she signed and motioned to the sleeping cadets. "You said they knew something was wrong in the library. Maybe they can see what we can't?" she added cryptically.

Pete's dad waved his hand over the cadets; they yawned, stretched and woke up. Martha left for the other room so as not to distract the cadets.

"Sir, we," George mumbled, as he scrambled up and the others followed. "Something is wrong, sir. Please you have to believe us," George said, pleading.

The Viceroy lifted his hand.

"Yes, I know and we need your help. We can't identity what is attacking us. It is spreading quickly across the station. Tell me what was wrong in the library," he asked intently.

"It was the librarian, sir. She wasn't our librarian," Emily chimed in.

"And when we questioned the new librarian on it, she denied it, sir," Gus added.

"She knew, we knew, sir," Andy added.

"Sir, Pete, Nick, and the others, well sir, we scanned them after you had come and scanned us. Sir, there was nothing in their minds; only emptiness, no thoughts, nothing there," George said, lowering his head.

The Viceroy leaned back against the edge of the door to think, his head nodding. Martha screamed, dropping her pie. It smashed on the floor of the kitchen, shattering. George looked up, grabbing hold of Gus and Emily as Andy yanked the Viceroy down from the doorway.

George thought of nothing and they all disappeared again. CORE officers rushed into the room. They were hidden, for the moment, against the back wall of the room.

"The scanners will have us chasing ghosts all day!" the CORE officer grumbled.

"There aren't any Calshene left, we have them all now," the other CORE officers said happily.

The CORE officers left, George uncloaked as Anna and Emily opened an archway and door into the caves behind them. Gus and Andy leaned back and they all fell through into the cave.

"George, you OK?" Andy asked.

He didn't answer. He was slumped over–too weak from cloaking the team three times in less than one day. Most Viceroys might have been able to pull it off once or twice in a day; however, three times was unheard of and a full team each time was unbelievable!

Pete's dad wanted to know where George was drawing the energy from; however, there was no time to ask. Gus flipped George over his shoulder like a sack of potatoes. Andy nodded and command was transferred. Anna and Emily took off running.

"Where to?" the Viceroy signed.

"There is only one place left for us to go to get off this station," Andy said.

"No, Andy. There is still one more way before we go there," Emily signed.

"Go where?" the Viceroy asked, lost in their cryptic signs.

He didn't know about the tunnel hog cave, and they wanted to protect the beings of white light and the secrets of the second cavern at all cost.

"Then there is only the fighter training port," Anna said, worried as to what they might find.

"Yes, it isn't an escape route they would think of so there should be only a few guards," Andy agreed.

"We can't escape in a fighter, cadet!" the Viceroy said firmly.

They all looked at each other, smiled, and then laughed.

"If it hadn't been for training fighters, we would have died long ago, sir," Emily signed.

"It is our main mode of transportation; regardless, of how impossible the distance to cover, sir," Anna added, as the other cadets grinned and ran.

The Viceroy was stunned, he hadn't known.

Anna and Emily turned the next corner and dropped to the ground. Their original thoughts wrong. Training port was filled with officers walking around.

Pete's dad scanned their minds. The officers had no thoughts; they lacked any focus.

"Look there's our fighter," Emily said, pointing across the port.

"No, Emily, not again. Can't we have a new shiny one this time?" Gus whined.

Emily smiled. "No, that's the one we need," she signed.

Off to the side was a rather dented training fighter.

"Emily can you do some sort of computer thing and make a diversion?" Andy asked not as specific as George, however, he was trying and that was all that really mattered.

"I'll need some hands-on time with a computer terminal," Emily said formally, winking.

Andy smiled this time.

"Gus, you take George, Sara, Anna, and the Viceroy to the fighter Emily has chosen. Get it ready for takeoff. I'll make the first distraction, Emily will make the second. When we come running, you have to be ready to leave," Andy said, giving orders like George.

"Got it," they all signed.

"Let's go," Andy said, and the Viceroy grabbed his arm, stopping him.

"Stop, cadets. What kind of plan is that? We need to discuss what each person will be doing and when to execute the plan," the Viceroy signed, confused by their simple plan.

"This plan will save our lives and yours, sir. However, you have to follow Sara, Anna. Gus's lead or we will all be captured. Got it, sir?" Andy said firmly.

Andy was in command and there was no time for a detailed explanations, everyone knew what to do. Their lives now depended on the Viceroy doing as he was told by a bunch of young cadets; not the easiest thing for an adult to do. Andy slid a staff weapon out of each sleeve and the Viceroy shook his head.

Emily crept over to a computer terminal near one of the main corridor archways and waited for Andy's sign. Gus readjusted George over his shoulder. Crouching together, the Viceroy and somehow George made them all disappear again. They ran in a straight line for the tiny fighter, knowing their cover wouldn't last more than a few seconds. The Viceroy reached the fighter first and flipped up the port door. Sara, Anna, and Gus leapt over the edge of the port door and slid across the floor. Quickly, the Viceroy lowered the door, but he didn't lock it. Gus laid George down in the Viceroy's lap.

"Take care of him, sir," he said, then spun around and placed his hands on Sara and Anna's shoulders.

Gus did his best to calm their fears. All the while, the Viceroy sat in amazement. He thought he was going to save them, and they thought they were going to save him.

With the others safe, Andy nodded and Emily stood up at the computer terminal. Andy spun around launched two precision red energy spheres from the end of each staff weapons. The blasts knocked him to the ground on his behind. Shooting energy weapons looked easier than it was.

Across the spaceport cavern, the red energy spheres hit their targets. Two large transport ships burst into flames. The hulls exploded at the impact, sending sections of metal hull flying through the air. The officers scattered and then ran back with fire extinguishers, trying to put out the flames.

With the officers distracted, Emily's hands raced across the computer keyboard. She launched a dozen fighters and transport ships into the air inside the spaceport cavern, and started the opening sequence for the spaceport doors.

With so little space in the cavern and no actual pilots in the ships, the ships wobbled and bumped into each other in mid-air. Soon the ships were bouncing off each other like balls on a pool table. It was getting dangerous in the spaceport. It was time to leave.

She loaded program after program into the station's mainframe computer network. An officer grabbed Emily's shoulder from behind, catching her by surprise. She screamed! Andy rolled over, sending a red sphere blazing through the air and striking the officer in the back of the legs. He crumpled to the ground in agony.

Emily returned to her computer terminal as if nothing had happened. Andy straightened up to improve his aim and launched two more volleys of red spheres from his staff weapons. Again, he was thrown to the ground.

The first two shots were precision shooting, however, these shots were haphazard at best. One sphere hit another transports and it burst into flames. The second sphere hit the cavern ceiling, sending rock and dust raining down on the ships below. It was the big diversion he wanted, and he ran over to get Emily.

She pushed the execute key as he lifted her off the ground, throwing her over his shoulder as he raced toward the tiny fighter. The fighter lifted a few inches off the ground and the port door swung open. Emily's pad had slipped from her hand when Andy lifted her up. An officer, who was right on their tail caught it, racing to give it back to her. He reached them at the port door of the tiny fighter. Emily touched his hand as she took the pad.

"Thoreans!" she whispered.

Andy waved them forward and five more officers raced across the port for the tiny fighter. Body after body, Andy and Gus grabbed onto them and pulled them inside.

"Any others, sir?" Andy asked.

"No, we're all here, Andy," Toma replied.

"Now Anna, we're ready," Andy said firmly.

The port door was slammed shut and locked.

"Hang on, this is going to be a bumpy ride!" Anna yelled.

"Now Emily," Andy said loudly.

Emily slipped out her pad and the entire fleet of training ships lifted off the floor of the spaceport. Some spun wildly and crashed while other shot up and out of the launch doors into outer space. Inside the ship, the extra weight was nearly more than the tiny fighter's engines could lift. The engines choked and sputtered, trying to lift the extra load.

George opened his eyes. "Andy, I need your help," he whispered, as Pete's dad, Viceroy Petrosky helped him straighten up.

"You're not strong enough George," Andy whispered, instantly concerned at what he knew George was going to do.

"Then share some of those flaming red energy spheres of yours," George whispered weakly.

Andy grabbed Gus and pulled him back over the Thoreans to George. He made his first red energy sphere and handed it to Gus. Gus sent the energy to George through their link and the ship lifted higher into the air.

"More, I need more!" Anna yelled.

Andy's next red sphere was bigger and hotter. The girls flew the fighter across the port as George passed more energy into the ships engines. The Thoreans turned off their holographic bars and Cal started feeding Gus energy spheres with Andy. Viceroy Petrosky grabbed onto George's shoulder to help calm and focus his mind.

Toma and the other Thoreans grabbed hold of the ship's hull and it became invisible as it rose up and out of the spaceport. Emily was whispering to Anna and Sara new directions as they flew. Rising out of the pull of gravity from Asteria station, the engines were able to maneuver the tiny fighter more easily.

Toma, Darri, Sheta, Gabe, and Tillie used their own strength and energy to cloak the fighter as Anna and Sara guided the training fighter ship through the Calshene asteroid field. An hour passed before they reached Emily's new landing location. It was a crater-marked piece of rock, slowly spinning in the asteroid field.

As they guided the fighter down toward the surface, Anna and Sara understood why it was so important to land on this rock and not on any another. Below them, hidden in one of the craters, was the transport ship Pete and Frank's teams had rescued them with earlier in the rotation.

Emily may have launched the empty transport ship earlier; however, she didn't destroy it. She hide it! Anna docked the fighter with the transport ship and Emily sent the unlocking code to the transport ship computers. The port door rolled open. The three jubilant girls spun around beaming.

Their smiles turned to gasps when they saw the mound of bodies behind them. The captains and cadet were exhausted from cloaking the fighter and feeding the engines. Sara ran from cadet to captain, checking for life signs.

"We need to move them to the hospital quickly," Sara said, a tear running down her check as her emotions welled up inside her.

"We can do this again," Emily said, hugging Sara.

"I know. I'm just so tired of running from evil that when it's not evil and it's something else, it just doesn't seem fair," Sara said, whining a little.

"We are all tired, but, we have work to do," Emily added with a little smile.

The three young cadets dragged one captain at a time into the transport hospital. The Thoreans were heavy and they dropped Cal and Gabe, bumping their heads on the healing table edges as they lifted them each into place.

"That's' going to leave a bruise," Anna said quietly.

"Hope he is not too mad," Sara replied, as they hurried back to the fighter for the cadets and the Viceroy.

Three hours later, the girls had everyone was out of the fighter and into the transport ship's hospital room.

"Are they OK, Sara?" Emily asked, as they laid George on a healing bed last.

"Oddly, yes. I'm sure the Viceroy had something to do with that," Sara answered, turning on all of the yellow healing beams.

"They gave us a lot of energy to escape," Anna added, combing back Gus's hair over his forehead.

"You know, I missed everyone so much over the school year. Now so much has happened to us this rotation. Sometimes I wish we were just normal cadets. You know?" Sara said, her fear creeping into her thoughts.

"Us too," Anna said, and the three girls hugged each other.

"We need to stay focused to save them," Emily whispered, trying hard to lead and focus her thoughts better. "Besides we have already done this at the beginning of our rotation, remember?"

"I was trying to forget that part," Anna said, joking a little.

Their link was strong and they had done this before. They could do it again. Emily stared at the captains, boys, and Viceroy. Then she stared at Sara and nodded for her report.

"The last time this happened we were on Mahadean and Shadoo, they almost died. So on a scale of one to ten with ten being dead, I'd say they are about a six," Sara replied rolling her hand.

"Good, I'm tired of always nearly dying," Anna said, laughing.

"Me too!" Emily said, laughing.

With everyone transferred into the hospital room and the fighter tucked neatly away in the cargo hold, Emily, Anna, and Sara walked to the command deck to eat a ration and share a bottle of water.

"So where are we going, Emily?" Sara asked, as every time George and Andy had slipped from them, Emily had risen to the challenge of leading their team.

"Where did George want to go?" Emily asked, kindly drinking her water.

"To the planet of the translucent librarians," Sara answered, smiling.

"No one seems to know what is going on here and we need information. So that's the plan. Anna if you would load the stellar coordinates into the navigational computer, we can get started on our way. However, until we clear the asteroid field, we will need to look like a drifting rock. Please fly rock-like.

After that, we will be a comet again and we can fly in a straight line. Sara, will you check on our captains, team, and Viceroy please?" Emily said, folding up the ration wrapper as they all stood up.

"On my way," Sara replied, walking out of the command deck as Emily and Anna walked over to the main command console.

Emily loaded a program and the transport ship shimmered and looked like a large chunk of rock, breaking off the asteroid as they lifted the transport ship off the asteroid in a drifting-rock-kind-of-way.

"Do you think we should call Max or grandfather, Emily?" Anna asked, worried that no one knew where they were going.

"No, we don't know where they were when whatever took over. It might lead the wrong people to us," Emily replied.

Anna nodded and flew cautiously; gliding passed small and large boulders. Together they used the gravitational pull of the larger asteroids to slingshot themselves along, increasing their speed each time.

At the edge of the asteroid field, Anna started the main engines and the transport ship and traveled in a parallel direction for a while. Then, they made a ninety degree turn and disappeared, becoming a comet that didn't pass too close to the asteroid field so it wouldn't have been trapped by it gravitational fields.

"How far away is the planet of the translucent librarians?" Emily asked.

"At our current speed, we will be there in four days. And yes, that's with your previous modifications," Anna replied and smiled.

Emily nodded leaving Anna on the command deck heading off to check on Sara. In the corridor between Anna and Sara, she stopped.

"Max, I know you are there, somewhere. I'm not as confident without George's help and right now he is resting. I know it is you who is helping me and I know you will not answer, it doesn't really matter. I only wanted to say, thank you," she whispered to the air.

She entered the hospital room and watched Sara dart from one captain to the next.

"How are they doing?" Emily asked.

"You need to learn to say report, Emily," Sara said, correcting her.

"Oh alright, report," Emily said, more George and Pete like.

"They are all doing rather well. They need a day's rest, and then they should be fine. How far are we from the librarian planet?" Sara asked.

"Anna said four days," Emily replied and smiled.

"Good, there will be enough time for everyone to recover by then," Sara said, nodding her head.

"We'll need to sleep in shifts tonight to keep the ship on course," Emily said.

Sara nodded and Emily headed back up to the command deck. Twice on this rotation, Emily had taken command of their team. It made her uncomfortable and she wondered how George could do it so easily. So many decisions to make all of the time, never a true moment of rest, and the fate of their teams resting on the decisions she had made. The responsibility was overwhelming; fear crept into her mind again.

"Calm and focused is your path," was the thought that suddenly popped into her mind.

She spun around, looking who was near. The corridor was empty.

"Max, grandfather, are you here?" she asked to the air again.

Chapter 27

INFORMATION IS POWER

By mid-afternoon the next day, the cadets, captains, and Viceroy Petrosky were starting to wake up. Sara had been injecting them with nutrients and vitamins since shortly after they had left the asteroid field. Now, they were recovering and growing stronger; somehow, she could sense their strength grow.

Viceroy Petrosky, George, and Toma were the first to wakeup. However, before they could say a word, Sara was pushing dark brown cereal on them to eat. Within an hour, all of the captains, Gus, and Andy were awake and eating the dark brown cereal.

"Sara, you need to learn how to cook," Andy said, joking and the others smiled.

"No, this way you will all appreciate Gus and Gabe's cooking," Sara said, grinning as she called Emily on the ship's systems.

Within a few minutes, Emily appeared at the door, looking very leaderish. She looked at Toma.

"Report, sir. What were you and your team doing on Asteria station?" Emily asked, as firmly as she could.

Inside she was nervous. They had spent very little time with Toma and his team. Toma was often the leader of their triad when they were all together. Now, she was the leader and needed some answers.

Toma crinkled his eyebrows and the Viceroy slightly shook his head. Emily, Anna, and Sara had guided them to safety and they were owed their respect. Toma dipped his head to the Viceroy, straightened up, and focused on Emily.

"We returned from our mission early and had only entered the spaceport a few moments ahead of your team. We knew something was wrong when we saw your team cloak and then run for the fighter. We knew we should be leaving with you, ma'am. Also, your diversion plan was well-executed, ma'am," he said kindly.

Emily nodded her head and Toma turned his attention toward Andy.

"Impressive staff work, Andy. Cal will instruct you further," Toma said and then paused, refocusing on Emily. "Ma'am, may I ask what is your team's status?" Toma asked formally, still recognizing Emily as the leader of their team until leadership transferred.

"We are headed for the planet of the translucent librarian, sir. We look like a comet. Our crew is now revived and this is the same transport ship that Pete and Frank rescued us with earlier this rotation, sir," Emily reported.

Andy smiled and nodded his head.

"You're going to like this, Cal. This ship has all the extras, sir," he whispered.

On their last use, the transport ship had been restored and its food, power, and armaments had been enhanced.

"Sir?" Emily said, and motioned to Viceroy Petrosky, Pete's dad, to report to the team.

He had been very quiet. They all turned and stared at him. He smiled.

"Emily, George, Andy, Gus, Sara, and of course Anna, whom I am assuming is guiding the ship right now, Martha and I thought we would need to rescue you, instead, you have rescued us. I have never seen such remarkable teamwork. I am very proud of you all. Emily, you, Anna, and Sara have done an exceptional job without your team leader. I am very impressed. I know Martha would be equally impressed with your work and ingenuity," he said kindly.

He held out his arms wide and the two girls rushed him like they rushed grandfather. Toma, Cal, and the others couldn't believe what they were seeing, a Viceroy hugging fourth year cadets and praising them for their strength. Toma leaned back to think for a minute about what the three young cadets had done on their own, without their leader or second; it really was downright impressive.

He understood why the Viceroy said and did what he did. Not many junior officers could have done what these fourth year cadets had done and none of them could have done it without their team leader.

Toma was pleased with their triad. It had been the right choice to make. He hadn't seen them last year when the cadets planned the attack against the Mahadean. His team had been captives and Frank and Pete's teams had watched and helped them. Now it was up to his team to guide them and discover the truth to set Asteria station free. Sara released her patients and soon everyone was busy with new work. George called Sara, Emily, and Anna together in a small room off the main command deck.

"You all did very well, a second time!" he said, smiling. "You keep this up and Gus, Andy, and I are going to retire!"

"Ha, what fun would that be? Andy won't have anything to blow up," Emily replied.

"Yes, he wouldn't like that at all," George replied, hugging the girls. "Good work. You are all amazing."

"I transfer leadership to you George and I don't want to do this again. So stop exhausting yourself, enough is enough," Emily said, as seriously as she could.

"Yes, ma'am," George replied and then hugged the girls again.

He knew this was hard on Emily, but, he was happy she was willing to step-up and lead when it was needed. The girls left the small room, feeling better and appreciated. They could help and make a difference.

Toma stood at the door, watching and waiting for George. George nodded and Toma entered. Waving his hand, two seats rose from the floor and a holographic projector type table grew up from the floor in the center of the room. The sector of space they were traveling through appeared. Toma said nothing; he only sat down. A long pause followed.

"Well, sir?" George whistled, a little impatiently.

"Well, what?" Toma whistled back.

"Well, Pete usually says something, sir," George said impatiently again.

"Well, I'm not Pete," Toma replied, rather matter-of-factly.

Another long agonizing pause followed.

"George, think. What would Pete say if he was here now. Think before you answer," Toma said encouragingly.

Toma really wasn't like Pete at all. Pete may have grown up with rules upon rules all his life, however, he knew when to let the rules slide a little. George actually knew very little about Toma and the other Thoreans in their triad. They had spent precious little time together, if you didn't count running for your life and trapped within stasis tubes. Until that moment, George had never noticed how much they had missed.

"Sir, tell me about you and your family. About where you come from, sir," George asked, staring at Toma.

Toma smiled. "Why?" he asked.

George hated having to be totally honest; however, he knew if Toma could die for them then he owed them the respect of a true friend.

"I have never asked. I simply assumed you were like Pete and Frank. I never even bothered to find out who you were or who Cal was or the others. I just assumed I knew. I was wrong. You aren't Pete or Frank and right now, I need your council to formulate a plan. To do that, I need to know who you are, so I can understand your point of view, sir," George replied, dipping his head.

"I like honesty sometimes. Other times, it seems so inconvenient," Toma whistled, trying to lift George's spirit.

"Yes, on that we agree, sir," George whistled, grinning a little.

"I grew up the second son of a powerful ruling family on my planet. I have lived a privileged life all of my life. Pete may have had rules, however, from time to time he, shall we say, stretches them. Most Calshene do, regardless of what they say. On Zalhala, stretching the rules isn't allowed. You can be punished severely for even thinking of bending the rules. My only escape was here, in space. And yet even here, I find it hard to break the rules," Toma said, telling George a part of the truth about his life and why he was in space.

"Toma, you have broken the rules a dozen times with us, sir," George said, chuckling.

"Not really. We have simply done what was required to protect you and your team," Toma replied seriously.

"Call it what you will, sir. I'm going with breaking the rules, sir," George said, grinning. "So what happened to your older brother, sir?" George asked kindly.

"He is on Zalhala. He wasn't allowed to escape his duty to our planet," Toma replied, his face looked sad.

"You miss him, sir?" George asked kindly.

"Yes, of course, he's my brother," Toma replied, grinning.

"And the others on your team? Are they also all escapees from the rules of Zalhala, sir?" George pressed, now that he had Toma comfortable and talking about home.

"Yes, George, it was the only way for all of us to live our lives," Toma replied seriously.

"But you made a triad with us. Doesn't that rather limit you and create another set of rules, sir?" George asked, thinking he and his team now had more rules to follow.

George didn't really understand what following the rules of a protocol officer meant, and that all the rules they followed in space and for their triad was nothing compared to having nearly every moment of your waking life scheduled by a protocol officer.

"Actually, it has freed us from a life of public service on Zalhala. A life that is not of our own choosing," Toma replied quietly.

"What does your brother think, sir?" George asked curiously.

"He is proud that I had the courage to stand up and change my life. To become who I was meant to be instead of someone that the protocol officer said I was supposed to be," Toma answered, and smiled at the thought of his brothers parting words.

George was stunned. His life had never been filled with obligations and duties to people other than himself and his family. He thought getting dressed up for a family wedding was a big deal. At that moment, he thought it made him seem shallow.

"Toma, do you know what the people on the planet of librarians are called, sir?" he asked.

"They are the Celestian. Why do you ask?" Toma asked calmly.

"That is where we are going, sir," George answered, thinking about their librarian.

"Why there George?" Toma asked kindly.

Toma already knew where they were going; however, he wanted to know why George and his team had chosen the Celestian home world as their destination.

"We don't know what is wrong on Asteria station. We only know something is wrong. We can't fight an enemy we don't know. So we need information. Where better to get information then a planet of information technologists, sir," George replied, matter-of-factly, pleased he could explain.

"How were you going to get this information from the Celestian?" Toma pressed, thinking George had not fully thought out his plan.

"Why, ask them, sir," George replied, frowning and not understanding why Toma was asking the question.

"Ask whom, George?" Toma pressed, raising an eyebrow.

"Well, whoever is in charge of the information-keeping-computer-stuff-thing, sir," he said, his voice trailed off as he realized what Toma was really asking.

"You can't fly in and ask for some obscure information and leave. They don't know you, nor will they trust you to read their archives by yourself. We will need a tactical plan," Toma replied, more captain like, now that George was beginning to understand.

"It sounds like we are going into battle, sir," George said, wanting to know more about what Toma knew.

It might have been easier and taken less time for Toma to tell George the answer outright. However, by making George reason out his initial plan, Toma was hoping he would learn a new lesson. Sometimes, things that appear simple on the surface are more complex under the surface.

"In a way, we are going into battle. Only this time, they are a lot smarter than we are, and we need them to help us," Toma replied, raising an eyebrow.

"Has the evil that destroyed Calshene and taken over so many other galaxies ever attacked the Celestian, sir?" George asked, thinking.

"No. I don't think mindless minions have a chance against the Celestian people," Toma replied, chuckling at the thought.

George heard Toma's answer; however, he was captured in the moment. Patiently, Toma sat and watched George think. At least, that's what Toma thought was happening.

"We need the others," Toma whistled, pushing George a little.

"Yesss," George answered, his voice trailing off as if lost in thought.

Suddenly, Gus and Andy burst into the small room, tackling George. Gus made a link with George and Andy before they hit the floor. In his mind's eye, Andy let loose with one extra hot red energy sphere into George's link. The boys crashed to the ground, flipping and sprawling across the small room. George shook his head.

"Who was in it, George? Toma, who was it in the link with George, sir?" Andy yelled, wanting immediate answers.

"What link? What are you talking about?" Toma asked stunned, jumping to his feet.

"The link with George, someone attacked him in a link, sir," Andy repeated.

"There is no one here or in a link," Toma said, turning around and calling for Cal and Gabe to come immediately.

Andy spun around invading Toma's mind.

"Stop that, cadet!" Toma yelled, in an instant, Toma was a captain again. "I don't know how you were able to sense George was in trouble, but, from now your team will remain in a continuous link. Am I clear, cadet?" Toma said, staring directly at Gus and Andy sprawled across the floor.

Toma was stunned and worried. He could sense when Andy tried to invade his mind, but, he hadn't know George's mind was been attacked. This was not good.

"Yes sir!" Gus and Andy replied quickly.

The boys leapt up off the floor, pulling George off the floor, still shaking his head. Cal and Gabe came running up to the door of the small room. With George upright again, Andy and Gus raced out of the room, grabbing onto Cal and Gabe as they ran. Their new link would need to be a strong link and they ran to join the other cadets in it.

"Report, cadet!" Toma said loudly.

He had turned serious in an instant. Someone had just tried to hurt one of his cadets under his protection, and he was unable to sense or stop whoever it was.

"I don't know who it was. It wasn't like any link I've been in before. This was smooth as silk, sir. I didn't sense my mind being invaded or a link even being formed. It was like when we were on Earth. It happened there the first time, before our rotation even began. Have you ever heard of anything like that, sir?" George asked, rubbing his head.

Toma's forehead crinkled.

"Maybe. Only a few Senior Viceroys I know of can do what you are describing," he said, frowning.

"Wouldn't be the first time a Senior Viceroy tried to hurt us. But, this time it was, well, this was different, Toma, like on Earth. I know what it feels like in my mind when someone is invading. Been there, done that. This was smooth as silk, sir," George said, carrying on and on, repeating himself, hoping it would help him figure out what had happened.

"Only a true master can do what you're talking about," Toma replied solemnly.

"You mean like David Lu, sir?" George whispered, not wanting to imply any wrong doing.

"Or Pete's grandfather or my grandfather. They are all strong enough to do it," Toma said seriously.

"No. It wasn't them. I know what they are like in my mind. It was someone we haven't met~yet. Someone that is as strong as our grandfathers and David Lu, sir," George replied, thinking.

Toma reached over and pulled George over to the chair to have him sit and focus on their first task before them again. The answer to find George's mysterious link would have to wait since it would be difficult to figure out, and they needed a plan for the Celestian first.

"We need a plan for when we arrive at the Celestian home world," Toma said, refocusing George.

"Toma, does your family have any connections to the Celestian people?" he asked oddly.

"I don't know. Perhaps, my father or Cal's father has spoken to them from time to time. I'll see what I can find out from my brother," Toma replied, and turned to pull up a computer terminal.

"See if they can get a way onto the planet too, sir" George added.

Typing quickly, Toma composed a letter and sent it to his brother on Zalhala, his home planet. Gus was back at the door of the small room when Toma turned back towards George.

"It's time to eat, sir," he said, nodded and left without entering the small room.

They got up and Toma slid his arm over George's shoulder. Cal followed Toma's example and leaned in to talk with Andy as they left the room and headed for the galley.

"This is going to be harder than before, isn't it, sir?" George half asked as they walked.

"Depends on your perspective, George. The task is more complex than our adventures in the past. I'll grant you that. However, there are always alternatives, decisions, and choices to be made. Perhaps, the answers to the questions we ask will lead us to our plan," Toma replied, walking down the hallway to the galley.

Everyone else was in the galley by the time the four arrived. George hardly noticed Toma's team had their arms over his team's shoulders as they sat down. The food before them was more than rations, however, not the meal they had been expecting. George raised his eyebrow and Gus smiled.

"We don't know how long we will be traveling this time. We are conserving early," Gus replied a little serious.

George had to agree, this was an unusual trip indeed. They all started to eat and tell Toma and the others captains about the odd events on Asteria station while they were gone.

"I will need reports from everyone in two hours. Same as always; however, this time your answers will determine our path," George said between bites.

Emily smiled and rolled her eyes. She had no idea what they would need on a planet of librarians. Her standard set of programs seemed inadequate. She worried she would not be able to come up with something this time to help their team find the information they needed.

Sheta picked up her fork in her other hand and slid her arm over Emily's shoulder again. Oddly, Sheta could barely sense Emily's trouble. She only knew she needed help focusing by the expression on her face.

They sat in silence, thinking for a few minutes as they ate. George was lost in random thoughts, grasping at anything that popped into his head. Still, his random thoughts did have a pattern and he was beginning to put the puzzle together.

"We need an edge, sir. Something and right now, we don't have it, sir," George whispered then turned suddenly, staring directly into Toma's eyes.

"You can't sense us or read any of our thoughts. Can you, sir?" he asked bluntly.

Toma stared at the captains and each one nodded in turn.

"No, we can't sense you anymore. We could when we first woke up. Now, we barely can," Toma replied, honestly and a little surprised the captains hadn't noticed until now.

"You're all infected with the whatever that is on Asteria station," George replied, getting worried.

"I don't see how. We were on Asteria station for less than half an hour. If it has affected us, our minds are still intact," Toma replied thinking.

George nodded to Sara, she needed to figure out if their captains were infected. If the captains were infected, their trip could be in trouble.

"Makes you wonder how the Viceroy and Mrs. Petrosky managed," Andy added.

"It had to be hard. Hiding their thoughts and guiding us to them, sir," George said.

"Do you think it was them who helped you and your team?" Toma asked.

"Yes, too many coincidences for it not to be them. Where is the Viceroy now, sir?" George asked, looking around the galley.

"Doing what Viceroy's do," Toma answered cryptically.

"What, sir?" George pressed, not understanding what Toma meant.

"He is guiding the energy of the universe," Toma replied.

"I thought that's what Senior Viceroys did, sir?" George questioned.

"They do; however, something is wrong right now, and they must need his help," Toma added.

"How do you know if you can't sense us, sir?" George asked and Toma smiled.

"His mind is exceptional strong, even we can sense his presence," Toma whispered.

"He must want you to. I can't sense him at all, sir," George replied.

"Clear your mind, focus your thoughts, think of calm and peace," Toma whispered.

George closed his eyes and focused his thoughts. Slowly, he found the Viceroy's thoughts. The energy in their sector of the universe was flowing through him, surrounding him filling his mind with peace and calm. In an instant, Andy flew across the table, landing on George, knocking him to the ground.

"George, George talk to me. You alright?" Andy said, shaking George's shoulders like crazy.

George could hardly answer. "Andy, stop I'm fine. Really, stop."

"I looked up and you had that dazed-look-thing going. I thought someone, well you know," Andy said and sighed.

"No, I was simply focusing my thoughts, that's all, nothing to worry about," George replied, as Andy reached forward and pulled George up off the floor with one arm.

Andy's flying leap ended lunch.

"I need reports in two hours everyone; and Gus, the Viceroy will need food too," George said seriously.

Turning he left the galley and met Toma in the hallway.

"We still need an edge, sir," he said, a little worried as they walked through the hallway.

"It will come. Give it time. Remember, the Celestian will know all about you and your team. They are the information archive and brokers of the universe," Toma whispered.

"Then it is their greatest strength and their greatest weakness, sir," George muttered.

"An interesting perspective, George. I'm not sure I would have said information was a weakness," Toma said, questioning his thought.

"Sure it is. They have all that responsibility for the care and management of all that information, sir," George replied, as they entered the main command deck and walked into the small room.

In that instant, George had started the plan and information was the root.

Chapter 28

PATH IS THE PLAN

They sat back down in the small room off the command deck and their sector of the universe appeared on the holograph in front of them. Sara and Darri appeared at the doorway early and waited, whispering to themselves. George nodded and they entered as Toma raised two more seats.

"Andy and Cal need to be here," Toma whispered.

"They're on their way, sir," George answered, as the two appeared at the door.

He waved them in and Toma raised two more seats against the outer wall. Sara and Darri sat in the center of the room with George and Toma.

"The hospital stores are full and everyone has recovered. However, we could all use a good rest. I have the same computer virus from before, but I'm at a loss as to what we will actually need. I don't think they will be easily tricked by any of my programs," Sara said a little worried.

"True, Sara; however, we have one thing they don't," he said, leading her down a path.

"What, George?" she asked, curious about what he knew.

"We know how to make the viruses and they don't," he said and Sara smiled.

She hadn't thought of it that way before. She liked the idea.

"And the other thing?" George asked cryptically.

"Nothing yet," Sara replied as cryptically, answering his question from before on if the captains were infected.

Sara and Darri left as Gus and Gabe walked up to the door. Again, George waved them in and they took their place in the center of the room.

"The stored are full so we have four weeks of food without conservation," Gus reported.

"And you can extend us to?" George asked, knowing he had more say.

"Ten weeks, maybe eleven weeks, depends. However, I'm not sure what I can help with on this planet. I don't think there will be any poor slaves to feed," Gus said, staring at the floor.

"Maybe not Gus, however, we have the recipe of your red drink to trade with," George suggested.

"The old one or the new one?" Gus asked with a grin.

George was surprised.

"The old one of course, we'll keep the newer one for us," he answered, grinning too.

Gus was beaming. He hadn't thought he could help much on this trip.

Anna and Tillie appeared at the door next. Gus high fived Anna as George nodded them inside. Anna and Tillie sat and adjusted the holographic image of the universe in front of them.

"This is our position, here," she said, pointing and marking it with a floating green dot. "Here is the Celestian home world. We are about two days from their home world now. It is a massive planet, twice the size of Earth. Gravity will be an issue for us, it's going to weigh us down and make us tired- -even with our suits on," she said and waited. "Come on, that was a perfectly good joke. Not even a grin."

Anna didn't tell jokes often so any joke was a major accomplishment.

"OK, ha, ha. Happy?" Andy chimed in.

"How do we approach Celestian?" George asked kindly, refocusing their thoughts.

"Like Asteria station, we will receive instructions on our approach. If they accept our answers, we will be given landing coordinates. We will know how valuable we are or if we are honored guests to them, depending on where we are told to land. And yes, I have that all loaded into everyone's pads and the transport ship's systems," Anna answered.

"Thank you, Anna," George said nodding.

They left. Emily and Sheta weren't waiting at the door.

"Emily where are you?" George thought.

She didn't answer, nor did Sheta. He glanced at Andy.

"Go pick her up, Andy. She knows better," George said calmly.

Andy and Cal took off out the door in search of Emily and Sheta.

"She will not come willingly, George," Toma whispered.

"Why, sir?" he asked, studying the latest navigation chart floating in front of him.

"She doubts her ability to help her team," he replied. "Remember, she is going to a planet where everyone is very intelligent. She thinks she will not~what do you say~ measure up, and you will no longer need her," Toma whispered.

"What? That's ridiculous. I will always need her council, sir," George said, staring at Toma.

"She needs to know that," Toma said bluntly.

"I've told her that before, sir," George replied, not understanding why he should state what was obvious to him.

"Then perhaps, you need to say it again, cadet," Toma said more captain like.

"Yes sir," George replied, thinking it was about being supportive of his team at this moment, and if that is what Emily needed, then he needed to say it again and not just assume she knew.

Andy appeared at the door with Emily, struggling, over his shoulder. George shook his head and they all entered. He dropped her down on the seat in the center of the room.

"It was only a figure of speech, Andy," George said, trying to hide a grin.

"She wasn't coming otherwise, George," Andy said, taking his seat.

"Emily?" George's voice softened.

"I have nothing to say and nothing to add. I told this brute that when he hoisted me up over his shoulder. There is no point for me to even be here. I have nothing that a planet of brainyacs doesn't already have," Emily said, huffing.

"Emily, you're our brainyac and that's all that matters to us. What programs did you write?" George asked softly, holding her hand to help focus her thoughts.

"Oh just the basics; stealth, distractions, diseases and a few computer network destruction sequences," she said, rambling on.

"She is on our side, right?" Cal asked, whispering to Andy.

"Ya, Cal, she is, sir," Andy whispered back.

"She looks so normal and all," Cal replied, staring at Emily.

"Na, she wicked like the rest of us, sir," Andy whispered and smiled.

"No argument there, Andy, no argument there," Cal whispered.

"Emily, do you have anything on decryption and you know?" George asked cryptically.

"Yes, I still have that particular decryption program. But, you know I can't use it. I promised, George," she replied, concerned as to why he was asking about the prophecy decryption program.

"True, however, it might give us something to trade with. After all, they don't have one. If they did, the Viceroys would have used it long ago, you know what I mean, for—well, you know," George said cryptically and grinned a little.

Emily glowed.

"I can do that. I could write a few basic planet defense programs too. I bet their computer systems are as open as the cadet stations. Then they could...," she said happily, her voice trailing off as she thought.

"Report back tomorrow, Emily. Anna said we only have two days," George added.

"I know, I was listening," she said, as she and Sheta left the small room, whispering and planning as they walked down the hallway.

"What was that all about?" Toma asked.

"What, sir?" George asked surprised.

"George?" Toma said, raising his voice and giving him a captain-type look.

"Emily decrypted the entire prophecy scroll in less than one day, sir. She wrote the decryption program long before she even saw the prophecy scroll, sir," George replied, not thinking anything of it.

"So you really did read the prophecy, the whole thing?" Toma asked in awe.

"Yes sir," George replied, wondering why Toma was asking.

"Twice, sir," Andy chimed in.

"So what did it say?" Toma asked.

"We don't remember, sir," George sighed.

"However, we were suppose to die already and so was our triad, sir," Andy added and grinned.

"The prophecy changed because we lived. We heard Pete's grandfather and dad talking about it a while ago, sir," George added, telling Toma and Cal something he thought they already knew.

"I can't say I've ever heard of that happening before," Toma said and smiled as best he could.

"You escaped Zalhala and we escaped the prophecy, sir," George said bluntly.

"It's not that bad," Toma said and frowned.

"It is if it tells you when you're going to die, sir," Andy replied.

"True enough," Cal replied for Toma.

"Andy, report," George said, changing the subject to prevent Toma from diving any deeper into his and Emily's cryptic discussion.

"We have a full set of cannons, a few torpedoes, plenty of staff weapons, and six holographic bars. We can all look like translucent librarians if we have too. Emily has us looking like a comet for now so we are fairly safe from discovery," Andy said.

"Good, then we have our plan," George said.

Toma frowned. "What plan is that?" Toma asked firmly.

"We will request landing privileges and then trade our information for theirs. I have only one big concern, sir," George said puzzled.

"And that is what?" Toma prodded.

"How do we hide the Viceroy from the Celestian, sir?" George said, thinking.

"Hide him. I would have thought you would want him to gain access to the power of the Celestian high council," Toma said, surprised by George's decision.

George grinned.

"No sir, that's you and your team. As you said, you are from a powerful family of Zalhala and so you will all rate a dignitary's welcome. We will not. We are only cadets on a training mission. They can't know who we really are, sir. You are the distraction, while we trade with minor librarians who want to improve their status. This way we can get the information we need, sir," George said, explaining the whole plan as he thought perhaps he was to brief in his explanation a few moments before.

"A clever plan, George, very good. Now let's see what my brother was able to arrange," Toma said, opening the computer screen and calling up the message he had sent earlier.

"We have an answer. My brother sent a message to the Celestian that we were emissaries from Zalhala in need of a remedy for an illness that has befallen our planet. You will all need to become Thoreans before we land," he added.

Gus appeared at the door. "You know, sir, time to eat."

In the hallway George spoke up, "I need to see the Viceroy first. Please go ahead, sir," George said quietly.

The others entered the galley and George walked on to the next turn. Andy followed George a little ways behind. George sat down outside the Viceroy's door, while Andy stood leaning on the wall around the corner. Calming his mind as Toma had shown him, he focused on Viceroy Petrosky.

"We have a plan to get the information we need, sir; however, you must stay hidden, sir," George thought.

"An odd request, George," Viceroy Petrosky answered.

"I can sense the energy you are controlling. You don't need another distraction, sir," he replied.

"And what else, cadet?" Viceroy Petrosky pressed.

"I don't know if we can protect you and accomplish our task, sir," George said bluntly.

The Viceroy smiled thinking it was odd that they thought they would need to protect him. "As you wish."

George stood up and left for the galley.

"What do you think, Andy?" he asked, rounding the corner.

"He will have a hard time not interfering if something goes wrong," Andy replied.

"Agreed." George nodded.

They all ate quickly, whispering back and forth their thoughts. After dinner, they all disappeared, planning extra options and proposals for George and Toma.

"We all need to rest," Toma said, when they had returned to the command deck.

"I will call them, sir," he replied, beginning to focus his thoughts.

"No, I want you to think about your request and let your mind open to their thoughts instead. Let them find you on the waves of energy of the universe," Toma suggested.

"What, sir?" George asked, not understanding.

"Focus and calm your mind," Toma said calmly.

Toma sat down on the floor with George in the small room off the command deck again. With Toma's help, George opened his mind to the ebb and flow of the energy around them. His team and the others found George. It was as if their thoughts were floating in a sea of ideas. They were exchanging thoughts in a whole new way, not as forced and planned as a link, instead freeform. The energy was calm and smooth as silk.

They all understood George's request and made their way back to their sleeping rooms. George was learning, but, it took a lot of focus and control. He slumped to the floor asleep. Toma carried George out of the small command deck and laid him in one of the rooms to sleep. When he returned, Cal was waiting for him.

"Amazing, how did you get George to do it?" Cal asked.

"I don't know. I didn't even know if George could do it," Toma answered, cryptically and as surprised as Cal.

"Do you think he will notice," Cal pressed.

"He didn't; although, I'm sure he'll figure it out," Toma replied cryptically.

"Can you do it, Toma?" Cal asked.

"No, it isn't a skill I possess, yet," Toma said, shaking his head.

"I have never felt anyone blend thought and energy so smoothly. It is incredible," Cal said, in awe.

"Now, he needs to figure out what he has been taught so he can defend against it the next time he is attacked," Toma whispered.

"Can't you tell him?" Cal pressed.

"No, I took the oath not to tell; however, it never said anything about teaching them about it," he replied.

"Toma, you are bending the rules that govern us," Cal said and raised an eyebrow.

"No, I am exploiting a loophole to protect our cadets," Toma said, correcting Cal.

"This path you have chosen is a very fine line," Cal said, reminding him.

"True. We will need to step carefully so we don't to cross it," Toma said, raising an eyebrow and agreeing with Cal.

Perhaps, George was right and Toma had broken the rules to protect them. At that moment, Toma wondered if George had been right all along. The Galactic council's rules were rigid and often out of date, no longer seeming to apply to the situations and issues in their modern universe. While some rules still applied, many didn't. Now the rules seemed to slow their culture's ability to adapt to the changes occurring today. Through the night, the captains watched over the cadets and calmed their minds.

George woke early and went to the cargo bay to stretch and swing from a few vines. Andy appeared and began Chen Lo. George spun down his vine, joining Andy at level two. By the twelfth level, all of the captains and cadets were in fluid motion, following Andy and Cal. The thirteenth level was more difficult, slowing them down.

"It would be easier if David Lu was here," Andy said to Cal.

"He does make it seem so much easier," Cal whistled, agreeing with Andy.

"Maybe we have a hologram of him in the computer," Sheta answered, stepping out of the rhythm and over to a computer terminal.

A minute later, a hologram of David Lu appeared. It bowed and started at level twelve. It was easier, however, not as good as the real thing. At level thirteen, the captains and cadets were nearly flying around the room. However, as they weren't in the flow of the energy of the universe, the room didn't bend and twist, fading into the sea of energy around them.

They crashed into each other and fell to the ground over and over, trying to complete the moves and combinations. Toma rolled and flipped Sheta through the air. Cal caught her before she hit the ground. Toma waved his hand across the computer terminal, stopping the program. A thunder of thuds followed as the captains and cadets fell to the ground, groaning and breathing hard.

"OK. Maybe we are not ready for that level without David Lu," Andy said, rubbing his shoulder.

From the floor of the cargo bay, they all nodded in agreement, helping each other up. George rolled over so he and Andy could lift each other up off the ground. George stopped in mid-air.

"Something is wrong. We need to get to the Viceroy, now!" he yelled, suddenly worried.

They rushed from the cargo bay. George and Toma yelled orders as they ran. Sheta, Emily, Anna, and Tillie ran passed the Viceroy's room to the command deck. Sara, Darri, Gus, and Gabe ran to the hospital to get medicine for the Viceroy. George, Toma, Cal, and Andy opened the Viceroy's door. The Viceroy was a mere shadow of a being-- nearly translucent.

"He is not, Max. They can't expect him to focus all of the sector energy. It will destroy him!" George said, stepping forward to lift the Viceroy up as Cal, Toma, and Andy formed a circle around George.

Calming his mind, George opened his thoughts to the universe--the way Toma had taught him the night before. George looked at the Viceroy. Viceroy Petrosky's didn't remember, he didn't understand what to do. The whatever had now fully affected his memory. Before, he was guiding the energy, now he was trying to control the energy, instead of letting it flow free; only guiding the energy around this sector of the universe as needed.

Stepping into an open link with the energy of the universe could destroy them. Had they been any other cadets and captains they may not have attempted such a dangerous move. However, Pete's dad needed their help; and they couldn't stand by and do nothing, and let him die.

They concentrated and focused their thoughts on the energy of the universe. Gus, Gabe, Sara, and Darri entered the room. Gus stepped through the glowing white light as if it wasn't there. Sara handed him a vial and he helped the Viceroy drink down the blue liquid. The others joined the link, and slowly, Viceroy Petrosky regained his strength. The Viceroy watched George pass the energy through himself. Viceroy Petrosky remembered, his father, and the other Senior Viceroy's didn't control the energy of the universe, they merely directed the energy. It was a hard task, although, not nearly as difficult as trying to control the energy.

Pete's dad reconnected with the other Viceroys and re-taught them last year's lesson that George had remind him of this year. Soon the flow of energy smoothed out in their sector of the universe. The cadets and captains stayed that day and into the night, until the Viceroy was again strong enough to guide the energy. Gabe, Gus, Sara, and Darri stayed as George, Andy, Toma, and Cal backed out of the flow of energy. They were all tired and needed to rest.

"We can't leave him alone again, George," Sara signed.

"Help and protect him," George replied and Toma nodded.

In the corridor, George thought only of Max. And what guiding the energy of the universe had done to him on their last rotation when they had rescued the Galactic council from the Mahadean. He focused his mind, thinking only of Max. Toma placed his hand on George's shoulder and they sat down in the middle of the hallway. Sheta came skidding around the corner, tripping on George's foot and flipping over him in a nearly perfect summersault. She slammed against the hallway wall, falling forward next to George and Toma.

"George, you can't do this alone," she said scolding him.

"But Gus is busy, ma'am," he replied apologized.

"Then you should have asked me," she said firmly.

"Yes, ma'am," he replied, lowering his head.

Andy and Cal added their hands to George's shoulder. Then Sheta backed away.

"What's he doing, Sheta?" Toma asked.

"He's making a link Toma, can't you tell?" Sheta asked.

"Yes, I know he is making a link. But no, I can sense almost nothing now and I am having great difficulty even concentrating," Toma replied, staring at Sheta.

"You are fully infected with, well, with the whatever it is, aren't you? How did you or we get it? Why has it affected you so quickly?" Sheta asked worried about Toma.

"I think so. I don't know how though. We weren't there long enough to breathe enough in or you would all be fully infected too," Toma said puzzled.

"What did you do that was different from the rest of us?" Sheta asked.

"I stopped that officer. I grabbed his arm and neck and flipped him to the ground," Toma replied then paused.

"You touched his skin! That's it! It must spread by contact. Hurry, we have to get to the hospital," Sheta said, jumping up from the floor.

"I have hugged or shaken hands with everyone here. Everyone is now infected," Toma replied, gasping as he realized that he was the carrier of the whatever.

"Maybe, but now we know how it's spread! I can work with this," Sheta said, hurriedly as they ran to the hospital.

"Cal, stay with Andy and George," Toma ordered, and then ran after Sheta.

George's thoughts were out in the universe, searching for Max and the beings of white light. He found Max in the place they couldn't be.

"Max, what are you doing here, we need you?" George asked in their link, thinking he would have been on Calshene.

"I can't interfere or in any way help this time, George. You must leave. You aren't strong enough to be here now," Max replied firmly.

"I know; however, you are our friend and you are worth the risk to us," George replied.

"George, I can't help," his said firmly with his head hung low.

"Then we will help you," he replied, twisting his thoughts and looking for a new approach.

"You have no idea what you are saying," Max said firmly, trying to get George to leave.

"Oh, of that I'm sure. However, the whatever is not evil, I can sense that. It is something else, nearly malevolent. It almost seems as if this was an accident that the whatever attacked," George said and then paused a long pause ~ his mind racing to put the pieces together.

"It isn't an attack at all! That's why you can't help," George said suddenly surprised.

His mind cleared and he pieced Max's non-answer together with his other random thoughts from earlier in their trip.

"Thanks, Max," he whispered.

"I haven't done anything," Max replied firmly, as if answering the same way because he was being watched.

"You let me see your perspective," George said calmly.

From the Viceroy's room, Gus ended the link with Max.

"What perspective?" Max asked for effect, knowing George was already gone.

"What did he say, George?" Andy asked, as only he had spoken to Max in the place they couldn't be.

"George, what did who say? Who did you link with?" Cal asked, hardly able to sense that the link had ended.

"Max. I needed to know why Max wasn't with us, sir?" George replied calmly.

"Well?" Cal pressed impatiently.

"The whatever, is well, it's not an attack. This was an accident," George said, stunned by his own words.

Cal and Andy's faces dropped.

"This means we can't destroy the whatever to save ourselves," Andy muttered.

"It changes everything, Andy," George replied shocked.

Sheta and Toma launched a blue gas into the transport ship's air system and burst out of the hospital room, running down the hallway holding a small blue vial with a lid on top.

"We've got it. We can destroy the whatever without destroying us! Toma is no longer infected. In a few minutes none of us will be i.n.f.e.c.t.e.d....," Sheta said beaming then slowing her words as she looked at George eyes.

George, Cal, and Andy looked up meeting their eyes. Toma stopped, he could sense George again and clearly read his thoughts. His face dropped.

"No, it can't be!" he said, stunned at what he read in George's mind.

"It is true. It is all an accident. This isn't an invasion," George answered solemnly.

Toma sat on the floor next to George and called their teams and the Viceroy. He and George explained what was going on. This wasn't an invasion.

The Viceroy relayed the information to the other Viceroys in the sector to help them prevent the spread of the whatever. Now, they would need a cure, that wouldn't kill them or the whatever. Sara and Darri left the Viceroy to join Emily and Sheta in the hospital. The whatever carried on the captains and cadets had been destroyed. Sheta had only one small vial of the whatever left.

They were one day from the Celestian home world now. Their plan would remain the same; however, the information they were searching for had changed. The Viceroys were now directing energy in their sector of the universe~instead of controlling the energy, and the invasion of Asteria station was now an accident.

The path they were walking along was narrow indeed. They knew how to destroy the whatever, and save the infected people across their sector of the universe. However, to do it, they would have to kill the innocent whatever. It wasn't hard, yet, George knew it was wrong. Sheta had cured Toma and everyone else on the transport; however, she didn't know it had been a mistake. Now they knew. It changed everything.

In the end, would they destroy the whatever to save their people or would they stand by and watch all of the civilizations of their universe disappear? Toma stared at George.

"Defining moment?" Toma said solemnly.

"I have doubts that everything we have been trained to do and understand can prepare us for this cosmic of a decision. Do we destroy the whatever, wiping it from our universe, to save our civilizations or do we let it run its course and destroy ourselves?" George said, still stunned by the new problem.

"We can call Max. Perhaps he can help us?" Toma asked, not knowing George had linked with him earlier.

"No, Max pointed the way to understanding, but, I don't think he knew he did it," George replied seriously.

"Another accident?" Toma pressed.

"I don't know this time~maybe, maybe not," George replied.

Max had been firm with George; yet, he wondered if it had really been a show for the high council.

"Toma, we need you," came Anna's voice over the transports communication system. They pulled each other up and ran down the hallway to the command deck.

Chapter 29

CELESTIAN HOME

On the view screen in front of them was the Celestian solar system. In the center was a star similar to the primary star of Earth. However, the Celestian home world was far from the heat and energy of their sun. Their cities were buried beneath miles of frozen gasses.

They slipped the transport ship behind one of the outer planets and turned off Emily's comet disguise. On the opposite side of the planet, two Celestian warships met them. Emily's comet disguise may have fooled the rest of the galaxies; however, they didn't fool the Celestian.

Toma and Cal called the warship commanders and relayed the information his brother had sent earlier. George, Andy, Emily, and Anna cleared their minds and thought only of helping the Thoreans. The warships parted and flew off each side of the transport ship, guiding it to the Celestian home world.

A sea of frozen gasses swirled high above the ninth planet's surface as they approached. The first warship dove down into the center of the swirling gasses. Tillie and Sheta dove the transport ship into the swirling tornado of gasses, following behind the first warship. The second warship followed closely behind the transport ship. Down and down they dove into the center of the swirling gasses. The first warship slowed its decent and turned, hovering horizontally. Tillie and Sheta followed the lead ship and hovered next to the first warship. When the second warship was in place, they landed together. The swirling tower of gasses disappeared and a solid layer of frozen blue gasses formed three hundred feet above the landing port ~ no escape.

Tillie tried to open the port door and lower the gangplank; however, the port door wouldn't open. A bright red light pierced the hull of the transport, scanning the entire ship. As the red light touched the Thoreans, they fell to the floor of the command deck, writhing in pain. There was nowhere to run. George, Andy, Anna, and Emily were next to crumple to the floor, twisting in agony.

Sara shoved her sample of the whatever into a status chamber as the red light crossed through the hospital room. She and Darri fell to the floor in pain. Gus and Gabe writhed in pain too. Oddly, Viceroy Petrosky was oddly unaffected.

When the Celestian bio-decontamination cycle was completed, the port door opened and the gangplank extended into the Celestian spaceport. The holographic bars the cadets wore shutdown.

"It will have to do," Toma signed to the cadets. "Follow Cal's orders from now on," Toma signed firmly.

George and the others didn't understand. Protocol was everything here and George and the others had had very little training. Toma and the other Thoreans had received formal protocol training since they were small children. In an instant, Toma's protocol training kicked in. His behavior changed suddenly from their captain to something else, something extremely formal, regal even. In reality, it was years of training re-surfacing. He would do whatever he had to help the cadets and save Asteria station.

Toma, Cal, and Tillie lined up at the top of the gangplank first followed closely by George, Andy, and Anna, who now appeared as Earth cadets.

On the floor of the spaceport, stood two rows of officials in fancy robes. Toma walked down the gangplank first, with Cal, following close behind. He stopped at the end of the gangplank before stepping onto the Celestian ground.

"Welcome Captain Heto," the official greeted Toma, bowing low.

"Greetings from the Thorean planet," Toma replied confidently, not bowing as he looked over the rank of the officials that were there to greet them.

Toma and the other Thoreans rated a full dignitaries greeting and Toma would tolerate nothing less. It was the only way they would get the help and information they needed.

"We welcome you as honored guests of the state," the Celestian official said and then carried on and on with his welcome.

Each time the Celestian paused, Toma replied in an equally grand fashion. George knew the importance of Toma's protocol greetings. They stood at the port door patiently waiting, thinking of nothing except helping the Thoreans.

Toma seemed so at home with the protocol. It wasn't even an effort for him to properly respond to the official's greeting. After thirty minutes, the officer nodded and the ground in front of the gangplank solidified into a light blue carpet of frozen gasses. Toma stepped onto the frozen gases and thought in their link for the others to follow in proper protocol order down the gangplank to the frozen carpet. Gus, Gabe, Sara, and Darri stayed on the transport ship with the Viceroy as the others followed Toma off onto the frozen gases.

"It is an illusion, it's OK," Cal signed behind his back, fearing that the cadets may not step off the gangplank.

Tillie followed Cal and then came George, Andy, and Anna. Sheta and Emily caught up to them as Anna stepped off the gangplank. George, Andy, and Anna stopped and stepped aside. Sheta was of higher rank. She glided passed them and took her place behind Cal. In single file, they walked between the two rows of Celestian officials.

George felt someone trying to worm her way into his mind. He smiled, glancing around and blocked the worm's attack of himself and his team.

Finding the worm in the crowd, George replied to the official's mind, "I know it's you."

The official jerked back, not expecting to have been found out. Andy and the others nodded to her as they passed by. She scowled her face, turning away from their stare.

"Odd," Emily puzzled until she caught George's sign.

"Nothing, help Toma," he signed in their new sign language, afraid their old sign language would be too easy to read.

As they reached the end of the rows of officials, Toma lifted his arm and a translucent official placed her hand on his arm. Next, Cal raised his arm and another official placed her hand on his arm. Sheta didn't raise her arm, instead a translucent official raised his arm for her. Gently, Sheta held her hand over his arm not wanting to bruise it from the weight of her hand. Anna and Emily studied what Sheta and then Tillie had done and held their hands just slightly above their official's arms when their turn came. Toma and the others knew what to do and the cadets followed their lead.

Down a long white corridor, they walked in silence. The group entered a large glistening white dome through an immense archway. It was the largest archway in the dome. The Thoreans were prized guests indeed.

In the center of the dome was a sparkling blue platform of frozen gases with six kingly looking officials dressed in shimmering blue and white flowing robes. They standing on the third and highest step of the platform.

Sheta stepped forward, passing Cal and ending up directly behind Toma as they were paraded across the glistening dome. Rows and rows officials lined their walkway.

At first, the cadets didn't get it, Sheta wasn't as high a rank as Cal. At least they didn't think so based on how they walked through the corridor to the dome.

Cal glanced back at the cadets. He was now giving orders to George, Anna, Andy, and Emily. The cadets weren't allowed onto the platform in the center of the dome.

"You have no rank here. You must show respect," Cal thought to the cadets.

In an instant they understood, Sheta was blocking for Cal. He needed time to explain what was going to happen and what they were going to do in only a few moments. Moments, Sheta was buying for Cal. George and the others nodded, thinking only of helping the Thoreans.

When they reached the platform, the officials pushed back from the platform's edge for all to see how high up the platform the lead Thorean would walk.

Without stopping, Toma walked up the first two steps of the platform and stopped. Sheta stopped on the first step with Tillie right behind her. Cal stepped passed Sheta and stood directly behind Toma. George stopped before the first step and knelt down on one knee, lowering his head. Andy, Emily, and Anna stopped behind George, knelling down on one knee. Their order showed their rank to the gathered officials.

The center kingly looking official, standing on the third step, walked forward, seeming to glide above the platform. At the edge of the rise, he stepped down one step to Toma's level, the crowd of officials gasped. He was a tall and slender being like their librarian. Standing directly in front of Toma, he reached forward with his palm down towards Toma. Toma knelt down on one knee, lowering his head and extending his palm face up.

The protocol was excruciating for Andy. It was mind numbing and dull; yet entranced, he knelt silently, watching and learning with the others. He wondered how Toma had had the strength to leave for the freedom of the stars. A blue glow formed between the palm of leader of the Celestian people and Toma's palm. The leader ever so slightly smiled. He's eyes seemed to curl up, following his mouth.

The other five kingly officials nodded and their eyes seemed to smile with the lead official. With a nod from the leader, Toma stood up and two new officials walked up next to him. They turned facing the crowd of the officials in the dome. They quietly cheered and the six kingly officials stepped passed the Thoreans, nodding to each of them as they left the platform and exited across the dome. Toma and the captains were lead back across the dome and out the same enormous carved archways.

A younger translucent Celestian official walked up to George and the cadets still kneeing next to the platform.

"Forgive them Cadet Hawkins. They are not accustom to visitors of your level," she said, and motioned them to follow her out of the dome and through a smaller archway.

He stood up and raised his arm to her. She smiled.

"You do me a great honor, Cadet Hawkins," she said kindly, taking his arm.

"Perhaps, it is an honor long over do, ma'am," he replied kindly.

Into an icy white corridor they walked, turning, and twisting as if a labyrinth designed to confuse the traveler. Anna had much of the planets corridors and features mapped within a few minutes. Thanks to one of Emily's computer programs. The mainframe computer system of the planet was hardly protected. Emily accessed the information easily as they followed George and the translucent official.

"Do you know the librarian on Asteria station, ma'am?" George asked quietly.

"How do you know of the Celestian librarian on Asteria station? You are all so very young," she replied softly, as if a whisper was too loud.

"We have been there and read from the ancient scrolls. Our librarian is missing. The librarian that is there now is kind; however, she isn't our librarian, ma'am," George whispered kindly.

"How can you know this? None have ever noticed before," she asked, puzzling that a non-Celestian would even notice the change of a librarian.

"Is she sick ma'am? May we see her? We have come a very long way, ma'am," he asked as softly as he could.

To find their librarian and get the help they needed, they would need this young official's assistance.

"Well, there is some time before dinner. We will have to hurry," the translucent official said softly, and started to very nearly hurry through the corridors.

Within thirty minutes, she stood before a large archway. Emily signed there were medical symbols carved into the doorframe around the archway. The young official pushed on the door; however, it wouldn't open.

George signed behind his back to Emily, while he looked concerned to their young official. Emily stepped forward and bumped into Andy. He spun her around and she touched the door near the floor as Andy lifted her back up to her feet.

The door flew open quickly, slightly frightening the official with all of the commotion. They hurried through the open door. Emily twisted her wrist on the other side of the archway and the door glided closed without a sound.

In the hospital wing, the official led them through another corridor to a second smaller archway. Emily twisted her wrist and this time the door opened easily for the young official.

Inside the room, on a long silver bed, laid their librarian from the Asteria library. What appeared to be doctors and medics scurried around her. Her skin was a pale pink and she looked more solid than translucent. The cadets approached with their official and the doctors and medics backed away.

"We have missed you in the library, ma'am. It's not the same without you, ma'am," George whispered.

"Why are you here, Cadet Hawkins?" she whispered, trying to smile a little.

"To find you, ma'am, we were worried when the other librarian appeared and you were gone, ma'am," George whispered.

"How can you know this?" she asked, staring at the cadets.

"We know you, ma'am. We are here to help make you better," he said, lowering his head.

"You are so young, there is little anyone can do," she said, turning away as a tear glistened across her cheek.

"You aren't dying, ma'am. You are only sick and need to get better, ma'am," he said softly, as encouragingly as he could.

George nodded and they circled her silvery bed. The cadets had made healing circles with and without their triad before. They knew what to do now to help their librarian. They started to concentrate on their librarian being well. A bright yellow sphere glowed around them as Sara and Gus appeared in the room with them. George was sure Viceroy Petrosky was helping calm their minds from the transport ship.

The librarian started to glow a bright pink, then orange, and finally red. She seemed to be in pain; however, she made no motion or sound, only her eyes wept glistening drops. Twenty minutes passed, and their glow turned into a cool, blue-white light. Sara and Gus faded from the room.

"You need to rest now, and eat something or you know Gus, he will not be happy, ma'am," George whispered.

"Thank you," their librarian whispered.

She was nearly translucent as the cadets backed away. The doctors and medics gasped.

"Please ask them to make sure she eats before she rests. It is very important. Also, they can't tell anyone what they have seen today, as it isn't permitted, ma'am," George said to their official, as they backed further away from her bed.

George needed their abilities kept a secret so telling a little white fib about it not being permitted seemed OK at that moment.

"Yes, of course, Cadet Hawkins," their official replied, and then turned toward the doctors.

The young official spoke in whispers to the doctors and medics, explaining what Cadet Hawkins had requested. They nodded intently, hanging on her every word as they stared at George and the other cadets standing by the door. The young official finished and walked toward the cadets in the archway.

George raised his arm and the young official took it. Their librarian smiled. They were learning. Silently, out the door they went. This time the young official was in a real hurry. She walked quicker when no one else was around then slowed to a casual walk if someone was looking.

"We can't be late. It will be very bad if we are late. It's all my fault for letting you go to the hospital," she said nearly frantic inside.

George spun around in front of her.

"Please stop, ma'am," he whispered, as the others gathered closely around their official. "Close your eyes and picture where we are supposed to be and I mean exactly the place. Now think of a small room near where we must be," he whispered softly.

She stared at him and closed her eyes. George concentrated as Andy placed his hand on his shoulder. In a flash of white light, they appeared, standing in a small room next to the grand banquet dome they had entered earlier in the day. They stepped out of the small room to enter through one of the smaller archway entrances. The young official was stunned.

"You, you... How did you do that? The Thoreans shouldn't be the honored guests, you should be," she whispered, staring at George.

"Please, ma'am. You must keep our secret. We don't know protocol like the Thoreans do and right now, our galaxies need help. Only the Celestian have the information needed to save our galaxies. Please keep our secret, ma'am," George whispered, kneeling down on one knee.

He offered his hand palm side up, his head lowered. A few officials entering the grand dome gasped. She held out her hand and cupped it under his, rolling his hand closed.

"You do not know what you are offering and how low a level I am," she whispered, blushing.

"I do know your level and the sacrifice you are making being seen with us ma'am," George whispered, fibbing again.

He had no idea what their social structure was; however, their being forgotten when they arrived, meant the cadets were at the bottom. Perhaps lower, only Emily would know for sure.

The young official smiled and he unrolled his hand. This time she held her palm over his and a glowing yellow white sphere formed between them.

"I will keep your secret, your confidence, and help you save your galaxies," she whispered kindly.

George stood up and again offered her his arm as they walked into the grandly decorated dome. Emily and Anna stood on either side of Andy with their arms raised, following George and their official inside.

"Do you have a name, ma'am?" he whispered, stepping around a fountain of red and yellow gases.

"Ma'am is appropriate," she whispered softly.

She passed several tables with small fountains of red and purple gases bubbling up from the center of the tables. The colored gases spilled out making the table tops appear to float in mid-air. The floor was the same frozen blue gas they had stepped onto earlier that morning. Three other young officials stood near a table with a white and yellow fountain bubbling out over the top.

The table and fountain colors were in matching rings around the dome. The platform in the center had an enormous blue and white fountain that spilled out over the table and platform covering the steps.

"We are sitting with the Celestian officials in front of us, George. Offer our official a seat first," Emily thought in their link, as she read the protocol from her pad.

Quickly, she sent a stream of the messages to George in their link. They may not have been honored guests, but they knew protocol rules still had to be followed.

"Will the officials in front of us help us, ma'am?" George whispered softly.

"I do not know; however, I will find out this evening over the course of events," she replied kindly.

The other officials smiled as they approached.

"How did you get here so fast?" one of the officials asked when they got to the table.

The three officials chattered away never acknowledging the cadets presence. Their official went to sit down and George pulled back her chair for her. She was startled and then realized she hadn't introduced her guests. They had been standing, patiently waiting.

"My apologies, Cadet Hawkins," she said, dipping her head.

"Why are you apologizing to them? They are so low they make us look high," one of the young officials quipped, and the others chuckled.

"What do you see when you look at them?" she asked the other young officials as if the cadets weren't there.

They all turned, staring impolitely at the cadets.

"Thorean royalty hanger-on-ers, servants maybe, that's all," the first one replied rudely.

"Didn't you see who they came with? I've never even seen the Celestian chancellor and the high council before. To say nothing of a Thorean crown prince!" the second one said.

"And the regional prince next to the crown prince. Who would have thought that we would ever have seen them? It must be one bad virus on Zalhala, for two princes to travel across the galaxies to us here," the third official said, not even answering the official's question.

"Well, I don't care who they came with. I see potential in them," their official replied kindly.

"Suit yourself. It's your demotion. We'll sit with you, now, but you're on your own after that," the third one replied harshly.

George wanted to drop his mouth open, followed closely by Andy, Emily, and Anna, although, protocol prevented it. They were stunned that Toma was a crown prince of Zalhala and Cal the regional prince! Toma's story of leaving behind a powerful family on Zalhala had a whole new meaning now.

They all sat and the three other officials did most of the talking and very little listening. Andy couldn't figure out why their official was even friends with these other officials. They had no manners what-so-ever.

Slowly, the immense dome floor filled with higher officials, all chattering away. The lights in the dome dipped and the officials all stood up, craning to get a better look. Through the largest archway into the dome paraded the Celestian chancellor, the high council, and the Thoreans.

Cal sent a thought to George. "Concentrate and focus on the task. We are no help to you. You have two days."

George shook his head as Andy grabbed his shoulder.

"Where's the link?" Andy whispered.

"It's Cal, we have only two days to get the information we need," George thought through their link.

"How long will this state dinner last, ma'am?" George asked their official politely.

"There will be many speeches. It will be late before it is done," the official whispered.

The cadets nodded. Toma and the others finally arrived at the head table in the center of the room. The chancellor raised his arms and all of the flowing gas fountains shimmered. Suddenly, all of the gasses flowing across the tables turned to a brilliant blue and white at once. The officials gasped and dinner began.

A new speech was given between each course of food. Course after course, speech after speech, the dinner dragged on late into the night. All the while, the officials sitting with them talked on and on, ignoring the cadets.

"Mindless drivel," Andy signed in their new sign language, bored from the young official's discussion.

"Listen for the bits of information we need. There is always a jewel of information among the chatter," George signed between servings of food.

During the evening, between courses, Emily and Anna searched for an officer's library of sorts, for a special library where these foolish young officials had never been. Something like the officer's library on Asteria station perhaps.

"Ask if there is a great master type library," Emily thought in their link to George.

"Have you been to all of the great libraries of study on Celestian, ma'am, sir?" George asked, kindly when there was a pause in their chatter.

"Yes, of course, or we would not have made it this far, this fast," one official arrogantly replied.

He was lying and George could sense it. Andy wormed his way into one of the other official's minds to find the one place they hadn't been. It was tedious and time consuming; however, by the end of the night, Andy had found the one section of the planet none of the officials had ever been to. He signed his information to George and the others over the dessert course.

"That is where we must go," George signed, taking a bite of his fizzing ice blue dessert.

Finally, the Chancellor, council, and Thoreans stood to leave the dome. George knew Toma was tired, and that, there was nothing George or the others could do to help him.

After the Chancellor and honored guests left, the young officials at their table left quickly. Their young official led George, Andy, Emily, and Anna through a maze of corridors to a small, icy-white sleeping room. The cadets were stunned. It was the size of a closet!

"So we really are nothing," Andy signed.

George shook his head and thanked their young official for the sleeping room.

"Focus!" he signed, firmly behind his back.

The door closed and the cadets went to work. There was no computer terminal in the room and no beds that rose from the floor for them to sleep on. They sat on the floor, leaning against the back wall of the room. The walls weren't cold, but they weren't warm either. Emily felt no presence like in the caves of Asteria station as she ran her hand over the wall and floor.

"Andy, you know why we are here. You need to stay focused," George said abruptly.

He was tired and short with Andy. This was the level they had chosen to be at while on Celestian, and they had to play along to find their answers. Their Asteria librarian was now healed; however, she wouldn't able to help solve their mystery.

"Are there any caves on this planet, Anna?" George asked, changing the topic.

"Not like on the cadet stations, George. Here, the caves are all natural formations and there are no tunnel hogs. It is a planet of frozen gases with a small metal and rock core," she replied, studying her pad.

"Tell us about the place the young officials have never been to, Emily," George asked.

"It's rather like the Calshene officer's library. I don't think most of them even know of its existence. It holds their most important documents and information. Access is limited to a very few officials," she replied, snuggling in next to George for warmth.

"Cal said we have two days. We need to get into that library and find the information before our time runs out. However, right now, we need to rest," he said, wrapping his arm around Emily's shoulder to warm her.

Andy followed his lead and wrapped his arm around Anna to keep her warm. Anna and Emily rested on the boys on the floor of the room, leaning on each other to sleep.

"Sorry, it won't happen again," Andy signed, to George when the girls fell asleep.

George nodded and they reached out on the energy of the universe to their triad. Sara and Darri were no closer to a remedy for the whatever than they had been the evening before. Gus and Gabe were watching the Viceroy, making sure he was OK. Yet, Gus and Gabe were both worried inside. Max was stronger and Pete's dad wasn't nearly as strong as Max. Even with their help, the Viceroy was tiring.

Toma and Cal met George and the others in their link.

"We found the library we need to enter. They call it the master's library; unfortunately, we have no way of entering. It is one of their greatest secrets. Very few ever get access," George said directly.

"I will get us in tomorrow; however, you will need to be quick. I will insist we need you to look up information for us. Don't let your guard down, the scanners here are more skilled and stealthy than most," Toma added.

Andy and George nodded and lowered their link with Toma and Cal. They would sleep in shifts through the night to protect their team from the scanners. Late in the night, George was concentrating, focusing on the energy of the universe when a smooth invader entered his mind. Inch by inch the invader started reading his thoughts. George shook his head, as if he was trying to blow away a buzzing fly. Andy rolled over and hit George's leg. Their link increased. Together, they could see the invader and George started manipulating his thoughts.

George thought of how cute one of the young officials was. He carried on and on in his mind, thinking about her, and what he would say if he saw her again. All the while, Andy was slipping into the invaders mind, reading his thoughts. The invader got nothing; unlike Andy who had gotten a lot of information on the Chancellor, the high council, the master's library and where they needed to go to in the morning. When they had the information they needed, Andy sent a small red sphere flailing into the invaders mind. It wasn't enough to destroy, however, the invader would have one heck of a headache the next day.

How cold and unfeeling they had become. Andy thought nothing of the event, but George worried. Had evil's relentless attacks turn them hard against others? Were they losing their compassion and humanity?

Chapter 30

MASTER LIBRARY

Early the next morning, the young official came to their door and knocked. Emily opened the door as the cadets stood up.

"We are late. The chancellor wants to show the Thorean princes one of our most guarded libraries of knowledge and you have to be there to assist your Thoreans. We should have left last night," she said worried.

"Do you know where they are now and where we are supposed to meet them, ma'am?" George asked kindly.

"Well, yes, but...," she said when George cut her off.

"Think like you did last night. Think of a place near the library that we can enter from without being noticed, ma'am," he whispered.

"But your gift, everyone should know," she answered.

"No ma'am. We only use it to help others and right now, we need to help you. It seems to us like someone should have told you last night about the change in plans and they didn't. Perhaps, they want you to fail so they can take your place, ma'am," George said, smiling kindly.

The young official twisted her long slender neck and thought. "You do have a point," she whispered.

"Can you picture the room we need to be in? Focus, ma'am," George whispered.

"It is a long way away from here," she said a little worried.

"It will be OK. Focus only on the room, ma'am," he said, as they all huddled close together.

She closed her eyes and in a flash of white light, they appeared in a tiny room. She peeked out the door and then rushed the cadets out of the room, hurrying them down the small hallway to the main entrance of the master's library.

The main entrance was a huge cavern with swirling gasses of every color, creating the dome over the cavern. The walls were arched and standing on pillars of blue ice. The floor was a translucent white that shimmered and changed color, reflecting the colors of the swirling dome. The young official placed the cadets at the base of a grand translucent white staircase that sprawled out onto the dome floor. The great-carved doors beneath the tallest archway rolled open and the Chancellor, Toma, the high council, Cal, Sheta, and Darri paraded up to the steps. The floor turned blue as if a carpet had been rolled out before them to walk on.

George, Andy, Emily, and Anna knelt down on one knee. The young official stood behind them with only her head lowered.

"Why do you kneel?" she whispered to George.

"It is what is expected, so we give them what they want to see, ma'am," he replied softly.

She smiled and lowered her head further.

The dignitaries glided over the flowing steps and the main door to the library glided open-gently. George glanced up, catching a glimpse of the mind invader from last night. It was one of the council members! He lowered his head and stared at Andy.

"It was one of the council members," he signed. Andy nodded.

As the last dignitary entered the library, the doors started to close. The young official raced up the stairs to stop the doors from closing. Emily twisted her hand and held the doors open just long enough for their official to touch the door and for them to enter the master library.

The main entrance may have been grand; however, the master library was beyond their imagination. Emily wanted to run from room to room, losing herself in the books and information. In front of them was an immense cavern with hallways and corridors leading off at every angle for six levels, reaching high into the ceiling of the cavern. They stood at the side of the cavern entrance in awe of it beauty and size. Corridors with ornately decorated archway lines each level.

The floor was the same translucent white, reflecting the swirling gasses in the domed ceiling above them. Toma and the others were a quarter of the way through the cavernous library. The floor below them was blue, as were the swirling gases above them. Around the young official and the cadets, the floor was a glowing golden reddish-yellow with a ceiling of swirling golden yellow and reddish gases.

"Ma'am, is there a special room you have heard rumored about in this library? A room that no one is sure even exists, and yet, it is the place all knowledge is known, ma'am," George whispered, remembering what he and Andy had read in the council members mind the night before.

"Yes, of course, however, it is only a child's story. It's not real," she replied, and paused, staring at George.

"Ma'am, it is real and we are inside the master library of your child's story. Now we need to find the room that the story speaks about. Can you describe it to us or tell us the story, ma'am?" he asked politely, lowering his head as other officials walked by, staring at the untidy group.

"Well, yes. Although, I don't know what good it will do you," she replied, puzzled.

"Please, ma'am, try," George whispered kindly.

"The room is small and unassuming, humble even. It has no grand entrance or swirling doors. It is hidden among the mightiest symbols, and yet, holds the greatest of information of all," she said, reciting the child's rhyme.

"I got it," Anna signed, pointing to a smallish corridor a quarter of the way through the library's main cavern.

"Can you get us to that small corridor over there, ma'am?" George asked calmly.

"Well, OK. Although, I think there are bigger corridors with better information than that one," she said, shaking her head not wanting to believe the children's story was even true.

"We aren't chancellors or princes, ma'am. We are only cadets and servants. The smaller corridor is best for us, ma'am," he replied humbly.

"Perhaps, you are right," she said, staring at the cadets.

She walked off the main aisle way over to the small corridor, the golden yellow reddish swirls beneath their footsteps. The small corridor was lined with many ornately decorated archways, each white archway connecting to the next. Halfway down the corridor was a plain archway with the least amount of decoration. George stopped in front of the plainest archway and door.

"This is the room we want to enter, ma'am," he said, staring at the young official and smiling slightly.

"Are you sure? It's so dull and uninteresting," she said, pointing to the other more decorated archways.

"We are only cadets, ma'am, and not accustom to luxuries. Simple is best for us, ma'am," George said softly.

"As you wish; however, I think another room would be more interesting," she replied, raising her translucent hand.

The door didn't open.

"It should open easily, I don't understand," she said aloud, a little frustrated.

"Try again. Perhaps the door isn't opened often and it is only stuck, ma'am," Emily encouraged, lowering her head.

The young official turned around and reached forward again. This time George and Andy had their hands on Emily shoulders as she twisted her hand behind the young official's back. The door slid open.

The young official smiled, "That's more like it."

They entered the small white room. Like their sleeping room, there was nothing inside. The young official looked disappointed; however, George, Andy, Emily, and Anna smiled.

"There's nothing here, we should find another more interesting room," she said turning to leave.

"Yes, there is something here, ma'am. It is only hiding. Close your eyes and imagine what should be inside this room, ma'am," George said encouragingly.

She closed her eyes. When she opened them, a small reading room appeared. As she sat down at the center table, a scroll rose from the table. She studied the scroll, smiling at her discovery, "I've always wanted to see this information," she said, her voice drifting off in thought.

Emily pulled up a computer terminal and Anna spun open a holographic array of maps and charts. George smiled, walking to the back of the room. Andy stood next to him. He calmed his mind and focused his thoughts. Andy placed his hand on George's shoulder.

Buried within their minds was the knowledge of the beings of white light, the space between good and evil and the control of the raw energy of the universe. George knew he could call on all of this information within this room. Instead, he and Andy focused only on finding a cure, something that could save their galaxies from the whatever and save the whatever from them.

He opened his mind and read from scrolls written for the last hundred thousand years, looking for information on a similar event in time. He found nothing. An hour past and then another, soon it was late and Gus was calling through their link from the transport ship.

The Viceroy was getting weaker. He seemed somehow infected with the whatever. George thought of Max and the energy between the spaces. He thought of the atoms, electrons, protons, and neutrons that made up the building blocks of the universe. He found the quarks and gluons and then the strings of energy hidden within. The space between was hidden with more energy and the strings were like the stars we can see in the night sky. The voids between the strings of energy were not empty but filled with energy too small to see~like the countless planets, asteroids, and moons between the stars.

"We live in a sea of energy, pushing and pulling, twisting and turning. The fuzz of energy is everywhere. Its cohesion or sticking together, gives us life. The whatever is looking for energy; a source of food to sustain its life," George signed to Andy.

Andy stared at George. "You mean like Gus feeding the green fungi with his purple liquid?"

"Yes, it is a temporary fix to the mosses food and energy problem. We are a temporary fix to the whatever's food and energy problem," George added.

"So to permanently fix the problem," Andy said and George finished his sentence.

"We need to give the whatever a better source of energy that will sustain it so it will leave willingly from the galaxies," George answered.

They had the answer to their problem. Now, they needed to make the path for the whatever to follow. However, they had stayed too long in the plain white reading room. The room used the energy of the cadets to create all that they had seen. Without Gus to feed them energy, the cadets and the young official fell asleep. The room went dark. They had found the answer and no one knew.

Late in the night, Viceroy Petrosky worsened. The energy he directed shattered, slicing through the air, crackling, and fracturing in the room around him. Out of desperation, Gus, Gabe, Sara, and Tillie began Chen Lo to stop the energy of the universe from total destruction. By the tenth level Toma, Cal, Darri, and Sheta joined in the rhythm of Chen Lo. At the twelfth level, the energy in the room began to bend and twist. They could see George, Andy, Emily, Anna, and the Celestian official trapped in the library reading room.

In a flash of white light, Toma appeared in the reading room next to George and the others. Carefully, he pulled the cadets and the official into the hallway. Then slowly, he guided the raw energy of Chen Lo into the cadets. As each cadet revived, they joined the Chen Lo rhythm Gus and Sara had started.

Soon, George was in the center of their Chen Lo, focusing their thoughts, and their strength increased.

At the thirteenth level, the rooms around them were gone. The air was alive with energy, twisting and turning. The energy taken by the white room was fed back into the cadets and young official. Everything was a blur of energy in fluid motion around them. George thought of grandfather and David Lu to help with the raw energy of the universe; however, there was no answer, only silence.

Gus lifted up Viceroy Petrosky and joined him into their link. His focus calmed their minds as his strength increased. Pete's dad was a Chen Lo master and knew what they had done. He understood the power and raw energy of the universe the cadets could now control and the warning of his father, the Senior Viceroy.

"Focus, only the goal, George. Use the energy to solve the problem at hand. Focus, only the problem," Viceroy Petrosky thought to George alone.

The Viceroy didn't know that George had wielded the full power and energy of the universe with their triad before and that they had willingly given up the control of that power.

In a way, it was frightening to the Viceroy, all that power in the hands of a young boy and his team. He had to keep George focused only on their task.

George thought about the whatever and the energy they needed to survive. He had to give the whatever a better source of energy. He focused on the raw chaotic energy of the universe and made a concentrated beam of energy. One end of the beams swept out over their sector of galaxies and the other end of the energy beam focused on a small rocky planet near a main sequence star.

As the energy passed through the galaxies, the whatever began following the energy stream to the rocky planet. Slowly, the whatever left the cadets, officers, and creatures that lived in their sector of galaxies. Within a few hours, grandfather, Senior Viceroy Petrosky, and David Lu joined their link and their Chen Lo.

"Your work is done," grandfather said, in their link as the other Senior Viceroys on Asteria station took over, guiding of the energy of the universe back from Viceroy Petrosky. They never saw George and the others in the link. Toma's grandfather, also a Senior Viceroy, hide the teams from anyone's view.

With the whatever gone and the guiding of the energy of the universe transferred, George and the others lowered their Chen Lo levels. Soon, Toma, Cal, Sheta, and Darri left the link as did Gus, Sara, Gabe, and Tillie. Only George, Andy, and grandfather, Senior Viceroy Petrosky, were left in the link.

"Your team has done well, forget not where you are. Complete your task," the Senior Viceroy thought to them as he faded from their link.

"Cryptic again. Why can't he just tell us what he means?" Andy lamented, sitting on the corridor floor in the master library.

"Don't know," George replied, looking down staring at the swirling red and yellow gases in the floor beneath them.

He knelt down in the hallway to help their translucent official. She opened her eyes and jumped from his arms straightening her flowing robes. At first, her face was stern and then she caught his eyes and her face softened.

"You were right, this is the room of the children's story," she said, her voice was soft and a little shaky.

Carefully, Emily lifted the young official's hand and placed it on hers and then she touched the door. The door opened and closed easily.

"Now you can open this door whenever you want to, ma'am," Emily whispered.

The young official smiled, understanding what Emily had been doing.

"We will need to leave, I'm sure we are late for something," she said quickly.

Hurrying, they left the corridor and returned to the enormous main cavern of the master library. George raised his arm and the young official gently placed her hand over it. They may have been in a hurry, but protocol was protocol. George focused on their young official and they hurried across the main floor.

With the chancellor and others gone, the high-ranking officials accustom to using the master library alone were busy with their work. As the group hurried across the main library cavern, the white floor beneath their feet turned a bright golden yellow with a swirl of red and the dome above them glowed a soft golden yellow reddish to match.

The high-ranking officials who had no color change beneath their feet stopped what they were doing and stared. Only the Celestian chancellor and high council could color the gases of Celestian by their mere presences. Yet here, this lowly young official, herding the Thorean's Earth cadets was changing the color of the gases.

The whispers grew as the group quickly walked to the great archway. The young official headed toward a smaller archway; however, Emily shook her head. Placing the young official's hand on top of hers again, she touched the immense main door. In a swirl of golden yellow gases, the door opened and the cadets and the young official ran down the main stairs.

"Now you can come back anytime you want to and open the doors to read and learn, ma'am," Emily said kindly and smiled.

"Thank you," she whispered.

She led them back to the little room. In a flash of white light, they were gone. A few officials that had followed them out of the library, peeked into the small room, it was empty. The whispers grew into a story about the young official and her herd of Earth cadets.

It was their last night on Celestian and another grand dinner was planned for the Thorean crown prince and chancellor. The young official had George bring them to the small room off the grand dining cavern where they had eaten when they first arrived. The group slipped out and weaved their way between the flowing swirling fountains coloring the tables until they reached the same table they had sat at two nights before.

"How did you know there would be a dinner?" George asked quietly.

"There is always a dinner when heads of state visit. This must be your last night. It will be especially grand," she said, pointing to a particularly large fountain flowing down from the ceiling of the enormous dome.

It lofted over each head table changing colors like a rainbow. Over their table, a golden yellow fountain swirled high into the air, spinning in great loops before flowing over the tabletop. George glanced at Emily.

"Not me," she signed, slightly shaking her head.

The three young officers they had sat with the first night came, running up to the table nearly knocking their official over.

"What did you do?" the first young official asked rudely.

"Everyone is talking about you and them," another said and motioned to the cadets, without actually acknowledging their existence.

"How did you get into the master's library?" the first official asked.

"And you brought them and not us?" the second official said, pointing at the cadets.

"I heard you glowed. One of the guys, who knows a guy, who knows an official, who is friends with a high-official said he saw it himself," the third young official said.

"So tell us, what happened?" the first official asked.

"No one glows except the chancellor and the high council, what gives?" the second official asked, pushing for an answer.

The three young officials chattered on asking question after question not waiting for any answers.

Soon the cavern was full of whispers and pointing officials. The lights dipped and the Celestian chancellor, high council, Toma, Cal, Sheta, and Darri entered through the great archway. The noise in the cavern stopped immediately, then rose to quiet whispers between the officials.

Halfway across the dome the chancellor stopped, the cavern fell silent. He waved his hands in the air and all of the swirling fountains over the tables turned a brilliant blue. The official's oooo'd and awwww'd at the magnificent feat. Well, that is, all but one swirl of gasses turned blue. The chancellor looked up and saw the swirling golden yellow gases above the young official's table.

"So the rumors are true," he whispered, to one of the high council members.

Raising his hand, the officials in front of him parted, opening a path to the table with the swirling yellow gasses. Leaving the main blue gas carpet, he walked straight to the young officials table, turning the white floor beneath his feet blue as he walked.

George knelt down on one knee, lowered his head, and raised his arm for their official to rest upon as the chancellor approached. The three other young officials ran up to the chancellor; however, he waved them away.

Standing in front of the young official, the floor turned a vibrant green as the blue and yellow gasses mixed. The chancellor reached out his arm and the young official took her hand off George's arm and placed her hand above the chancellor's arm. She turned and motioned for the cadets to follow them. George and the others froze. They had no idea what to do.

"Think of Cal," Andy signed quickly.

"Cal, help," George thought.

In a flash, George knew what to say.

"We are only humble cadets in service to the Thorean's, ma'am. Please forgive us," he said, to the young official, not to the chancellor.

However, the chancellor smiled, a proper protocol answer, he was pleased. Her flowing white robe turned to a golden yellow as the chancellor walked her over to Toma and the others. The gasses swirled a vibrant green as the chancellor and their young official walked across the cavern. They continued their procession to the rise in the center of the cavern. A new chair at the end of the head table rose from the floor for their young official. The officials all sat and the festivities began.

George and the others stood up and turned to take their seats at the same table they had on the first night; however, the three young officials had already taken their seats and invited five other friends to sit with them. The cadets turned away and weaved their way out of the grand cavern. At the small archway, George glanced back and saw their young official, running towards them. The floor beneath her feet turned a golden yellow with each step she took.

She laid her hand on George's arm as she reached them and led them to the first row of tables before the riser. The chancellor waved his hand and a new table rose from the floor with only four chairs. She sat them down and stared angrily at her friends that had taken their seats. Then she returned to her new seat on the end of the table next to the chancellor.

George suddenly knew what grandfather had meant by his cryptic words. They were not the honored guests, and they had to finish playing their part until they left the Celestian home world. The evening lasted late, and finally the chancellor, Toma, and the others walked out of the great cavern. High-ranking officials now led George, Andy, Emily, and Anna out on their arms as they were now in the front row.

Toma stopped at the gangplank of their transport ship. Cal signed the cadets to enter first and stay hidden inside. Darri, then Sheta, then Cal and finally Toma entered the ship. The gangplank retracted and the port door rolled closed. A Celestian warship took off, hovering over of them and the towering swirl of gasses opened up above them. Their transport lifted off and a second Celestian warship followed them up and out of the swirling gasses. At the edge of the solar system, the warships broke off their following flight and the transport ship turned into a speeding comet headed for home.

Chapter 31

EVIL'S REVENGE

Outside the range of the Celestian solar system, George, Toma, Viceroy Petrosky, and the others formed a link. They called their triad and the Senior Viceroys. Viceroy Petrosky calmed their minds, helping them focus their thoughts. The whatever was gone and the cadet stations were up and running as if nothing had happened. No one even seemed to know they had been infected.

Toma reported out formally to the Senior Viceroys, his grandfather, and Pete's grandfather. George was amazed. He had never seen a full, formal report to the Senior Viceroys before. Usually, they were reporting out to a Viceroy or walking and talking to the Senior Viceroy after leaving the hospital. Toma's report was long and filled with information. He answered each question precisely giving as much detail as possible.

An hour later, their report to the Senior Viceroys ended and Gus closed their link. The captains were exhausted. Protocol was hard and tedious, and three days on Celestian had worn them out. The teams retreated to their sleeping rooms while the Viceroy flew the transport ship for home.

The Viceroy was now free from holding the energy of the universe and joined his triad's link when the captains and cadets were asleep. Toma's father and grandfather, George's father and Pete's grandfather were in the link with him.

"Report," the Senior Viceroy said seriously.

"The energy and power they wield is unbelievable. I don't think they understand at all what it means," Pete's dad reported. "It was amazing to watch, and yet terrifying. They have buried the information about the universe deep within themselves; nevertheless, they can still access the energy at any time. I don't think they know that others can't use raw energy of the universe like they do," he added with a little concern.

"Surely, they know how different they are by now?" George's dad said surprised.

"No, they don't know. The knowledge has been hidden from them. It is too much information for them right now. They need time to grow up. It must remain a process of discovery for them," Pete's grandfather said firmly.

"What of the young official they met?" Toma's grandfather asked.

"She may have read the ancient scrolls and now possesses the abilities of the Celestian high council. I will have Pete and Toma asked George for some more details," Pete's father said.

"And their chancellor and high council? What of them?" Toma's grandfather pressed, worried damage had been done.

"The chancellor has assured me they will add her into their circle and protect her until she is of age," Pete's father answered.

"There was no mention of a new council member in the prophecy until the cadets went to Celestian," Toma's father added.

"They are rewriting the prophecy," George's father said and sighed.

"This can't be good. It will be harder to protect them this way," Pete's dad added.

"Then we will need to change with them. The Galactic council is already changing. We must change, too, or we will be left behind like the dinosaurs on the Earth," the Senior Viceroy concluded. Late in the night their link ended.

The next morning everyone was up early, feeling rested.

"Someone must be helping us," George said to Andy, stretching.

Soon all of the cadets and captains were up and busy working around the transport ship until Gus and Gabe had breakfast ready. George sat with Toma, Cal, and Andy in the small room off the command deck.

"Why didn't you tell us you were a prince of Zalhala, sir?" George asked bluntly.

"I did," Toma answered, twisting his head.

"And you a prince, too, sir?" George asked Cal.

Cal smiled and whistled, "Yes," and hesitated.

"But what? I can see you almost saying it, but, you are what, sir?" Andy pressed.

"Our rank on our home planet is not important here. We are your captains. It is of greater importance," Cal whistled rather matter-of-factly.

Andy thought his answer was cryptic and so it meant it was important. Over the last three rotations, he had learned the more cryptic the answer, the more important it was to understand. Toma glanced at Cal. Cal stood up to leave and Andy stayed seated.

"Andy you need to leave. We have work to do," Cal ordered. "George will be here with Toma, he will be safe," Cal added.

George nodded and Andy reluctantly stood up. He never liked leaving George alone. The door closed and Toma stared at George.

"What happened in the master library on Celestian? Who was the glowing, golden yellow official you were with?" Toma asked seriously.

"I don't know who our young official was, sir. We meet her the day we arrived. She took my arm. Her friends teased her that we would get her demoted. Yet, she stayed with us. She got us into the master's library just behind you and the chancellor. If she hadn't repeated the child's story, we would never have found the right reading room, sir," George answered.

"That reading room nearly destroyed you," Toma said firmly.

"True, but the knowledge inside it was amazing, sir," he said, lost in the thought.

"Was the answer to the whatever inside?" Toma asked.

"No, it wasn't, sir. It only gave us the path to follow. It wasn't until Gus started Chen Lo, and you pulled us from the reading room that Andy and I knew the answer to saving our galaxies without destroying the whatever, sir," George answered, drifting off in thought again.

"Odd," Toma said and George refocused on Toma.

"What's odd, sir?" George asked drifting again, then focusing again.

"The master's library didn't have the answer. Did you ask any other questions while you were in the reading room?" he pressed.

"No sir. Don't worry, we stayed focused on our goal. Although, right now I can't remember how, sir," he said and paused. "I don't even know what Anna and Emily read or what our young official read," George said, trying to think and remember. "Something must be stopping my memory of the reading room, sir," he whispered, glancing off in space as if lost in a thought for a few minutes.

Toma stared at George waiting.

Suddenly, Andy and Gus burst into the small room, tackling George to the ground and making a nearly instantaneous link. Andy sent a small red energy sphere through the new link between George and someone else. The link broke abruptly. Immediately, Gus joined Andy and George in another new link then spun around, running from the room to return to the galley.

"I'm gone for thirty minutes and someone tries to knock you off George. Stop it! No more screwing around, George!" Andy yelled in a huff, as Cal caught up to him at the door.

"What is going on? What are you talking about? Report!" Toma said, suddenly became a captain again.

"It's like, every time my link is lowered, someone slips in to my mind and tries to destroy me. It's really getting annoying, sir," George replied matter-of-factly.

Toma's jaw dropped open. How could George be so casual about someone trying to destroy him, all of the time?

"Then don't lower you link with Andy again. Is that understood?" Toma said firmly, hardly believing he was saying the words.

"Yes sir," George replied, not understanding Toma's concern over a now common occurrence.

Anna popped her head inside the doorway. She, too, seemed unaffected by Andy and Gus's actions and that someone had tried to hurt George in a link again.

"Gabe called, said it was time to eat, sirs," Anna said, and left down the hallway.

Cal helped George and Andy from the floor and dragged Andy out of the room toward the galley.

"The young official you were with, did you get her name?" Toma asked, focusing George back on the master's library.

"No, she wouldn't tell us, sir," George replied, wishing she had said her name.

"The golden yellow gases she made were something," Toma added casually.

Toma's grandfather and Viceroy Petrosky had sent a message to him to find out more about the young official from the cadets.

"She turned the gasses yellow in the master's library as we walked across the main floor after you passed by. She could do it even before we entered the small reading room sir. It got really bright after we left. I was a little worried someone would follow us as it was a little hard to hide, sir," George said calmly, thinking back.

Toma stared at George and nodded. Yet, he didn't quite understand. Most beings would shout it from the rooftops that they had power or were seen with someone famous. But, these cadets went out of their way to hide it.

Trying hard not to use someone else for their fame and trying to protect the beings from harm.

"So where are we going, sir?" he asked, as he and Toma headed for the door.

"Back to training, cadet," Toma replied seriously, staring at George.

"Where exactly, sir?" George asked cautiously.

"You know where," Toma replied oddly puzzled.

George lowered his head, "Don't tell Andy, sir. He thinks we are going to Indus station, sir," George whispered.

"Why would he think that?" Toma asked at the door.

"You said we were going home, so he thought you meant your home," George whispered.

"Then we will not tell him until we absolutely have too," Toma replied and laughed.

George and his team would have liked to rest for the transport ride back to the cadet station; however, Viceroy Petrosky had other ideas. The Viceroy knew the captains and cadets had spent far too much time on transport ships and far too little time in real training classes.

Early the next morning, Toma was in their sleeping room with bowls of officer cereal for the cadets.

"Hey, this is like a regular training morning on one of the cadet stations, sir," Andy said laughing, as he sat down for a bowl of officer's cereal.

"That's good Andy, because it is a regular training morning. The Viceroy doesn't want you to lose anymore training days so he has set up some training for us in the cargo bays," Toma replied.

"No, really. You're kidding. Right, sir?" Andy said, pleading as he stuffed cereal into his mouth.

His words did no good. When they had finished their cereal, Toma stood up and walked to the door, motioning the cadets to follow him. They walked in silence to the cargo bay. The door slid open and a replica of Colonel Moawk's training dome stood in front of them. Toma's team was already lined up in the dome when they entered.

"The Viceroy is good," Gus whispered to Andy, marveling at the detail of the room.

He stopped when he caught Cal's stare. The cadets lined up and a holographic image of Major Doyzel appeared in the center of the training dome.

"This is the Thorean yellow captains training level. Everyone be careful," Andy signed, in their old sign language so the captains could read their conversation.

"Captains, this lesson will be on tactics. This is the art of knowing when to use your armaments training," said the holographic Major Doyzel.

Seats rose from the floor of the room. They looked more like tree stumps than chairs. However, they were better than sitting on the floor in the dirt.

Andy shook his head. "We're being watched," he signed to their team.

They each nodded and focused intently on Major Doyzel's descriptions of tactical details. The lesson was dull and boring. It made the previous lecture from Mayor Pennelo on the fighter's structure and armaments seem nearly interesting. Even Andy was bored and he usually liked blowing things up!

After a few hours of lecture, with no break for lunch, the training program projection glitched and changed from lecture to participation.

"Cadets, captains, armament training will introduce you to the basic weapons we use in defense. Tactics will teach you when to use this training," the holographic Major said, repeating the start of the lecture.

However, this time Major Doyzel flicked his wrist and slid out a staff weapon. The captains and cadets stood up and followed the Major's direction. With the flick of their wrists, staff weapons appeared in the captains and cadets' hands. Gabe shook his head, a little surprised. Cal didn't even blink, of course their cadets had their own staffs, no need to get the training staffs!

A holographic image of Colonel Moawk appeared and Major Doyzel's image turned to face him. They raised their staffs and began hand-to-hand attack and defensive moves. With each move, Major Doyzel called out the command, and the Major followed through with the action. George and Toma, Andy and Cal, Emily and Sheta, Darri and Sara, Anna and Tillie, Gus and Gabe all faced off. Move after move they attacked and defended.

The Thorean captains were stronger than the cadets; however, the cadets were quicker. George rolled and jumped with the other cadets. They couldn't take a direct hit from Toma and the others. An hour later, Emily, Anna, and Sara were pinned and the Major motioned them out. The Colonel yelled command after command to the remaining cadets and captains as if he was in the cargo bay with them, watching their moves.

Andy leapt to the cargo bay wall and flipped over Cal. Cal countered with a wild spin, clipping Andy in the leg. Andy fell, landing on Gus. Gabe pinned Gus and Cal pinned Andy as they skidded into the other wall of the room.

Only George and Toma were left standing, as once pinned you were out of play. Cal knelt down and lifted Andy up, while staring at Toma.

"What's up sir?" Andy whispered.

"I don't know. Something isn't right. That's not Toma's fighting style," Cal whispered, studying Toma.

George and Toma circled each other in the center of the cargo bay. Major Doyzel yelled command after command to Toma and Colonel Moawk yelled counter commands to George.

Suddenly with full force, Toma struck at George. George flip away and Tomas staff shattered when it impacted the floor of the cargo bay. Toma slid out a second staff springing forward toward George. Again, George flipped his body, this time, landing on Toma's back. Toma swung his staff around over his head, trying to knock George off.

"Say goodnight, Toma," George whispered, as he grabbed Toma's shoulder.

However, he didn't fall asleep. Toma's staff hit George and he flew off Toma's back, stumbling as Toma spun around for another strike.

"This isn't right. Toma would never hurt George," Cal muttered, as Toma connected with George's shoulder.

The cracking of George shoulder bones echoed across the cargo bay. Cal bolted forward to stop Toma as the Colonel and Major continued yelling command after command. Andy jumped up and knocked Cal to the ground; bits of dirt flew through the air crackling in red energy beams. Cal had narrowly missed being hit by the red beams. Cal's staff cracked as it rolled across the floor thru the red energy beams.

Toma swung his staff in a circle and impacted George's body again. This time it was with George's ribcage. George crumpled to the ground in agony. Again, Toma turned around for another hit.

"Stop Toma! He'll kill George!" Sara yelled frantically.

Emily was already trying to shut down the holographic computer program with Sheta. Gabe ran to the galley and returned a few minutes later with a green powder. He shook some into the air and fanned it with his wings. The cargo bay was alive with criss-crossing red energy beams.

"It's a cage!" Tillie yelled.

"Someone is using Toma to destroy George," Anna added, gasping.

"We need a link now!" Cal yelled, as Toma tossed George into the air.

George grabbed a ceiling support with his good arm, yelling out in pain as his other shoulder swung around dangling at his side.

Gus, Gabe, Darri, Andy, Cal, and Tillie instantly made a link.

"I can't break in. Something is stopping us," Gus thought through the link.

"Andy, can you sense anyone else in your link with George?" Cal asked.

"I don't have a link with George. Cal, it's gone!" he yelled.

Emily, Sheta, and Anna were plotting a path through the red beams. Toma turned his staff towards George and shot a red energy sphere into George's back. He let go of the ceiling, falling down onto Toma and knocking him to the ground. George's body laid sprawled out on the floor. Toma lifted himself up off the floor and raised his staff above George's body.

Cal shot red sphere's at Toma to stop Toma's attack. However, his spheres disintegrated before they reached Toma.

"That can't happen," Cal said stunned.

Both holograms yelled orders for Toma to strike at George again. Andy ripped a silver, barrel-shaped cover from the cargo bay wall and dove through red beams. The holes became slits as the red beams cut through the barrel. Streaks of blood marked Andy's path. Toma's staff came down on what was left of the barrel cover, shattering the remaining pieces.

Andy jumped to his feet, sliding out a blue staff. Cal ran over to the other side of the cage, careful to stay on the outside of the red beams. He matched Andy's staff position with a blue staff of his own. The others stopped in their tracks. They didn't remembered ever seeing blues staffs before.

Toma whistled a blood-curdling whistle. The cadets and captains fell to their knees in pain. Andy and Cal stood their ground and turned their staffs horizontally. Toma fell to the ground. The evil that possessed Toma wouldn't let go. He whistled again and the cadets rolled on the ground of the cargo bay in agony. Still, Cal and Andy stood their ground as blood trickled from Andy's ear. Control fields took a lot of energy, and Cal and Andy weren't being fed any energy. Soon, they would weaken.

Sara frantically grabbed for Gus's backpack, searching for her disc. Two rotations ago, they had been trapped in a medical office, and Sara had found a small silver disc. She had searched nearly every drawer in the office to find it. Gus didn't know what it was at the time and had even forgotten that he had it in his backpack.

Sara pushed the center of the disk out and threw the outer disc into the control field Cal and Andy had set up between their blue staff weapons. It spun and rolled on its edge, spinning to a rest near Toma's clawed foot. She dropped the centerpiece and smashed it with her fist. A purple gas rose from the outer disc. Toma choked and coughed, collapsing to the ground with a thud.

With Toma unconscious, the holograms faded and the red energy beams stopped. Andy and Cal spun their blue staffs vertical again, slipping them back up their sleeves. Sara and Darri rushed to George's side, forming a healing circle while Gabe and Gus dragged Toma's body out of the cargo bay to the small brig. Sara's gas may have knocked Toma out for the moment; however, they didn't want to chance him regaining consciousness.

Sara and Darri had their healing circle formed and Gus and Gabe joined the link from the brig. Sara didn't call on the energy of the universe to help her; instead, she used the energy of their triad. From Asteria, Pete, Frank, and the other captains joined their link and Sara's yellow sphere grew. George drew a deep breath as Darri set his shoulder bones. An hour passed and Sara lowered her sphere. Andy was next to be healed. His surface skin wounds healed much quicker.

Soon Pete, Frank, and their teams were released from their healing link. Cal carried George to the hospital room. Sara and Darri stayed with him.

"Where's the Viceroy?" Andy asked.

"Odd, he had to have known something was wrong," Cal whistled.

Cal and Andy left the hospital at a run.

"Emily, Sheta, Anna, Tillie find out where we are?" Cal yelled, passing the cargo bay at a run for the Viceroy's room.

Emily stared at the others; "how long have we been in here?"

Chapter 32

NOT HOME

They bolted from the cargo bay, heading for the command deck. A few moments after arriving, Anna and Emily's hands were racing across the controls as Sheta and Tillie brought up Emily's navigation holograms.

"Where are we?" Sheta asked, staring out the view screen, looking for familiar stars.

"Shouldn't we be almost halfway to Asteria station?" Tillie added.

"Yes, but we're not?" Anna replied.

"Then where are we?" Sheta asked, staring at Anna's charts.

They all puzzled, rotating their star charts and galaxies trying to find anything familiar to triangulate their position.

In the Viceroy's room, Andy and Cal found Viceroy Petrosky in a near coma state. He was barely breathing. They lifted him from the floor and raced to the hospital room with him hanging between them. Sara and Darri gasped when they saw the Viceroy.

"It's as if the life has been pulled right out of him," Sara whispered.

"It can't be here. George made it go away," Andy replied cryptically.

"What? Report cadet!" Cal yelled, most uncharacteristically.

Toma was their leader. He was the calm and focused one. Cal was not. Unlike George's team that traded leading the team on a moment's notice, the Thoreans changed leadership only when absolutely needed. Cal was more reactive to changes than Toma.

"Once before, we have felt this cold feeling. It was in the labyrinth on Jupiter station. Grandfather said it was from the evil being. It nearly pulled the life out of another group of cadets and the walls of the labyrinth itself. It can't be here, not now. George made the evil that hunts us leave, sir," Andy said, shaking his head.

"How do you know George made evil leave? Where did he send evil? No, Andy, it's not possible. Really, how could George have sent evil anywhere? What you are saying can't happen. It doesn't make any sense, Andy," Cal said, shaking his head as if something was forcing him to fight against the idea.

Andy stared at Cal, something was wrong. Cal was on the edge of spinning out of control, and Andy didn't know how to help him. Andy needed Cal. He couldn't save everyone without his triad. It was too much. Quickly, he changed Cal's focus to the issue with the Viceroy and Cal stared at Andy, refocusing his thoughts.

Sara and Darri made another healing circle and again their triad joined the link. It was weaker now, not stronger as they had expected. In a few hours, the Viceroy's color had returned to his skin and like George, he was breathing easier.

"We all need to eat, sirs," Gus said, releasing everyone from the healing link.

Andy went to the galley with Cal to get rations and water for everyone, since Gus and Gabe were still watching over Toma in the brig. Cal and Andy picked up the water and rations and distributed them to the hospital and brig first. Then they ran to the command deck to find the others.

They ran into the command deck with their arms loaded with water and rations. Anna, Emily, Sheta, and Tillie were frantically scanning space and calculating their position.

"Report!" yelled Cal, over the commotion in the room.

The girls spun around. They looked drained as if life itself was being pulled from them in the command deck. Instantly, Cal and Andy dropped the rations and water. Cal and Andy bolted forward, grabbing onto Anna, Emily Tillie, and Sheta arms and dragging them from the command deck. The door slammed closed and they all fell to the floor in the hallway. The girls shook their heads staring at Andy and Cal.

"What happened, Emily?" Andy asked.

"Andy, we don't know where we are," Emily said frantically.

She and Anna looked like pale shells and Sheta and Tillie looked as bad.

"Explain, remember I don't do cryptic, that's George," Andy replied.

She smiled weakly. "I wasn't cryptic, Andy. We really don't know where we are?" Emily answered.

Sitting on the floor of the hallway, the color was coming back into Emily, Anna, Tillie, and Sheta's faces. They were getting oddly better. Andy stared at Cal and then at them. He knew this one and it wasn't that cryptic.

"Emily, the command deck seems to be like the one place we can't be. It seems to make your body sick if you stay too long," Andy said cryptically, thinking about them getting better simply because they left the room.

Emily stared at Andy and then at the others. She sighed, breathing in deeply regaining her focus.

"You mean like the room wants us to leave because it knows something is wrong, and it's the only way it knows how to get our attention," Emily said, more to herself than to Andy and the others.

"Anna, remember the race?" Andy asked, looking for options, as they could no longer go into the ship's command deck.

"Which one, Andy?" Anna asked and laughed.

"The Sandue race in space that you flew with me. You said I could fly the fighter from the galley computers if I had too. Can you fly this transport ship from the galley computers?" Andy asked.

"Well, yes, but, well, we could," Anna started, and then Emily finished her thought.

"We could reroute the main control systems to a dumb file and lock them away. Then with a separate computer, load the data from our pads and reroute the power," Emily added, sliding out her pad.

Within minutes, the four girls were planning again. They understood the command deck wasn't hurting them now, it was trying to get them to leave. It didn't matter why at that moment, only that they had to leave. They lifted each other off the floor of the hallway and Emily, Sheta, Anna, and Tillie hurried to the galley to reroute the computer system controls.

Cal and Andy set up a warning device to prevent anyone from entering the command deck undetected. In their link, Cal informed the others what had happened and what the new plan was for navigation.

Toma had regained consciousness in the brig and was yelling at Gabe and Gus when Andy and Cal entered. Gabe and Gus left for the galley to help Anna and the others. Andy and Cal stayed to watch Toma.

"So I am told he lives," the being within Toma taunted, it's voice low and raspy.

Andy and Cal didn't answer.

"You will all die soon enough and I will become a prince over the universe," he said.

"You already are a prince, sir," Andy replied calmly.

"You lie. No matter. You will all be dead soon!" the being inside Toma yelled.

"You left being a prince for the freedom of the stars, sir," Andy said.

"Again, you lie. All will bow before me," Toma said, standing up straight and waving his arms and wings high into the air.

"All except one, sir," Andy pressed.

"A third time, you lie," he replied.

"No sir. I don't. You have been lied to by evil itself. How can such a being place you above itself, sir?" Andy said firmly.

He had the being within Toma thinking. Andy was the distraction as Cal wormed his way into Toma's mind. It was working; the being was beginning to doubt what he had been told.

"The evil being that guides you, now controls your every thought? Can you trust a being like that? A being that uses you and then discards you when you are no longer needed to serve its purpose. Your master wants only the team of the prophecy. Does it not?" Andy said seriously, distracting the being inside Toma.

His voice was low, trying to push the being inside Toma into doubt.

"Yes, and I will bring you to him. I will be the prince of the universe!" the being said triumphantly, stuck on only one thought~ one focused mission.

"Can't your master take away, as easily, as he gives the treasures of the universe?" Andy pressed.

"I have earned my reward. No one can take it from me," the being said, getting agitated. It was what Andy and Cal wanted.

"Can't the master take away Toma's body and give it to another, more deserving than you?" Andy taunted.

"No one is more deserving than me!" the being said yelling and ranting, not even trying to disguise its gruff voice.

Cal nodded and they walked out of the room as Tillie and Anna entered to watch Toma.

"Who possesses, Toma?" Andy asked.

Cal frowned. "It's like someone is forcing Toma to do all these things, and he has to watch unable to stop whomever it is. A strong mind link from... Well, you know the Earth expression," Cal answered seriously.

"You mean a stealthy mind link that was smooth as silk, like the Senior Viceroy master that keeps attacking George," Andy said, piecing the thoughts together.

Their run in with the command deck seemed to have cleared Cal's mind. His focus and control had returned.

"Good work. That's close to what it is," Cal said, pleased at Andy's reasoning ability. "However, Toma is strong enough to stop even the most formidable of mind invasions, even the stealthy smooth as silk ones. This is more like evil itself," Cal said, thinking.

"Been there, done that. Toma isn't going to like the cure," Andy replied, remembering when he, George, and Cal had been touched by evil on their second rotation.

Gus and Gabe came around the corner and handed Andy and Cal ration packs and bottles of water before entering the brig. Tillie and Anna left and returned to Emily and Sheta in the ships galley. Andy and Cal followed them. The girls had wires pulled out of the walls and ceiling of the galley with small monitors and holographic emitters tied to the walls with bandages they had taken from the hospital supplies.

"The time has come, let's see if it works," Emily said, doubtful of their work.

The others didn't seem to hold out much hope either.

"It will work Emily. Focus on the task at hand," was the thought that crossed her mind.

Cal and Andy nodded, and the girls started flipping control switches, one at a time. A holographic image of their part of the universe appeared. They found their position and breathed a sigh of relief.

"Someone or something must have messed with the main command deck computers," Emily said with relief.

"So, where are we?" Andy asked.

"Well, we traveled passed Asteria station more than a day ago and it looks like our heading is for the second kitchen. Yet, I don't know how we got here so fast, we should still be days away from Calshene," Emily answered and then shook her head.

"It's kind of like the beginning of our rotation, when evil moved our transport ship near the center of the universe in less than a week," Anna added, and they all started muttering to themselves, planning their next move.

"Can you turn us around and take us back to Asteria station?" Cal asked.

They all looked up at once, then, they looked down and changed some controls around.

"Yes, we can trick the computer and make it think it is going to the traders planet, when in reality, it is going to Asteria station," Emily replied, not looking up from her screens and controls with Sheta.

"Change course for Asteria station," Cal ordered, and he and Andy left the galley.

"They hate us there you know," Andy said, in the hallway after they had left the girls.

"I know," Cal said, not even trying to fib like Pete, Frank, George, or Toma.

Cal was blunt and direct.

"You have to look passed their hatred and look for the little positive changes, Andy," Cal counseled.

They walked to the hospital next as if they were making rounds.

"Cal, if you are not a crown prince on Zalhala, what are you? Really?" Andy asked as bluntly as Cal.

"A regional prince," he replied.

"And that means what?" Andy pressed.

Cal stopped in the hallway. "Toma is a crown prince. In our culture, line of succession is flipped back and forth so no one family rules forever. Toma's uncle, my father, is the chancellor of our planet. His sons are regional princes as they can't become the next chancellor. Toma's dad's sons are the next in line to become chancellor. His older brother is in training now to assume the role of chancellor when the time comes. Another family will be chosen after Toma's brother becomes chancellor. Like the Celestian, we have a high council. However, ours is made-up of more than four hundred people. They represent the people of different regions on our planet."

"But Toma is a crown prince," Andy pressed for more information.

"If Toma's brother dies, then Toma will the chancellor of Zalhala," Cal replied, wondering why Andy was so curious.

Andy thought for a moment. "Your father is the chancellor of your entire planet?" Andy said, nearly speechless as the words Cal said sunk in to his mind.

"Yes, and I can see by your reaction, you shouldn't have been told," Cal said, shaking his head.

"No sir, it's OK. I'm not too weirded out by it. You just have to give me some time to settle the information. I'm a country boy that grew up on a farm out in the middle of nowhere. The whole protocol thing is hard enough for me to swallow. You being rich and famous and a prince is going to take some time to get used to and then you wanting to leave all that to chase around the galaxies protecting us? Incredible. On Earth, people dream all their lives of being a rich and famous prince and princesses of the world. They would never even think of leaving it after getting it," Andy said, sighing thinking of how much fun it would be to be that rich.

"You will have to come and live with the protocol officers on Zalhala for a while. I'm sure they will change your mind," Cal said, giving his best Thorean grin. "Besides you're ..., ahhh, nothing," Cal said, stopping mid-sentence and staring at Andy.

"What, I'm what, sir?" Andy pressed, wanting to know what Cal almost slipped up and said.

"Nothing, I forgot for a moment, cadet, that's all," Cal replied seriously, entering the hospital room.

Andy shook his head and followed him inside. "So close, and yet, so far," Andy muttered.

George and the Viceroy were awake when they entered. They both looked tired; however, they were sitting up, eating dark brown cereal. George smiled and the Viceroy nodded.

"Report," George whispered.

"We are running the ship from our second operating base, as we did on Sandue. We are now about three days less the one we missed from Asteria station," Andy said, reporting out cryptically enough that George knew what was really going on and the Viceroy would be one-step behind.

The command deck didn't get messed up by itself and Toma was never alone long enough to do it. The Viceroy was the only one who had been alone, guiding the ship!

"Three days, cadet," Viceroy Petrosky repeated.

"Ah yes, sir. We will be there very soon, sir," Andy answered, without directly lying.

George nodded, understanding Andy's cryptic report.

"And Toma?" the Viceroy asked.

"There is little we can do, sir. He is lost to us as Gus was to the master on Sandue, sir," Andy answered formally.

"Gus honored the master?" the Viceroy asked, gaining an odd interest in their cryptic conversation.

Cal stared at the Viceroy and then glanced at Andy. Cal wanted Andy to be the distraction while he wormed his way into the Viceroy's mind. Someone was controlling the Viceroy like Toma. Cal was now sure of that.

"Yes sir, it took everything we could do to pull Gus back from the master. He would have done anything for the master. Truth be told, we each felt the pull of the master. He was so kind and welcoming. He wanted us to come to him and share in his riches," Andy said, leading the Viceroy on.

"And you rejected the master, how is that possible?" the Viceroy asked, entranced by Andy's words.

With each word the invader controlling the Viceroy said, he was giving more and more of himself away.

"It was hard and Gus didn't want too. But, the master took interest in someone else and then left us on Sandue. We were alone and very frightened so we had to come back to the Galactic Union, there was nowhere else for us to go," Andy said, his story getting longer and more twisted with each word.

George was now blocking Cal's thoughts and Andy as embellished his story to keep the Viceroy distracted.

"We were so alone–the master was gone. Sadness overtook us. We had to get medicine for Gus or he wouldn't have survived," Andy whispered, lowering his head.

Cal rolled his hand over, motioning Andy to continue his story.

"Have you ever been in the master's presence? There is nothing you wouldn't do for the master. You are guided and given the path to follow. Everything is planned out and there is nothing to do, but, think of the treasures and rewards you will get when you return from your mission to be with the master," Andy said. His words were hypnotic to the invader, possessing the Viceroy.

"Yes, yes, I know the feeling. It is lonely without the master near," the invader replied, dropping his guard.

In that moment, Cal dove into the Viceroy's and the invader's mind. He sent one flaming red energy sphere after another until he had nothing left. Cal's body collapsed to the floor as Andy followed Cal into the Viceroy's mind. Andy also sent flaming red energy spheres at the invader, pounding the invader and the other invaders ready to take his place if he should fail in his mission.

George was feeding Andy energy in their link. Where George was getting the energy from, Andy couldn't tell, only that the energy seemed endless. The invaders link stopped and Andy fell to the floor, shaking, his eyes glowing a fiery red. George was unconscious, as well as the Viceroy, Darri, and Sara.

Anna and Sheta, Tillie, and Emily never left their station in the galley. It took all of their skills to pilot the transport from a few small monitors and one holographic display in the ship's galley. Toma ranted and raged all the while Gus and Gabe kept watch.

Another day passed and the cadets and captains stayed where they were- too focused on their tasks to move or eat. The transport ship took a hit and Emily spun the ship around.

"I can't see the asteroids! There're coming in too fast!" Anna yelled.

"I'll spin us around again. Look and remember, like in the labyrinth, Anna. You remember how we did it on our first rotation," Emily said, her voice calm and quiet.

"Spin us around again. I think I can do this," Anna answered calmer.

Tillie had laid her arm over Anna's shoulder, helping her calm her mind and focus her thoughts.

"We can do this together," Tillie whistled softly.

They stared intently at the little monitors as Emily and Sheta spun the transport ship slowly around again. Emily slowed their speed by one-half and Tillie used the gravity of a large asteroid to slow them down further.

"We're almost there. The Calshene administrator should be calling soon," Anna said sighing, relieved they had made it to Asteria station. Suddenly, her face went blank. "We can't answer the administrator from here!" Anna yelled replied.

Horror raced across their faces.

"They'll destroy us before they will let us land without clearance," Emily said frantically.

"Grandfather. We need to call grandfather. He can help us," Anna said, hoping he was nearby.

"Only if he's close. I'm not as strong as George and Andy," Emily replied, thinking they may need to go find George, yet, there wasn't really enough time, they needed help, now!

The girls joined arms and focused their thoughts, reaching out with their new link to find their Senior Viceroy Petrosky, Pete's grandfather. Their link was weak and they found only silence. A moment later, Emily spun away from the others and ran from the galley.

"No!" screamed Anna, Sheta, and Tillie.

With the twist of her wrist, Emily broke open the lock on the command deck door from the hallway, racing up to the command console. The lights on the main console were all lit-up and the communication lights were blinking. An administrator was calling. Emily's hands raced across the keys with lighting speed. The administrator was having difficulty keeping up. Suddenly, Emily's answers stopped. The administrator called again~ no answer. Emily lay on the floor of the command deck unable to move, her body shaking as she tried to fight back an evil mind invader.

A huge Thorean warship over took the transport ship. The sound of grappling hooks attaching to the ship's hull echoed through the hallways. Tillie, Sheta, and Anna left the galley and ran to the weapons lockers. They didn't know who had grappled onto them, however, they would defend their ship. It was all they had.

Inside, Sheta was worried. Cal and Andy didn't come running to defend when they heard the grapples on the ship's hull.

The transport was lifted into the Thorean warship's immense cargo bay and the cargo bay door closed, echoing as they clanked, clunked, scrapped, and thudded shut. The three were ready to defend, standing at the main port entrance. The port doors spun open and Thorean guards were rushing into the transport ship.

The guards grabbed onto Sheta, Tillie, and Anna. In a flash of white light, they were gone! The guards methodically searched room after room on the transport.

In the brig, the Thorean guards surrounded Toma with blue staffs and in a flash of light, he too, disappeared as medics followed them in to help Gus and Gabe. The medics carried them away to the hospital onboard the Thorean warship.

In the transport ship's hospital room, Andy and Cal bodies lay twisting and shuttering on the floor. George was dangling off the side of his bed, as if reaching for Andy. The Viceroy was nearly translucent slumping over on his bed, his head nearly touching the floor. Afraid to separate the group, the medics whisked them away in a huge flash of white light.

The Thorean officers ran up to the command deck doors and backed away as a cold shiver ran up their spines. The lead officer tore open a section of the wall and cross-connected several wires. The door opened. Emily lay on the floor, shaking. Her skin was a translucent color.

A few officers ran to the galley and pulled out the wiring from the small command center the captains and cadets had set up. Two of the Thorean officers weaved the wires together, making a long rope as they ran back to the command deck. Somehow evil was strong in the command deck and the officers knew they weren't strong enough to enter the command deck. They called for help.

In a flash of white light, a Viceroy appeared in the hallway outside the command deck. The Viceroy made a cowboys lasso from the wire. The Thorean officer opened the door again. With all his strength, the Viceroy stood in the open doorway and threw the wire lasso across the command deck. It landed a few feet short of Emily's foot.

"I need more wire!" he yelled, recoiling the lasso and closing the door again with a quick twist of his wrist. The Viceroy knelt down to rest.

"Are you alright, sir?" the lead Thorean officer asked.

"Yes, yes, I'll be fine. The evil within is difficult to fight off," the Viceroy replied nodding. "I don't know how Emily was able to answer the administrator's questions or how she has lasted as long as she did," he added, admiring her strength.

Another officer returned with more wire and the Viceroy made the wire rope longer. The door opened again and the Viceroy threw the lasso with all his strength. This time it landed over Emily's foot. Carefully, the Viceroy pulled the lasso over her foot. It caught!

Quickly, he dragged Emily from the command deck. The door closed and medics rush forward and then backed away. The Viceroy knelt down and lifted her up in his arms as shivers ran up his spine.

"Oh child, what have you done," he whispered, disappearing in a flash of white light.

Chapter 33

GALACTIC UNION

They may have been on their way to Asteria station; however, their rescue by the Thorean warship, out in open space, changed everything. The cadets and captains had been able to change their course away from the second kitchen. However, the administrator they were talking with was in a remote asteroid field far from the Calshene solar system and far from the Asteria station.

The Thorean warship had been on its way to Asteria to greet Toma and the other Thoreans with a message from Toma's brother. The Thoreans had answered the Calshene outpost's called for help when the transport ship spun around the Calshene's first asteroid beacon.

With the transport ship loaded inside cargo bay, the Galactic Union council ordered the commander of the Thorean warship to a new destination. They were not to return their new cargo to Asteria station. Instead, the warship blazed across the galaxy, far from home, to an un-named Nebula and a planet, spinning slowly around a red dwarf star. They were to head straight for the Galactic Union.

Across the universe, there were many sector Galactic councils. All of which sent representatives to the Galactic Union. The Galactic Union was the central governing body of all the sector Galactic councils. The delegates were the most Senior Viceroys and Chancellors from the member galaxies across the known universe. This council of elders of the Galactic Union over saw the activities of the Galactic councils in all sectors of the universe.

The Galactic Union council of elders had watched the progress of George, his team, and his triad over each of their rotations. Each time evil had attacked the team, the Galactic Union council of elders had been told - this time was no different.

The evil that hunted them now possessed a strong Viceroy, the strongest captain of George's triad, and one of the cadets. The triad was nearly destroyed trying to stop evil and had failed to stop evil from controlling its members.

Inside the hospital room on the Thorean warship, the captains and cadets were placed in stasis tubes. Once again, evil possessed members of George's triad; a powerful triad that the Calshene Galactic council and the Galactic Union council now feared.

The Thorean warship was fast and needed no clearance to land on the Galactic Union Nebula planet. Instead, it circled the planet from space, the cadets and captains were extracted from the stasis tubes in flash after flash of white light. It was a stunning display of power from the Galactic Union members on the planet surface.

The Thorean warship left the planet the instant the last captain was whisked away. The commander sent the transport ship barreling into the red dwarf sun to destroy it as they left the Nebula.

On the planet below, the medics didn't place the cadets and captains into yellow healing tubes in the hospital. Instead, each cadet and captain was laid out on a gleaming silver bed. A dozen Senior Viceroys that glowed with bright white auras surrounded each one.

The Senior Viceroys concentrated and George and Andy stopped shaking. Slowly, one by one, the cadets and captains were healed and every trace of evil was stripped from their minds. Then the medics carried each cadet and captain to another room in the hospital to sleep and rest. Toma, Emily, and Pete's father were last.

The Senior Viceroys looked tired; yet, they wouldn't give up. They each summoned their individual triads. Quietly, the room filled with 216 Viceroys and Inner Circle Officers. The Viceroys knelt on one knee when they saw the circle of Senior Viceroys. Never had so many come together, peace and calm filled the air as if peace was an energy unto itself.

"Arise, sons and daughters of the universe. Evil has come too far this time and we need your help to push it back," Senior Viceroy David Lu, spoke in a whisper.

He reached out to Pete's grandfather, Toma's grandfather and father, and Frank and George's father and they moved across the white room to where Pete's dad lay on the shimmering silver bed. Pete's grandfather, Senior Viceroy

Petrosky, lifted him into his arms as Toma's dad and George's dad made the link and felt the pain and agony within Pete's dad.

"We will not lose another to evil. Not this time," George's dad thought through their link.

The room glowed with a blinding white light and Pete's dad drew a deep breath. Two hours passed and evil fled the Viceroy's mind. Two other Viceroys lifted Viceroy Petrosky up as another Viceroy moved the Senior Viceroys and Viceroys over to Toma's silvery bed.

The Senior Viceroy Heto, Toma's grandfather, lifted Toma into his arms next.

"Toma hide not your actions from us. George forgives you as it was not you who hurt him. You must forgive yourself as all is forgiven here. Face the fear and it will have no place to hide," Senior Viceroy Heto whispered.

Toma opened his eyes. They were a blaze with the look of red fire and fear.

"I can't forgive myself for hurting George," Toma whispered, through gritted teeth, struggling against the evil still hiding inside him.

"You can and you will, as the oath you freely gave does not end when things get difficult. You must trust in the strength inside you and know the path you have chosen is good. Believe in yourself and trust those around you. Within all of us is the capacity to change and learn from our experiences. It is one of our greatest inner strengths. Use it to free yourself from the evil and fear, hiding inside you," the Senior Viceroy said, his voice but a whisper.

His father helped Toma stand up and walk over next to his grandfather. His grandfather placed his hand on Toma's shoulder and his mind began to focus. Deep inside, he believed in himself, their triad, and the others. His strength increased and he shared his energy with the Viceroys and released the fear and regret he held inside. Together, they glowed a brilliant white light again. The light died down and two other Viceroys lead Toma away to another room to rest with the others.

Senior Viceroy David Lu turned and walked toward the last silvery bed in the room. At the edge of the Senior Viceroy's circle, he stopped; and Toma's and Pete's grandfathers joined him. The aura of evil was strong, as if, it was there in the room with them. He lowered his head. The three Senior Viceroy's circled Emily and a brilliant white light burst across the room. Quickly, it died down.

"We are not strong enough to save her life and take the evil from her," David Lu whispered, a tear running down his cheek as he spoke the words.

In a shimmer of white light, Max appeared next to Senior Viceroy Lu, Heto and Petrosky. The Viceroys and Inner Circle officers in the room gasped. Many had never seen a being of white light before. Max solidified and placed his hand on Lu and Petrosky's shoulders to help steady their focus and restore their calm.

"You and I know there is only one among us strong enough to save her life," Max whispered. "George," he said in their minds only.

"The cost is too high, Max, and you know it or you would not have come to stop them," Senior Viceroy Petrosky whispered, as sadness filled his heart.

"Stop them we must. As this is what the evil truly wants more than their deaths. It is control over the cadets lives that evils wants the most," Max whispered.

They couldn't see Emily's seed of hope buried deep inside her mind. However, it was too late for the Senior Viceroys and Max. From the other room, George and the others had already made a link with Emily.

"Chen Lo," Andy said in their link as the triad stood up from their silvery beds.

"We will need David Lu this time as we will need to go higher then before," Toma signed.

"He will not come. We must do this on our own," George signed back.

The cadets and captains slipped off their beds as the medics ran from the room fearing for their lives. These cadets and captains shouldn't have even been able to stand. Anna locked the doors.

Andy, Gus, George, and Toma started out on level one in their minds, and then Cal, Sheta, and Anna followed, all moving only their arms, not their feet. Soon Tillie, Gabe, Darri, and Sara joined in, and the room started to become alive with energy. They reached out on the energy of the universe and found Emily. It was as if her entire being was somehow being changed into pure evil, and only a small tiny part was left, fighting back.

George focused on the little tiny bit of good left within Emily. It was her seed of hope. Their seed of hope was the only thing that had saved the cadets when all had seemed lost in the past. It was the cadets most guarded secret.

At the thirteenth level, as the room bent and moved with the energy of the universe. George stepped forward and opened his arms. Emily faded from the circle of Senior Viceroys. Max and the Senior Viceroys spun around, staring at each other. Emily reappeared in George's arms and the energy warped around her. Toma and Gus focused and guided the energy to George.

"Noooo! You don't have the control you need to do this!" Senior Viceroy Petrosky yelled.

Running from the healing room to the sleeping room the cadets and captains had been placed in, the officers beat on the doors.

"No children, you don't understand," Senior Viceroy Petrosky said.

"You will all be destroyed and evil wins. Please children," Senior Viceroy Heto whispered, thinking the energy of the universe was too strong for them to control.

The other Senior Viceroys beat on the doors and corridor walls. They couldn't enter room, not even on a stream of energy. David Lu spun around and glowed with a brilliant white aura.

In a flash of white light, Pete and Franks teams physically appeared in the room with George and the others. Quickly, they joined in the Chen Lo. Their triad was complete and the raw energy of the universe ebbed and flowed around them.

"Why did you bring them?" Senior Viceroy Heto asked as Senior Viceroy David Lu's aura faded and he slumped over a little.

"You are right. They don't have the control that they need to guide the raw energy of the universe and Max can't interfere. However, with their whole triad together, perhaps, they may have a small chance to live," David Lu replied hopefully.

Level fourteen, fifteen, sixteen, and seventeen whizzed-by. Soon the triad was at level eighteen. Their motions were fluid and seamless, flowing in and out of the space between the raw energy of the universe. The room was gone and the raw energy danced between them, twisting and turning. With great sweeps of their arms, the energy rolled and spun, flipping and turning in the air. George held Emily in his arms and focused only on her thoughts and mind.

"I have you now!" Evil screeched through Emily.

"As you wish," George replied, smiling a devilish grin.

Toma, Frank, and Pete nodded as if of one mind. George opened his thoughts and mind to evil. Through evil's link with Emily, George sent all of the uncontrolled raw energy of the universe careening into the evil being and washing across the universe.

George and the others knew their triad couldn't control all of the raw energy of the universe alone! The uncontrolled energy washed over a hundred thousand of the evil's most powerful minions, knocking them unconscious.

Without its' minions to direct and guide the energy of the universe to it, the evil being was defenseless and quickly lost its hold on Emily ~ evil faded away.

George stared at Emily. She smiled and slipped out of his arms. She held his hand as she stepped out of the center and into their Chen Lo, as if she had been a part of it from the beginning.

The triad thought of the Galactic Union council, Senior Viceroys, Inner Circle Viceroys, and Viceroys. Together, the triad streamed energy to them to help them recover from the events of the last two years. Without the drain of energy from evil, the energy of the universe smoothed out, calming and flowing across the galaxies.

In the corridors, the Senior Viceroys and Viceroys felt their strength and energy returning. Emily unlocked the room with a wave of her hand. However, only one was allowed inside, as the triad knew the raw energy they still guided was uncontrolled. David Lu appeared in their link, stepping through Chen Lo with them.

"You need to release the energy very slowly now, captains and cadets. This will take much longer than you are used to. Do not hurry or what is it Captain Petrosky says, ah yes, the universe will have one big headache. Calm and focused, you will slowly release the energy of the universe back into the ebb and flow of life," he said calmly. His voice was melodic and focused.

Slowly, over the next twenty-four hours the triad stepped down their Chen Lo levels, releasing the energy of the universe. Toma, George, and the others sat down on the floor of the sleeping room as they finished.

"I thought we had lost you, Emily," George whispered, holding her in his strong arms.

"I knew you would come for me. I never gave up my seed of hope," she whispered, blushing.

"George, I'm sorry," Toma whistled, lowering his head.

"Nothing to be sorry about, sir," George whistled, nodding.

"No, there had to be something inside of me that let evil get a hold of my thoughts," Toma said, dipping his head lower.

"No sir. Cause if there is, then it's in all of us as we are all connected," George answered.

"You know that somehow all of this will only lead to more special training," Gus added.

"Sure does seem that way," Gabe whistled.

The door of the room opened and the Senior Viceroys and Viceroys rushed inside to find the captains and cadets sitting on the floor and David Lu standing behind them. Senior Viceroy Petrosky nodded and David disappeared in a flash of white light. The other Senior Viceroys and Viceroys backed out of the room. The door closed and the cadets raced forward to the Senior Viceroy Petrosky, hugging him as the captains stood up. The Senior Viceroy raised his hand and silver seats appeared in the room. Soon, the cadets left grandfather and sprawled out across the floor as the captains sat in the seats.

"I am proud of all of you," Senior Viceroy Petrosky said. "However," he paused. "It was a very risky move for the universe," he added, raising an eyebrow.

"Yes sir," Toma answered for the teams, lowering his head and the others followed.

"Giving evil what it wanted, a very novel idea, George. I can't say I have ever heard of someone giving evil exactly what it asked for. We will need to add it to our tactical training," the Senior Viceroy said, pleased to have a new defense against evil.

"You are all at risk now and very vulnerable to suggestions from the evil. As that is now the issue, you will remain here for the duration of your fourth rotation. A decision will be made as to when you may return," the Senior Viceroy said spoke firmly, as if no further questions or comments were needed.

"Where are we, sir?" Emily asked, before George or Toma could stop her.

"Yes sir, where is here?" Anna added quickly.

"Here is somewhere safe," the Senior Viceroy said, standing up.

Toma's dad entered the room and he and Senior Viceroy Petrosky vanished in a flash of white light. The chairs started to change into beds and the cadets and captains stood up.

"Are we in isolation on some far away outpost, sir?" Anna asked.

"A mystery to solve another day, sleep now," Toma whistled.

They laid down on their silvery beds and yawned. A great calmness filled the air between them. George knew someone was watching out for them that night. He would have to remember to thank them if he sensed their presence again.

Morning came early, Pete, Frank, and Toma were sitting at long silver picnic tables, signing as George, and the others started to wake up. George and Andy didn't recognize their new sign language as they slid onto the seats next to Toma and Cal.

"Report," was the only word Pete said.

George relayed the events of the last few weeks to Pete and Frank, confirming what Toma had told them.

"So the rumors of the new Celestian council member emerging early are true?" Frank said, more than asked.

"I guess. She was the only official who would even be seen with us, sir," Andy added.

"Then you have a true friend. One who stays with you when others shun you and turn away," Pete said sincerely.

"It was a good thing you all did," Niels added.

"We didn't do anything, sir," Anna spoke up sitting down with Gus.

"Honest, we only followed protocol, sir," Emily added hugging George's arm.

"Well, kind of," Gus added, waving his hand in the air.

"Toma, Cal, Sheta, and Darri did all of the hard rule-following-work, sir," Andy added hugging Sara.

Pete smiled. They did something; they simply didn't recognize it, yet. They had healed their librarian and protected their young officer from those that tried to harm her by making her late.

Chapter 34

RETRAINING ?

Pete, Frank, and Toma stood up from the table, stretching.

"We have all been assigned new sleeping rooms. Each morning we will assemble and go to our original training classes. However, our training will be in one dome near our sleeping rooms. We will train together and you will train only at our level from now on," Toma said, giving orders like a captain again as they left the hospital sleeping room.

Emily reached out to touch the corridor wall, and the wall bent back from her hand. Frank glanced down and shook his head.

"Not here, Emily," Nick signed, in the cadets sign language.

She pulled her hand back from the wall and lowered her head. It would be hard with no one to play simple games with she thought.

George held her hand to comfort her a little. The corridors were all white and it was hard to tell when they left the hospital for the other places on the station. There were very few doors and no signposts to read. They passed officers who were more absorbed in their own thoughts and didn't even try to read their thoughts.

Two more turns and Toma lead them into a dome slightly larger than Colonel Moawk's training dome. There was only an archway, no door. The captains and cadets walked inside and lined up as a holographic image of the Major Doyzel appeared.

"Where are we, sir?" George asked.

"In a place that is safe," Pete replied, not even raising an eyebrow; however, Toma shook his head.

"This is tactics training today captains. Extend your staffs," Major Doyzel began.

A second holographic image appeared. It was Colonel Moawk and the two images raised their staffs to the vertical position.

"The staff weapon is used for defense and offense. It can absorb a staff blast if properly aimed," the Major said.

He shot a small blast at the Colonel and the Colonel caught it with the end of his staff. The captains faced each other and George and his team faced each other. They took turns, shooting small blasts with the staff at each other.

Gus winced and missed his catch. The blast caught Nick in the back of his knee, dropping him to the ground. Sara and Rachael raced over to heal Nick's injury. Toma motioned and Cal and Niels repositioned Gus against one of the walls of the dome so if he missed again, no one would be injured. Gus apologized as best he could from across the room.

With Nick healed, Pete started the holograms again and their lessons continued. They were taught about the horizontal positions, the vertical positions, and the meanings of each move. At lunch, Frank stopped the holograms and they left, in silence, for their lunch of dark brown officer's cereal in the officer's dining room. No one spoke a word, no thoughts, nothing, only silence. They walked back to the dome and Frank started a new holographic program.

"We will continue with the Major's lesson tomorrow. This afternoon we will have training from Colonel Payate. Remember she teaches first aid and basic survival," Toma whistled firmly.

The holographic projection started and brown first aid kits appeared before the captains.

"In all first aid kits are the basics for caring for an injury. Now, carefully lift out the inside box in the first aid kits you have before you. Not all kits will have these inserts," the Major spoke, pointing to the bottom of the kits.

Sara lifted hers out and gasped.

"What Sara? What are these little vials?" Andy asked, picking one up and shaking it in the air.

Sara jumped up and grabbed it from his hand. "Andy don't touch it, if you don't know what it is," Sara said scolding his harshly.

"What?" Andy said, shaking his head and George raised his eyebrow.

"It's poison Andy, and a strong one if I say so myself. It isn't something I would have expected to see in these kits," she said, a little concerned.

Everyone carefully set down the vials and jars they had been touching.

"Thank you, cadet," the holographic Colonel said directly to Sara.

Sara blushed and the lesson continued. George listened; however, he wondered how a prerecorded image could answer Sara directly. With mind-numbingly detail, the Colonel described the contents of each vial and jar on the inside of the first aid kits. Toward the end of training, even Sara was getting bored.

Eventually, Toma stopped the projector and they followed Pete back to the dining room for more dark brown officer's cereal. After dinner, the cadets were lead to their sleeping rooms, three cadets per room with one captain. There would be no extra training tonight, no exploring the planet, or finding caves. Nothing, only sleep, calm, quiet, peaceful, and safe sleep.

Morning came and each captain lead the cadets back to the dining room for more dark brown cereal and then on to the training dome again. Pete brought up an image of Colonel Moawk. He started them out running as vines fell from the ceiling. Command after command the cadets followed the captains. The Colonel didn't believe in lunch and ran the captains hard right up until dinner.

Again, they left in silence, not even making a link or signing any thoughts. Their new isolation was hard and boring. On the third day, Major Doyzel's training was continued and then Colonel Payate again after lunch.

Day after day, they repeated the cycle at an excruciatingly slow pace. They each knew they could have finished the entire training sequence in less than a week. Yet, as before, when they had tried to be regular fourth rotation cadets, they endured.

There was nothing to talk to and Emily grew sad. Andy was nearly bursting with energy. Anna wanted to know so badly where they were, she could hardly contain her thoughts by the seventh day. Gus needed to cook and Sara needed to help people.

Each night George only focused on his team, calming their minds and helping them focus their thoughts. No one read their thoughts and they read no one else's thoughts. This had to be what the Galactic council meant by isolation, George thought.

Pete was right, his team didn't like it and they wouldn't last much longer in isolation, safe isolation. Even the evil that hunted them couldn't have come up with a better torment to break their will.

The days became a blur and George and others could no longer focus. They simply followed orders as mindless minions, hoping to make it through another day. Pete's grandfather appeared outside their training dome on the twenty-first day.

"They are ready, sir. They are following orders without question now," the watching officer thought to Senior Viceroy Petrosky.

"I am not convinced this is the right path," Senior Viceroy Petrosky replied.

"The Galactic Union council of elders has ordered their isolation and retraining, sir. They have lasted longer than most, sir," the officer replied, trying to be comforting.

"That doesn't make it right," the Senior Viceroy replied, lowering his head and disappearing in a flash of white light.

George looked up, he felt the change in the energy and the sadness within the energy.

"May we practice Chen Lo this evening, sir?" George signed to Toma as they walked to dinner after the day's training ended.

"No cadet," Toma signed back.

"Possum, sir," George answered.

"What?" Toma replied, still walking through the corridor, not turning into their dining room.

"Possum, sir. We are being retrained. Our spirits are nearly broken, and we are without hope or any end in sight, sir," George signed.

Quickly, Frank translated possum into the new sign language of the captains. It had to be something very new they had only recently created.

"Then we will continue to play possum until they think there are only shells of beings left," Toma signed, entering the dining hall.

They sat and ate in silence with their knowledge and seed of hope buried deep inside them, hiding it from anyone's scan or view.

On the twenty eighth day, a hologram of David Lu appeared before them in the training dome. Only, it wasn't a hologram at all. He was real. They knew him, like Pete's grandfather. He had a strong mind and would discover they were playing possum once they began their Chen Lo training.

"Gus, you must hide our seed of hope. You are the only one who can do this and still remember our seed of hope," George signed as David Lu turned away to begin Chen Lo.

"Remember, it is what grandfather said, 'you are the one'," George signed quickly.

Gus smiled. Grandfather's cryptic words from so long ago, finally made sense. Gus nodded and hid their seed of hope from the cadets and the captains.

Chen Lo started and David Lo started scanning and searching their minds as they reached level twelve. At level thirteen he stopped. The captains and cadets stopped and stood in formation facing the open doorway as if waiting for their next instruction. David Lu left the teams and walked out into the corridor. Senior Viceroy Petrosky and a dozen other Senior Viceroy's appeared next to him in flashes of white light.

"There is nothing left, their minds are blank," he said. A great sadness filled David as he spoke the words. He lowered his head and disappeared in a flash of white light.

As the Senior Viceroys talked, Gus sent the seed of hope back to the captains and cadets standing in the dome. With his hands behind his back, Andy signed the Senior Viceroys entire conversation to the triad, not once thinking about the words, only sending the information.

The time had come, they weren't sure how much more they could endure—even with their seed of hope. As they walked to dinner that evening, Toma passed by the dining room. George understood his cryptic signal. The time had come for them to escape, if only for a few hours.

"Remember, we are being watched," Toma signed, as they walked in circles through the corridors.

"Anna, I need a tunnel hog cave in this sector of the universe. Think of it's location, however, only for a moment, like Emily's computer flash," George signed, in their new sign language, knowing the captains couldn't read it and so they wouldn't actually know where they were going; just in case they were caught when they returned.

Toma waved his hand through the air at the front of their line to Cal who was at the end of their line. Cal placed his hand on Darri's shoulder and so on until all of the captains and cadets were physically connected. Anna thought the location of the tunnel hog cave, and in a flash of white light, they were all gone. They reappeared on a deserted asteroid far, far out in empty space. The cavern they appeared in looked like the cave Sid, Mid, and the twins slept in.

A small green glow from an adjoining cave told them where they had to go. George turned to Pete, Frank, Toma, and the other captains, while the other cadets turned toward the second cave.

"This is our most guarded secret; it is the one place no one can ever go. It has been lost for over the millennia. Even the Galactic Union council of elders doesn't know about this place and they must not be told. It is a place that must be discovered. Only this cave is safe. You must not enter the other cave for now. This is the only place that is safe," George said firmly and cryptically, trying not to tell them where they really were; and yet, trying to tell them how important a place it really was.

"We will wait here, in this cave for your return," Toma replied, a little worried by George's odd words.

"Don't touch the green fungi, it bites," Andy added, and Cal pulled his hand away.

Gus poured some purple liquid on the edge of the moss and it glowed a warm green. Emily dipped down and ran her hand across the ground.

"It is safe to rest on the ground. It will protect you now," she whispered.

George and the others walked into the other cave; and in a flash of white light, they were gone.

"What is this place," Nick asked, stunned by George's words.

"Where the heck are we?" Cal asked.

"We have been here before. It was when we were looking for George on Asteria station. Gus brought us here or at least it was a place like it," Han replied, looking around the small cave.

"So this is the place they have always considered safe," Pete said, looking around.

"Each time they have gone missing, they have come here," Toma said.

"Or a place like it," Frank added, piecing together the cadets adventures of the past rotations.

"How many caves are there?" Niels asked.

The others captains nodded, thinking the same questions.

"So this is their hiding place," Toma added, thinking and nodding with Frank and Pete.

Cal, Nick, and Niels understood what their leads were talking about. Yet, they didn't like George and the others just disappearing.

"I wonder why they think this is safe, for them?" Cal added, staring around the cave. Nick and Niels nodded, thinking the same thing.

"We come here and they leave. It is as if it is only a stop on their way to somewhere else," Nick added.

"So where did they actually go?" Toma asked, staring at the second cave.

"It is an interim place and it was hidden for a millennia," Pete said, repeating George's words.

Frank, Pete, and Toma were good with cryptic words. This was a puzzle meant for them.

George and the others appeared on a swirling cloud of gases and dust. Again, the beauty of the universe appeared before them, a multitude of nebulas and galaxies, spinning and swirling across the universe. Gazing out over the universe, a shimmering white light appeared next to them.

Andy glanced at George. "Like on Earth, George. When we were with the medicine people and Tara appeared," he signed.

George smile, "Yes, I agree," he signed.

A being of white light solidified and stood next to George.

"We are looking for the one we call Max. Is he here, ma'am?" George asked, turning to face her and lowering his head.

Tara stared at George. "He is here; however, he cannot help you, child," Tara replied softly.

"We have come to help him, ma'am," George replied quietly, as if not wanting to disturb the spinning gasses with the vibrations from his words.

"You cannot stay here, child," Tara pressed.

"Yes, ma'am. We will leave now. We only came to help Max, ma'am," George said, and they all dipped their heads.

In a flash of white light, they were back in the second cave. Gus spun around and looked at George.

"Why did you say that to the being of white light, George?" Gus puzzled.

"I think Max needs us right now, more than we need him. I wanted him to know that we knew he needed our help," George whispered, trying to explain the words he spoke to the being of white light. Only Andy and George knew Tara's name.

"Too cryptic, George," Emily said, shaking her head.

George turned and stared at his team. "The being of white light that spoke with us will speak with Max and tell him we were there, in the place we can't be, looking for him. When Max asks why we came, the being of white light will say we asked how he was. Max will know and the other white light beings will not understand," George said smiling, thinking his explanation was exceptional clear.

Andy smiled and wrapped his arm over George's shoulder. "George, trust me when I say, only you and Max know what's going on," he said, chuckling.

Emily, Anna, and Sara smiled and turned their heads away, hiding their smiles. Together, they walked out of the cavern and came face to face with the Senior Viceroy Petrosky, and Senior Viceroy David Lu. George stopped in his tracks and lowered his head. The other cadets followed his lead and lowered their heads, waiting to see what would happen next.

"How do you know of this place?" Senior Viceroy Petrosky asked firmly.

"I can't say, sir," George replied, straightening up a little.

"Did Max tell you of this place?" he pressed firmly again.

"No, sir. It was our own discovery, sir," George answered, his head still lowered.

"And the second cavern, do you know what it is for?" the Senior Viceroy pressed harder.

"Yes sir. We can't ...," George started to answer, however, grandfather raised his hand.

"I did not ask," he said firmly, stopping George from answering.

"How did you know we were here, sir?" George pressed back, looking up a little.

"George, you used the energy of the universe to bring everyone here. We were on the Nebula and knew when the raw energy of the universe was disturbed. Since David and I are the only ones on the Nebula right now that can use the raw energy in this way, we knew it was your triad that did it," the Senior Viceroy replied bluntly.

"I read deep within all of your minds, there was nothing there?" David Lu questioned, staring at the captains and cadets. Wondering how they had fooled him.

"Yes sir, there WAS nothing there sir," George replied, without answering his question.

"You're not answering my question, cadet," David Lu pressed firmly.

"I have been taught by the best, sir," George replied, his head still lowered, but using David Lu's own words from before.

David smiled; "then, you have a good teacher."

"Sir, why are we being retrained, sir?" George pressed Senior Viceroy Petrosky, seizing on their moment of distraction.

"The Galactic Union council thinks that your teams have too much power and that you and your teams have no checks and balances," Senior Viceroy Petrosky replied seriously.

"Absolute power, corrupts absolutely," Emily whispered.

"Yes, Emily, and it does," David Lu added, agreeing with Emily's words.

"Will they let us leave the Nebula, sir?" Andy asked, wondering how afraid the Galactic Union really was.

"They now believe you are ready to be retrained. When they are convinced you can become red cadets on your fourth rotation again, they will allow you to leave and return to Asteria station," the Senior Viceroy answered bluntly.

"You know that will not happen, sir. We have tried. We can't go back that far, sir," George replied a little sad.

"Maybe we could talk to them, sir?" Emily asked hopefully, thinking the council wouldn't be so afraid of them if they could talk to the members.

"No, Emily. They are afraid of you and your speaking with them will only scare them further," David Lu replied, his voice not as serious as before.

"Why, sir?" Gus asked, knowing it was important to know the cryptic answer.

"It shows strength of character and confidence in your abilities. Many beings are not as confident in themselves and their abilities as you and your teams are. They think your confidence is frightening, whether they admit it or not. Their fear makes them think you want to take their position away from them," Senior Viceroy Petrosky answered bluntly.

"That's not actually rational, sir," Andy said, crinkling his eyes.

"Rational or not, you will need to learn how to dealt with it," David Lu said firmly.

"Sounds like Captain Stiles," Anna added, thinking back to their second rotation.

"Who?" Pete asked, staring at Anna.

"No one important, sir," Sara whispered to Pete.

"However, a good lesson we need to learn," George replied, more thinking than answering.

David Lu turned his head as if looking out a window. "You must all return now. They will know you are missing in another minute," he said urgently.

The cadets and captains made their physical link, and in a flash of white light, they were back circling aimless around in the corridor, looking for the dining hall.

"What do you think?" Senior Viceroy Petrosky asked, turning toward David Lu in the cave.

"George moved their entire triad by himself, and he wasn't weakened. He and his triad have become exceptionally strong. The council's fears are not all unfounded," David replied. "Yet, George seems to be missing the true understanding of what they can do," he added.

"Perhaps it is Max's doing. He may be stopping they from figuring it out right now. But you have something else in your mind, what?" Senior Viceroy Petrosky pressed.

"I think George and the others know they can leave at any time and they are tired of being treated with disrespect by the council," David answered bluntly, talking about the Galactic Union council members.

"Why don't they leave now?" the Senior Viceroy asked, pressing for his opinion.

"They truly don't know where to go if they left. All that power and nowhere to go. So much unhappiness I sense within them," David answered, sadness filling his thoughts.

"Then we must give them a place to go before they get frustrated with the Galactic Union council and leave without any purpose," the Senior Viceroy said, wrapping his arm around David, calming an odd sadness rising within David's being.

An officer found the captains and cadets wandering through the corridors and directed them to the dining hall. They ate in silence and sat in their seats until another officer came and brought them to their sleeping rooms. The next ten days were mind numbing, while George and the others were retrained to the cadet and captain level by the Galactic Union re-trainers.

All the while, the teams endured, holding tight to their grain of hope. On the eleventh day, the teams were walked onto a Thorean warship and slipped into crystalline tubes.

When they awoke, they were in a hospital room on Asteria station. Two Inner Circle officers led the cadets and captains out of the hospital to their sectors of the station. They all walked in silence through the corridors, no thoughts shared. No ideas or plans created-only mind numbing silence. The Inner Circle officers never even tried to read their thoughts.

"Nothing to read, they had been re-trained," one Inner Circle officer thought to the other Inner Circle officer as they left each of the captain teams in their separate captain sleeping rooms.

"Lock your door and get some rest. It was a long journey," the Inner Circle officer said kindly, as they left cadet's sleeping room.

Moments after the Inner Circle officers left, Pete, Frank, Toma and the others burst through the cadet's door. They crowded together in the cadet's sleeping room. Emily reprogrammed the station computer within minutes. The station sensors would now show the captains and cadets, sleeping in their rooms with the doors locked~ just in case anyone was looking. In a flash of white light, they were gone.

Chapter 35

HOPE RESTORED

Instantly, the teams reappeared in the tunnel hog cave where Sid, Mid, and the twins slept.

"Another cave?" Pete asked.

"Yes, there is more than one cave in the universe, sir," Anna answered seriously.

"Why here?" Frank asked.

"It is the only safe place, sir," George replied, as Gus fed the green fungi purple liquid.

"The station seems sad," Emily whispered.

"It is as if their hope is gone. I thought that would have been fixed when the whatever left," Sara added curiously.

"Yes, Sara. Me too," Andy replied, sliding his arm around Sara.

"That is the answer. It is why the civilizations across the universe have stopped evolving. It is why they're development is stagnating," George said cryptically, changing the topic.

"What answer?" Andy asked.

"What question?" Gus asked George, wanting to understand.

"Without hope and a goal to work towards, life can be one boring, tedious set of events after the next," George said oddly sad.

"So the galaxies stopped evolving. They lost their hope for the future," Emily said.

"They thought they had accomplished everything and so Earth was able to catch up to the other beings in the universe," Anna added.

"But now, something is wrong, even more wrong than before the whatever was here," George said, puzzling as if the captains weren't there.

"What about Sport?" Gus asked pressed.

"A distraction for the young perhaps," Cal replied.

George wandered into the second cavern as the others talked. Andy followed, sitting down on a few fallen rocks near the cavern entrance watching. Cal sat down across from him.

"What is George doing, Andy?" he asked.

"Just thinking, it has been a long time since he was able to even have a thought. Somehow we need to put everything back, back to the way it's supposed to be, sir," Andy said.

"What do you mean?" Cal asked.

"Cal, this isn't right and George knows it. All of this is wrong. Like our little grain of hope. You have to have it and work toward a goal, Cal. We have no goal. Nothing is left and now even hope is gone from here. We need to somehow put things right, sir," Andy replied, staring at George.

Cal looked at Andy. He only understood about half what he had said. It was as if the universe was sad and the sadness was everywhere, creeping into their thoughts and distracting their focus. The sadness was making them lose track of their hopes and dreams. As if, without hope and a goal, there was nothing left for them.

In a flash of white light, George was gone. Andy jumped up and ran into the second cavern.

"You know better, George. If I didn't know where you were, I'd be ticked," Andy yelled inside the empty cave.

He left the second cavern, returning to his seat on the rocks. He knew he could stay in the second cavern, but, he didn't want Cal to enter the cave and get sick.

"Where's George?" Cal asked, not having moved from his rock.

"Not here, but safe, sir," Andy replied grumpily.

Cal didn't like Andy's answer, but pressed him no further.

The others were oblivious to George, Andy, and Cal. They were enjoying their first freedom in weeks. Emily talked to every rock and Gus and Sara feed the fungi, running their hand over it as if petting playful kittens. Anna opened her star charts, trying to find the Nebula they had been held at. She was looking for a hub of sorts.

"Where has Major Gatte never had us look?" Anna whispered to herself.

Karmen, Maria, and Tillie leaned in towards Anna and expanded their pads.

"Let us help," Karmen whispered and the others smiled.

Pete, Frank, and Toma sat on one side of the cavern concentrating, keeping their thoughts hidden from anyone's view.

George appeared on their now standard swirling cloud of gasses and cosmic dust. He turned and looked around, a glowing being of white light didn't appear. The universe seemed sad~ without its hope. It wasn't evil that now covered over the universe like a cloud. It was a loss of hope as if the universe was without focus and a goal. George thought of Max~ nothing.

"I need to find, Max," George said aloud~ still no answer.

He spun around and waved his hand through the air like the Senior Viceroys. Suddenly, his team appeared, all together, on the cloud. In a second flash of white light, they were gone from the cloud. They reappeared on a barren asteroid, standing among a hundred glowing beings of white light. Emily leaned over and touched the ground. She shuttered and a tear formed in her eye.

"Max is dying and so is their hope," Emily signed, standing up.

"What?" George turned toward Emily.

"Somehow Max represents hope to his people," Emily signed.

"How do you know?" Andy pressed, needing to understand.

"I can sense it in the rocks and the soil of this asteroid. It's like a sad aura," she replied, her eyes filling with tears.

George turned and stared at all the beings of white light. He paused, thinking. He knew the answer to sadness.

"Hope!" he said, as the others turned and stared at George. "Hope is what the team of the prophecy represents~hope to our galaxies and universe," George whispered, beginning to understand what the team of the prophecy was truly about.

"We can save Max, George. We have done it before," Gus said suddenly, remembering the events of the past. The cadets all nodded as their minds filled with the hidden memories.

"Yes, we did save Max before, but this time is different. It is as if he's dying of old age," Sara whispered, seeming to sense his being.

"Without hope and focus, there is nothing left for the beings of the universe," Emily added.

"Max isn't old. He has only lost his hope, his focus," George said, frowning.

"This is all wrong, George. You know it and I know it. We have to change this," Emily whispered.

"I know," George replied, looking down at the ground.

"Why are we here? I mean here, here. There are no others like us here?" Gus asked, looking around.

"How can we even breathe? Why aren't we dead?" Andy pressed.

"They knew we would come and they made a space for us, Gus," Anna said, nodding her head as she looked around the asteroid.

"They knew, that's why no one came to get me on the cloud," George said, figuring out their cryptic message. "Now we need to do what is needed to save Max's life, like he saved ours, and restore hope to the universe," George added, lowering his head.

We will need the others," Andy whispered, placing his hand on George's shoulder.

A moment later, Pete, Frank, Toma, and the others appeared on the asteroid's surface in the center of the beings of white light. Toma, Frank, and Pete dropped to one knee, lowering their heads. The other captains followed his lead.

The captains were stunned. They thought they had never seen the beings of white light other than Max in his human form. Now the images George had share with them started to make sense. They didn't know Max was a being of white light as the memory had been taken from them from before. They had assumed he was a stronger Senior Viceroy like Pete and Toma's grandfathers or Senior Viceroy like David Lu.

The beings of white light commanded great respect from the civilization across the universe and they wielded great power and strength. George had always known the beings of white light only as counselors and friends.

George walked over to Toma and held out his palm. A small yellow sphere danced above his palm. Toma held his hand over George's hand and stood up.

"We are in the place we can't be, sir. The space between space, where only pure energy exists. Our triad is here with the beings of white light to restore hope to the universe as the prophecy has said," George whispered.

The others stood up, following Toma.

"Your team is truly the team of the prophecy," Toma whispered.

"No, Toma, our triad is the team of the prophecy. The Viceroys read the prophecy scroll wrong. The team of the prophecy is the entire triad. It is only together that we are strong enough to restore hope to the universe, sir. It was never about destroying evil. It is about hope sir," George replied.

"Then we should begin as I am sure we can't last long here in the energy between the space," Toma replied, moving his hand across the open sky of the asteroid pointing out into open space.

"Andy, I need your strongest thought of hope for the future," George asked.

George stood in the center and Pete, Toma, and Frank stood in the first circle. Then Andy, Cal, Nick, Niels, Emily, Jennifer, Sheta, and Kate stood in the next circle. After them came Sara, Anna, Lucita, Tillie, and Rachael, Gus, Gabe Sven, Han, Maria, Darri, and Karmen in the outer circle.

The beings of white light backed up, making room for their circles across the asteroids surface. George, Pete, Frank, and Toma began Chen Lo and the beings of white light backed up only slightly more. At the second level Andy, Niels, and the others in their ring began. At the third level, the last ring began. They had done Chen Lo when they were healthy, with their whole triad physically together before, however, often the memory was hidden from them afterwards.

Usually, when they had started Chen Lo, they weren't all together and their triad teams appeared as they were needed. Now, they were together and they could sense the difference.

At the twelfth level, the surface of the asteroid began to bend and warp. By the thirteen level, they were standing in a sea of energy, twisting, bouncing, and spinning around their circle, crisscrossing the asteroid's surface. At the fourteenth level, George thought of David Lu and Pete's grandfather. Suddenly, they were in the center of the circle with George. David Lu nodded to Cal, Niels, Nick, and Andy and they progressed through the eighteenth level. Grandfather smoothed the raw energy of the universe and George and David Lu guided it, letting it flow threw them.

The asteroid was a blur of energy and Andy and George thought only of hope for the future. The energy spread out in waves, washing across the asteroid and the beings of white light. It touched Max as it spread. Max faded in and out with the ebb and flow of raw energy of the universe.

Finally, Max appeared next to grandfather, helping smooth the raw energy of the universe. Ripples of energy became waves of energy, spreading further out across the galaxies. The uneasiness George and Andy had felt on Earth so long ago was ending. Hope and focus were being restored.

The waves washed over the galaxies of good and evil, even evil's hope was restored. The ebb and flow of the universe returned. David Lu nodded to

George and he started to slow their triad, stepping down through the levels of Chen Lo, slowly releasing the energy back to the universe ~ days had past.

For a brief moment, George and the others knew all that was. This moment in time was what made them the true triad of the prophecy. The waves of energy calmed and the asteroid reassembled before their eyes. Max lowered his head to George and the others. In a flash of brilliant white light, they were all gone.

The cadets and captains awoke five days later in the CORE hospital on Asteria station. George lifted his head and a medic ran to his side. She smiled as she handed him a bowl of dark brown cereal.

"Thank you," he thought to her.

"So who won this time?" he teased, knowing the medics were now betting on when this odd team would return.

The medic pointed to one of the doctors who tipped his head in George's direction.

"You need to be more careful when your team is practicing for Sport. You need to keep your energy up better, you came to us too weak," the medic whispered and then left to help Andy.

He didn't feel weak as he looked around the room. He saw only his team of cadets in the hospital room and thought of Pete, Frank, and Toma. He couldn't tell where they were, only that they were OK.

A commotion in the center of the room caught George's eye. Pete and Nick had walked in. They wanted their cadets released. They were ranting and raving that the cadets had missed too much training.

At first, George didn't understand, then he saw how many medics, doctors, and CORE officers were focused on Pete and Nick. They were the distraction. George slid out of his bed and stepped back. Senior Viceroy Petrosky caught him and he spun around.

"Can you walk with me, George?" the Senior Viceroy asked.

"Is everything OK, sir?" George whispered.

"Calm is our path. All is well," Senior Viceroy Petrosky replied calmly.

George walked to a small room off to the side of the hospital room as Pete and Nick continued to distract everyone else with great flourish. Two seats rose from the floor of the small room and they sat down.

"George, do you understand what has happened?" the Senior Viceroy asked.

"For one brief moment on the surface of the asteroid we all did, now everything is gone, sir," George answered and lowered his head. "Except, for hope and focus, sir. I remember hope has been returned to the universe, sir," George replied thoughtfully.

"Yes, hope has been restored. It is a good thing you and the others did. In the process of restoring hope to the universe, the prophecy has been truly fulfilled. Oddly, your triad has lived," the Senior Viceroy said puzzled.

"Why is that odd, sir?" George asked, needing to know.

"It has never happened before George. We have always thought it was only one lead team that was the team of the prophecy. It was your team that figured out the prophecy was really about the triad as a team, and now, your team and triad lives," he said wistfully.

"What will become of us, sir?" George asked.

"There is a plan; however, the details will need to be refined. However, right now, I think you need to return before Peter and Nicholas bust an artery. I think that's what you young people say today," the Senior Viceroy said, telling a joke.

George smiled and nodded. They stood up and George walked to the door. He turned to say good-bye; however, the Senior Viceroy was gone.

George slipped back into his bed and his cereal bowl slipped off the silvery cover, flipping over and hitting the floor, spilling cereal everywhere. The officers in the room turned toward George. Pete and Nick threw their hands into the air and left the hospital room. A medic ran to George to clean up the spilled cereal and bring him a new bowl.

Andy smiled, seeing the distraction for what it was. He asked George no questions. The next morning, Pete came alone to collect his cadets. He walked over to George.

"Report, cadet!" he yelled.

George and the others jumped up. He didn't wait for George to answer.

"This is your last week cadets and it will be particularly grueling as you have all been relaxing in bed for the last few days!" he said firmly.

"Yes sir," George answered formally.

The medics backed away and Pete led the cadets from the hospital room.

In the corridor, Andy spoke up, "so you were just kidding right, sir?"

Pete spun around and faced the cadets. "Did you forget where you are? This is Asteria station and you are fourth rotation cadets. Your thoughts are to be controlled and no, I was not kidding, cadet," he said with every bit of his captain's voice.

George knew Pete was saying it mostly for show and to give them a place to focus their minds. Pete spun back around and the cadets lined up silently behind him. He was right, they had been gone so long they had forgotten their protocol. Hope may have been restored to the universe; however, Asteria station had only slightly changed.

Who knew if they would get to go back to Earth after their fourth rotation? Right now, it didn't really matter to George. They had survived being captured by evil, racing to near death, infected by the whatever, escaped from the Celestian reading room, lived through retraining on the Galactic Union nebula, and restored hope to the universe. The triad of the prophecy was alive and well as they sat in a dining room far across the universe full of whispering captains with hope for the future.

The End

Made in the USA
Middletown, DE
10 April 2023

28501925R00217